Emma Dorothy Eliza Nevitte Southworth

Lilith

A novel

Emma Dorothy Eliza Nevitte Southworth

Lilith
A novel

ISBN/EAN: 9783337027322

Printed in Europe, USA, Canada, Australia, Japan

Cover: Foto ©Andreas Hilbeck / pixelio.de

More available books at **www.hansebooks.com**

LILITH

A Novel

A Sequel to "The Unloved Wife"

By MRS. E. D. E. N. SOUTHWORTH

Author of "The Bride's Fate," "The Changed Brides,"
"Cruel as the Grave," "The Hidden Hand," "Ishmael,"
"Self-Raised," Etc.

A. L. BURT COMPANY
PUBLISHERS   ∴   NEW YORK

Copyright, 1881 and 1890
By ROBERT BONNER'S SONS

LILITH

Printed by special arrangement with
STREET & SMITH

LILITH

CHAPTER I

OLD ADAH'S SECRET

So at last shall come old age,
Decrepit, as beseems that stage.
How else should we retire apart
With the hoarded memories of the heart?
—*Browning.*

Oh, for the touch of a vanished hand,
And the sound of a voice that is still!
—*Tennyson.*

It was a lovely morning in May, when Tudor Hereward sat, wrapped in his gray silk dressing-gown, reclining in his resting-chair, on the front piazza at Cloud Cliffs.

He had had a hard fight with death, and had barely come out of it with his life.

Physicians and friends alike ascribed his illness to nervous shock upon a system already run down under the long-continued pressure of work and worry.

He was convalescent now, yet he seemed the mere shadow of his former vigorous manhood.

By his side, on a stand covered with white damask, stood a basket of luscious strawberries in a nest of their own leaves; also a vase of fragrant spring flowers—hyacinths, tulips, jonquils, daffodils, violets and heart's-ease. Yet he neither touched nor tasted ·flowers or fruit.

Before him stretched the green lawn, shaded by acacia trees in full bloom, which filled the air with their rich aroma.

Farther on, the woods swept around the grounds, a semi-circular wall of living verdure.

Beyond them stood the cliffs, opal-tinted in the sunlight, misty where their heads were vailed by the soft white clouds which gave them their name.

Birds trilled their song of rapture through the perfumed air.

It was a lovely morning in a lovely scene. A morning and a scene that ministered to every sense, yet it was more than a mere material paradise, for its many delights combined to fill the soul with peace, joy and thankfulness, and so to raise it

"From Nature up to Nature's God."

Especially to a convalescent, coming for the first time out of his sick-room, must such a scene of summer glory have brought a delicious sense of new life in fresh and keen enjoyment, making him think that even of this material world it might be said, to some less favored people of some other planet: "Eye hath not seen, nor ear heard, nor hath it entered into the heart of man the things that God hath prepared for them that love Him."

But this was not the case with Tudor Hereward. To his sick soul, as to the diseased mind of another, the beauty of the earth and the glory of the heavens were but

"A foul and pestilent congregation of vapors,'

for all the pleasure he could take in them.

His wife Lilith was gone—dead—murdered.

This was to him the death-knell of nature. His mental suffering was not now sharp. He was much too weak to feel acutely. His sorrow had settled into a dull despair—a cold and lifeless misery.

Lilith was gone.

If she had passed away peacefully in her bed, attended by friends, sustained by religion, though he must have mourned for her, he could have borne his loss; or if, as had been at first supposed, she had accidentally fallen into the creek, and met a sudden, painless death, still, though he must have suffered much more, yet he could have endured the blow; but she had been butchered—cruelly butchered by some night-prowling ruffian, whose identity was neither known nor suspected, and whose motive for the monstrous crime could not even be imagined.

Lilith had been slain, and the blackness of darkness had settled upon the soul of him who felt that he had driven her forth that bitter winter night to meet her awful fate.

Yes, the blackness of darkness seemed to have fallen like the clods of the grave upon his dead and buried soul. In other deaths the body only dies; the soul lives on. In his case it seemed the soul that died, while the poor weak body lived on.

He had not been deserted in his misery and despair. As soon as the news of the discovered murder at Cliff Creek had flown over the country, spreading horror everywhere, friends and neighbors had flocked to the house, with profound sorrow for the murdered wife and sympathy for the awfully bereaved husband, and earnest proffers of assistance in any manner in which their services could be made available.

And when it became known that Mr. Hereward himself had been suddenly stricken down by dangerous illness, the ladies of the neighborhood, skilful nurses all, carefully trained to their duties as their mothers before them had been—and as all the mistresses of large plantations necessarily were—came in turn to stop at the Cliffs, and to take care of the desolate master.

The Rev. Mr. Cave, his old pastor, had come every day to visit him, and as soon as his condition warranted, to administer religious consolation.

Every one mourned for Lilith, every one sympathized with Hereward, and served him in every possible way. They "pulled him through," as the doctor phrased it, though it was but the shadow of the man they raised.

And even now that he was convalescent he was not left to himself.

Mrs. Jab Jordon was now the volunteer housekeeper and nurse, as she had been for the week past, and as she meant to be for the week to come, and her fine health and good spirits and judicious management were as beneficial to the stricken man as anything could be under these adverse circumstances.

It was her hand that had arranged his reclining-chair on the piazza, and placed the stand of fruit and flowers by its side. It was her will that had kindly forced him out of the gloom of his sick-chamber into the sunshine and fresh, fragrant air of that lovely May morning. It was her precaution that still kept from him the loads of well-meaning letters of condolence that he could not have borne to read as yet.

And even now the good woman was upstairs superintending Cely and Mandy in the work of preparing a new room for the patient, who was not to be taken back to the old sick-chamber, which was dismantled and, with all its windows open, turned out, so to speak, to all the airs of spring.

It was a little surprising to all who knew old Nancy, the colored housekeeper who had so long ruled supreme at Cloud Cliffs, that she was not jealous of this invasion of the house by the ladies of the neighborhood. But in fact, Nancy was grateful for their presence and their help.

"'Sides w'ich," as she confided to Cassy, the cook, "dis ain't no time fer no po' mortil to stan' on deir dignity. De 'sponsibility ob de case is too mons'ous; let alone my heart bein' broke long ob po' dear Miss Lilif goin' to glory de drefful way she did! an' me fit for nuffin'. It would be flyin'—'deed it's de trufe—flyin'."

So Nancy put herself under the orders of Mrs. Jordon, as she had done under her predecessors.

The pale convalescent, sitting in his resting-chair, gazed with languid eyes over the lovely lawn, with its fragrant blossoming trees, and its parterres of flowers in sunny spots, on to the encircling woods filled with birds and bird songs, and beyond to the opal-tinted, mist-vailed cliffs, and to the deep blue sky above them all; yet seemed to take in nothing of the brightness and the beauty.

At length his listless, wandering eyes perceived a figure, at strange variance with the bright summer scene.

Creeping around from the rear grounds, emerging from a side grove of acacia trees, winding between parterres of hyacinths, tulips, daffodils, and other spring flowers, came a very aged woman, small, black, withered, poorly clad in an old brown linsey gown, with a red handkerchief tied over her head and under her chin, and leaning on a cane, she drew slowly near the piazza, climbed the two or three steps and stood bobbing, but trembling with infirmity, before the invalid master.

"Well, Aunt Adah, I am pleased to see you abroad once more," said Hereward, kindly.

"Young marster, I t'ank yer, sah. An' I is t'ank-

ful! Oh, my Hebbenly Lord, how t'ankful I is in
my heart to fine yer sittin' out yere!" earnestly responded the woman, reverently raising her eyes and
trembling through all her frame.

"Sit down, Aunt Adah. You are not able to stand,"
said Hereward, kindly, stretching out his emaciated
hand to reach and draw a chair up to the weary old
woman.

"I t'anks yer, young marster, I t'anks yer werry
much, an' I will sit down in yer p'esence, since yer's
so 'siderate as to 'mit me so to do; fer I is weak,
young marster—I is weak. I has been yere a many
times to see yer, young marster, but dey wouldn'
leabe me do it, no dey wouldn', an' I 'spects dey was
right. Yer wa'n't well 'nuff to be 'sturbed," said the
old creature, as she lowered herself slowly and carefully into the chair, for all her joints were stiff with
extreme age.

"You were very kind to come to inquire after me
so often," said Hereward, gently.

"An' w'y wouldn' I come? An' how should ebber
I hear ob yer 'dout comin' myse'f to 'quire? It'd be
long 'nuff fo' any ob dese t'oughtless niggers yere
come 'cross de crik to fetch me any news! Me, as
has been a savint ob de Tudors for 'mos' a hund'ed
years an' is by fur de ol'est savint on de plantation!
'Deed it's de trufe, young marster. I was ninety-nine
years old las' Can'lemas Day," continued the old
woman, stooping to lay her cane on the floor.

Hereward smiled faintly. He knew from old farm
records that Aunt Adah was even older than, with
the strange pride of her race in extreme longevity,
she claimed to be; and that for the last few years she
had steadily called herself ninety-nine years old last
Candlemas Day, sticking at that imposing number and
seeming to forget that every year increased it; hon-
estly to forget, for old Adah would have been per-

fectly delighted if any one had opened her eyes and
explained to her that she might truly lay claim to a
hundred and seven years.

"You have certainly been a most faithful follower of
the family, Aunt Adah," said the young man.

"Yes, honey, fai'ful!" assented the old creature.
"Dat's me, fai'ful!—fai'ful froo fick an' fin, froo good
'port and ebil 'port, fai'ful fer ninety-nine years las'
Can'lemas Day! I didn't 'mancipate de plantashun to
go off to Cong'ess like so many ob dem riff-raff, low-
life brack niggers did! No, sah! Aunt Adah Mungummerry had too much 'spect fer herse'f, let alone
'spect fer de ole famberly ob de Tudors, to 'grace
herse'f dat way! 'Sides w'ich, young marster, to tell
de bressed trufe, I wouldn' 'a' lef' my log-house in de
piney woods 'cross de crik, wid my good pine-knot fire
in de winter time, an' my cool spring ob water outside
de do', no, not fer all de Cong'ess in de whole worl'!
'Deed, 'fo' de law, it's de trufe!"

And, inasmuch as Aunt Adah had been long past
labor and was living as a pensioner on the family at
the time of the emancipation, any stranger hearing her
boast might have thought that policy and not principle
was the secret of her fidelity to native soil and friends.
But such was not the case. At no age would she have
left the home and the family to whom she was so
strongly attached.

Her bondage was that of love, from which no act
of Congress could emancipate her.

"Would you like a glass of wine, Aunt Adah?"
inquired the young man, reaching his thin hand to a
silver call-bell that stood upon the stand near him.

"No, honey; no, chile, not yit; not jis yit! I'd like
a tumbler ob good b'andy toddy, bimeby, but not yit,
caze I's got somefin on my min'," replied the old creature, so very solemnly that Hereward withdrew his
hand from the bell, lifted his head and looked at her.

"Something on your mind, Aunt Adah?" he inquired.

"Yes, young marster, somefin werry sarous on my min'," repeated the aged woman.

"What is it, Adah? Speak out, my good soul. Don't be afraid!" said Hereward, kindly.

"I ain't afeard, young marster! 'Tain't dat! But it is somefin berry heabby on to my min', as been wantin' to get offen my min' by tellin' ob you; an' dat's wot fetch me yere mos' ebbery day since yer's been sick; on'y dey wouldn' leabe me see yer, no way, and I 'spects dey was yight. But I sees yer now, young marse, an' I wants to tell yer."

"Very well, Aunt Adah, tell me what it is now," said Hereward, in an encouraging tone.

"Young marse, it is a solemn secret, beknown on'y to me an' one udder gran' wilyan! But I was boun' not to tell anybody on dis worl' 'fo' I could tell yo' fuss. Dough, indeed, it ought fo' to be tole long ago, on'y it wasn' in my power to tell it at de yight time, caze I was all alone in my house, laid up long ob de rheumatiz, an' didn' know wot was gwine on yere at dis place; an' w'en I did come to fine out, it were too late fer dem, an' I come to tell yer, but yer was too ill to be 'sturbed, an' dey wouldn' let me see yer, an' I 'spects dey was yight; but I was 'termined to keep dat solemn secret in my own heart, an' not to tell nobody wot I knowed to make a stracshun in de place, till yo' got well so I could tell yo' fuss, an' let yer do wot yer t'ought bes'."

"Yes, yes; but what—what is it that you have to tell me?" demanded Hereward, becoming more impressed by the words and manner of the woman.

His excitement alarmed the poor creature, who pulled herself up suddenly, saying:

"Hole on now, Adah Mungummerry! Hole on,

ole lady! Yer's a rushin' ob it on too rapid on to
a sick man. Hole up, now!" she said, talking to herself, as is the habit of the extremely aged.

"Tell me at once what you have to tell," said Hereward, with a sudden terrible suspicion that her communication might concern the murder of his young
wife.

"Well, dear young marster, but yer mus' have
patience and 'pose yerse'f, sah! 'Deed yer mus',
young marse, or yer'll make yerse'f wuss, an' wot
would Mrs. Jab an' de udders say to me ef I made
yer wuss? I's gwine to tell yer, young marse, w'ich
I come yere fo' dat puppose; but I mus' tell yer
werry graduately—so as not to make yer no wuss.
Well, now, le's see—le' me see, now. Le' me be
cautious. Sort o' break de news little by little. Young
marse, yer know dat mornin' wot yer come to my
cabin to 'quire 'bout Miss Lilif?"

"Yes," breathed the young man, beginning to
tremble with anxiety in his extreme weakness.

"Well, young marse, as I telled you dat mornin' I
'peats now. She hadn' been dere, nor likewise nigh
de place dat bressed night, as w'y should she come,
w'en—listen now, young marse! w'y should she come
w'en it warn't ne'sary; caze she had sent Nancy long
ob dat po' misfortunit young gal, to fetch me money,
an' close, an' wittels, an' drink, an' ebbery singerly
fing as heart could wish."

"So you told me before," said Hereward, impatiently.

"So I did, my dear young marse, an' I ax yer pardon fer tellin' ob yo' ag'in; but I does it to make
yer ax yerse'f w'y should Miss Lilif do such a unne'-
sary fing as to come to my cabin dat cole night for
nuffin? No, young marse! She didn' come to no cabin
dat night."

"But she started to go!" exclaimed Hereward, with a cry of anguish.

"No, young marse! An' dis is wot I war tryin' to come at, soft an' grad'al, not to s'prise yer too sudden. Now listen, dear marse, an' year wot I tell yer, 'caze it's de bressed trufe—Miss Lilif nebber come to de cabin dat night, nor likewise she nebber started to come, neider!" solemnly declared the old woman.

Hereward sprang up, stared at the earnest speaker and then fell back faint and trembling.

" 'Pose yerse'f, dear young marse; dere ain't nuffin to 'stress yer, but quite deffrint," soothingly murmured old Adah.

"What—what do you mean? She certainly did go to the creek, because—because——" faltered the speaker, but his voice broke down in silence.

"Caze dere was a body foun' dere? Dat wot yer were gwine to say, young marse?"

"Yes," breathed Hereward.

"Yes, so dere was, Marse Tudor, so dere was. But dat body wa'n't dear Miss Lilif's!"

Hereward, trembling as if stricken with palsy, and with his hands clutching the arms of his chair, bent forward and stared at the speaker.

"It's de trufe, as I s'pect to stan' 'fo' my Hebbenly Judge at de las' day, Marse Tudor! Dat body war not Miss Lilif's, as I could hab edified to de Cow's Jury, ef I had a knowed wot was gwine on yere an' could a come up 'fo' it. 'Stead of w'ich I war laid up long ob de rheumatiz at home, an' no one came nigh me to tell nuffin."

"Not—not—Lilith's——" muttered Hereward, falling back in his chair quite overcome.

Old Adah, in her well-meaning, blundering manner, had tried to "break the news," but had not succeeded. She was alarmed at the looks of the young man.

"Le' me yun in de house an' fetch yer a glass of wine, Marse Tudor! Please, sah!" she pleaded.

"No, no, no, do not move!—I want nothing—I want nobody to come. What did you say?—It was not——"

"No, Marse Tudor, it war not hern, no mo' an it war your'n or mine," impressively replied old Adah.

"But—it was identified as such by—by——"

"By de long, curly brack ha'r, so I years, an' by de gown, an' de unnerclose wid her name on 'em, an' de putty little F'ench boots wid her name on de inside. Wa'n't dat wot yer war gwine to say, Marse Tudor?"

"Yes."

"Well, dat were all jes' so. De booful ha'r war like Miss Lilif's, shuah nuff, an' de warm casher gown, an' de unnerclose, an' de pooty F'ench boots war all Miss Lilif's. But dat war jes' all dere war ob Miss Lilif's. It wa'n't hern."

"Adah! what is this you are telling me, and what reason have you for saying what you do?" demanded Hereward, with a great effort.

" 'Caze I knows all about it, young marse, an' I knows whose 'mains dey war as war foun' in de crik."

"Whose, in the name of Heaven, were they?"

"Dey war doze ob dat po', des'late young creeter wot war murdered by her man, an' t'rowed inter de crik dat same night, as I could a testimonied at de Cow's Quest, ef I had been sent for or eben ef I had known wot war gwine on yere at de time. But no one t'ought ob sendin' for me, a ole 'oman cripple up wid de rheumatiz an' not able to creep no furder dan to fill my bucket at de spring outside de do'! 'Deed, I nebber heerd nuffin 'tall 'bout wot happen till it war too late to edify de Cow's Jury. Soon as I did year it, I creeped up yere to tell yer wot I knowed; but yer war too ill to be 'sturbed—so dey said, an'

I 'spect as dey war yight. So I 'solved to keep de secret till yer war able for to year it; 'caze I didn't want to make no mo' stracshun in de neighborhood wid no mo' news till I could 'vise long ob you 'bout it, sah. An' so I come up yere two or three times ebbery week, but dey wouldn' leabe me come to yer —no dey wouldn'! I's moughty t'ankful as I has cotch yer to-day, Marse Tudor."

CHAPTER II

NEW HOPE

HEREWARD was suffering from terrible excitement. We said a little while since that his soul seemed dead within him. And as resuscitation is always more distressing than asphyxia, so the infusion of a ray of hope that gave new life to his spirit caused much anguish.

It required all his recovered power of mind to control his emotion.

"Adah!" he said, "what you tell me is so strange, so startling, so incredible, that I have the greatest difficulty in receiving it! What good reason have you for believing—believing that?"

Again Hereward broke down.

"Dat de 'mains foun' in de crik wor not doze ob my dear young mist'ess, but wor doze ob dat young gal wot wor made way wid by her man? Yer see I kin 'lude to dem 'mains d'out lozin' ob my head 'caze I knows dey wor doze ob dat po' murdered gal. Ef I eben s'picioned as dey wor doze ob my dear young mist'ess I couldn' speak ob dem, no, no mo' dan yer can yerse'f, Marse Tudor."

"Yes; but what proof—what proof have you?" breathlessly inquired Hereward.

"I's gwine to tell yer, Marse Tudor, ef yer will on'y 'pose yerse'f an' hab patience. 'Deed, I 'spects as Mrs. Jab'll take de head offen my shou'ders fo' 'citin' ob yer so."

"Yes; but what proof? what proof?"

"I's gwine to tell yer, Marse Tudor, 'deed I is. Yer 'member dat mornin' w'en yer come 'quirin' at my cabin 'bout Miss Lilif?"

"Yes, yes; you asked me that question some time back."

"So I did, Marse Tudor; an' I ax ob yer pardon fo' axin' it ag'in. It wor on'y to 'mind yer of de day, marse. Yer 'member as I tole yer how de young mist'ess had gib dat po' gal lots ob wittles an' drink, an' close, an' money, fo' herse'f an' me, too? Yer 'member dat, young marse?"

"I do."

"An' likewise as I tole yer how her man come in unexpected dat same night, an' eat up all de good wittles, and drunk up all de good licker, an' tuk all de money, an' 'pelled her to go 'way 'long o' him dat same night?"

"Yes, I remember. Go on."

"Well, Marse Tudor, I tole yer all dat; but I didn't fink ob tellin' ob yer all de little trifles w'ich 'peared no 'count—sich as he makin' ob her dress herse'f in her close to go 'long ob him—dose berry close wot Miss Lilif gib her—dat warm cashy gown, an' de nice unnerclose, an' de pooty French boots, an' de little hat—all wot was tied up in de bundle—did he make her take out an' put on to go 'long ob him genteel. No, I didn't tell yer dat; nor likewise as how she 'beyed him in 'spect ob de close, but 'posed him when he tuk ebberyfin' out'n de house an' lef me nuffin'. An' dey bofe went 'way quarrelin'—

quarrelin' werry bitter, an' I yeard 'em at it till dey got out ob yearin'—an' next minit I heerd an awful screech, an' den anoder, an' anoder. An' I say: 'Dere, now,' I say, 'he's beatin' ob her, de brute!' An' den dere was silence. An' I nebber t'ought no wuss ob it, dan it wor bad 'nuff, but not so uncommon as to keep me 'wake."

Old Adah paused for breath, while Hereward waited for her next words with intense anxiety. At length she resumed:

"I nebber tole yer 'bout dese las' mentioned fings, 'caze I t'ought den dey was on'y trifles; but, Lor', who kin tell wot is trifles, or wot trifles is gwine to mount up to 'fo' dey's done wid yer? It wor dem berry trifles, w'ich I t'ought ob no 'count, as would indentified dem 'mains wot was foun' in de crik for doze ob dat po' young gal, ef on'y I hed been sent fer to edify de Cow's Quest. Dere! My Lor'! now what is I done?" cried the old woman, rising in alarm and peering into the face of the young master, who had fallen back into his seat in what seemed to be a dead swoon.

She took up the hand-bell, and was about to sound an alarm for help, when her wrist was feebly grasped, and her name faintly called.

"Adah—no—don't ring! Wait—I shall recover presently. Give me—time," whispered Hereward, making a great effort to rally.

After a little while he said:

"If what you tell me is true—and I have no reason to doubt your word—then it was really the body of that poor girl which was found in the creek, and your mistress is still living. But, Adah, I commend your discretion in keeping silent so long; and I advise you to the same course. Speak to no one of this matter. Let it remain for the present a secret between you and me."

"Old Adah, highly flattered by the thought of having a secret in common with her master, kept from
all the rest of the world, warmly responded:

"I kep' dat secret to myse'f all dis time, waitin'
fo' yer to be well 'nuff to hear it, an' I will keep on
keepin' it, marster, an' red hot pinchers shouldn' pull
it out'n me till yer say so."

"I do not want any more neighborhood gossip or
excitement over this matter. I do not want the
sacred name of my wife bandied about from mouth
to mouth in speculating as to what has become of
her. I must confer with my own tried and trusty
friends and the local authorities, and we must take
counsel together. You understand, Adah?"

"Surely, surely, young marster, I unnerstan's so
puffect dat dat wor de reason w'y I kep' wot I kno'd
to myse'f till I could tell it to yo', Marse Tudor."

"Very well. Now I think I must be alone for a
little while. Do you go into the kitchen and tell
Nancy or Cassy to give you—whatever you would
like in the way of refreshments."

"Tank yer, Marse Tudor; I will go. Yer was allers
so 'siderate to de po'," gratefully replied the woman,
as she stooped and picked up her stick, slowly arose
and hobbled away towards the rear of the house.

Hereward, left alone, pressed his hands to his head.

"Am I dreaming?" he asked himself. "Is this one
of those delirious visions that tortured or delighted
me during the progress of my fever? Lilith—not
dead? Lilith living? Oh, Heaven! can such a happiness be really still possible to me, that I should see
Lilith again in the flesh? Oh, Heaven! that this could
come to pass! All evils of life would be nothing if
only Lilith could, peradventure, be restored to me
living. I would no longer care for all the fame and
glory that this world could give me, if only my child
wife could be returned to me! But can this be pos-

sible? What balance of proof is there in favor of her continued life, in the face of the verdict of that coroner's jury? I do not know; I cannot weigh evidence to-day! I am weak! I am weak! Kerr will be here soon. I will ask him what he thinks about the matter. I will tell him all and I will take his opinion."

As Hereward communed with himself in this manner the door opened, and Mrs. Jab Jordon came out on the piazza, bringing in her hands a silver waiter upon which was arranged a china plate of chicken jelly, another plate of delicate biscuits, a small decanter of port wine, and a wine glass.

She set the waiter with its contents upon the little stand beside Hereward's chair, and then, looking at the invalid critically, she inquired:

"What is the matter with you? You have been worrying and exciting yourself about something. And you know that is not good for you. Come, now, I want you to eat all this jelly and drink at least two glasses of wine, and then, as the sun is coming around this way and it is getting warm, I want you to come in and take your noon sleep."

Hereward smiled faintly and tried obediently to do as the lady bade him; but it is doubtful whether he would have accomplished the task before him had not Mrs. Jab drawn up a chair and drilled him into compliance.

When he had finished his light meal she took his arm and led him into the house and upstairs to the new room that had been prepared for him, and made him lie down on his bed.

Meanwhile, old Adah had gone into the kitchen, where she found Nancy superintending the preparations for dinner, while Cassy and the two younger negro women were engaged in paring potatoes, shelling peas, and capping strawberries.

"Mornin', chillun! How does all do dis fine mornin'?" said the old woman, as she slowly and stiffly lowered herself into the nearest chair and laid her stick on the floor.

"Mornin', Aunt Adah!" returned a chorus of voices, as the three women stopped their work and came around her.

"Glad to see de young marster out ag'in!" said Adah.

"Yes, he is out ag'in—wot's lef' ob him! 'Deed it's awful! Makes me fink ob my latter en'," said Nancy, with a deep sigh.

"Yes, it's a warnin'! It's a warnin'!" put in Cassy, without exactly defining what "it" meant.

" 'Deed I gwine look out an' see ef I can't j'in some more s'ieties. I 'longs to sebben or eight now, but I ain't satisfied in my own mine w'ich is de yight one, or eben ef any ob dem I 'long to is de yight one. An' dere can't be but one yight one, no way."

"Chile Nancy, I fink as yer 'longs to too many s'ieties. Now, one is 'nough for me, w'ich dat is de Rebbernt Marse Parson Cave's s'iety, w'ich is good 'nough for me, 'caze arter all it is de Lord I trus' in and not de s'iety," humbly suggested old Adah.

"G'way f'om yere, ole 'oman! Yer dunno wot yer talkin' 'bout! In dese yere drefful times I want to be on de safe side; so I j'ines all de s'icties I kin flue so as to get de yight one! I done hear ob two more s'icties way out yonder some'ars, w'ich I mean to j'in soon's ebber I get de chance."

"Two more s'ieties, A'n' Nancy!" exclaimed Cely opening her eyes to their widest extent.

"Yes, honey; yes, chillun! W'ich one is—le' me see now—wot's deir names a'gn? One is called de Shakin' Quakers. An' dat s'iety would suit me good, leastways in some fings; 'caze I doan beliebe in marr'in an' gibbin' in marridge no mo' dan dey do;

an' as fer de res' ob it, w'y, ebbery time I gets de fever'n' ager I ken shake an' quake wid de bes' ob 'em! An' dere's dat oder s'iety, 'way out yonder som'ers, as is called de More-men. But I misdoubts as dat one kin be de yight one, 'caze dey's just opposide to de oder one, an' beliebes in a doctrine called Pulliginy, an' libs up to it, to be sure, w'ich is mo' dan some s'ieties do deir doctrines."

"Wot's Pulliginy, Nancy, chile?" inquired old Adah.

"Pulliginy is de More-men perswashun. It means as a 'oman may marr' as many husband's as she kin take care ob! An' marster knows dat wouldn't suit me at all. I never could hab patience 'nuff wid de po' he-creeturs to marr' one husban', much less a whole pulliginy ob 'em. No—I can't say as I 'mire de More-men doctorine. Dough I is much exercise in my mine fear it might be de on'y yight one. Sure 'nuff, it must hab crosses 'nuff in it ef dat would sabe a soul."

"Nancy, chile, w'y can't yer trus' in de Lord, an' not trouble so much 'bout de s'ieties?" inquired old Adah.

" 'Caze I wants to be zactly yight an' sabe my soul an' go to Glory. But as for you, Aunt Adah, wot do you expec' as nebber goes inside ob any church?" demanded Nancy.

"Honey, I hum'ly hopes de dear Lord will sabe my soul, 'caze I can't go to church in my 'streme ole age—ninety-nine years old las' Can'lemas Day. Can't walk nigh so far, honey, an' can't sit so long; but I trus' in de Lord."

"An' you, 'lectin' de s'ieties as you do s'pects to go to Glory?" demanded Nancy, full of righteous indignation.

"No, honey, no—not to Glory. I nebber 'sumed to fink ob sich a fing as dat. But I do hope as de dear Lord will let me in to some little place in His kingdom

—some little house by some little crik running up
out'n de Ribber ob Life, whey I can lib in lub 'long ob
my dear ole man an' our chillun wot all went home so
many years ago. Dat's wot I hum'ly trus' in de Lord
to gib me."

"A'n' Adah, wouldn' yer like a bowlful of beef
soup?" inquired Cassy, breaking in upon this discussion.

"Yes, chile, I would, w'ich de young marster said as
I might hab a tumbler ob b'andy toddy, too."

"All yight. So you shall. An' yer'd better stay all
day wid us an' get bofe a good dinner an' a good supper, an' Cely an' Mandy 'ill take you home."

"T'anky, kindly, Cassy, chile, so I will," concluded
the aged woman, settling herself comfortably for a
whole day's enjoyment.

Early in the afternoon the Rev. Mr. Cave and Dr.
Kerr drove over together to see Tudor Hereward.

They were shown at once to his chamber, where
they found him reclining on a lounge near the open
window.

"You have been sitting out on the piazza this morning, I hear," said the doctor, after the first greetings
were over.

"Yes, for two hours," replied Hereward.

"Too long for a first effort. You have overtasked
yourself."

"No, it is not that, doctor. Please lock the door,
to prevent interruption, and draw your chairs up to
me, both of you. I have some strange news to communicate, which I received this morning," said Hereward, in some nervous trepidation.

"Yes! and that is just what has excited and exhausted you," said Dr. Kerr, as he complied with
Hereward's request, sat down beside him and felt his
pulse.

"And yet it was good news, if I can judge by the

expression of your face, Tudor," put in the rector, wondering, meanwhile, what good news could possibly have come to this awfully bereaved man.

"Yes, it was good news, if true; and there lies the great anxiety," replied Hereward.

And then to these two oldest of old friends and neighbors, the pastor of the parish and the physician of the family, Tudor Hereward told the story that had been told him by old Adah.

The two gentlemen were not so much amazed as the narrator had expected them to be, yet they were most profoundly interested.

"There must always be a doubt in these cases where the proof of identification seems to be in the clothing only, and not in the person," said the doctor.

"That is certainly so. Clothing may have changed hands, as in this instance," added the rector.

"I want your decided opinion, if you can give it to me, on this subject. It is no exaggeration to say that if it can be shown that the remains identified before the coroner's jury as those of my wife, were in reality not hers, but of another person, I should be lifted from death and despair to life and hope. For look you, my friends, in all the long and dreary days and in all the long and sleepless nights, I say to myself, that whoever struck the fatal blow, I, and I only, am the original cause of Lilith's death," said Hereward.

"You are so morbid on that subject that I despair of ever bringing you to reason," sighed the rector.

"At least until I have brought him to health! The body and mind are so nearly connected that when one is weakened or diseased, the other is apt to be so too," added the doctor.

"You are both mistaken. My remorse and despair have nothing to do with health of body or mind. They are both normal and natural. Listen to me.

If I, in the madness of the moment, had not insulted, outraged, and driven my young wife from my side, she would never have gone forth that bitter winter night to meet the cruel death at the hands of some midnight marauder—according to the verdict of the coroner's jury."

"But you did not send her to the creek," said the doctor.

"No! but I might as well have done so! Oh! I knew how it was—or might have been—for I will still hope that it was not so. She knowing that she was about to leave the Cliffs for an indefinite time, thought of the poor old woman who might suffer in her absence, and determined that she would pay her a last visit and leave with her provision—in money, which could be easily carried—to last her for a long time. In her feeling of mortification at having been cast off by her husband, she chose to go alone, so as not to expose her distress to any one—not even to a faithful servant. So, before setting out on her long journey, she started to visit old Adah, at the creek cabin, and met her fate—through me."

"If she did meet her fate! But, Hereward, I am inclined to believe the old woman's story," said the doctor.

"And so do I," added the rector.

"There is only one doubt," replied Hereward, "and it is this: The identification by the clothing only must still be unsatisfactory. Lilith was in mourning for my father. Her dress was always black, and of one pattern—that is, her ordinary dress, I mean, of course. It seems that she gave a suit of her clothing to that poor girl. What of that? She had other suits of the same sort of clothing, and wore one of those that same night, for she wore no other sort on common occasions. And the fear is that when she set out to visit old Adah at the creek cabin, she was met, robbed and murdered by this tramp and his girl, and that it was her screams that old Adah heard. For remember, that Lilith's watch and purse have never been found, nor any trace of Lilith herself, unless that found——" Hereward's voice broke down, and his head fell back upon his pillow.

Dr. Kerr went to a side table and poured out a glass of wine, which he brought and compelled his patient to drink.

"At any rate, Tudor, there is a very reasonable hope that Lilith still lives. Let this hope sustain and not exhaust you. Leave the matter in the hands of Divine Providence, first of all, and in the hands of your two friends as his servants and instruments. Say nothing of this to any one else. It would not be well to open up such a subject of discussion in this neighborhood. Wait until we have used every human means of discovering the whereabouts of your Lilith," said the rector, earnestly.

"Yes, that's it! Leave the affair to us, under Providence! We have no certainty; but the new hope is better than despair," added the doctor.

And to support moral teaching by physical means, he made up a sedative draught and left it with his patient.

The doctor and the rector went away together, much wondering at the new aspect given to the Cliff Creek tragedy by the revelations of old Adah.

They kept this revelation to themselves, and went about secretly trying to get some clew, either to the whereabouts of Lilith, or of the young girl to whom she had given a suit of her own clothes.

They visited old Adah in her cabin, and using her young master's, Tudor Hereward's, name, questioned her closely on the subject of the events that had transpired in her cabin on the night of the murder.

They cross-questioned her with a skill and persever-
ance that Hereward, in his weakened condition, could
never have shown. And old Adah answered them by
revealing freely all she knew and all she suspected.

They came away from that interview thoroughly
convinced that the body found in the creek was that
of the gypsy girl to whom Lilith had given a suit of
her clothes.

They were again together to Cloud Cliffs, and told
the suffering master of the house of their new and
strong convictions on the subject.

"Lilith lives! Be sure of that! No stone shall be
left unturned to discover her, and her restoration to
your arms is only a question of time, and of a very
little time also," said the doctor.

"Bear up, Tudor! It rests with yourself, under the
Lord, to recover your former health and strength of
body and mind. Rouse yourself! Be the calm, strong,
firm man that you have heretofore shown yourself,"
added the rector.

And Hereward grasped their hands and thanked
them warmly for their sympathy and services.

"But though we feel sure that Lilith lives, and
that we shall find her before many days, yet still, to
avoid giving rise to a sensational report, we have
determined to continue our first policy of reticence
until we shall really have found Lilith and restored
her to her home. Do you not approve our plan, Hereward?" inquired the doctor.

"Yes, certainly, that is the best," answered the
young man.

The two friends took leave of the patient and departed.

".All the same," said the doctor, as they walked
out together and re-entered their gig, "if Lilith is

not soon recovered, Tudor must die. The strain upon
him is too great to be borne."

"Let us trust in the Lord," said the rector, "and
hope for a happier issue."

CHAPTER III

THE NIGHT-PASSENGER'S NEWS

Rise! If the past detain you,
  Her sunshine and storms forget;
No chains so unworthy to hold you
  As those of a vain regret.
Sad or bright, it is lifeless ever,
  Cast its phantom arms away,
Nor look back but to learn the lesson
  Of a nobler strife to-day.
The future has deeds of glory,
  Of honor—God grant it may!
But your arm will never be stronger
  Or the need so great as to-day.

A. A. P.

THE Rev. Mr. Cave and the good Dr. Kerr, both
devoted friends of Tudor Hereward, had promised
him to leave nothing untried that might lead to a
clew to trace the fate of the missing women. For—
to reach the truth more promptly and effectually—it
was deemed highly important to institute an exhaus-
tive investigation into the movements of both the lost
ones, from the day of their disappearance.

One of them lay in her grave, in the village church-
yard; and the other had vanished.

But which was the dead and which was the living,
no human being at Frosthill could prove.

The negroes and the neighbors had identified the

body thrown up by the spring flood from the bed of the creek and found in the ravine as that of young Mrs. Tudor Hereward; but they had identified it only by the clothing and by the long, black, curling hair—only by these; for "decay's effacing finger" had blotted out every feature beyond recognition.

And this held good for the truth until old Adah declared in the most solemn manner her conviction that the remains were those of the poor gypsy girl Lucille, giving strong reasons to support her statement.

Lucille was dressed in a suit of young Mrs. Hereward's clothes, which had been bestowed on her by that lady.

Lucille had left Adah's hut that fatal night, in company with her ruffian husband, with whom she had ventured to remonstrate on his robbing the poor old woman of the goods sent her by Mrs. Hereward; and they had gone away quarreling until they were out of hearing; soon after which, and at about the time they might have reached the point where the path through the woods passed over the bridge crossing the creek, a piercing shriek rang through the air followed by another and another, startling the bed-ridden old woman in the hut and filling her soul with terror.

Then all was still as death.

Old Adah had not at that time suspected the man of killing his wife, but only of beating her brutally, as he had been in the habit of doing.

Never until she heard of the body that had been found did she think of murder.

Then, at the first opportunity, she had told her story and given her opinion to the convalescent master of the Cliffs, who, in her judgment, was entitled to the first information.

Tudor Hereward's "wish" was certainly "father to the thought" when he gave so ready a credence to old Adah's story, and called his two oldest and most faithful friends into counsel as to the best means of ascertaining the truth.

And they, without committing themselves to any positive opinion—for, in such a case, they could have no just grounds for entertaining one—had pledged their words to leave "no stone unturned" for discovering the truth.

To do so, they knew that they must search for clews for both the missing women.

And they searched long, thoroughly, but fruitlessly, until near the end of May.

They ascertained from the accounts of the ticket agent at Frosthill that two passengers only had bought tickets for the midnight express on that fatal 21st of March. One was a ruffianly young man, he—the agent—was sure, but the other he could not describe at all.

Now who were those two passengers?

The uttermost efforts of our amateur detectives failed to discover. They could find no one in the village or in the surrounding country who had taken the train that night.

The "ruffianly young man" mentioned by the ticket agent was probably the husband of the poor gypsy girl; but who was the other passenger? Was she his wife, traveling with him, as they had set out from the hut to do, or was it Lilith, who was a mere accidental fellow-passenger?

No one could tell.

And so the time passed in fruitless search and heart-sickening suspense, until late in May, when one morning, as Dr. Kerr was seated in his office, the door opened and a stranger entered.

The doctor, believing the visitor to be a patient, arose and offered him a chair.

"Thank you, sir. I dare say you are surprised to

see me, sir," said the man, as he seated himself, took
off his hat and wiped his face.

"Not at all. Strangers sometimes honor me with
a call," blandly replied the doctor.

"Yes, I know, for medical advice, with a fee in
their hands, and then they have a right to come, and
you are glad to see them. But I don't want any medical advice whatever, and I haven't brought any fee;
and that's the reason why I am afraid you will think
I am intruding."

"Not at all, if I can serve you in any way," politely
replied the doctor.

"Yes, but you can't even do that! I don't stand in
need of services."

"Then will you kindly enlighten me as to the circumstance to which I am indebted for this honor?" inquired the doctor, with a smile of amusement.

"Do you mean to ask what brought me here?"

"Yes, if you please."

"Well, I don't mind telling you. I should have to do
it anyway, because that is what I came for. My name
is Carter, and I came from Maryland."

"Yes?" smiled the doctor.

"And have been traveling through the country here
looking for land."

"Quite so, and you have found a great deal."

"I mean, and to buy. I hear that land is very good
and cheap about here and the climate very healthy."

"All quite true; but I fear I cannot help you in the
least in that matter. You had better take counsel with
Lawyer Jordon, who acts as land agent occasionally,"
said the doctor.

"Did I ask you to help me? I told you first off that
I didn't want any service."

"Then what in the name of——"

"Sense have I come for?"

"Yes, if you please."

"Why, I am telling you, man! Being in search of a suitable farm, I have been traveling about these parts considerable. Last night I came here and put up at 'The Stag.' Good house that!"

"Pretty good. Yes."

"Well, I did hear of a rum case. The body of that young woman being found, and there being a distressing doubt whether it be that of young Mrs. Tudor Hereward, who disappeared from the neighborhood on the 21st of last March, or that of a little gypsy tramp, who bore a great personal resemblance to that lady, and who was suspected of having been made way with by her ruffian of a husband!"

"Yes, yes," eagerly exclaimed the doctor, all his listless indifference vanished. "Yes! You have heard of that affair. You have been traveling about in this region. Is it possible that you may be able to throw some light on that dark subject?"

"I think I may; that is what has brought me here this morning. Perhaps I ought to have gone out to the place they call the Cliffs to see Mr. Tudor Hereward himself; but they told me it was a matter of six miles from the village, and that perhaps I had better see you, as you were interested; and so here I am."

"I am very glad you did. Now tell me quickly what you have to tell, for I am extremely anxious to hear," said the doctor, eagerly.

"Wait a bit! Let us see how the land lies first. You say young Mrs. Hereward and the gypsy girl looked alike?"

"In size, figure, and the unusual length and beauty of their hair—yes!"

"And that both disappeared from the neighborhood the same night. At least so I heard from the talk at the Stag."

"It was true."

"And a young woman's body was found near the creek a month afterwards?"

"Yes."

"But so far gone that it could not be identified except by the clothing?"

"True."

"And that clothing was recognized as having been young Mrs. Hereward's?"

"Yes."

"And that proved to the coroner's jury the body to be also young Mrs. Hereward's."

"Yes."

"Until a certain old woman comes with a tale that young Mrs. Hereward gave those clothes to the gypsy girl?"

"You have a correct account."

"And so the doubt remains, which of the two missing women was killed and thrown into the creek, and which levanted from the neighborhood?"

"Yes, that is the situation at present. Can you help us to clear up the doubt?" anxiously inquired the doctor.

"Well, I rather reckon I can clear it up pretty decidedly, if not satisfactorily."

"What do you mean? Speak!"

"You were much interested in young Mrs. Hereward?"

"I was very much attached to her, having known her from her infancy."

"Then I am afraid I am going to grieve you. I am indeed," said the man, gravely and hesitatingly.

"Oh, what do you mean?"

"It was that young gypsy girl who took the train at Frosthill at midnight of March 21st," said Carter, in a low tone.

The doctor stared gravely for a moment, and then inquired:

"How do you know this?"

"Because I was on that very same train, and sat in that very same car along with her."

"Man! Is this undoubtedly true?" demanded the doctor.

"Well, I will tell you all about it, and then you will see that it is true. I took the train at West-bourne and traveled on until we got to Frosthill, which it reached at midnight, and where it stopped for one minute. Two passengers got on—a young man who looked like a young devil, saving your pres-ence, he had such a dark, scowling, lowering face. He was clothed in a rough overcoat, and had his hands thrust into his pockets, and never offered the least assistance to the young woman, who came creep-ing and cowering behind him. I couldn't help but notice them both, and saw at a glance that they were man and wife, and that they had had a row, in which the woman, of course, had come off second best. He looked so wicked and sullen, and she so frightened and broken-hearted. He just threw himself into a seat, and stretched out his legs over the top of an-other one; and she slunk away into a corner, and turned her face to the wall, and cried fit to break her heart. And he never took any more notice of her than if she had been a dog. I wanted to kick him all around the car. There was plenty of room to do it, too, because there weren't a half a dozen people in that car, all told. I got out at Snowden, about twenty miles farther on, where I stopped over a day to look at a farm, and I never thought any more about that ruffian husband and gypsy wife until I came here to Frosthill last night, and heard the whole story of the mystery at the Stag. And then I thought I would tell you what I had seen at the Frosthill sta-tion, at midnight, on the twenty-first of March," con-cluded the visitor.

"I thank you very much. Still, still, there may be ground for a faint hope. How was this girl whom you saw in the man's company dressed, do you remember?" inquired the doctor, with increased uneasiness.

"Oh, yes; I remember quite well. She was clothed in a red suit, with something dark about her head and shoulders. And Mrs. Hereward was in deep mourning, they say, for her father."

"Yes, she was," said the doctor, as the faint hope died away. "And this red suit," he added, mentally, "was, of course, the very suit that she used to wear before she went in mourning, and which, of course, she must have given to the girl in preference—upon every account of economy and fitness—to giving her a black one."

While the doctor was turning these hopeless thoughts over in his mind the visitor arose and said:

"Well, sir, I have told you all I came to tell, and now I must go. But I shall be in this neighborhood for a few days longer, if anybody wants to ask me any questions about this matter."

The doctor also arose and said:

"I thank you, Mr. Carter, for the trouble you are taking, and shall, perhaps, have occasion to see you again. You will be at the Stag?"

"Yes, mostly, for the rest of this week; but I shall be riding round a good deal in the daytime, looking at land, but always at home—leastways at the hotel —at night, and shall be glad to see you or any one you send. Good-morning, sir."

"Good-morning, Mr. Carter."

And the visitor left.

The doctor sat ruminating over what he had heard for some time after he had been left alone.

At length, when his office hours were over, instead of taking his noontide meal and rest as a preparation for his afternoon round of professional visits, he rang for his servant, ordered his horse, and started on a ride to the Cliffs.

He did not go to the mansion house, but taking a narrow bridle path through the woods to the creek, he crossed the little rustic bridge, and drew up at the log hut in the thicket on the other side.

Here he dismounted, tied his horse to a tree, and went up to the door, where he found old Adah sitting in the sun, and busy with her knitting.

"Well, auntie, how is the rheumatism to-day?" he inquired cheerfully, as the old woman stood up and courtesied.

"T'anky, Marse Doctor, sah. Dis warm sun hab melted it all out'n my bones. 'Deed it's de trufe. Will you come inter de house, Marse Doctor, or take a chair out yere?" she inquired, politely.

"I will stay out here," replied the doctor, as he settled himself on a little bench outside the door.

"Have anyfing been yeard 'bout po' dee Miss Lilif, Marse Doctor?" anxiously questioned old Adah.

"No. Not since the verdict of the coroner's jury," significantly replied Dr. Kerr.

"Oh, Lor', Marse Doctor, dat want nuffin. Dat hadn' nuffin to do long ob Miss Lilif. Dat war de gypsy gal wot war foun' in dem woods, and war sot on by dat jury. I done tole Marse Tudor Her'ward all bout dat a mont' ago," said old Adah, speaking with the utmost confidence.

"Yes; I have heard so from Mr. Hereward himself. I know all the evidence you have brought forward in rebuttal of the evidence given before the coroner. I would to Heaven it had been as conclusive as you thought. But we will not go into that. I only wish to ask you a few questions."

"Go on Marse Doctor. I'll answer de trufe. I ain't got no secrets from nobody."

"Well, then, did you see the clothing worn by the gypsy girl on the night she left the hut in company with her husband?"

"Yes, Marse Doctor, I did. I yeard her say how Missis Her'ward had gib it to her, an' I seed her put it on, an' tie her ole close—nuffin but duds dey was—in a bundle."

"What was the color of those clothes?"

"Dem wot she took off an' tied into a bundle?"

"No, no; those given her by Mrs. Hereward."

"Oh! dose as she wo' 'way?"

"Yes."

"Wot was it yer ax me 'bout 'em, Marse Doctor?"

"I asked you what color they were?"

"Oh! Dey was sort o' dark."

"Dark red?"

"Now, dey mought o' been. Or dey mought o' been dark blue or dark black. You see, Marse Doctor, it was sort o' dark in de house, an' it made eberyfing look dark."

"Had you no light?"

"Nuffin' but a tallow dip—dat didn' show much."

"And you can't be certain about the color of the clothing?"

"No, Marse Doctor; on'y it were dark. I sort o' t'ought it were dark black, but I dessay it were dark red, jes' as you say."

The doctor asked a few more questions, and then arose to depart. He put a half dollar into the hand of the old woman, who thanked him heartily. And then he remounted his horse and rode away along the same bridle-path that led back through the thicket to the little bridge crossing the creek, and by a circuit through the next woods up to the mansion house.

He found Tudor Hereward walking up and down on the front piazza. He had convalesced so very slowly that he had not yet been strong enough to take a ride.

Hereward dropped heavily into a chair as the doctor dismounted, threw his bridle to Steve, who came up to take it, and walked up the steps.

"Any news, doctor?" anxiously inquired Mr. Hereward.

"Not a trace of Lilith yet. No, I did not come to bring news, but to make a few investigations here in the house that may lead to something."

"Very well, doctor; you have carte blanche. But what is the nature of the investigation in this instance?" wearily inquired Hereward.

"Into the wardrobe of your wife, to see what is missing, and what is left."

Hereward sighed, as if he were very weary of a hopeless subject and then faintly replied:

"Why, you know that has been done, thoroughly, and there is nothing missing but the one black waterproof cloth suit that was found on the body of that poor murdered gypsy girl."

"And that was Lilith's usual walking-dress when in the country, was it not?"

"Yes, it was; but she gave it to that poor girl upon whose dead body it was found."

"She gave a suit; but you do not know that it was the waterproof suit she gave. She would not have been likely to have given the suit that she was in the habit of wearing, and that she could not very well do without," suggested the doctor.

"Ah! but she did give it. It was found on the body of the girl."

"You still feel so sure that it was the body of the gypsy girl which was found?"

"Yes, I do. Oh, doctor, why do you doubt it?" demanded Hereward, with the fretful querulousness of an invalid.

"Because we cannot be sure until the other miss·
ing one is found. Until the living one turns up we
cannot prove who is the dead," gravely replied the
physician.

"How much proof do you want? The dress that
Lilith gave to the gypsy girl was found on the dead
body."

"But you do not know that the black waterproof
cloth was the dress that was given by Lilith to the
girl. I repeat, that it was not likely that Lilith should
have given away a suit that was so necessary to her
own comfort, when she might have given others."

"But that is the only one missing from her ward·
robe."

"The only one missing from her wardrobe?"

"Yes. I have told you so twice before."

"Then, if Lilith is living, what dress did she wear
when she left home?" significantly inquired the doctor.

Hereward started, turned paler than before, and
stared fixedly at the questioner. He had never asked
himself that question. He stared, but did not speak.

"Tudor, my dear boy, we must look facts in the
face. And now I ask you, was the discarded ward·
robe of your wife examined when the investigation
was made?"

"The discarded wardrobe?" questioned Hereward,
with a perplexed look.

"Yes; I mean the colored clothing that she left
off and packed away when she went into mourning
for your father?"

"Of course it was not touched. She would not
have been likely to wear colored clothing in her deep
mourning."

"No, of course she would not. But she would have
been very likely to give that left-off colored clothing
to the gypsy instead of the mourning suit, which
would have been unsuitable to the girl."

Again Hereward started, changed color and gazed
at the speaker, but without uttering a word.

"Come, Hereward, let us send for Nancy and have
her search through her mistress' left-off clothing, to
see if any portion of it is missing. Shall I ring?"
inquired the doctor.

"If you—please," faltered the young man, sinking
back into his chair.

Dr. Kerr rang the door-bell which was soon answered by Alick, who had reinstated himself in his
place as butler at the Cliffs, but who was still a poor,
broken-hearted old man, grieving for his young
mistress, and accusing himself of being her murderer.

"Go and tell Nancy to come here," said Dr. Kerr.

Alick ducked his head and disappeared.

Nancy soon stood in his place.

"Aunty," said the doctor, speaking for his young
friend and patient, "I wish you to open all Mrs. Hereward's boxes of colored clothing, and examine every
article and find out if any be missing."

"Berry well, sah," said the woman, turning and
going to do her errand.

The doctor followed her into the house, went to
the corner buffet in Lilith's parlor, and took out a
certain liqueur case, opened it, and proceeded to mix
a strong, restorative cordial, which he brought out
and placed on the stand beside Hereward's chair,
saying:

"Drink half of that now, Hereward, and leave the
rest."

The young man obeyed, and then, as he put down
the half emptied glass, he inquired:

"What is it that you expect to prove by this new
search, doctor?"

"Wait and see, dear boy! I do not yet know what
myself."

About half an hour passed, and Nancy came down-stairs.

"Well, auntie, have you missed anything?" inquired Dr. Kerr.

"Yes, Marse Doctor. Miss Lilif's red cashmere dress, w'ich was her mos' favorite home dress, an' w'ich she wo' de werry day 'fo' she was marr'd, an' 'fo' ole marse died, an' nebber wored since den."

"And are you sure it is gone?"

"Yes, Marse Doctor, sure, 'cause I knowed whey I packed it away, an' nobody ebber went to dat trunk 'cept it was me an' Miss Lilif."

"And what do you think has become of it, Nancy?"

"Well, Marse Doctor, I s'pose as po' dee Miss Lilif give it to dat po' gal wot come beggin'. I know she did give her a bundle of close, 'caze I helped dat gal to carry dat bundle t'rough de woods an' 'cross de crik to ole Aunt Adah's house."

"Did you see what was in the bundle, Nancy?"

"No, Marse Doctor, not I. I warn't upstairs in Miss Lilif's room w'en she give 'way dem close, I war downsta'rs in de store room packing ob a bas-ket wid tea an' sugar, an' bread, an' meat, an' fings, to tote to po' ole Aunt Adah, 'cordin' to Miss Lilif's orders, an' I nebber seen dat bundle till dat gal fotch it downsta'rs, an' I nebber seen wot war in-side ob it; but de gal tell me, as I went along wid her, how de young madame had gib her a good dress, an' dat it must a been dat red cashmere dress wot de young mist'ess couldn' wear herse'f, 'stead of bein' de black mournin' dress wot she could wear; let alone de fac' dat de young gal wouldn't a-liked to 'cepted a mournin' dress, not bein' in no mournin'. It wouldn't a been lucky."

"You are right," said the doctor. "It was the red cashmere dress that Mrs. Hereward gave to the girl,

and that the girl wore when she left the neighborhood that night."

"Oh, most merciful Heaven, doctor! Do you mean
to knock from under me the last prop of hope that
sustains me?" groaned Hereward, sinking back pale
and faint as any woman might have looked at such
a crisis.

"Hush, Tudor! Drink this," said Dr. Kerr, placing the glass of restorative cordial to his lips.

Hereward emptied the glass, and the doctor set it
down, and continued:

"I deprive you of no real hope, Tudor, but of a
false hope which, instead of being a prop to support
you, is a burden that is wearing you out with anxiety.
The sooner you give up all hope the sooner you will
be able to resign yourself to the inevitable and find
peace and rest for your spirit."

"But I cannot! I cannot resign all hope! I cannot!" passionately exclaimed the young man.

"Listen to me further. Hear all that I have to say
and you must do so," gravely and tenderly replied
the doctor.

"What have you to tell me now? You said you
had no news to bring me of Lilith. You said so when
you first came in and I asked you the question."

"And I spoke the truth," patiently replied the old
man. "I had no news of Lilith. But I had news of
the gypsy girl, which—ah me!—leaves me no doubt
as to whose remains they were that were found in
the woods."

"Oh, Heaven! Oh, Heaven!" groaned Hereward.
"But tell me all! I can bear it! Yes, I can bear it!"

"There is a man by the name of Carter now stopping at the Stag, who was in the train at midnight
of March 21st, when the strolling player and his
gypsy wife got on board. He was a sullen ruffian in
coarse clothing. She a pretty, dark-eyed gypsy,

with black hair, and she was dressed in a red suit, with something dark about her head and shoulders. They were the only people who got in that train at Frosthill. They had been quarreling, and the man had a scowling, ferocious look, while the woman seemed terrified and broken-hearted. Does not this coincide perfectly with all that we have heard about the poor girl and her ruffianly companion?" gently inquired the doctor.

Hereward replied only by a groan.

"Come, Tudor! I must take you upstairs. You must lie down, and I will send Cave to you," said the doctor, with gentle firmness.

But it was with considerable difficulty that the doctor finally prevailed on his deeply stricken patient to seek the rest and retirement of his own chamber.

Then Dr. Kerr, leaving Nancy in charge of the sick-room, went downstairs, got into his saddle and rode off, dinnerless, to make a round of professional visits on a circuit of at least thirty miles. It was very late in the afternoon when he finally reached Frost-hill.

Even then, before going home, he stopped at the rectory and had half an hour's interview with the Rev. Mr. Cave, in which he told the latter of all the news he had received and all the discoveries he had made concerning the fate of Lilith, during the day. He ended by asking the rector to go with him to the Stag to see and question Carter.

Mr. Cave put on his hat and walked with Dr. Kerr the short distance that lay between the rectory and the hotel.

They found Carter smoking in the little reading-room. He willingly accompanied the gentlemen to the parlor, at their request, and closeted there, he readily answered every question put to him, but, after all, they elicited nothing more than had been told to the doctor that morning.

At the end of the interview they thanked Carter and took leave of him.

"And, after all," sighed Mr. Cave, "the verdict of the coroner's jury was right."

"Yes," assented the doctor, "it was right! And now I do not think we have far to look for the dastardly murderer of Lilith Hereward."

"Whom do you suspect?" inquired the rector, in a low, awe-stricken voice.

"The ruffian husband of the gypsy girl who was on the creek the same night of her death."

CHAPTER IV

A STARTLING VISIT

EARLY next morning Mr. Cave, in accordance with the request of Dr. Kerr, went to the Cliffs to spend the day with Tudor Hereward. He found the young man too ill to leave his room, seated in a reclining-chair near the open window.

The effects of alternate hope and fear ending at last in despair deepened by remorse.

Mr. Cave sat down beside him and essayed to comfort him; but he did not succeed. Loss, sorrow and disappointment may be consoled, but remorse and despair are beyond comfort.

"The truest, gentlest, fondest child that ever blessed man I drove out that bitter night to meet her cruel death! It is that which is killing me," he said, in reply to Mr. Cave's well meant efforts to rouse and cheer him.

"You are morbid, Hereward. You are too severe

on yourself. You are not rational and consistent. You should remember, my dear friend, you did not mean to drive her away."

"Ah, but the taunting, insulting, unpardonable words I hurled at her, heaped upon her head, overwhelming her—no true woman could have borne them! If she had been the creature I suspected and accused her of being, she might have borne them and remained here for profit; but Lilith had no alternative but to leave the house! And I drove her from it as surely as if I had taken her by the shoulders and put her out and turned the key against her!"

"I do not think you should consider it in that light. Besides, for the words you used, you would do wisely to remember now the provocation you received," gravely suggested Mr. Cave.

"Not from her! Not from Lilith! She was ever true, meek, gentle and wonderfully self-controlled for a being so young. No! I never received provocation from that child," said Hereward, with a deep sigh.

"Then from false appearances!—false appearances which would have driven a much older and wiser man than you quite beside himself."

"But against which I should have set Lilith's life and character then—as I do now. No, Mr. Cave, you need not talk to me of comfort. I will not receive it!"

"Ah, Tudor, you hug, cherish, and cultivate your sorrow."

"Not my sorrow! Sorrow is a matter of time, and it may be consoled. But remorse is a thing of eternity, never to be comforted."

"You seem to nourish this remorse as a matter of duty and conscience."

"Yes, I do. I will not take comfort."

"Tudor, my dear boy, there never was a case of insanity in either branch of your family. Their brains were too strong and too well balanced, else I should fear for you. But at any rate you really must go away from this place," said the minister, very earnestly.

"Well, and if I should, it would be only to wander over the earth as aimlessly and drearily as the legendary Jew," replied the young man.

Mr. Cave remained with him until nearly dark, and then went away, promising to come and see the solitary mourner in a very few days.

The next morning the invalid, with the assistance of the two men-servants, got downstairs and into the front piazza, where he sat in his favorite reclining-chair, with a little stand beside him.

He was still sitting there alone, gazing vacantly out upon the lovely summer scene of mountain, valley, woods and waters spread out before him, when the sound of a strange footstep, a firm and ringing footstep, fell upon his ear.

In another moment the figure of a young man, dressed as a gentleman, emerged from the footpath through the alder bushes, and came into view.

In that moment, with a start of surprise, Hereward recognized the form and face of Mr. Alfred Ancillon.

The young wanderer came up the steps, and standing in front of the pale and fainting invalid, took off his hat, and in a stern voice demanded—as if he had the most sacred right to demand:

"Tudor Hereward! Where is Lilith?"

"Lilith! How dare you utter that name!—the name of the lady whose destruction you have compassed?" faintly yet indignantly demanded Hereward.

"No! not I, sir! I never wounded her by a word! I never wronged her by a thought! Your senseless jealousy has wrought all this ruin! Only ten days ago, in the remote Southwestern town where I was fulfilling an engagement, did I happen to pick up an

old copy of the New York *Pursuivant,* and read the
account of her dead body having been found three
weeks after she had disappeared from her home! I
threw up my engagement and came here with all
speed, for well I guessed that you, and you only, had
the secret of her disappearance and her death. For—
'Jealousy is as cruel as the grave!' "

"Had I no just cause for jealousy?" demanded
Hereward, thrown upon his defence, trembling with
weakness and scarcely conscious of having instinctively put the question.

"No!—as the Lord is my judge and yours! A better,
truer, purer woman than Lilith never lived! A holier
tie than that which bound us never united man and
woman!" retorted Ancillon. "Utterly blameless,
though reckless folly and egotism, if not even insanity,
placed her in a false position, created false appearances about her. But should all this have led you to
suspect Lilith? Lilith, who was brought up at your
good, wise father's feet, and by your side? Lilith,
who was so carefully trained in all wisdom and goodness? Lilith, whose religious and self-sacrificing spirit
you knew so well? Should any false appearances have
shadowed the brightness of Lilith's image in your
eyes?"

"Man! Hold your peace! I am passing from earth,
soon to meet Lilith in the better world, if repentance
and faith can take me there. I wish not to quarrel
with you now!"

"I will not hold my peace! I came here to ask you
—Where is Lilith?"

"And you ask it in the tone in which the minister
reads the question: 'Cain, where is thy brother Abel?'
Lilith is in her grave," moaned Hereward.

"Yes, she is. And you have put her there. You
have as surely murdered your young wife as if you
had plunged a sword through her bosom, like that

black brute, Othello, whom I never could consider a
'noble' Moor, and never would personate to please
anybody. Othello, when he found out his mistake,
had the decency to kill himself—the only decent
thing he ever did do! But you, Tudor Hereward—
the law cannot hang you for driving your young
wife out to death. Why have you not had the manhood to hang yourself?"

"Man, spare your reproaches! I am passing from
earth, and if repentance and faith avail me, going
to that other world, where I shall receive my dear
one's forgiveness. You may spare your reproaches,
as indeed I do not know how, or by what right, you,
of all men, dare to make them," said Hereward, with
more dignity than he had hitherto shown.

"I speak by the most sacred right that a man could
have to speak," solemnly replied Ancillon.

"What are you to Lilith, or what was Lilith to you?
A man may not know all his wife's relations. You
may be of Lilith's kindred—and, indeed, I notice a
likeness between your faces—but you cannot be of
very near kindred."

"No?" queried Ancillon, with a wistful look.

"No!" repeated Hereward, with more emphasis
than he had yet used in speaking—"No! for you are
not her brother. I knew her father and mother;
they were young people just married a year when
Lilith was born. She was not only their first, but
their only child. The father—ah me!—lost his life
while rescuing me from drowning, a few days before
Lilith was born. Her mother, shocked to death by
the sudden bereavement, gave birth to her child and
died. My father took the infant orphan from beside
the dead mother, and brought her home to be his own
adopted daughter. So that Lilith was an only child,
and you could not be her brother."

"No, I am not her brother," assented Ancillon, with the same wistful look.

"And if you are merely her cousin, or even her uncle, the relationship in either case would not give you the right to take such liberties with her name and memory as you have taken, and are taking now."

"But I am not either her uncle or her cousin," said Ancillon, with the same inscrutable look.

"Then, in the name of Heaven, man! what are you, that you have dared to do as you have done?" demanded Hereward, with an excitement for which he was to pay in a dangerous reaction and depression.

"Mr. Hereward," said Ancillon, with more gravity than he had lately exhibited, "I came here not only to ask that question which first I put to your conscience, but also to place in your possession a secret that I have hitherto guarded with the most jealous care, not only for my own sake, but even for yours, and most of all, for Lilith's, that no sorrow should come to her gentle heart, no reproach to her spotless name; but now that she is gone I care not at all what doom may fall upon me, or what shame may confuse you."

Ancillon paused and smiled grimly.

"Speak, man! Speak, man—speak! What is it you would tell me?" demanded Hereward, trembling with agitation.

"I would tell you nothing!"

"Nothing?"

"Nothing; for you might not believe my words. But I will give the means of discovering my secret for yourself—of learning my story, and proving its truth beyond all doubt," gravely replied Ancillon.

"Well? Well? Well?"

"Do you happen to know of an old trunk, the property of Lilith's parents, filled with family relics and correspondence, bundles of yellow letters, photographs, trinkets, prayer-books, Bibles, old diaries, newspapers, pamphlets, and other rubbish? Do you happen to know of such a depository?"

"I think I do," said Hereward, reflectingly. "Yes; I am sure I do," he added, confidently.

"It seems to have been packed and preserved by your father's orders, after the death of Lilith's mother and for the possible pleasure or benefit of Lilith's after life. Ah, dear! It was anything but a pleasure or a benefit to the poor child. It was never opened from the day it was packed until the day after your father's funeral, when you had gone to Washington, leaving Lilith alone in this old house. Then, she having received the key of the trunk for the first time, as a legacy from your father, sent for the trunk and opened it. And then she learned the dire secret of her family, even before she ever saw my face. It was an accident that brought me to the Cliffs, that night, Mr. Hereward."

"I heard that it was—the storm——"

"Not so. The storm kept me at the Cliffs, but did not bring me here. I was a guest at Rushmore, and at the supper table chanced to hear, in the gossip of the ladies, the story of Lilith Wyvil's adoption and marriage. To me it was a revelation. I determined to see her. I did so, and was storm-bound for a week at the Cliffs."

"Ah!"

"That trunk, Mr. Hereward, is at your disposal. All necessary information can be found within it. Seek and know and prove it, all for yourself! When you have done so, you may deliver me over to the British authorities as a fugitive from justice and send me back to England, under your favorite extradition treaty—to penal servitude for life! I care not one farthing now that Lilith is gone!"

"Man! Man! in Heaven's name, who and what are

you?" demanded Hereward, pale and shaking with emotion.

"I am known to the British police authorities as John Weston, the mail robber; to the keepers of Portland prison, Z. 789; to the play-going public as Mr. Alfred Ancillon, tragedian, comedian, tenor and athlete; in diplomatic circles in Washington as Señor Zuniga, nephew of the P—— Minister; but to Lilith I was known by another name, and in a sweeter relation. There! I have said and done all for which I came here. I am going now. Good-bye! I shall be at the Antler's in Frosthill all this week, waiting your pleasure;" and the visitor put on his hat and walked off by the way through which he had come.

He had seen Mr. Hereward drop back in his chair; but neither knew nor, if he had known, would have cared that the invalid had fallen into a deep swoon.

In this condition Dr. Kerr found him a few minutes later.

After using prompt means for his recovery, and seeing him open his eyes and breathe again, the doctor made him swallow a cordial, and then asked him what had caused his swoon.

"Weakness, I suppose," evasively answered the invalid.

The doctor took him into the cool, shady drawing-room and made him lie down on the sofa.

And then, when his strength was somewhat restored by the cordial he had swallowed, the doctor produced a large envelope with an official stamp, and said:

"I brought this from the post-office for you. I hope it may contain good news that will rouse you up."

Hereward thanked the doctor, and, without lifting his head from the sofa pillow, opened the long envelope and took out a letter partly in print and partly in writing. His pale face flushed a little as he read the paper, and he passed it over to Dr. Kerr, saying:

"You see it is a letter announcing my appointment as secretary of legation to the new embassy to the court of ——, and requiring me, in the event of my accepting the mission, to be ready to sail with the party by the Kron Prinz, on the first of June."

"And you will accept it, Hereward? The sea voyage and the change will be so good for you."

"Yes, I shall accept it."

CHAPTER V

LILITH'S FLIGHT

Do you think, because you fail me
　And draw back your hand to-day,
That from out the heart I gave you
　My strong love can fade away?
It will live. No eyes may see it;
　In my soul it will lie deep,
Hidden from all; but I shall feel it
　Often stirring in its sleep.
So remember that the true love,
　Which you now think poor and vain,
Will endure in hope and patience
　Till you ask for it again.
A. A. Proctor.

WHEN Lilith left the presence of her husband on that fatal night of their parting, her mind and heart were in a whirl of confusion and suffering.

He had accused her of unspeakable, of incomprehensible evil! He had repudiated her! He had told her that in a few hours he should leave that house

—his patrimonial home—never to return to it while she should "desecrate it by her presence."

Her love was wounded to the quick! Her pride was trampled in the dust.

What remained for her to do?

First of all to leave the house which he declared that she "desecrated with her presence."

Yes, that was the first and the most urgent duty that she owed to him who had repudiated her and to herself, and her own honor and self-respect as well.

It was good to know what first to do. It saved useless brooding and loss of time.

As soon as she reached her room, therefore, she locked the door to secure herself from interruption, and then she began to prepare for her departure.

For she determined to go at once and to take with her nothing, no, not the smallest trifle, that Hereward had ever given her.

So she took off the deep mourning dress that had been one of Hereward's first gifts, hung it up in the wardrobe, and replaced it with a crimson cashmere, the gift of his father, which since Major Hereward's death had been packed away with other clothing, left off when she first went into black.

From the same depository she took a gray beaver cloth coat, a gray felt hat, gray barege vail and a pair of gray gloves. These she laid out upon the bed.

Next she took from her casket the few jewels given her by her foster-father, and the few hundred dollars she had saved from the liberal allowance Major Hereward had made her during his life. All these, together with her comb and brushes, a few pocket-handkerchiefs, and a single change of underclothing, she packed into a hand-bag.

When her small preparations were all complete, it

seemed to require a painful wrench to tear herself
away.

Her husband had outraged and repudiated her indeed; yet she felt that she could not leave the house
without writing to him a few words of farewell. She
meant to write only a very few words, not half a
dozen lines in all, only enough to remind him that she
went not of her own will, but by his will.

Yet, when she sat down at the table and commenced her letter, a flood of thought and feeling bore
her impetuously onward to a fuller utterance, and
she poured forth her soul in that touching. pathetic,
yet dignified letter that he afterwards found upon her
dressing-table, and which, after perusal, and with
reckless anger, he committed to the flames.

When she had finished her task, sealed her letter,
and pinned it to the pin-cushion where he could not
fail to find it, she put on her gray beaver coat, hat,
vail and gloves, took up her hand-bag and left the
room.

She paused for a moment in the upper hall, and
looked over the balusters to see if any one were in
sight or hearing below.

But there was no one. The coast was clear. There
was no danger of interruption.

So Lilith went softly down the stairs, opened the
hall door and passed out into the night.

The sky was clear and the stars were shining
brightly down on the snow-covered earth.

All the servants, horses and carriages attached to
the place were at the young mistress' order; but
she chose to avail herself of none of them. She would
walk to the railway station. The clear, starlit sky
and the snow-white earth rendered her road light
enough for convenience. As for danger, there was
none of any sort. No act of violence had ever been
known to occur in that primitive, rural neighborhood,

which might almost have been called Arcadian in its
simplicity and innocence. She knew that she could
easily walk the six miles in two hours and catch the
ten o'clock train. So she walked bravely on until she
came to the outer gate. Just as she was in the act
of opening it she was startled by a rushing sound behind her, and turning, saw Lion, the large Newfoundland dog, at her side, evidently bent on following her.

"Yes, good dog. Good, good dog, you shall go!
And then if there could be any danger you would
guard me with you life. Wouldn't you, good dog?"

Lion assured his mistress, in much eloquent pan-
tomime, that he was her own devoted dog and would
die for her if necessary.

Lilith went on, the dog trotting by her side, over
the stubble fields, into the dense forest, out again,
through the narrow mountain pass, out again into the
fields, and finally in sight of the lights at the railway
station.

Here Lilith stopped to draw the vail more closely
around her face, for she did not wish to be recognized by any acquaintance who might ask her questions. Here, too, she must part with her dog. It
would not be well to take him with her to the railway station, either for her sake or for his own. So
she must send him home; but she wished to part
pleasantly with her fourfooted friend—not to drive
him away from her, but to send him on an errand for
her; so she opened her hand-bag and took off a paper
which had been wrapped around her brushes, breathed
into the paper, rolled it up to a convenient size and
gave it to the dog, putting it between his jaws, pat-
ting him on the head, turning him with his nose
towards the Cliffs, and saying:

"Good dog! Good dog! Good fellow! Carry it
home! Carry it home!"

And Lion, delighted at having an important commission to execute, set off at a run.

Lilith dashed a tear from her eye and hurried on to the railway station. There was not a soul there except the ticket agent and a rough-looking passenger.

Lilith knew exactly the price of a ticket to Baltimore, and had her change ready. She went into the musty office, pushed the money on the ledge of the ticket window, and said, from behind her vail:

"One, to Baltimore."

The agent, behind the partition, drew in the money and pushed out the ticket, without seeing or caring to see whether the passenger standing aside in the shadow were man, woman or child, but taking a man for granted.

Lilith got on the train while the railway porters were throwing off and throwing on mail bags, and by the time she had dropped into her seat, midway in a nearly empty car, the train started again.

The car was but dimly lighted, and there were but five other passengers in it besides Lilith. They were all strangers to her—probably country merchants on their way to the Eastern cities to buy their Spring goods—mostly clothed in heavy gray overcoats, with their hats pulled low over their foreheads, and their hands thrust into their pockets. They seemed more inclined to doze than to talk, and seldom spoke, except to remark how very cold the weather was, opine that the mercury was at zero, and declared that such a thing had never occurred in that neighborhood so late in March within the memory of man.

And then they hugged their overcoats more closely around them, pulled their hats down lower, and relapsed into silence and dozing.

Lilith, now that the hurry and excitement of her sudden departure was over, and she was seated in the car, with nothing to do, suffered a natural reaction into depression and great discouragement.

What was before her? Whither should she go? What could she do? What was to be her future life? Who were to be her future friends or companions? She was leaving her old familiar home, leaving all the friends of her youth, going among perfect strangers, without one single letter of introduction to any one. What would be the end?

Had she done right to take the responsibility of her future into her own young, inexperienced hands? Would it not have been better to have borne the reproach and humiliation she suffered at Cloud Cliffs, and to have remained there and patiently waited for events? She would at least have been safe.

But in answer to these thoughts came the memory of her husband's cruel words hissed into her ears:

"In a few hours I shall leave here—leave my father's house—never to return to it while you desecrate it with your presence."

And she felt that it was better to go out into the bitter world of strangers than to lose the last remnant of her self-respect by remaining in the home which her husband had scornfully declared that her presence desecrated.

Then Lilith broke down for the first time since that crushing blow, and wept bitterly though silently behind her vail.

Her fellow-passengers did not seem to notice the weeping, or even if they did, they probably thought her tears were only caused by some ordinary parting with friends, a mere matter of course, too trifling to cause remark or sympathy.

The motion of the cars often has a soporific effect upon passengers, and especially upon a woman traveling alone and at night. So it came to pass that Lilith, poor, tired child that she was, cried herself to sleep, and slept soundly, rocked by the swift, smooth motion of the train.

She dreamed a very vivid dream, that seemed a very graphic reality. In her dream her husband was seated by her side, and they were traveling to Washington together. Her promise of secrecy had been canceled, and her tongue had been loosed in some strange way, possible only in dreams, and she was telling him, with her head upon his bosom and her arms around his neck, the wonderful story of her parents' youthful life and love and sorrow, and the true story of her own birth.

And he, holding her in his arms, pressed her to his heart, was listening with such affection, sympathy and admiration. He was saying so earnestly:

"And you, my brave little darling, you have borne all this misconstruction, all this humiliation, rather than betray your trust. But I love you more than ever for all that you have borne and suffered, my Lilith."

A shock startled Lilith out of her deep sleep and dispelled her beautiful dream.

What was this? Where was she?

On the train, indeed—on the train, that had just stopped at a crowded junction and taken on additional cars, which had joined with a shock that waked her. But——

Where was Tudor?

Not seated by her side, certainly. Not even gone out to stretch his limbs. Ah, no! he had vanished with the dream.

Again her eyes overflowed with tears, and she sat back in her seat and wept bitterly in the loneliness and desolation of her heart. She missed the Tudor of her lovely dream. She longed for him with an infinite, agonized longing. She felt an almost irresistible impulse to leave the cars at that junction, and take the next train to her home, where she could arrive by morning—where she could throw herself upon her husband's mercy and remain in peace.

But then again the memory of his cruel words pierced her through the heart, and left her helpless —wounded to the death, as it were. Those words were ringing through her spirit:

"No; I thank Heaven that I never loved you! I married you only to please my father! I never loved you! That dishonor has been spared me! In a few hours I shall leave this house—my father's house— never to return while your presence desecrates it!"

Oh, no! With the sound of these degrading words still reverberating through her soul, she could not go back any more than she could have remained when she was there.

The car was now filled with passengers, and even the seat by her side was taken by a fat woman with an immense bundle in her lap, who crowded Lilith close against the side. She turned towards the window, drew her thick vail closer over her face, and wept silently but bitterly until once more overtasked nature yielded to weariness and to the smooth, swift, soothing motion of the train, and she slept; this time a dreamless sleep, that lasted until the train ran into the Baltimore station.

It was now six o'clock, and the eastern horizon was flushed with the coming sun.

Lilith awoke to find the train at a standstill, and all the passengers in motion. She roused her stupefied faculties and realized that she was at Baltimore, and that she wished to continue her journey to New York.

She arose and took up her hand-bag and left the car, went to the ticket office and inquired when the next train would leave for New York.

"At six-fifteen," the busy agent replied.

Lilith glanced at the large station clock. It was now five minutes past six. She bought her ticket, got a cup of coffee at the refreshment counter, and then followed the throng who were crowding through the gates to get on the New York train.

She got a corner chair on a Pullman car, wheeled it around towards the window, so that her back would be turned to her fellow-passengers, and gave herself up to thought.

She had been driven from her home in dishonor, and her flight and the letter she had left behind had cut off all retreat, and made a voluntary return impossible.

What were they doing at Cloud Cliffs this morning? Her husband had not probably received her letter until this morning, because he had not, she thought, entered her room during the night.

What would he think of her letter? How would it affect him?

She could not conjecture, especially as she could not remember what she had written, in the white heat of her emotions, when about to leave him, perhaps forever.

And old Nancy! What would she think of this sudden flight? Would Nancy be very sorry for her? And the other domestics, who had known and loved her from her babyhood—would they care?

Oh, yes, indeed, she felt and knew that all the servants, old and young, would grieve for her, and all the animals would miss her.

Then Lilith fell to weeping again at the thought of all human and brute that she had loved so well, and yet had left, perhaps forever.

Her paroxysm of tears exhausted itself, but her distressing thoughts continued.

What would the neighbors think or say about her disappearance? They would certainly ask a great many questions. Country people always do. They would question and cross-question Mr. Hereward.

How would he answer them? Would he tell them the truth, or would he evade inquiry? And oh, above all, would he, could he, be any happier now that she was gone? Would he not sometimes remember how much she had loved him? How hard she had tried to please him? How diligently she had worked to help him, answering his letters, copying his speeches, searching out his authorities, and through all this secretary work keeping his one room in the attic of the crowded hotel neat, bright and attractive, and always taking such pure delight in being useful to him? Would Tudor remember these things, and think more kindly of her?

Ah, no! for he did not love her; he had told her so, and thanked the Lord that he did not love her! So all that she had tried to do had failed to please him.

Again the child Lilith wept as if her heart were breaking; and there was no one to comfort her.

CHAPTER VI

LILITH'S FIDELITY

LILITH sat in one corner of the Pullman car, with her chair wheeled around, her shoulders to all her fellow-passengers, and her face fronting the large mirror on the wall. She sat quite still, and wept silently.

Now there happened to be in the same car a lady who, in this year of grace 1882, might be called a Benevolent Crank; but the term had not been invented in her time. She was a large, rosy-cheeked, handsome matron, of perhaps fifty years, of the class called "motherly;" with such an exuberance of life, health, vitality and happiness as rendered her kindly affectioned, sympathetic and confiding towards every fellow-being.

She had got on the train at Baltimore and had ever since been sitting in the opposite corner to Lilith; not with her chair wheeled away from her fellow-passengers, but fronting them all as fellow-beings in whom she took a friendly interest, and looking with her kindly, smiling face, half shaded by the black plush bonnet, and her portly form wrapped in her fur-lined cloak, the very picture of comfort, contentment and benevolence.

She did not find much, however, in the seven men who shared the car to interest her—every one of them the incarnation of "business" or "politics," as far as she could judge from physiognomies half hidden by the large, open newspapers they were reading.

Next she turned her social attention on the only woman beside herself in the car, and who sat in the opposite corner.

What she saw there was the red back of the chair, and a pair of pretty, sloping shoulders, in a gray coat and a little, graceful, bowed head in a gray hat and vail, and—the reflection from the mirror.

It was this last that attracted and fixed the attention of the lady. She could not withdraw her eyes from the picture reflected there—a pale, lovely child-face, with soft brown eyes, suffused with tears, and budding red lips, quivering with grief.

The lady watched this picture with growing interest and sympathy. Then she turned her head around to look at the passengers to see if by any sign she could judge whether any one of them could perhaps be the father, or grandfather, or uncle, or other male protector of this lonely and grieving child.

But no; she felt sure that they were all strangers to the little one. Besides, two chairs behind hers were vacant.

Still she watched the weeping girl, but hesitated to address her; it was such an unusual, such an unwarrantable thing to do, and the little lady might not like to have a stranger intrude on her distress when to hide it she had turned her back on the world —of the Pullman car—reasoned the good woman, as she watched the woful picture, and sighed, and sighed and watched, until she could scarcely sit still in her seat.

"Suppose it were my own dear Edith or Clara left alone in the world, with no one to care for her, traveling alone, with no one to speak to her? Oh, dear!"

She looked and saw pretty shoulders rising and falling with half-suppressed sobs, and she could stand it no longer.

"I must go to her! I must, indeed! I can't be like the swimmer who would not rescue the drowning boy because he had never been introduced to his father. I must go to that child even if she should take me for no better than I ought to be and repulse me!"

So saying to herself, the good woman arose and left her chair and went and took the chair next behind Lilith.

Laying her hand gently on the girl's arm and speaking very tenderly and deprecatingly, she said:

"My dear, you seem to be traveling alone, and——"

Lilith lifted her head with a startled look, and raised her soft brown eyes inquiringly to the face of the speaker, thereby embarrassing the good woman, who began all over again:

"You seem to be traveling all alone, my poor darling, and—and—and—you don't seem very well. Can I do anything for you, my dear?"

"Nothing, I thank you, ma'am. I thank you very much. You are very kind to notice me," said poor, solitary Lilith, in an unmistakably grateful tone.

"My poor darling, I should have been a brute—and worse than a brute, for brutes do have feelings—I should have been a stock or a stone, not to have noticed you and not to have felt for you, and me the mother of children of my own, too," said the kind creature, ungrammatically, but very affectionately.

"You are very good, ma'am, and I thank you very much."

"I wish you would let me do something for you."

"There is nothing to do, thank you—nothing," sighed Lilith.

"Oh, yes, there is, plenty, plenty! Now I see you so pale and weak that you are scarcely able to sit up, and if you are going to New York—— Are you going so far?"

"Yes, ma'am."

"Well, New York is a long way off yet, and you are not able to sit up all the way. Now in the next compartment—a little compartment right behind us—there is a sofa and two chairs, all unoccupied. Let me take you in there, and you can lie on the sofa and I will sit in one of the chairs and keep you company. Will you come? I will carry your bag."

Lilith hesitated.

"Well, I declare," said her new friend, "you look like the girl in the song—

'Half willing!—half afraid.'

But you have no cause to be afraid of me, my dear. I only wish to be a help to you. I would not hurt a hair of your head," said the good woman, earnestly.

"Oh, indeed I am sure you would not. You are very, very kind. And I am very thankful to you. I am not afraid of you, but of the conductor," said Lilith.

"Of the conductor!" exclaimed the lady, with surprise and then with a laugh. "Why, on the face of the earth, should you be afraid of the conductor, my child?"

"He might accuse us of trespassing, if we should go into that vacant apartment, for which we have no tickets, and I don't know what the law for trespassing may be on the cars," said Lilith.

"Well," laughed the lady, "it is nothing very dreadful—it is not hanging, nor penal servitude for life, nor even fine or imprisonment. It is simply to be politely requested to vacate a position to which you have no right in favor of some one who has a right —supposing such a one should turn up. Otherwise you may keep the place to the end of the journey. But if it would make you feel any better, I will speak to the conductor next time he passes through the cars. I have traveled this road so many times—how many you may know when I tell you that for the last seven years I have had one daughter married in Brooklyn, one in Jersey City, one in New York and one in Boston, and I spend nearly all my time in going backwards and forwards between my home in Baltimore and their homes. Think of it, my dear! There are four of them, and every one of them has a baby every year. And I have to go on every time a baby is expected, and then have to be there a month before the baby comes, and stay a month afterwards. But, as I was saying, I have traveled this road so frequently that I know all the conductors, and I like the one on this train better than any of them; for there is nothing in the line of his duty that he would not do for me, or for any woman."

"Are you going on now to meet an expected little grandchild?" inquired Lilith, who, child-like, had ceased to weep when she became interested in something else besides her sorrows.

"Oh, no, not exactly now; though there will be such a harvest of them between this and Christmas that it will be hardly worth while for me to go back home this year. Eh, me! Ponsonby might as well be a full widower, for he has been a grass-widower most of the time since our girls have been married. True, the two youngest girls—Edith and Clara—are at home, and they keep house for their father while I am away. But you were asking me about the cause of my journey. It isn't a baby this time; it is a wedding. My Boston son-in-law's sister, who lives with him, is going to be married on Thursday, and all the family connections are to meet at his house. I and my three other married daughters are to go on to-morrow morning. I shall stay at my son-in-law Saxony's house to-night. Here comes the conductor. Mr. P——," she said, turning to that officer, "this young lady is not well. Is there any objection to my taking her into that vacant compartment where she can lie on the sofa?"

"No objection at all, Mrs. Ponsonby; the compartment is not engaged," replied the polite conductor.

The lady arose and gave her arm to Lilith and took her to the sofa, where the exhausted girl was glad to lie down. Then she returned for her own and Lilith's light luggage, which she transferred to the new seats.

As the conductor passed through the drawing-room car on his return, a stout passenger with iron-gray hair, who had sat three seats off from Lilith and her friend, on the opposite side of the car, and had watched the interview between the woman and the girl, and had heard as much or as little of their conversation as their low tones would permit, and had formed his own opinions on the subject—beckoned the officer to approach, and looking solemnly over the top of his spectacles said, impressively:

"Conductor, I want you to keep an eye on that pair who have just gone into the next compartment. That young girl is traveling alone. That stout woman first accosted her. She has some evil designs on that girl, I am sure of it! Robbery or worse! She has every opportunity to chloroform and rob the girl, or to drug her and take her away for something worse!"

"All right, sir! I know the old party! She is Mrs. Ponsonby, of Baltimore. And she will be met at the depot by her son-in-law, Mr. Saxony, of Number —— Street," replied the amused officer.

"Oh, very well, if that is so! But her extraordinary proceedings of accosting a strange young lady in the cars very reasonably aroused my suspicions. I am glad it is no worse," said the Detective Crank, in a tone of disappointment that illy accorded with his words.

In the meantime, Lilith reposed on the sofa and her new friend sat by her side and chatted to cheer her up.

With a rare delicacy she refrained from asking Lilith any questions as to the cause of that distress which had drawn the good woman to the girl's side, until they were drawing near to New York. Then she inquired:

"Is there any one to meet you at Jersey City, my dear?"

"No, no one," answered Lilith.

"Nor any one the other side?"

"No, no one is to meet me anywhere," said the desolate girl.

"My dear child! Some one ought to meet you! It is not right or safe for a young girl traveling alone to enter a city at nightfall, with no one to meet her! But I suppose you know exactly the number and street of the people you are going to see," said the good and sorely troubled woman.

"I am going to no house. I have no friends or even acquaintances in the city," said Lilith.

"Then why on the face of the earth have you come here, my poor child?" inquired Mrs. Ponsonby, in surprise and distress.

Lilith, like the baby into whose state she sometimes relapsed, burst into tears, covered her face with her hands and wept bitterly.

"Now what have I done? Now what is the matter? Oh! what is the matter? Tell me, my dear. I am very sorry for you. I will help you all I can. Indeed I will, for Edith and Clara's sake," said Mrs. Ponsonby, bending over and caressing the girl, who, between her sobs and tears, tried to answer.

"I came," she gasped, "because I have lost everything in the world. I have suffered cruel, cruel reverses, and could not bear to stay in the place where I had seen such happy and prosperous days so suddenly turned to misery and destitution."

"Poor, poor, poor dear! Was it through the war, my dear?" inquired the woman, in tender, compassionate tones, while the tears stood in her kindly eyes.

"No, it was not through the war. It was since the war."

"Oh, yes! My dear child, tell me all you wish, but no more than you wish. I will help you in any case. Indeed I will. Are you an orphan, my dear?"

"Oh, ma'am, I am much worse than orphaned," said Lilith.

"Dear me! Poor child! How worse than orphaned, my dear?"

"Oh, ma'am, I cannot tell you now. Indeed I cannot. Do not blame me, and do not be angry. It is not my fault that I am so desolate and that I must be so reserved about my past life," pleaded Lilith.

The lady fell to musing.

"I wonder what has happened to the child? That she is good I can see for myself. Nobody could make a mistake about her. I wonder what she means by worse than orphaned, now. I wonder if her father was hanged or sent to prison for life, or anything like that. There are so many men who ought to be gentlemen, but who come to that sort of end now, that I should not be surprised that it was so. Why, there is always something of that sort going on in some city or other, some bank defaulter, or some forger, or manslaughterer, or something. And so it seems more than likely that her father may have disgraced his family in that way, and be in prison, or in a felon's grave, and that's what she means by being worse than orphaned. But her mother—— Is your mother living, my poor child?" she inquired, suddenly breaking the long silence and addressing Lilith.

"No, ma'am. My mother left this world a few hours after I came into it," said Lilith.

"Poor, dear darling!" said the good woman, who then relapsed into silent thought, drawing her own conclusions.

"Yes, that is it!" she said to herself. "The mother gone, the father worse than dead! That must be it, or she would not talk of being worse than orphaned."

Lilith, perhaps mistaking her continued silence for mistrust, said at length:

"You have been very kind to me, a perfect stranger to you, ma'am, and I thank you from my heart; but do not trouble your kind soul about me, ma'am. It is not worth your while, indeed."

"Oh, it is easy to say that, my dear; but I can't help troubling myself about you! Suppose you were my own Edith or Clara? But don't be afraid, my dear; I won't ask anything about your past; what I want to know is your future. You said when you started for New York that you wished to get away from painful associations; now what I wish to ask is, where do you intend to go in New York, and what do you intend to do?"

"I shall go first to some hotel, the only place a stranger can go to, I suppose, and then I mean to look out for some employment."

"Then, my dear, you are all wrong. In the first place, you must not go to a hotel," said Mrs. Ponsonby.

"But why?" inquired Lilith.

"Because you would go as a lamb among wolves. That is why."

"Then I suppose I must try to find a private boarding-house."

"Worse and worse! A respectable boarding-house would want references, and if you happened to apply to any but a respectable one——"

"That is the reason why I wished to go to one of the first-class hotels. They are always very respectable. No one can make a mistake about them, and they take strangers without references."

"Yes, my dear, at ruinous prices. Unless you have got a great deal of money, you would be quite penniless before you could get any employment. And, by the way, what sort of employment do you expect to find?"

"I hardly know. I might be an amanuensis for some lady or gentleman——"

"For no gentleman. I put my foot right down on that. Let the men alone, my dear—unless they happen to be your very nearest male relations. And to enter a lady's employment you would have to have good references. I do hope you have references, my dear?"

"No," said Lilith, "I have none; not one; and circumstances are all so adverse that I cannot hope to get one."

"Dear me!" said Mrs. Ponsonby, taking a long look into Lilith's face. "But you are all right. I am sure you are all right. You are not the sort of child to run away from your father or mother to seek your fortune. I tell you what I will do; I will be your referee. That is—do you write a fair hand, spell words correctly, and compose sentences grammatically, as an amanuensis should do? For, you know, you may have to answer letters as well as to write from dictation."

"Yes, ma'am, I can indeed. I have been accustomed to do all that for my dear lost foster-father. The next time the train stops I will write a specimen and prove it," said Lilith.

"Very well, then," said the Benevolent "Crank," "I will be your referee. And as to your lodging in New York, I will take you to a cheap but very respectable house kept by the widow of a Methodist minister. She has no fashionable boarders, my dear, for she lives on —— Street, near —— Avenue, and fashion has left that part of the city these fifty years or more. She boards some of the public school teachers. I will take you to her house to-night before I go to my daughter's, mind you. If Saxony comes to meet me, and is in a hurry, he may go home in the street cars, and I will take the carriage and carry you to Mrs. Downie's," said the new friend, who had worked herself up into a benevolent fever on the subject of the desolate young creature.

"Oh, how good you are to me! How wonderfully good! How do you know that I am deserving of your goodness? How do you know that I am not an impostor?" said Lilith, catching her friend's hand and covering it with grateful kisses. "Yes! how should you know but that I am a very foolish, wicked girl?"

"Good Lord, child! how do I know anything, for that matter—how do I know light from darkness, except through my eyes and my understanding? That is the way I know you from an impostor. How I thank the Lord that I met you before you fell into the Lion's Den of this great city!"

"And do I not thank the Divine Providence—oh, do I not? And thank you, oh, so much!" exclaimed Lilith, clasping her hands in the fervency of her utterance.

"Now, here we are at Jersey City! Gather your traps, my dear, and be ready to get off. Don't be afraid. The dragon's mouth is always wide open, but you shall not fall into it!" said Mrs. Ponsonby, as the train ran into the depot.

"And there's Saxony's carriage, but I don't see him," she said, when they had crossed the ferry and passed out on Desbrosses Street.

"Where's your master, Patrick?" she demanded, when she had dragged Lilith through the crowd to the door of the carriage.

"If you plaze, ma'am, Misther Saxony is dining out this evening, and Misthress Saxony requisted me to mate you in the carriage meself, ma'am," said the Irish coachman, who resented the term "master" as applied to his employer.

"Very well. I am glad of it. Get in, my dear. And, Patrick, do you drive first to Number 10 —— Street, near —— Avenue. It will not be much out of your way," said Mrs. Ponsonby, as she put Lilith into the carriage and followed her.

The short winter twilight was fading into night, and the streets were beginning to be lighted with gas.

"Suppose," said Lilith, "suppose that your friend should not have a vacant room for me?"

"Then you must put up with a bed for this one night."

"But if she has not an unoccupied bed?"

"Then she must find one for this night, anyway," persisted Mrs. Ponsonby.

It seemed a long ride through the crowded city streets before the carriage at last drew up before the door of a plain, dull-looking, three-story brick house.

Mrs. Ponsonby—without waiting for the coachman to get off his box, for, indeed, Patrick was so indolent that he always made an excuse that he "darn't" leave his horses to open the door—alighted, and assisted Lilith to alight, and led her up to the house and rang the door-bell.

A female servant answered it.

"Is Mrs. Downie at home?" inquired the elder lady.

"Yes, ma'am," replied the waitress, opening a door on the right, and showing the two ladies into the long but plainly furnished parlor, where they sat down.

"Will you tell Mrs. Downie that I would like to see her on business for a moment?"

"Yes, ma'am. What name?"

The lady handed the waitress a card.

"Mrs. Downie is at tea now, but I dare say she will not be long," said the girl, as she left the parlor and ran down the basement stairs.

In a very few minutes the mistress of the boarding-house came up, with a warm, exuberant welcome for an old friend. She was a short, fat, good-natured looking woman, of about Mrs. Ponsonby's own age, and she was dressed in a clean but rather dowdy black gown, all in keeping with her general aspect of careless good humor; and her pretty, soft, silvery gray hair was gathered into a knot behind, and as much disheveled all over her head by nature as it could have been done by the most fashionable hair-dresser.

"Why, goodness me, Em'ly Ponsonby! This ain't you? I never was so surprised in all my life as when Mary gave me your card! And we have just this minute sat down to tea; and you will come down and have some?" said the landlady, in the softest and most caressing voice, that seemed to be perfectly natural to her.

"No, thank you, Sophie Downie," replied Mrs. Ponsonby, as she arose and embraced her fat little friend. "I am in the greatest hurry that ever was, and only called here on my way from the depot to Sam Saxony's to bring you a new boarder, a very dear young friend of mine, who came with me from Baltimore to get something to do in New York here. Miss—— Good Lord of mercy! I don't know the child's name!" said the good woman to herself, as she arose and went to Lilith, and whispered:

"What name, dear—what name?"

"Wyvil," answered Lilith, in the same low tone.

"My young friend, Miss Wildell, wants a quiet, respectable home just such as you could furnish her," resumed Mrs. Ponsonby, rejoining the landlady.

"Oh! Another Southern orphan, ruined by the war!" said kindly Mrs. Downie.

"Ah! poor thing!" replied the Baltimore lady, in a non-committal way. "I hope you can take her. She has some little money left, I think."

"And she wants to get in one of the public schools? Poor girl! there ain't the least chance."

"No, I don't think she wants to teach—but the question is, can you accommodate her?"

"I must 'commodate her somehow or other. I haven't got a room; but if she could put up with a cot in my room——"

"Of course she could, until you can do better for her. And now I must go, for I am keeping you from your tea, while they are waiting for me on —— Street. Miss Wilde, my dear, I leave you in good hands, and if you ever want a friend, call on me. Sophie Downie, you see I am due in Boston, at my daughter's, to-morrow. That's why I am in such a hurry now. Good-bye!"

And so saying, the dear woman kissed her old friend, and then kissed Lilith and left a card with her address in the girl's hand.

The next instant she was gone, and Lilith was alone with the landlady.

"Come, my dear, come upstairs to my room and take off your things and wash your face and hands, if you wish; and then we will go down and get some supper. My dear, I hope you will feel at home here. Most of my boarders are young people. Two young ladies who are public school teachers, and one who is a colorer of photographs, and then I have a young Methodist minister who has a parish near this. He is going to be married soon, though, as ministers must, you know, and then we shall lose him. And then, my dear, if you are still with us, you shall have his room and be comfortable."

So talking, the landlady led Lilith upstairs and so installed her in the home that was to be hers for many months to come.

CHAPTER VII

LILITH'S STRUGGLES

Perhaps in some long twilight hour,
  Like those we have known of old,
When past shadows round you gather,
  And your present friends grow cold,
You may stretch your hands out towards me.
  Ah! you will—I know not when.
I shall nurse my love, and keep it
  Faithfully for you till then.

A. A. Proctor.

LILITH found her new home a safe enough retreat. Let any young woman go into a strange house, in

a strange city, under the circumstances in which
Lilith entered the Widow Downie's, and if she feel
compelled to observe a strict silence concerning her
own past life, she need not tell her story. Her neighbors will make up one to fit her, and, what is more,
will believe in it.

Try to get at the origin of such a story, and you
may trace it to "They say," but no farther.

The advent of Lilith in the boarding-house of Mrs.
Downie caused a great deal of gossip, in which,
strange to say, there was not a word of ill-nature,
of criticism, or of adverse reflection upon the young
creature.

She was so childlike, so pretty, and so desolate,
that the hearts of all her fellow-lodgers were drawn
towards her.

By "putting this and that" together, by unconsciously exaggerating all they heard, and by involuntarily drawing upon their imaginations, they had
formed a theory, which they took for fact, in regard
to Lilith.

The talk ran something like this:

"Mrs. Ponsonby, a very dear friend of Mrs. Downie,
brought her from the South, to try to get something
to do in New York."

"They say her father was a rich planter, who was
totally ruined in the late war."

"Not at all. He was a wealthy banker of Rich-
mond, who failed in '65."

"A great mistake. She was the only child of a
Baltimore broker, who——"

"Oh, no! A Washington merchant, who became a
bankrupt last year, and——"

And so forth, and so forth.

At last, however, the chaotic story came into form
and shape and permanent existence, as follows:

Miss Wilding—for that was the way in which Mrs.

Downie had heard and repeated the word when
Lilith, remembering that her husband had forbidden
her to use his name, had replied to the landlady's
inquiries by giving the one to which she had the next
best right, and saying, "My name is Wyvil," whereupon the landlady thought she said, "Wilding,"
and thought, from her childlike appearance, that she
was, of course, a single woman, and reported her as
Miss Wilding—Miss Wilding, then, according to the
crystalized gossip of the house, was the only child
of a wealthy Virginia planter, who had been ruined
by the war, and had died, leaving his motherless
daughter entirely destitute. Mrs. Ponsonby had become so much interested in the young orphan that
she had brought her to New York to get something
to do, and had very wisely brought her straight to
Mrs. Downie's boarding-house, and had very prop-
erly become surety for her board, for Mrs. Downie,
with all her goodness of heart, was too poor to lose
the board money, which Mrs. Ponsonby was quite rich
enough to pay without feeling it.

Lilith was also spared troublesome questions, because the inmates of the house, though poor enough
in this world's goods, were too refined openly to intrude upon the reserve of the young stranger; and
also because, when once the good landlady, in the
motherly kindness of her heart, had questioned Lilith
concerning her troubles, the poor girl had burst into
such a passion of tears that Mrs. Downie became very
much distressed, and after doing all she could to
soothe the mourner's sorrow, she not only resolved
never again to allude to the subject, but she warned
all her young inmates to observe the same caution.

" 'Cause she can't bear it, my dears. She can't, indeed. It 'most kills her to hear it mentioned. And
no wonder. Them tender Southern girls as has never
been used to anything but love and softness and

sweetness all their lives, to be suddenly thrown upon a rough, hard, bitter world, you know, my dears, it is very trying. We must never speak to her about the past, and never breathe a word before her about the war. I dare say her poor father was killed in battle, or died in one of them military prisons, or something like that, which it breaks her heart to think about. We must just try to make her forget it, my dears," concluded Mrs. Downie.

And her sympathetic hearers promised all she required, and from that time emulated each other in their kindness to the young stranger.

Mrs. Downie's household were in some respects a peculiar people, of whom the gentle landlady was the controlling spirit.

One word about Sophie Downie. She had been a wife, and was now a widow only in name.

Her late husband, William Downie, had been a Methodist minister of sincere piety and much eloquence.

They had been neighbors' children in a country village, and had been engaged to each other almost from their childhood.

He was "called" to the service of the Lord from his boyhood, and the two widows, Sophie's mother and his own mother, had joined their slender means to send him to college, to be educated for the ministry.

"For," said his own mother, "he is all that I have in the world, and why shouldn't I spend all that I can on him?"

"And," said Sophie's mother, "he is just the same as my own son, and he'll marry Sophie and take care of me when I get old, so why shouldn't I spend all that I can spare in helping him?"

So the boy was sent to college, and in due time went honorably through his course, graduated and was ordained.

He was to marry Sophie as soon as he should obtain his first parish.

Within a few months after his ordination he was appointed by the convention to the Methodist church in New York City near which his widow now kept her boarding-house.

He had held his pulpit but a few weeks, during which Sophie was busily engaged in preparing for their wedding and their housekeeping, when he was suddenly stricken down with a disease known to be fatal from its onset.

As soon as he knew that he was to leave this world he sent for his promised bride, and she came to him, accompanied by their two mothers.

And in the sick-chamber the long-engaged, faithful lovers were united.

He lingered a few days after his marriage, constantly attended by Sophie and the two mothers, and then passed peacefully away to the better world.

The three grieving women took his remains to their native village and laid them in their last resting place in the old church-yard.

Soon afterwards his mother departed and left all the little remnant of her savings to Sophie.

"For she is all the same as a daughter to me, and I have no other child," said the poor widow to the lawyer who drew up the will.

We live in a changeful country. Few of us have the good or the bad fortune to

> "Live where our fathers lived
> And die where they died."

It would be tedious and irrelevant to this story to tell of the various circumstances that finally led Sophie and her mother to sell out all their possessions in the little country village, and to open a boarding-house in New York, in the immediate vicinity of that church which had been the scene of William Downie's short ministry.

For many years the house was nominally kept by the elder lady; but it was entirely managed by the younger.

Many opportunities had the pretty little widow of marrying a second time; but she remained faithful to the memory of her first love.

She had never even permitted a lover to become a suitor; for as soon as her delicate perceptions discovered that this or that young "brother" in the church, or boarder in the house, had cast an eye of "favor" on her, the very shrinking of her nature threw such a sphere of coldness around her that, however gentle and courteous her manner might be to the aspirant, he dared not cross the invisible boundary of that circle.

One of her most ardent admirers said, when "chaffed" on the subject of his infatuation:

"She is as sweet and gentle, as kind and courteous as it is possible for woman to be; but it would take a fellow with more impudence than I possess to make love to her, or to ask her to marry him. There is a sort of 'Thus far, no farther shalt thou go' about her that I defy any man to transgress."

He was right.

And so, without any second love, without coquetry, and without vanity, the pretty, gentle girl-widow grew from youth to middle age. Then she lost her mother, and became the nominal, as she had long been the actual, head of the boarding-house.

It would be difficult to explain or even to understand how Mrs. Downie had managed to succeed in eliminating from the house and from her circle of acquaintances all persons who were uncongenial to her own gentle and generous spirit, and in filling them with those who were in perfect accord with her, and with each other. It was the progressive work of years, however.

But now, at the time that Lilith first entered her house, it was filled with a little society to whom she seemed less a landlady than a loving mother, and whom she absolutely ruled—not by force of intellect, or position, or power, but by unselfish goodness. Always, since her mother's departure, she had one or more of adopted children—little waifs, picked up in the streets of New York, and whom she lodged, fed and clothed, and sent to the public schools until they were old enough to be put out to learn trades.

When any hard-headed, practical brother or sister would expostulate with her on the extravagance of her benevolence and the imprudence of her neglect to provide comfortably for her old age, she would answer, simply:

"Why, Lor's, you know if my poor, dear husband had lived we should have had a large family of children by this time, most like. But as I haven't got none of my own, I feel as if I ought to take care of other people's orphans. Seems to me that people without children should take care of children without parents, so far as they can. And as for the rest of it, I know that if I take care of the destitute the Lord will take care of me."

Acting on this simple faith, the gentle little widow had brought up and provided for no less than seven girls and five boys.

And that is the reason why, at the age of sixty, she had not a dollar in the savings bank.

But oh! the treasure she had laid up in heaven!

At the present time she had a boy and girl, nearly grown up, and when these should be well provided for, by being put in the way of getting their own living, she meant to take two more to bring up—if she should live long enough to do so.

So much for the kindly mistress of the house.

Her circle of lodgers consisted of seven persons. First, there was the young Methodist minister, John Moore, who occupied the same pulpit that had once been filled for a few weeks by William Downie. And here let it be explained, that whenever there came to that church a young unmarried minister, he was always recommended to Mrs. Downie's boarding-house as to a haven where he would be perfectly safe not only from the harpies of business, but from the harpies of matrimony, where he would really find "the comforts of a home," and possibly the society of some fair, good girl, suitable to be the companion of his life and labor.

Next there was Mrs. Lane, the widow of an officer in the Union army, who had fallen in the battle of the Wilderness, and who eked out her small pension by decorating china for a large wholesale house, and supported a son at Yale College.

Then there was a Mrs. Farquier—the widow of a colonel in the Confederate army. She was an artist, and made drawings for the illustrated papers and magazines.

These two women, whose husbands had fallen on opposite sides of the same war, were great friends.

Next there were the two Misses Ward, orphan sisters, and teachers in the public schools.

Lastly, there was Lilith, who shared the landlady's room, and was expected to share it until the young Methodist minister should marry and take possession of the parsonage that was being fitted up for him.

Lilith, who had been madly driven from her home by the goad of her husband's stinging words:

"I never loved you! I married you only to please my dying father. In a very few hours I shall leave this house, never to return while you desecrate it with your presence!"

Lilith, who had fled away, without any definite purpose but to escape from the humiliations that had been heaped upon her, and to support her life, until she should die, by some honest toil—Lilith had now ample leisure to come to her senses and to reflect upon her past and her future.

Ample leisure indeed! Her days and nights were spent in solitude and meditation, for immediately after breakfast, every morning, her fellow-lodgers, workers all of them, scattered to their various occupations—the minister to study, to write, or to make duty calls; the two widows to their rooms to work at their arts; the two young teachers to their schoolrooms, and the good landlady to market, and then to her household duties.

Lilith, left alone, would wander through the parlor, up the stairs and into the room she shared with Mrs. Downie, and then back again, in an aimless, dreary manner. She could settle herself to nothing, take interest in nothing—

"Her past a waste, her future void."

Her life seemed to have come to a standstill. There seemed nothing to hope for in heaven or on earth.

There were days of such deep despondency that life seemed a burden too heavy to be borne, and she longed for death—days when the unrest of her soul craved the rest of oblivion in the grave.

There were moments, too, when athwart the utter darkness of her soul flashed the lightning of consciousness that she might change all this and bring renewed life, action and happiness to herself; that she might write to her husband, or return to her home and implore him to believe in her and to bear with her until she should be at liberty to clear up the mystery that rested as a cold, dark storm-cloud between them.

And at such moments she might have acted on the impulse and hastened back to Cloud Cliffs, but for the memory of his fierce, cruel, stinging words:

"I never loved you! I married you only to please my dying father. In a very few hours I shall leave this house, never to return while you desecrate it with your presence!"

Every time these words recurred to her mind they overwhelmed her with a fresh sense of unspeakable humiliation.

"Oh, no!" she said to herself—"no! my heart seems dying in my bosom, but I must not listen to its moan! I must not go back until he himself shall repent and retract and entreat me to return! I can die, but I cannot go back. I cannot."

And indeed existence for Lilith was now a mere death in life.

All her efforts to obtain employment by advertising and by answering advertisements had signally failed. There seemed to be no use for her in the whole world. No one on earth seemed to want her in any capacity.

Mrs. Downie, watching her with motherly tenderness, ventured one day to say:

"Honey, you must be awful lonesome here days, when everybody has gone about their business and left you by yourself."

"It does not matter, Mrs. Downie. Don't trouble yourself about me, dear heart," said Lilith.

"But I must! I can't help it! Emmy Ponsonby has never been to see you since that night she fetched you here, nyther, has she?"

"No, Mrs. Downie!"

"Well, I reckon she's still with the weddingers in Boston, or else there's another baby coming around somewheres. 'Mong so many married daughters there's always a baby coming 'round in Emmy's family, sometimes two or three of 'em in a year, and I reckon that is what's the matter now. 'Cause Emmy Ponsonby never forgets her friends or her promises."

"She was very, very good to me, and I had no claim on her," sighed Lilith.

"Oh, yes, but you had a claim on her, honey; as you have on me and on every grown-up woman as is able to help a motherless child like you," said Mrs. Downie, so tenderly that Lilith's eyes filled with tears.

"Mrs. Downie," she said, "I want to ask you something."

"Ask away, then, honey."

"You have taken me here a stranger in your house. I have been here four weeks and you have never given me your bill——"

"I was waiting till you got something to do, honey," interrupted the landlady.

"And—this is what I wanted to ask you: Suppose I should be here for eight weeks or for twelve weeks, without paying you?"

"Well, honey, it wouldn't so much matter as you might think; because, you see, dear, you don't occupy a room. You only sleep on a little bed in my room; so really your being here don't make no odds. I have six rooms as I let to boarders, and that is what supports the hoi se. They are all let, and you don't take up none of them, so your being in the house don't make no odds at all, let alone it being a comfort to have you."

"Dear Mrs. Downie——" began Lilith, with the tears running over her eyes; but her voice faltered and her words died in silence.

"Look here, honey, it is borne in on me as if you would just stop calling me Mrs. Downie—not but what I am fond of the name, and proud of it for

poor, dear Will's sake—but if you would just stop
ceremonials and call me Aunt Sophie, like the rest of
the children do, and would come closer up to me, in
your heart, like you would feel more at home with
me, and would be more better satisfied, and wouldn't
have no doubts nor troubles about board and such.
Couldn't you now, honey?"

Lilith left her chair and came and sat down in the
good woman's lap, dropped her head upon her bosom,
and put her arms around her neck.

"That's right, dearie. Now remember, I am your
Aunt Sophie," said Mrs. Downie, folding the young
creature in a close embrace.

"I never knew a mother or a sister or an aunt. It
comforts me to be allowed to call you aunt."

"That is right, dear. Now I'm going to propose
another thing; that is, for you to go to market with
me every morning, when you feel like it. It will
amuse you, and take your thoughts offen troubles it
is unprofitable to dwell on. And then, dearie, sometimes you might go to meeting with me in week eve-
nings. We often have a real good, warm time at our
meetings," said the good woman, with a cheerful glow
in her gentle countenance.

"I thank you, dear, dear Aunt Sophie. I should
like to go anywhere with you," said Lilith, as she
kissed her friend, and arose to her feet.

No more was said about the board bill, the subject of which had been introduced by Lilith herself.

But the next morning, as Mrs. Downie was putting
on her bonnet to go to market, she spied an envelope
directed as follows:

"To Aunt Sophie, from Lilith."

She took it from the toilet cushion upon which it
was pinned, and found three ten-dollar greenbacks
inclosed in a short letter, which she read:

"DEAR AUNT SOPHIE: If I were in need, there is no one in this whole world to whom I should be so entirely willing to be indebted as to yourself. And if I were in want, it would be to you, first of all, to whom I should come for help, feeling sure of obtaining it. But, dear friend, I am not so poor in funds as I am supposed to be. I have enough to keep me for a year at least, even if I should get no work to do. So, please take the inclosed without any qualms to your benevolent heart. I shall still be infinitely indebted to you for love, sympathy and protection.   LILITH."

Mrs. Downie read the note, looked at the money, and communed with herself:

"Now what did the child go and do that sort of thing in that way for? Trapping me into taking the money in that manner. She knew very well that if she had handed it to me I wouldn't have touched it. She a galliant soldier's orphan, too. And now I s'pose if I hand it to her she won't take it back, no way! Now I wonder if she has got a plenty of money, sure enough? Sufficient to keep her for a whole year, as she says? If she has, this would be a convenience, and a real godsend, just at this time, too. when I am trying to make up the rent. Yet I don't like to take it offen that poor child, nyther, and she only occupying a cot in my bed-room. Well, I'll go and try to make her take it back, and if she won't, why, she won't, and I'll put it to the rent money, and get that off my mind to-day."

So saying, the landlady went in search of Lilith, whom she found in the parlor, ready and waiting to go to market with her friend.

"Well, Aunt Sophie, we have a fine day for our walk," began Lilith.

"Yes, honey; but before we go you must take this back again," said the good woman, trying to force

the money into Lilith's hand, " 'cause I don't want
to charge you any board until I can give you a room,
my dear; and that won't be until Brother Moore gets
married and goes. And then I will take pay."

Lilith opened her hand with the palm down, so
that it could hold nothing, saying, at the same time:

"And I will not impose myself on you, dear Aunt
Sophie, until all my funds are spent, and then—I
shall continue to stay with you—perhaps—until you
turn me out."

"That would be forever, then, honey; or, leastways,
it would be as long as I should live, for I should never
do that cruel thing on no account," said the old lady.

And so the strife in generosity was ended, and the
two friends left the house together.

As they walked down the avenue, Mrs. Downie said:

"I think, dear, as you would be a great deal happier if you were to have some regular employment.
You came here to get something to do, didn't you,
now?"

"Yes, Aunt Sophie," said Lilith, sadly.

"Well, have you tried?"

"Yes, Aunt Sophie. I have advertised in the New
York papers, and I have answered advertisements, but
have not yet succeeded in getting anything to do."

"What did you advertise for?"

"For the situation of private governess in a family,
or assistant teacher in a school, or translator, or
copyist, or as companion for an invalid lady or an
elderly lady, or as amanuensis to a literary lady. For
all these situations I have advertised at various times,
and have received not one reply."

"Ah, dearie me! Every road to business is so over-
crowded! But you said you answered some of the
advertisements of such places as you would like to
take."

"Yes, but no notice was taken of any of my letters."

"Ah, you see, child, I suppose there were hundreds of applications for every place, and they couldn't answer all the applicants."

"No, I suppose not," said Lilith, patiently.

"And it costs so much to advertise," sighed Mrs. Downie.

"Yes," said Lilith. "And so I have given up advertising on my own account, and I only answer the advertisements of others. That does not cost so much; only the paper and postage stamp."

"Well, dear, I hope you will succeed at last," said the old lady.

"Yes. 'It is a long lane that has no turning,' as our homely proverb has it," said Lilith.

"Yes, dear, I know it. 'It is a long lane that has no turning,' and the worst of it is that when the lane does turn it doesn't always turn into

'Fresh fields and pastures green,'

but into some dusty highway a deal harder to travel than was the long lane itself! But there! I ought not to have said that. I don't want to discourage you, dearie," suddenly said Aunt Sophie, with a qualm of compunction.

"I saw an advertisement in this morning's *Pursuivant* that pleased me and that I have answered. I have brought my answer to drop it into the post. But I scarcely hope that anything will come of it."

"What was it for, dearie?"

"A companion for a widow going abroad. The applicant must be a young lady, healthy, agreeable, well-educated, competent to speak French, Italian and Spanish. Oh, I have all the list of requirements at my fingers' ends, you see."

Aunt Sophie stopped in the middle of the sidewalk, to the great annoyance of other foot-passengers, and stared in mild wonder at her companion.

"Now, where in all this wide world do that widow expect to find a young lady, accomplished as all that comes to, who is in need to go out and get her living?" she inquired.

"Oh, dear Aunt Sophie, there are many, many among the impoverished children of the South who, in the days of their prosperity, had received such education."

"And do you think you would suit, my dear?"

"I can but try. I must try, you know."

"Well, I hope that widow will be willing to give a high salary for all that she wants."

"The advertisement says that a liberal salary will be given; but also adds that the highest testimonials of character and competency will be required."

"Well, my dear, you can furnish them, anyhow."

"I don't know. I have my college testimonials, or could get them; but for the rest——"

"Well, you have Mrs. Ponsonby."

"But she knows so little of me," sighed Lilith, as she reflected how that good, credulous woman had come to her side in the spirit of compassion and had taken her respectability quite for granted.

"Well, honey, don't sigh, that's a dearie; because if you don't get the place it makes no odds. I dare say that widow is some poor, infirm old lady going to travel for her health, who would be no end of a trial to you. And you know if you never get nothing to do, you can always live long o' me and be comfortable always. 'Deed I feel so drawn to you, dearie, that I would like to adopt you if you would let me. It would make no odds, leastways not much at the end of the year. And I meant to adopt two more as soon as ever John and Mary are provided for. And I reckon I had better adopt one like you than another child. I mightn't live to see the child grow up, for I am getting old. Will you think of what I tell you, dearie?"

"Think of it? I shall never forget it so long as I live, dear Aunt Sophie," warmly responded Lilith.

"Here is the post," said Mrs. Downie, pausing at the pillar box, into which Lilith dropped her letter.

CHAPTER VIII

LILITH'S FIRST PLACE

My life you ask for? You must know
My little life can ne'er be told;
It has been full of joy and woe,
Though I am but a few years old.
A. A. Proctor.

A WEEK went by without bringing any answer to Lilith's application.

She scarcely expected to receive one, indeed. She was becoming inured to disappointment, for, in fact, she had known nothing else in connection with her efforts to obtain employment.

She was beginning to despair of success in this line of enterprise, and even to contemplate the possibility of remaining with Mrs. Downie for an indefinite time, and of becoming useful to her in some good way.

Lilith thanked Heaven that the rigor of her desolate doom was tempered with mercy in the person of Aunt Sophie. She was beginning to love the sweet old lady, with that satisfying affection which is born of esteem and perfect trust. Lilith knew that whatever evil fortune should be in store for her, it would not be the loss of Aunt Sophie's motherly care and protection.

She knew if she were to become quite penniless, and should be stricken with a long and tedious illness, that Aunt Sophie would never permit her to be sent to a public hospital, but would nurse her tenderly and skilfully at home.

And this was the dear woman at whom some people —not many, to the credit of human nature, be it said —had sneered, as too plain, homely and ignorant in looks, speech and manner, ever to have been fit for a minister's wife, though she was a minister's widow.

These people little know that all the spare money of the two widows—William Downie's mother and Sophie Wood's mother—had gone by mutual agreement to educate Willy, leaving Sophie to get what benefit she could out of the village school, which could never cure her of the quaint, old-fashioned, ungrammatical talk she had learned at her mother's knee and used all her life.

As for Lilith, she loved this homely speech, for it reminded her of her own country neighborhood, and she loved every peculiarity of the dear unselfish creature—even the carelessness of her dress, whose only redeeming quality was its perfect cleanliness, and the disorder of her fine, thin gray hair, which was as well disheveled as if it had been attended to by a fashionable hairdresser—because all these revealed in the active, industrious woman, not laziness or idleness, but utter self-forgetfulness in the constant service of others.

But she was growing old, and Lilith wondered if in the failure of all her efforts to obtain employment, and in the possible necessity of her having to remain with Aunt Sophie, whether she might not help her in some substantial manner; as to learn to keep the house, do the marketing, cast up the accounts and pay the bills.

It was Lilith's inspiration always to be useful.

It was late on Saturday evening that Lilith was sitting alone in the front parlor, all her fellow-lodgers being absent from the house or at work in their rooms, when the postman, on his last round for the night—and the week—rang the door-bell.

It happened that Aunt Sophie answered the summons. There was a little parley at the door, and finally the old lady came in with a letter in her hand, which she held out to Lilith, saying:

"Here, my dear, see if this is for you. The carrier is waiting to know. You see it is directed to the house all right, and the number and street all right, but the name is all wrong, if it is for you; though it is so like your name that it must be for you."

Lilith took the letter and looked at the superscription:

"Elizabeth Wyvil."

"Yes, Aunt Sophie, this is for me, and I think it must be in answer to my application," she said.

"Very well, my dear; I will go and tell the man," replied the old lady, as she went again to the front door to explain the case and dismiss the postman.

"Now then, dearie, is the answer favorable?" she inquired, as she returned and took a seat beside Lilith, who sat at the centre table reading her letter by the light of the gasalier.

"It is favorable; if it were not, you know, I should never have received it. Advertisers, I suppose, do not take the trouble to write rejections," replied Lilith."

"No, I reckon not, especially as in every case I have heard there are hundreds of applications for one place. Well, dearie, has the widow lady decided to engage you?"

"No, not decided; she has only appointed an interview with me on Monday at twelve noon, at the Constellation Hotel."

"Oh!"

"But that, you know, is very hopeful."

"Yes, I reckon it is. Well, honey, I hope you will find her a good, kind friend; but who is she, my dearie? Ah! here they come!"

Several of the boarders entered the parlor, and cut short the speech of Aunt Sophie.

Lilith left the room and went up to Mrs. Downie's chamber to read over her letter again.

It was very short, merely acknowledging the receipt of the applicant's letter, and asking for a personal interview at the time and place already specified.

Of course Lilith would keep the appointment and accept the position if it should be offered to her.

But, she asked herself, would she be justified in leaving the country, without first informing her husband and giving him the opportunity of seeking a reconciliation with her, should he desire to do so?

"I never loved you. I married you only to please my dying father. In a very few hours I shall leave this house, never to return while you desecrate it with your presence!"

These words came back to her in all their fierce, bitter, scornful cruelty. "Came back to her?" They had never left her. They smouldered in her memory always, and only blazed up in a fiery heat at the very thought of seeking any notice from the husband who had contemptuously cast her out; but whom—oh, woe—she still so deeply, so painfully loved.

No! he had turned her off, and she must not call his attention to herself in any manner. She must let him go his way, untroubled by her. As for herself, she could live—even in pain and sorrow—until she should be called away to the land of peace.

Lilith had ample time and opportunity for reflection between that Saturday night and the Monday noon when she was to wait on her possible future employer. So it was after mature deliberation that she decided to enter the service of the lady advertiser, supposing that she should be permitted to do so.

On Monday morning she set out to walk to the hotel. She arrived a few minutes before the appointed hour and sent up her card by a porter.

While she waited in the reception-room, many questions arose in her mind.

Who was this German baroness who had advertised for a lady traveling companion, and had appointed this meeting with her, and with a view to engaging her services?

Was she old, sickly, melancholy, ill-tempered and exacting, as Aunt Sophie, in her tender anxiety for Lilith's happiness, had feared that she might be?

Or was she young, handsome and fashionable?

Would the companion be required to nurse an aged invalid, or to amuse a young beauty?

While Lilith was anxiously considering these questions, the door opened and a little old gentleman, dressed in clerical black, and having a little, round, gray head like a silver ball and a fresh, rosy face like a baby's, came bowing into the room, walked up to Lilith, and bowing politely, said:

"Mademoiselle, Madame la Baronne desires that you will ascend to her apartments."

Lilith arose, trembling, bowed, and followed her conductor to the elevator, which in a few seconds brought them to the second floor.

Here the old gentleman took her out, along a handsomely furnished hall to a pair of folding black walnut doors, beside which sat a servant out of livery, who arose and opened them for the visitor to enter.

Lilith found herself in a spacious apartment, whose first impression was of gloom and splendor. Rich, heavy curtains vailed three lofty front windows; but between their openings long needles of light struck here and there on glowing crimson velvet, or gilded cornices or framework, tall mirrors, elegant vases, filled with rare and fragrant exotics, glimpses of rare pictures, statues, stands of every graceful form, and seats of every luxurious make, and under all a carpet that

"Stole all noises from the feet."

Shadow flecked with gleams of splendor; silence softly moved by the sighing of an invisible Eolian harp; cool air just slightly fragrant with the delicate breath of fresh, living flowers.

A pleasing awe, as of entering a chapel of the olden time, of incense and artistic decoration, crept over Lilith.

As her eyes became accustomed to the religious gloom, she saw the figure of a lady rise slowly from one of the reclining-chairs and stand waiting to receive her—a lady of majestic beauty and grace, whose perfect form was clothed from head to foot in a closely fitting, rich black velvet trained dress, without trimming or ornament of any kind; and whose beautiful head was crowned with an aureole of golden hair, which her widow's cap but half concealed.

Lilith approached and courtesied involuntarily as to a queen, so much did the grand beauty of this lady impress her imagination.

"Madame, I have the honor to bring you mademoiselle," said the old gentleman, bowing.

Lilith courtesied again, and glanced up at the lady's face—a beautiful face—somehow suggestive of the surroundings, shadow and splendor—perfect features, a brilliant blonde complexion, dark, glorious eyes, and golden-hued hair, the radiant beauty of the whole enhanced by the dead black of the mourning robe.

"Le Grange, you may retire," said the lady.

And the old gentleman, with another bow, withdrew.

The lady resumed her seat, and by a courteous motion of her hand invited Lilith to take another near her.

"You are much younger than I expected to find you, Miss Wyvil," said the lady, when both were seated.

"I am not Miss Wyvil, madame," said Lilith, who, since her marriage, had always written herself Elizabeth Wyvil Hereward, but who, having been forbidden by her husband to retain his name, meant to obey him by dropping it, yet who wished to avoid deception in representing herself to be an unmarried girl.

The lady looked somewhat surprised, gazed wistfully at the speaker for a few seconds, and then said:

"You are very young to be a widow."

"I am nearly eighteen, madame," said Lilith, without deeming it necessary to enter into farther explanations—for was she not, indeed, "a widow in fate, if not in fact?"

"And you look even younger than that. When did you lose——" the lady began to question, but seeing Lilith trembling and turning pale, she desisted, and after a little pause she turned the conversation.

"Mrs. Wyvil, I have had about two hundred answers to my advertisement for a companion. These have taken myself and my private secretary, Monsieur Le Grange, about a week to get through with examining, although at about two-thirds of the letters we only glanced to see that they were written by utterly incompetent persons, who could not, indeed, write a fair, legible hand or compose a grammatical sentence. Of the other third we selected about a dozen persons, whom we saw, in turn, by appointment during the week. None of them—not one of them—suited me. Several were evidently in bad health, fitter for an infirmary than for any other place. Several others, though they were fair English scholars, had little or no knowledge of other languages; and the others were so unlovely in looks and manner that I could not think of one of them as a companion. Your letter was one of the last I received, and you are the very last with whom I have appointed an interview. Your letter made a favorable impression on me, and your appearance has deepened it," concluded madame, who had evidently given these details only to afford Lilith the opportunity of recovering her composure.

Lilith bowed in respectful acknowledgment.

"The objection, as yet, seems to be your youth," continued the lady.

"As another in my case said: 'It is a fault that must mend daily,' madame," replied Lilith.

The lady smiled. She had a rare, brilliant, beautiful smile.

"You are apt at repartee and quotation," she said. "But now, about your knowledge of modern languages. I can see that you have all the other requirements."

"I am familiar with the languages mentioned in your advertisement, madame, and I have testimonials from professors to that effect."

"I would rather judge for myself. You will find writing materials on that table near your left hand. Translate and write out for me there, in the languages required, this text, which is the anchor of hope for the Christian:

" 'For God so loved the world that He gave His only

begotten Son, that whosoever believeth in Him should
not perish, but have everlasting life.' "

Lilith went and sat down at the table, took a sheet
of note paper and wrote slowly, and with some pauses
for recollection and selection, until she had completed
her task, and filled a page of note paper, which she
brought and gave to the lady.

She smiled, bowed, and read as follows:

"Car Dieu a tellement aime le monde, qu'il a donne
son Fils unique, afin que quiconque, croit en lui ne
perisse point, mais, qu'il la vie eternelle.

"Perciocche Iddio ha tanta amato il mando, c'egli
ha dato il suo unigenito Figliuola acciocche chiunque
crede in lui non perisca, ma abbia eita eterna.

"Porque de tal manera amo Deos al mundo que hayo
dado, a su Hijo unigenito; para que todo aquel que en
el creyere, no ce pierda, mas tenga vida eterna."

"I think these will do, Mrs. Wyvil. I am not a
very accomplished linguist, but I will submit these
specimens to Professor Le Grange for his opinion,"
said the lady, as she touched a golden timbré at her
side.

The door opened, and the man whom Lilith had
seen in the hall appeared.

"Request Monsieur Le Grange to come here," said
the lady.

The man disappeared, and was succeeded by the
little, round-bodied Frenchman.

"Monsieur, will you have the goodness to glance
over these translations, and give me your opinion of
them?" inquired the lady, handing the paper to the
professor, who bowed—he spent half his time in the
presence of his employer in bowing—looked over

the page, then read it carefully, and returned it, saying:

"The translations are correct, madame."

"Thank you, monsieur. That will do."

The professor bowed and retired.

"Now, Mrs. Wyvil, there remains but to ask for your references—a mere matter of form, my dear, for believe me I am very favorably inclined towards you."

Lilith's face flushed as she answered:

"I have such testimonials as I brought from college at the end of my last and graduating term. I have no other referees, except a lady of Baltimore, who gave me permission to use her name. She is a Mrs. Ponsonby, of Calvert Street, in that city, and she is frequently in New York here, where she has a married daughter, Mrs. Saxony, of —— Street."

"Oh! I know them both—mother and daughter. I have met them in Washington and at Newport. They will do quite well," said the lady, cordially.

"But, madame," said Lilith, as the painful flush deepened in her cheek, "I don't know Mrs. Saxony at all, and very little of Mrs. Ponsonby except that —that—that—she took me up on faith—and——"

"That does not matter. I can trust Mrs. Ponsonby; and, my dear, I can trust your candid, truthful face. Are you equally satisfied with me?"

"Oh, madame!" said Lilith, deprecatingly.

"Then we have only to speak of salary—twelve hundred dollars a year, paid quarterly. Are the terms satisfactory?"

"Oh, madame, they are very munificent. The salary is very much larger than I expected."

"It is not too large for one of your accomplishments, who is, besides, required to quit her country —to expatriate herself, perhaps, for years."

Lilith made no reply. She was beginning to tremble at the prospect of an indefinite exile.

"I expect to sail on the first of June. Can you be ready by that time?"

Lilith paused to consider. Should she take this plunge?

"I never loved you. . . . I shall leave this house, never to return while you desecrate it with your presence." As these stinging words arose in her memory, she roused herself and answered, firmly:

"Yes, madame, I shall be quite ready."

"Very well, my dear. Your duties will be very light—almost merely nominal. I wanted a young, pretty, accomplished and agreeable companion. I did not expect to find one. But I have found one in you. I will not detain you longer at present. Come in at this time to-morrow, if you please, and we will talk further," said the lady, rising.

"One moment, if you will pardon me, madame, I have not yet the honor of knowing the name of the lady to whom my services are pledged," said Lilith.

"Now is that possible? Well, my dear, if you were better acquainted with the world you would know one thing about me—that I am a very unbusiness-like individual," said the lady, as she placed a card in the hands of her companion.

Lilith bowed and read: BARONESS VON BRUYIN.

CHAPTER IX

LILITH AND THE BARONESS

Life is only bright when it proceedeth
Towards a truer, deeper life above;
Human love is sweetest when it leadeth
To a more divine and perfect love.

Learn the mission of progression duly;
　Do not call each glorious change decay;
But know we only hold our treasures truly
　When it seems as if they passed away.

Nor dare to blame God's gifts for incompleteness;
　In that want their beauty lies. They roll
Towards some infinite depth of love and sweetness,
　Bearing onward man's reluctant soul.

A. A. Proctor.

THE Baroness Von Bruyin, the name and title on
the card, bore no especial significance for Lilith.

She bowed as she took the enameled bit of paste-
board and withdrew from the room.

The little old Frenchman came from some other
room opening upon the same corrdior, and politely
escorted her downstairs and out of the hotel.

"Shall I have the honor to call a cab for you,
madame?" he inquired, when they had reached the
vestibule.

"No, monsieur, thank you. I prefer to walk," replied Lilith.

The professor stood aside to let Lilith go out.

Lilith "preferred to walk" that she might be alone,
and have a longer time for reflection and for self-col-
lection before reaching her boarding-house, and having to meet the kind inquiries of Aunt Sophie.

The die was cast, then. Her fate was sealed. She
had taken the step from which she felt there was no
honorable retreat—unless, indeed, her husband should
relent; should retract all his bitter charges against
her; should seek her out, ask her to return to the
home from which he had madly driven her, and set
up his own superior claims to her allegiance in opposition to those of madame, the baroness.

But this, Lilith knew, was a possibility far too remote to be thought of.

And so she was—or she tried to persuade herself
that she was—glad that her fate was decided for her
by circumstances beyond her control.

With all a very young girl's enthusiasm for an imperial beauty, Lilith admired the baroness, and felt
that, since she must take service with some lady, she
could be better satisfied with the companionship of
the beautiful and gracious Madame Von Bruyin than
with any one else.

Lilith walked so slowly that when she reached her
boarding-house she found that lunch had been over
for some time, and all her fellow-lodgers had dispersed to their business or to their rooms.

But Aunt Sophie was anxiously waiting for her in
the parlor.

"Take off your things down here, dearie, and then
come with me to the dining-room, and you shall have
a cup of fresh tea before you tell me anything, though
I am half dying to hear," was the greeting of the old
lady.

Lilith kissed her affectionately, and then followed
her to the basement dining-room, where a fresh white
cloth had been laid over one end of the long table,
and adorned with a fine china tea service—that had
been bought many years before for Aunt Sophie's
bridal housekeeping, but which was never, never
used, except on the most sacred occasions.

The kettle was boiling, and the tea was soon made
and brought in, with the accompaniments of light
biscuits and lamb chops.

But not until Lilith had drunk her first cup of tea
would Aunt Sophie, who sat beside her, watching her
affectionately, ask one question.

Then when she had refilled the cup for her young
guest, she inquired:

"And have you got the situation, honey?"

"Yes, Aunt Sophie."

"Oh, dearie me! I ought to be glad, but I ain't. I had a heap rather kept you here long o' me. And are you really going abroad, too?"

"Yes, Aunt Sophie. I cannot help going. I must."

"Oh, dearie me! dearie me! I hope you will do well, honey. When are you going?"

"We sail in the Kron Prinz on the first of June."

"So soon! Ah me! I shall never live to see you come back, dearie."

"Oh, yes, you will, dear Aunt Sophie. Your good and useful life will be prolonged for many years yet."

"Oh, how selfish I am! I ought not to think about myself, but about you. Dearie, I hope the lady you are going with will not be too hard on you. You are such a child! Is she real old and ugly?" anxiously inquired Aunt Sophie.

"Oh, no! She is young, and very, very handsome."

"Oh, then, I hope she is not haughty and tyrannical —so many of those rich, proud beauties are. But, oh, dear, how wrong of me to talk so, to discourage you. Though I did not mean to do that. It is because I am so anxious about you, honey. Just as anxious as if you were my own dear child."

"I know it, dear Aunt Sophie. But do not be uneasy on my account. I think the lady with whom I have engaged will be very kind to me. I do, indeed. Certainly during our interview she was very gracious and considerate. She gives me a very large salary, and tells me that my duties will be very light—merely nominal. That I shall have nothing to do for her but to keep her company," said Lilith, cheerfully.

" 'Nothing to do but to keep her company.' But that's the hardest sort of work with some people, my dearie. There I go again, discouraging of you, when I ought to be doing of the very opposite sort of thing. What an old fool I am, to be sure. Don't mind me, honey, but tell me what this lady's name is. Don't you know, dear, I have never heard that yet?"

"I never heard it until about two hours ago. I had actually engaged myself to her before I knew her name," said Lilith, with a faint smile.

"Lor'! Now that shows how very little you know of the world, and how unfit you are to be thrown, unprotected, upon it! But what is the lady's name, now you do know it?"

"She is the Baroness Von Bruyin."

"Von—Brewing? Brewing? 'Pears to me I've heerd that name before—connected with—connected with—some grand wedding to-do at the great cathedral, where the archbishop and ever so many bishops performed the ceremony. Yes, yes, I disremember her name; but she was a great beauty and a great heiress, being an only darter of some rich city banker, rich as creases; and he was a Mr. Brewing, another rich banker, a heap richer than creases; but older than her own father—so old, so old, as never was seen before at a wedding. And they said how, when he went back to Germany and took his beautiful wife, he paid the emperor lots of money to make him a baron, and it was all to please his wife, so she might be a baroness. Yes, yes! I remember now! And so she's a widow. And the old man is dead! Well, well, well, how things do turn about! Not much use in his getting married to a beautiful young woman and getting himself made a baron, when he was just ready to depart away from this life! Ah me! 'Vanity of vanities, all is vanity,' saith the preacher, and it is true!"

Lilith made no reply, and presently Aunt Sophie resumed:

"I see how it is! She don't like to shut herself up away from society, while she is in her first mourning, as she would have to do if she stayed in this city, where she was a sort of queen; so she is going

to travel to amuse herself until the time of fashionable mourning is over, and she wants a bright young
thing like you to keep her company! But in a year
or two she will be back here, and then we shall see!
But there I go again, sinning as fast as I can! I
wonder what makes me so uncharitable? I reckon
it is because I haven't been to class-meeting lately.
I'll go this very evening, when my class meets, and
I'll get the brethren to pray for me. It's a great
help."

And seeing that Lilith had finished her lunch, the
old lady arose from the table and began carefully to
gather her precious china and to wash it up to put
it away.

Lilith went up to her own room, to look over her
slender wardrobe, and to think over what she would
have to buy for her sea voyage and her European
tour.

While she was still engaged there, late in the afternoon, her fellow-lodgers were discussing the details
of a horrible and mysterious murder that had been
perpetrated in the city, the night previous, but only
discovered that morning. It was in all the evening
papers, forming the sensation of the hour.

In the same paper was a short paragraph, stating
that:

"The body of an unknown woman, suspected to be
that of Mrs. Tudor Hereward, wife of the Congress-
man from that district, a young lady who had disappeared from her home some weeks before, had been
found in the woods bordering Cave Creek, near Frosthill, in West Virginia. A wound on the back of the
head indicated that she had been the victim of
tramps."

That was all. If any one read it they paid but

little attention to it; their imaginations being engrossed by the details of the more shocking tragedy in their midst.

At dinner in the evening the dreadful occurrence was discussed.

After dinner, Lilith took up the paper from the parlor table, not to read the details of the murder—her whole soul shrank in loathing from such a subject—but to look at the Congressional news, as she had looked at it daily since her flight from her home, to see if any mention was made of her husband.

But there was none. Not once since she parted with him on that bitter night at the Cliffs had she seen his name. The once active, industrious, irrepressible Hereward seemed to have dropped out of the Congressional debates.

This continued silence sometimes caused Lilith serious anxiety. Was Tudor ill? she asked herself, and then quickly repressed her rising anxiety with the recollection of that bitter taunt, which, like a poisoned arrow, had left an incurable, festering wound which daily ate deeper and deeper into her spirit.

At length Lilith put away the paper, without having seen the paragraph that concerned her so much that it might have changed the whole current of her life.

The next day, at the appointed hour, she went again to the hotel to see Madame Von Bruyin.

As we said, the name of the baroness had no especial significance for Lilith, for when Tudor Hereward, in the first weeks of their married life, had told Lilith the history of his first love adventure, he had in delicate consideration abstained from mentioning the name of the lady or of the gentleman who afterwards became her husband. And although the gossips she had heard talking of the matter in

the parlor of the hotel had just once let fall the name
of Mr. Bruyin, it had made no impression on her
memory, and there was nothing to connect the personality of the baroness with that of the beauty who
had been the object of Tudor Hereward's first passion.

When Lilith reached the hotel and made inquiries
she found the polite old Frenchman waiting in the
parlor to conduct her to the apartment of the
baroness.

The lady received Lilith with a kiss, saying, as she
placed her in a comfortable chair and resumed her
own seat:

"My dear, I have been thinking of you ever since
I saw you last. I feel that I shall grow very fond
of you."

"You are very good, madame," replied the girl.

"Child, I hope that in going abroad with me you
are not leaving any one whom you will suffer in parting from?" said the baroness, in the gentlest tone.

"I am not leaving any one in the world who loves
me, except my landlady, and she has only known me
for a little while," said Lilith, with a slight tone of
sorrow in her voice that she could not quite repress.

"'Only known you for a little while!' And I for
a less. But it does not take long to learn to love
you, my dear. Will you tell me something about
yourself? I am very much interested in you. Indeed, I am filled with wonder and speculation concerning you. When I advertised for a companion,
young, agreeable and accomplished, as I desired her
to be, Monsieur le Professeur plainly told me that rara
avis was not to be found in the ranks of women who
were seeking situations; that such an education as I
required in my companion was the privilege only of
wealth and genius. And the answers to my call
proved that he was right. In about two hundred applications yours was the only one that suited me.

And you, my dear, have really excelled my most unreasonable expectations. Your extreme youth, which
at first view seemed an objection, is really an additional charm. Your having been married, too, seems
to draw us nearer together. Two young and recently
bereaved widows may surely sympathize with each
other. I hope, dear, that you will consider me as a
friend."

"You are very kind to me, madame. I have no
words to thank you, but I will try to make my actions
speak," said Lilith.

"And some time, dear, not now, but some time
when you feel that you can do so, I hope that you
will tell me something about yourself, something
about the circumstances that have forced you, a young,
beautiful and accomplished girl—you are little more
than a child, although you have been married—to
take the situation of lady's companion," said the
baroness, gently.

Lilith had a struggle to control her emotions; but
she soon conquered them, and replied, with forced
calmness:

"You are entitled to my fullest confidence, dear
madame, for you have taken me almost on trust, as
everybody has so kindly done since I left home——"

"Who could do otherwise, my dear? Who could
look in that pretty, tender, child-face and doubt you?
But go on, my dear, with what you were about to
say."

"Only this, madame, that some time, when I can,
I will tell you my little story. But now I can only
say this much—I am from West Virginia. A reverse,
a calamity, sudden and overwhelming as a thunderbolt or an earthquake, laid waste my life and destroyed all my happiness in an instant, 'in the twink-
ling of an eye,' and cast me alone upon the world.
I came to New York to get away from a scene so full

of miserable associations as my home had become, and seek a living here among strangers, all of whom have so charitably taken me on trust, when they might have put out the last spark of hope and life by unjust but reasonable suspicions," said Lilith, as if she deeply felt the truth of every word she uttered.

"Who could suspect a baby?" said the lady, gently; but nevertheless she inquired within herself:

"What can have happened to this girl? Has her husband killed her father and been hanged for it? Or vice versa, or what? There are so many homicides and hangings in this vast country that no one can keep trace of them all. Her words are very enigmatical."

Something in the lady's looks might have betrayed the drift of her thoughts, for Lilith, with a deepening color and in a low voice, ventured to say:

"There is one circumstance that I ought to have added to my statement, madame, and it is this: There has been no dishonor connected with my misfortunes, no dishonor of any one's. I have no way of proving this, but oh! as I hope to be saved, I am speaking the sacred truth!" she concluded, clasping her hands in the earnestness of her asseveration.

"My child, I feel sure that you do," answered the baroness, kindly; and then she changed the subject by asking Lilith if she had ever been abroad, and if she was a good sailor.

"No," Lilith answered. "My longest sea voyages have been from Baltimore to New York and from New York to Newport. But I am a very good sailor, for I have been in more than one storm on Chesapeake Bay and have never been seasick."

"That is very well. I hope you will be able to bear the unrest of Old Ocean as bravely," said the baroness.

And then she told Lilith what her experience had

told her, the outfit necessary for the comfort of the voyage, and the outfit that would be nothing but an impediment.

And then, when an hour had passed, Lilith arose to take leave.

Madame Von Bruyin would not allow her to go, but insisted that she should stay to luncheon, which was served in madame's private apartments.

It was a tête-à-tête feast, and Lilith much enjoyed the delicate fare set before her—the well-dressed game, the delicious salad, the dainty confectionery, the luscious fruits, and the pure, light Chablis.

When the repast was finished and the service was removed, the baroness went and took a guitar from its place on a stand in the recess, and sat down to play. She touched a few chords and then floated into a mournful solo from "Il Trovatore." Her voice was a deep, rich, full contralto, but so profoundly sad that Lilith felt her eyes fill with tears as she said to herself:

"Ah, madame has also suffered. I know it."

The baroness finished her song and laid aside her guitar without a word.

But presently she said:

"You love music, my dear? Bah! who does not?"

"I love music. That was a beautiful solo, madame, only so sad!"

"Ah, my dear! But never mind. You have promised to tell me your story some day. I may tell you mine before that. For in this case I feel towards you somewhat like the ancient mariner to the wedding guest."

"I shall be glad to hear, madame, very glad and grateful for your confidence," said Lilith, as she once more arose to take leave.

"Why is it that I feel as if you belonged to me,

dear?" said the baroness, as she took the girl in her arms and kissed her.

"It is because you are so good to me, madame. In an humble way, in my happy days at home, whenever I took any helpless creature under my care, I always felt as if it belonged to me, whether it did or not," said Lilith, simply.

"Come again to-morrow, my dear, if you can. If not, come any day at this hour. I am always at home between twelve and two," said the baroness, as she patted the cheek of her new favorite and let her go.

As before, the old Frenchman joined her in the corridor and escorted her downstairs and out to the sidewalk.

There she thanked and took leave of him.

Lilith walked home, where she arrived an hour later than on the preceding day.

"You have made a long visit this morning, honey," said Aunt Sophie, who met her in the parlor.

"Yes, the baroness detained me," answered Lilith.

"I am getting jealous of that there baroness. I am so," said Aunt Sophie, half in jest, half in earnest. "But take off your things right here and come down to lunch. I have got such a beautiful cup of broma for you."

"Thank you, dear Aunt Sophie. But I have had lunch. The baroness made me stay for it, with her," replied Lilith.

"Now I am jealous of that baroness—downright jealous, that I am," said Aunt Sophie, with such an aggrieved look that Lilith embraced her, and privately resolved never to be persuaded to stay to lunch with Madame Von Bruyin so long as they should remain in New York.

Lilith did not go to the baroness the next day, but she went down on Broadway to purchase the necessaries for her sea voyage.

When she returned to her boarding-house a great surprise awaited her.

Aunt Sophie met her at the door with a radiant, beaming countenance, and asked, with a very mysterious air:

"Well, honey! Who do you think has come? And is in the parlor waiting for you? You can't guess!"

Lilith's heart gave a great bound. For a moment she could not move, and her swiftly changing color and agitated features caused Aunt Sophie to laugh softly, as she added:

"Why, it is Emily Ponsonby, of course. She has just arrived from Boston, where she has been staying with her daughter ever since she left the city the morning after she brought you here. She reached the city last night, and is stopping with her other daughter, Mrs. Saxony. And this morning she came right down here to inquire after you. She came in just about ten minutes after you had gone out. Now come in and see her."

Aunt Sophie's long explanation had given Lilith time to recover from her mingled feelings of surprise, wild hope and disappointment. She quietly followed Aunt Sophie into the front parlor, where the ample form and rosy face of the good-hearted Baltimore lady met her view.

"Well, my dear, glad to see you again, and to hear from your good friend, Sophie Downie here, such splendid accounts of you," said Mrs. Ponsonby, rising and embracing Lilith.

"Thank you, madam; but all my good fortune began with yourself. If you had not spoken to me on the train and brought me to this house, I really do not know what would have become of me."

"Neither do I," replied Mrs. Ponsonby, quite frankly. "It was the wildest freak I ever heard of in all my life—a young girl coming to a strange city to seek her fortune! Ugh! It makes my very flesh creep to think of it!"

"It was a forced measure, dear friend. I had no choice. I was obliged to come," said Lilith, as she took a seat on the sofa beside the matron.

"Well, I suppose you were obliged to come, and so the Providence that takes care of the young ravens took care of you. But I tell you what, my girl, if you had come away from home from other impulse than stern necessity you would have gone to the deuce before this. It was an awful risk, my dear."

"I knew it was, but I could not help it," said Lilith, meekly.

"And Sophie has been telling me that you have just got a splendid situation with the Baroness Von Bruyin."

"Yes, ma'am."

"Why, I knew her! I met her in Washington when she was a Miss Von Kirschberg. I have not seen her since she married the old banker, Mr. Bruyin, who got himself made Baron Von Bruyin to please his wife, and paid a good round sum to Emperor William for the honor, you may take my word for it. Bosh! I like nobility when it is real, that is, hereditary; but I should care no more for a purchased title than I should for a paste 'diamond' or an imitation 'India' shawl. And the poor old man is dead, and dead, too, without an heir to perpetuate his dearly bought title."

"What sort of a woman is the baroness, anyway, to live with, do you think?" inquired Aunt Sophie, in anxiety for the happiness of her protégée.

"I think she is just about as good a woman as one could expect to find in an only child, a beauty and heiress, who had been petted and pampered and flattered and fairly idolized by everybody around her all the days of her life," emphatically answered Mrs. Ponsonby.

"I am glad to hear it," answered Aunt Sophie.

"And I think you will just have a splendid time with her, my dear. Why, you are really going to travel all over Europe. My! don't I wish I was going to Europe! But, there! what is the use of talking. When Ponsonby and myself were young, with a family of little ones around us, we promised ourselves just as soon as we had raised and settled them all, we would travel and see the world; but Lor'! before the last of them were married the grandchildren of the first wedded began to come on, and they are just as strong fetters and as heavy iron balls to hinder our travels as ever their mothers were. You are to be envied, my dear, I can tell you that!"

"I am thankful," replied Lilith. "But why should you have waited until your children grew up before you could go to Europe? Why not have taken them all with you?"

"Never saw the day when we could afford that, my dear. But I will live in hopes to see the old world some time or other before I die. Well, dear, I only called to inquire after you, and to see whether Sophie Downie had done a good part by you——"

"She is the best friend I have in this world!" hastily and warmly interrupted Lilith—"except yourself, Mrs. Ponsonby," she added, on reflection.

"And I don't doubt that Madame Von Bruyin will be a much more valuable friend than either of us," said Mrs. Ponsonby.

"No! no!" exclaimed Lilith.

"Well, at least I hope for your sake she may be. You cannot have too many or too good friends. Well, I must go, or I shall be late for lunch. I shall fetch Polly Saxony to call on you; and then we must have you to come and spend a day with us before you sail," said the Baltimore lady, as she arose, kissed Lilith good-bye, and left the drawing-room, followed by Aunt Sophie, with whom she chattered all the way out, and lingered to chat in the hall, and still loitered to chat on the stoop outside.

At length she was gone, and Aunt Sophie returned to the parlor.

"Wasn't that a surprise?" inquired Aunt Sophie, gleefully, as she re-entered the room.

"Yes; quite a surprise," assented Lilith.

"And now I have got another for you: John Moore has gone off to be married. The wedding is to be to-morrow, at the bride's mother's house, in Spring-field. And he is to bring his wife home on Saturday, and take her straight to the parsonage, which is all ready. And I have fixed up his room for you. You can have it at once. Ah! if you were only going to stay I could make you so comfortable!" said Aunt Sophie, with a deep sigh.

"Dear friend, I would like to stay with you, but you know that I cannot; I must take the employment that is offered me," gently replied Lilith.

"Yes, I know. Some of these days you will come back, though, and I hope I shall live to see you, and if so, you must come straight home to me, dear, do you hear?"

"Yes, Aunt Sophie; and I certainly will come to you first of all, if we both live," said Lilith.

And then the entrance of other persons ended their tête-à-tête.

The next day Lilith went to see the baroness, and was received with even more kindness than on the former occasions. But she declined an invitation to stay to lunch.

When she returned home Aunt Sophie met her with a smile, and put two cards in her hands, saying:

"They called while you were out, my dear, but they

didn't stay long. And they left an invitation for you and me to go and spend the day with them to-morrow."

Lilith looked at the cards, which bore the names of MRS. JOHN PONSONBY and of MRS. THEOBALD E. B. SAXONY.

"I think I'll go with you, my dear; I have not had a day out so long. I know Mary Farquier will look after the house for me one day."

And so Aunt Sophie and her protégée accepted this invitation; and the next morning, at a most unfashionably early hour, they presented themselves at the Saxony mansion, where they were very kindly re-received and hospitably entertained by the mother and daughter.

They met none of Mrs. Saxony's fashionable friends. It was not that lady's receiving day; so she was "not at home" to all casual callers, and she devoted herself to her mother's simple friends.

Aunt Sophie and Lilith returned in the evening, well pleased with their visit.

The next day the old lady invited Lilith to accompany her to the parsonage, where she and all her "family" were going, with many of the church people, to receive the young minister and his bride.

Lilith went, for she had resolved to give herself up to please Aunt Sophie for the short remainder of her stay with the affectionate woman.

They found the parsonage a very attractive home for the newly married pair. The house, which stood beside the church, had been newly papered and painted, and refurnished from top to bottom, and prettily decorated for the occasion. The church people had vied with each other in the choice of their wedding presents, which were tastefully displayed on the drawing-room tables.

The refreshments were laid out on the extension table in the dining-room at the rear.

The house was full, but not crowded, because the people dispersed themselves through all the apartments.

Aunt Sophie only waited long enough to welcome the young minister and his bride, to wish them all happiness, and to show them into their chamber, where they might change their traveling suits for festive dresses before going down into the drawing-room to meet their friends, and then she took leave.

She would have persuaded Lilith to stay with the company, but the latter insisted on going with her friend.

"You know I ain't young, honey, and gay and festive scenes don't suit me," she said, apologetically.

"And as for me, I wish to go with you, and to be with you as much as I can while I remain in the country," Lilith answered, affectionately.

CHAPTER X

IN HER TRUE COLORS

MADAME VON BRUYIN grew very fond of Lilith and would have had her new favorite with her every day, or even had her to come and live at the hotel.

But Lilith pleaded that she wished to stay with her kind landlady as much as possible during the short interval that would intervene before their sailing for Europe.

The baroness admitted the excuse and did not insist on Lilith's entering upon her duties of companionship before the stipulated time—June 1st.

But whenever Aunt Sophie was out on business, or very much occupied with her household duties, Lilith would slip away to pay a flying visit to the baroness, to whom she was now, at all hours, a most welcome guest.

One evening it happened that Aunt Sophie had gone to a protracted meeting at her church, and Lilith availed herself of that opportunity to go and see the baroness.

It was the first occasion on which she had ever ventured to call on that lady in the evening.

She found Madame Von Bruyin alone in her apartments, more lonely and depressed than usual, and more than ever pleased to see her unexpected but most welcome visitor.

She received Lilith with a warm embrace, and made her lay aside her bonnet and mantle, and sit down in the most comfortable chair in that luxurious room.

The gas had been turned down low, so that the whole room was in a subdued cathedral light very favorable for meditation or for confidential conversation.

How it was that Madame Von Bruyin glided into speaking of her own life neither she nor her companion ever knew.

It was in answer to some remark of Lilith's, however, that the baroness answered:

"Yes, I know. Of course there are many people who envy me, and I suppose that I may be considered in a very enviable position; but that is only the external view. Within myself I am not enviable. There are few women in this world less happy than I am."

"I am very sorry," said Lilith, in true sympathy. But she was much too modest to preach to this great lady, this spoiled beauty, and to tell her of the vast power her wealth furnished of doing good and finding her happiness in the happiness of others.

"Child!" continued the baroness, "the truth is that I do not know what to do with my life. If I were not in deep mourning I should take a plunge into

society and in its maddest excitements forget myself.
But as I cannot do that, I go to Europe, to make a
tour of the continent. But I ask myself, to what purpose? I have seen it all before. It will have no
novelty for me."

"Not the beaten track—the great cities, the great
centres of art, science and learning, the monuments
of antiquity—you have seen all those; not the high-
ways of travel, but the by-ways, madame—the remote
villages, the country people of each country. It seems
to me that these also might be very interesting," Lilith
modestly suggested.

"Possibly," wearily replied the lady; "but nothing
interests me, child—except yourself—nothing. With
every appliance of material good—with youth and
health and wealth—I have no interest in life, no enjoyment of anything."

"Oh, madame! what has brought you into such a
state as this?" exclaimed Lilith, speaking from the
irrepressible impulse of her great sympathy, and then
stopping short and blushing at the thought of having asked the baroness an impertinent question.

But Madame Von Bruyin did not seem to perceive
any impropriety in Lilith's words. She felt only their
deep sympathy.

"I must tell you something about myself and my
spoiled life, and then you will understand. Come
nearer to me, child."

Lilith left her easy-chair, drew a hassock after her,
and sat down on it at the feet of the baroness.

The lady bent her stately head until the golden
tresses touched the ebon ringlets of the girl. And
after this caress she laid her hand on Lilith's head
and whispered:

"I have been so wilful all my life. I can never
remember the time when my will was crossed—until

about six months ago. How full the last six months
have been of changes for me!"

The lady paused thoughtfully. Lilith might have
added: "And for me!" but she did not. The baroness
continued:

"I am an American, my dear, as you might know
by my speech; and I was born and married in America,
though my father and my husband were both sub-
jects of the Emperor William. I was the only child
of my widowed father, who had married very late
in life and who lost his wife in the same hour that
gave him his child. He never married a second time,
but devoted himself to me. In time I became the idol
of my father and of his dearest friend and insepar-
able companion, Mr. Nicholas Bruyin—who became
Baron Von Bruyin later, you understand."

"Yes, madame," said Lilith.

"I was never sent to school, but had teachers at
home, who taught me no more than I chose to learn;
masters and governesses who never mastered or governed me, but who had to submit to my will or leave
my service. And in all my self-will I was upheld by
the two fondly doting old gentlemen who held my
destiny in their hands. I learned music and dancing because I liked to do so; but I do not think I
should have learned anything else if it had not been
for the advent of Monsieur le Professeur Le Grange,
my present private secretary, whom you have seen."

"Yes, madame."

"He was engaged to teach me languages when I
was about thirteen years old, and more ignorant
than any girl of my own age and rank. Well, Professeur Le Grange certainly found out the road to
my conscience and affections, convinced me of my pitiable ignorance and became my teacher not only of
languages, but of science, history and general litera-
ture. I became very appreciative of his character

and abilities, and tried to profit by them. I think I
have shown my gratitude for his services by attach-
ing him to my household. He will never leave."

"He seems sincerely devoted to you, madame," said
Lilith.

"I think he is. There are spiritual fathers in the
church. Professeur Le Grange may be called my
intellectual father. When I was but fifteen years of
age I went to Europe with these three old men—my
father, my friend and my teacher, and with no female
companion except my old nurse and my maid. You
have never seen those two faithful women, dear?"

"No, madame."

"Yet they are still in my service. We made an
unusually extensive tour of Europe, and the professor, who, in addition to his other acquirements, was
a learned archæologist and antiquarian, was my most
valuable guide and mentor. Perhaps I derived more
benefit than most persons from my travels. If so,
I owe that benefit to the professor. He is to go with
us when we sail, as I suppose you know."

"Yes, madame."

"We returned at the end of three years, and I was,
soon after our arrival, introduced into society. Two
years of fashionable seasons, in the winter spent in
New York or Washington, in the summer at Newport or at some other fashionable resort. I was
nineteen years old when my father was attacked by
what he believed to be a temporary though very
sharp illness. But the physician who was called in
warned him of its real significance. Then my father
grew anxious to settle up all his worldly affairs, and
very anxious to see me married. I know not how it
happened, or who first suggested the plan—whether
it was my father or Mr. Bruyin—but the issue was
that I became the betrothed bride of Nicholas Bruyin
before I knew that I had a heart in my bosom. Mr.

Bruyin, though older than my father, was really a healthier and a stronger man, with the promise of a longer life. This betrothal took place just before I went to Washington last summer. Ah! if it had been delayed but a few weeks longer what a difference it would have made in my life; for there, in the beginning of that season in Washington, I was destined to meet the only man whom I could ever love; a man of whom you have probably heard, for his fame has gone abroad all over the country, the brilliant orator and rising statesman, Tudor Hereward."

Lilith uttered a low cry, so low that it escaped the notice of Madame Von Bruyin, who continued:

"I became so much interested in this gentleman that, unconscious of the danger into which I was running, I allowed myself to enjoy the heaven of his society and conversation, for it was heaven to me. One night—it was at the masquerade ball given by Senator and Mrs. S——, at their splendid mansion, on New Year's Eve—Mr. Hereward sought me out and proposed for my hand. Oh! not until that hour did I realize how much I loved him. But I had to explain that a betrothal scarcely less sacred than marriage bound me to Mr. Bruyin. He, my lover, Tudor Hereward, bitterly, bitterly reproached me for misleading him, and trifling with his affections. And we parted in wrath."

The baroness bowed her face on Lilith's curly black head and wept. The girl, unable to trust her voice to speak, took one of the lady's hands and fondled and kissed it in sympathy. The baroness recovered her self-possession, and continued:

"The next day I missed Hereward from all his usual places. And before the night came, my betrothed arrived from New York. He was shocked to see how changed I was. Child, it was my first sorrow, and I had no power to conceal it. The good old man,

who loved me with a totally unselfish love, won my
secret from me, at once released me from my engagement and left me free to marry the lover of my
choice. Then I watched for Hereward's return, and
when he arrived—child, I went to him, I humbled
myself before him; I told him that I was free, and
I offered him my hand. He replied in icy tones that
he was married. Yes, married, within two days after
having been rejected by me. He had married a young
girl, a child who knew no better than to take a man
at a moment's notice. The news was a thunderbolt
to me; yet even through that nervous shock how I
pitied that young wife."

"Oh, Heaven, yes. How much she was to be pitied!"
cried Lilith, in a tone of sharp pain.

"As for my miserable self, the kind guardian of
my peace and welfare saw that there had been no
happy meeting between me and my lover. Again he
won my secret from me. This time it was the secret
of my disappointment and humiliation. Then taking my hand, he said to me:

" 'My dear, the world knows nothing of this. The
world still believes us to be a betrothed pair. Let
things go on as they were arranged. You know me.
We will be married at the time appointed. I will
then take you abroad to the court of Berlin. Your
dear father will go with us for his health. You are
so young yet that you will outlive and forget this
trouble.' "

"Well, I consented. I was so confused and depressed between grief and mortification, that I was
easily led. Only a few days later we were married
in the cathedral in this city, and sailed in the Kaiser
Wilhelm for Germany. We had planned out a very
fine tour. But ah! while we were still at the court
of Berlin, and only a few days after Mr. Bruyin had
received his patent of nobility and become the Baron

Von Bruyin, he had a stroke of apoplexy that terminated his earthly existence. We laid him in the cemetery of the city that he loved so well, and then set out to return home. My father never reached these shores alive. His mortal remains repose in Woodlawn. There, my child, I have unburdened my mind to you."

CHAPTER XI

THE FAIR RIVALS

How am I changed? My hopes were once like fire;
  I loved and I believed that life was love.
How am I lost? How high did I aspire!
  Above heaven's winds, my spirit once did move
All nature by my heart and mind, to make
  A paradise of earth, for one dear sake.
I love—but I believe in love no more.
  I still aspire—but hope not. And from sleep,
All vainly must my weary brain implore
  Its long lost flattery now. I wake to weep,
And sit through the long day, gnawing the core
  Of my bitter heart, and like a miser keep—
Since none in what I feel take thought or pleasure—
To my own soul its self-consuming treasure.
Shelley.

AND thus Leda, Baroness Von Bruyin, had told her heart's history to Tudor Hereward's young wife.

No words can describe its effect on Lilith.

She sat in the "gloaming," silent and motionless, her still, white face invisible to the lady, who, after finishing her story, fell into thought, seeming to brood over the past.

This, then—mused Lilith—this peerless, regal beauty was the Miss Von Kirschberg, the woman whom Tudor Hereward had passionately loved, and by whom he had been cast off, only on the evening before he had married her—Lilith—to please his dying father, and to be revenged upon his false love! Oh! the bitter wrong! the bitter, bitter dishonor of the wrong!

Lilith pressed her hands upon her white face, in an anguish too deep for tears.

Madame Von Bruyin saw nothing of that in the gloaming. Presently she spoke again:

"Strange—strange; but since Herr Von Bruyin passed away I seem to understand his character better than I ever did before! More than ever before I seem to feel the pure, tender, unselfish love he lavished upon me, from my earliest infancy, even until the day of his death—'until the day of his death?' What am I saying? Uttering hastily, and with parrot-like repetition, false, unmeaning words—for there is no death and no limit to love like his. From his home above, he loves me still. And, perhaps, when I, too, shall reach that bright world in which there is no winter and no age, I shall find no disparity between us; but shall see and love him even as he sees and loves me! And that shall be my comfort and his reward."

The baroness spoke tenderly, meditatively, with her beautiful head bowed upon her hand, and her fair hair, escaped from the widow's cap, flowing down over her black-robed shoulders.

Lilith uttered not a word, but she thought:

"This is the woman whom Tudor Hereward denounced as vain, self-seeking, double-dealing; false to him, false to herself, false to her betrothed, and all because, to keep her plighted faith, she had rejected him."

And Lilith, through all her own deep pain, felt a tender sympathy with the desolate heart of her rival.

At length the baroness spoke again:

"You are very silent, petite. Of what are you thinking?" she softly inquired.

"Of the story you have told me, madame," gently replied Lilith.

"And what about it, dear?"

"It is very sorrowful. You are not happy, madame; and perhaps you never can be, unless, unless—by——"

"By what, my child?"

"By making others happy. You have such great power of doing good, dear lady!" earnestly replied Lilith.

"What good can I do? I seem of no use in the world!" sighed the baroness.

"By your great wealth, madame," modestly suggested Lilith.

"Oh, of course, I subscribe to all worthy charities that are brought to my notice. Le Grange attends to all that! That is, of course, my bounden duty, and I try to do it," said the baroness.

"Yes, I know you are very liberal and very conscientious, but——"

"But what, my dear?"

"There are so many, many cases of great poverty, sickness and suffering outside of these organized charities! Aged, or ill, men and women, and little children, suffering in extremity for want of the barest necessaries of life, helpless and dying for lack of help, even in the midst of all these organized charities! These do a vast deal of good, but they cannot do everything! They cannot reach all the suffering!"

"How do you know?" inquired the lady.

"I know from what I see, and hear, and observe

in the streets, and from what I learn when I go into the poorest tenement houses with Aunt Sophie."

"Aunt Sophie? Who is she, child?"

"Mrs. Downie. My good landlady. She is a Methodist minister's widow. She keeps a plain boarding-house, mostly for young ministers and teachers. She is very poor, but very charitable, and when she sees a poor, pale, ragged child on the streets trying to make a few pennies by selling matches or pins, she often takes such a child to its own home to see for herself into its circumstances and find out how she can permanently benefit it. She has adopted and brought up several of these forlorn children, and settled them respectably in life. She has always one or two on hand. She has one even now. Oh! if I had only plenty of money I would found a home for destitute children. I would set Aunt Sophie at its head with the carte blanche to take in all the needy children that the home could hold."

"But there are so many of these asylums, my dear."

"I know; but there are not enough, else why these poor, little, homeless and friendless ones in the street?"

"Well, petite, I do not feel just yet quite inspired to found such an institution, but, before we sail, I will place in your good Aunt Sophie's hands a sum of money to aid her charitable work among the friendless children of the street," said the baroness.

"Will you? Oh, will you, indeed? If you do, you will make a good heart so glad!" exclaimed Lilith, with a beaming face.

"I will, indeed! I will send Le Grange to the house with the check to-morrow," said the lady.

"Oh! give it with your own hand, dear madame, and you will see what joy you will bring into the dear woman's face."

"I hear what joy I bring into your voice, little one, and I am glad to hear it," replied the baroness.

In her deep interest in the subject under discussion, Lilith had for the moment forgotten her own griefs.

Even Madame Von Bruyin seemed in better spirits as she said, cheerfully:

"We must have lights now, dear."

She touched the silver timbre on the stand beside her.

An attendant came in and lighted the gas and retired.

Lilith arose from her low position on the hassock at the lady's feet.

The baroness also stood up, and drawing her companion's arm within her own, walked up and down the splendid, illuminated room in silence.

It happened that at each end of this room there was a broad and tall mirror that reached from floor to ceiling and reflected the two figures from head to foot—the grand beauty of the Baroness Von Bruyin and the petite grace of Lilith.

The young wife marked the contrast with a sinking and despairing heart. In her admiration she greatly exaggerated the power of her rival's queenly charms, and in her humility as much underrated the effects of her own sweet loveliness.

"Ah!" she sighed, from the depths of her desponding spirit. "No wonder he worships this lady, for she is the crowned queen of beauty! No wonder he could not love me, for who am I beside her? No more than a little yellow duckling beside a royal white swan! No! I cannot blame him for adoring her and not liking me. But oh! he might have let me alone. He ought not to have married me so lightly and cast me off so easily because I was a duckling and not a swan. Now I remember that he never said he loved me. He never professed what he never felt for me. And I was so blind I never missed that. Because he asked me to be his wife, I truly thought he loved me, and I did so joyfully consent—letting him see how happy and how glad I was of the honor he had done me, the delight he had given me. Oh, the sin of it! Oh, the shame of it! Oh, my angel mother in heaven, if you had been on earth you would never have let your child fall into such a trap. You would have taught her; you would have warned her. Oh, he ought to have been generous; he ought to have remembered that I had no mother; he ought to have let me alone!"

"What is the matter with you, dear child?" inquired the baroness, breaking in upon Lilith's grievous reverie. "You are so absorbed and distressed that you must be in some great trouble, either for yourself or for some one else. Can I do anything for you?"

"No, dear madame; nothing. My passing mood was not worth your attention. A vain regret given to lost treasures, or perhaps only to imaginary treasures that I never really possessed. I will try to overcome my tendency to fall into these moods," answered Lilith, with an effort to collect herself.

"Some day, my dear, you will tell me of your past life—a short story, it must be—as frankly as I have told you of mine. I will wait patiently until then. But, little one, we have talked and mused, and mused and talked, until the hours have slipped by us unheeded, and now it is so late that you must either stay all night, or allow me to send for a carriage at once to take you home."

"Oh, thank you, madame. I must go home. Late as it is, Aunt Sophie will expect me," said Lilith.

Madame Von Bruyin touched the timbre, and

ordered the attendant who answered the summons to procure a carriage.

While Lilith was putting on her hat and gloves the baroness said:

"You may tell this dear Aunt Sophie of the power I intend to place in her hands to help the poor little children."

"Oh, dear madame, how good you are! But I would rather not tell her. I would rather you should do so first, for the sake of seeing the happy surprise that will light up her face," said Lilith.

"Very well, then. You may expect me to-morrow morning at the house," said the baroness.

The attendant entered the room and announced the carriage.

"Ask Monsieur Le Grange to be good enough to step here," said the baroness.

The man bowed and withdrew.

"Monsieur," said the baroness, when the old secretary made his appearance and respectfully saluted the company, "will you do me the favor to see Mrs. Wyvil home? The carriage waits."

"With the greatest pleasure, madame," answered the old gentleman, with his habitual deep bow, as he gallantly offered his arm to the young lady to lead her from the room.

The baroness drew Lilith up and kissed her cheek before giving her into the care of the polite old secretary, who took her in charge, and bowed himself out of his lady's presence.

He led Lilith down the stairs, placed her in the carriage, took his seat by her side, and directed the coachman to drive to Mrs. Downie's, number so and so, such a street.

It was so late when they reached their destination that all the lights were out in the house, except those of the front parlor.

The old Frenchman left the carriage, helped Lilith to alight, and led her up to the door. Nor did he leave her until his ring was answered and an old lady appeared to receive the returning guest.

Then he bowed himself down the steps to the carriage and drove off.

"Oh, my dear, I was that uneasy about you; I was thinking of starting out to the hotel to inquire after you," said Aunt Sophie, as she went into the front parlor to turn off the gas.

"Why should you have been uneasy? What harm could have happened to me even if I had started to come home alone through the streets of a crowded city?" inquired Lilith, as they went upstairs together.

"What harm? Oh, child, you read the papers, and see how busy the devil is and how artful his children are. Every once in a while you see an account of some child or young girl kidnapped and made away with, and I suppose as there's many and many a case that never even gets into the newspapers."

"I am sorry to hear that, Aunt Sophie; but there was no danger in my case, for madame sent me home in a carriage, under the care of her aged secretary."

"So I saw. So I saw. And she was in the right of it. Well, my dear, it is after one o'clock, and I think we had better get to bed as soon as we can," said the old lady, as they entered the double-bedded chamber, which they still occupied together.

The room vacated by the minister having been taken by the organist.

Early the next morning, as Aunt Sophie, having got through with the breakfast, was preparing to go to market, Lilith said to her:

"I cannot walk out with you to-day, dear. I am expecting the Baroness Von Bruyin, and as I do not know at what hour she may find it convenient to call, I must stay in until she does."

"I am awful jealous of that baroness," said the little old lady, in a pathetic tone, shaking her little rumpled gray head.

"You need not be. There is no woman in the world I love half so much as I do you, dear Aunt Sophie," said Lilith.

"Well, then, why won't you live long of me always and be my child, instead of going off to foreign parts with that baroness?"

"Because it would not be right, dear Aunt Sophie."

"Eh, dear, it's a tiresome world. What's that baroness coming here for to-day?"

"To call on me, and I think she wishes to see you, too, so I shall keep her till you come back from market."

"No, you needn't! I don't want to see that baroness! That I don't," said Aunt Sophie, as she tied on her little mashed black silk bonnet, which, like her rumpled fine gray hair, and little baby face, was a part of her gentle personality.

"But I want you to see her, Aunt Sophie. I think you'd get over your prejudice against her."

"No, I shouldn't! I'm jealous of her. That's where it is. I'm awful jealous of her, that I am! But I'll hurry back from market to see her if you want me to. And if I have to do that I must hurry away now."

And the dear little woman folded her rusty Canton crape shawl across her bosom and left the room.

Lilith set the bed-chamber in order and then went down to the front parlor to await the coming of Madame Von Bruyin.

But it was twelve o'clock before the baroness arrived. Aunt Sophie had come home from market and "fixed herself up" to receive the great lady, by putting on her Sunday gown, a thin, rusty black silk, and tying a bobinet fichu crookedly around her neck,

but she could not sit in state to receive her visitor.
She was too busy overseeing the cook get dinner for
the boarders.

"Besides, what does she want to see me for, I would
like to know?" she asked herself.

So she was shelling peas in the kitchen when word
was brought to her that there was a lady in the parlor
waiting to see her.

She put the pan of peas on the table, took off her
"check" apron, shook down her dress and went upstairs to see the visitor.

She found a tall, beautiful woman, dressed in deep
mourning, the black crape vail thrown back, revealing a fair face, with delicately blooming cheeks,
large, soft, violet eyes, and rippling golden hair, just
visible under the borders of her widow's cap.

Gentle Aunt Sophie was won, despite herself,
by the sweet, pensive smile with which the lady received her own rather cold greeting, when Lilith had
introduced the parties to each other.

After some little preliminary conversation about
the early setting in of summer; the unusual warmth
of the weather for only the last week in May; the
prospective sea-voyage in June, and the probability
of fair winds and good weather, the main object of
Madame Von Bruyin's visit was artfully introduced.

It required some tact on the part of the baroness
and her young companion to deal with a woman as
shy, jealous and peculiar as the minister's widow,
under such circumstances as these.

But when Madame Von Bruyin briefly explained
that the news of Mrs. Downie's mission among the
street children had awakened her own interest to a
very great extent, and had inspired her with a wish to
serve them—which, owing to her swiftly approaching embarkation to Europe, she could not personally
carry out—and when she begged as a great personal

favor that Mrs. Downie would act as her almoner, with carte blanche to use the donation according to discretion, and ended by placing a check for a thousand dollars in Aunt Sophie's hands—

Well, she, good soul, did not utter one word of thanks!

But her whole form vibrated and her face beamed with joy and thankfulness. Tears of joy filled her eyes as she faltered, almost inarticulately:

"Oh! how much good you will do with all this, madame! How much good you will do!"

"If so, it will be through your hands, dear friend," replied the baroness, rising to take leave.

Mrs. Downie, with the most old-fashioned, time-out-of-mind hospitality, would have pressed her to stay to dinner, to stay to tea, to spend the whole evening, but the baroness smiled, pleaded a pressure of engagements, and departed.

"She's good! she's mighty good. But, oh! what a sinner I am. For I'm so awful jealous of her, all the same. But I can't help it, and it's all because of you, honey," said Aunt Sophie, as soon as she was left alone with Lilith. "I must get the brethren to pray for me," she added.

From that memorable evening on which Madame Von Bruyin had told her own heart history to Lilith Hereward, the two friends were drawn closer together in sympathy and affection.

It was strange that Hereward's young wife, though she admired her husband's first love so excessively, and underrated her own self so humbly, yet felt no great jealousy of her rival.

Perhaps it was because Tudor himself had been the first to tell her of that first love, that mad though "brief infatuation," as he had called it; and because, on referring to its object, he had spoken of her only in terms of contempt and displeasure; so, at any rate, for this cause or for that, Lilith, on cool reflection, saw no cause to be jealous of her beautiful rival. She felt even some compassion for her, as for a fellow-sufferer from Hereward's great injustice—for had not Hereward denounced her as a false woman, a self-seeker, a double-dealer, a coquette, a traitress, a jilt? And all because Leda Von Kirschberg, after having promised her hand, discovered that she had a heart, and tried to do her duty between the two!

CHAPTER XII

NATIVE LAND ADIEU

As THE day of sailing drew near, Lilith's heart sank into utter despondency.

Up to this time she had been almost unconsciously sustained by the recognized uncertainty of human affairs; by the deep-seated hope that "something might happen" to delay the voyage, or perhaps to put it off altogether.

She watched the newspapers for news of Hereward; but she found none. She knew that Congress was still in session in Washington, and she read all the Congressional reports in the hope of finding his name; but it was not there; not in any debate; not in any speech; not even in the mere rank and file of the yeas and nays when a vote was taken. It seemed to have dropped quite out of public affairs. What had become of that once shining beacon of liberty and light?

Lilith could not even conjecture.

She diligently searched the personal column of the *Pursuivant*; but no carefully worded appeal came to her.

Lilith could not understand this utter silence, even from Ancillon, who had himself fixed in this column as the medium of their intercommunication.

Ah! but Lilith did not know that a coroner's jury had pronounced her dead—and come to her death "from a fatal blow on the back of her head, inflicted by a blunt instrument held in the hands of some person unknown," and that she had been given up, if not forgotten, by all her friends.

So Lilith looked through the papers day by day, "hoping against hope" for some sign from her silent husband.

"He knows that I cannot make any," she said, despairingly, to herself. "He knows that he discarded me, and drove me from his home with insult and contumely. He knows that in my farewell letter to him I wrote that if ever he should review his course towards me, retract his charges against me, and permit me to return, I would go to him, and be to him all that I have been—wife, housekeeper, secretary, guardian of his home, and helper in his office. Yes, I would, for although he does not love me, oh! my Heavenly Father, I do love him, and I cannot help it! Oh! if I could but return to him! But he does not want me. He will not have me. If I had stayed at Cloud Cliffs he would have gone away never to return while I 'desecrated the house' with my presence! He told me so! And oh! oh! the scorn and hatred of his looks when he spoke those words! No! he will never relent. He will never retract. He will never permit me to return—never in this world. It is no use to hope. Nothing is going to happen to bring us together. Nothing ever happens that one either hopes or fears. A poor wretch condemned to death hopes something may happen to save him; but it does not, and he dies. A happy girl looking forward to her bridal, fears something may happen to stop it; but it does not, and she marries. And oh! my Father, I still keep on hoping against hope; looking against a possibility for something to happen to open my husband's eyes to show him how cruelly he has wronged me, to bring him to my side. Hoping and expecting with idiotic persistency. Yet I know that nothing will happen. I must 'dree my weird,' as the Scotch say."

All this time Aunt Sophie watched her favorite with a troubled face, and often with tearful eyes. At last one day she said:

"There's something on your mind, dear, that you never let on to any one about. What is it, dear?"

"It is nothing but vain regrets for all that I have lost, Aunt Sophie, and foolish, mad longings to recover the irrecoverable," replied Lilith.

The gentle old lady did not quite comprehend her; but she said:

"I don't believe as you want to go on this voyage, child. I have noticed as the nearer the time comes the worse you are. Now, if you don't want to go, dear, don't you go—don't you. Stay here long o' me!"

"Oh! Aunt Sophie, I do grieve to leave you, but I must go—I must," sighed Lilith.

And she held to her resolution in spite of all the good woman could say.

For Lilith felt that since her husband would not relent, would not retract, would not call her back, the farther she could get away from the scene of her suffering the more contented she might be. In change of scene and foreign travel she might forget her misery.

Aunt Sophie, since she could not persuade her favorite to stay with her, busied herself in helping in the final preparations for her sea voyage. She packed little jars of home-made pickles and acid preserves, and little boxes of delicate biscuits and cakes, for Lilith's private use.

"For," she said, "though I know them ocean steamers have all the luxuries that can be bought with money, yet I do think as these home-made things is better. And though you mayn't be downright sea-sick, honey, you're bound to be a little bit mawkish with the motion of the vessel, and then these little things might suit your appetite when nothing else would."

"I am sure of it, dear Aunt Sophie. Even a cup of tea is all the sweeter and more refreshing when it is poured out by a friend's hand," replied Lilith. Whereupon Aunt Sophie shed a few tears—weakly, not unhappily.

The last day before the sailing came. All the luggage was to be sent down on board the steamer that afternoon; and the next morning the baroness was to call in her carriage to pick up her companion on her way to the ship.

All that forenoon Aunt Sophie wept softly to herself, furtively wiping her eyes whenever she could get a chance.

"I don't want the child to see me cry. It will only make her feel bad," she said to herself as she dodged Lilith.

At noon Lilith's trunk was taken down to the hall, to wait for the expressman to call and carry it to the ship.

Lilith herself, with nothing at all to do, sat with Aunt Sophie at the front parlor window, saying those last, tender words that are always repeated over and over again for days and hours before parting, when there came a ring at the door-bell, followed soon by the entrance of Monsieur Le Grange, private secretary to the Baroness Von Bruyin.

The little old gentleman came in, bowing as was his wont.

Mrs. Downie got up to leave the room—thinking that the secretary might have brought some private message from the baroness to her young companion; but he prevented her by a deprecatory bow and a polite disclaimer:

"Pardon, madame! I have come but to say a word, to make an explanation. I have come from Madame la Baronne to her beautiful and accomplished dame du compagnie here," he said, turning with another bow to Lilith. "Madame desires me to say, to explain, that she goes not to Europe by the Kron Prinz to-morrow."

"She does not sail by the Kron Prinz!" exclaimed Lilith, as if in her surprise she could not comprehend the fact.

"No, madame. La Baronne has changed her plan. She sails not to-morrow."

"Has she changed her mind about going to Europe?" inquired Lilith, with new hope lighting her eyes at this reprieve.

"No, madame. She has not changed her mind, but only her ship. She will go by the Kaiser Wilhelm on Saturday."

"Dear me, what a pity! Why, she will lose all her passage money!" exclaimed Mrs. Downie, whose economical soul was dismayed at such a useless sacrifice of the "needful."

"She will lose the half of it, madame, for herself and all her suite, and that is considerable, as her suite is large. But she goes, after all, by a ship of the same line."

"Well, honey," said Aunt Sophie, turning to Lilith, "at least this will give me three days more of your dear company; and who knows?—before Saturday something may happen to prevent your going at all."

"Oh, no!" sighed Lilith. "Nothing will happen. Nothing one hopes or fears ever happens."

"Now, what was the reason why the baroness put off her voyage for only three days at such a cost as that?" inquired simple Aunt Sophie, asking a question that Lilith had longed to ask but had shrunk from putting.

"I do not know, madame. Her resolution was taken very suddenly this morning," said the secretary, rising to take leave.

"Has the baroness any commands for me?" inquired Lilith, also rising.

"No, madame, none," replied the secretary, bowing himself out.

"Well, of all the whims I ever heard of in my life!" exclaimed Aunt Sophie. "But, anyways, 'it is an ill wind that blows nobody any good.' And this here 'whim' has blown me the blessing of your company for three days more, honey, and something may happen."

Lilith shook her head incredulously.

She gave all her time to Aunt Sophie that day and the next day, when the old lady said to her:

"To think, now, if it hadn't been for the whim of the baroness you would now have been on the ocean, instead of sitting here beside me. And maybe you won't go on Saturday, neither, who knows? Something may happen."

But again Lilith smiled and shook her head.

In the course of the forenoon a note came from the baroness to Lilith.

"Come to me this evening, my dear, and I will tell you why I changed my ship. The news will astonish you, I think, and it may indeed change my whole destiny. Tell your good landlady not to expect you back soon, as I shall keep you until a late hour, and

then return you safe, as before, under the escort of Monsieur Le Grange. Answer by the messenger.
        "Affectionately,   L. V. B."

Lilith wrote a note to the effect that she would wait on the baroness at seven o'clock that evening, and sent it by the page who had brought the first.

Then she showed the baroness' note to Aunt Sophie, who, after hearing it read, was filled with curiosity.

"Now what on earth can she have to tell you that will astonish you so much? Maybe she is going to marry the old secretary, and wants you to be brides-maid!" said Aunt Sophie.

Lilith looked at the simple woman and laughed. It was the first time she had laughed since her heavy sorrow.

"Well, now, stranger things than that has happened, honey; let alone the fact that nobody can ever account for the whims of these fine ladies. And come to think of it, didn't she marry an old man for her first husband? Maybe she has a fancy for old men. Some women have, I know," said Aunt Sophie, nodding her head sagaciously.

"Perhaps," said Lilith, remembering Mrs. Jab Jordon, and being unable to gainsay Aunt Sophie's declaration—"perhaps; but I do not think Madame Von Bruyin is one of those women. She married the Herr Baron to please her father."

"She don't look to me like one as would do anything as didn't please herself just as well. She is a good lady, a mighty good lady, and a generous and a charitable one, and she give me a great deal of money for the poor children. And I shall always be thankful to her and pray for her, and get the brethren to pray for her; but all the same, she's got a will

of her own, my dear. She will have her own way—
you may depend she will.

'Gin mammie and daddie and a' gang mad,'

as the old song says."

"Well, I shall know to-morrow why she has delayed
her voyage," said Lilith.

"Yes, and if she is going to marry the old secretary—and a nice old gentleman he is, too, I will say
that for him—she won't want you, my dear. It's
only rich old maids and rich widows as wants companions—married women don't. And so she'll let you
off your bargain and pay you compensation, which is
no more than right and proper, she being wealthy and
generous and you being a young orphan. And that's
what's going to happen, maybe, to prevent your voyage, and I shall have you all to myself. Who knows?"

"I do not think that will happen, Aunt Sophie."

"Well, we'll see."

"Yes, very soon. This very evening."

"And if it is that which I said, of course we shall
all hear it. But if it is anything else that has made
her change her day of sailing, will you tell me?"

"Yes, Aunt Sophie, unless the communication of
the baroness to me should be of a confidential nature," said Lilith.

"How I do hate secrets! I never had one of my
own in my life," said Aunt Sophie, with funny simplicity.

When evening came Lilith set out to walk to the
hotel to keep her appointment with the baroness.

When she reached that lady's apartments, however, she was met by the secretary, who, after politely
greeting her, explained the absence of the baroness.

"Madame is ill! She is ill! Headache. Migraine,
you know," he said, in a very pathetic tone. "She

lies in a room pitch dark; her maid sits beside her, silent as death. It is a vault—it is a grave, for she cannot bear the faintest ray of light, or murmur of sound. She can see no one; but before she retired to her bed she bade me receive you here, excuse her to you, and say to you, in brief, that the reason why she changed her steamer was that there was a party going by the Kron Prinz with whom she did not wish to sail, and that she would explain further when you meet. Meanwhile, chère madame, all arrangements are completed for our embarkation on the Kaiser Wilhelm on Saturday morning. Our baggage will be sent on board on Friday evening."

Lilith thanked the old secretary for his information, left her sympathetic regrets for Madame Von Bruyin, and arose to depart.

"I will have the honor to see you home, madame," said the polite secretary, as he attended Lilith downstairs and out to the sidewalk.

There, as before, he called a carriage, put her into it, took a seat by her side and ordered the coachman to drive to Mrs. Downie's boarding-house.

He only left Lilith when he had seen her enter the hall.

"And now, honey, what is it?" inquired Aunt Sophie, as soon as the two friends were seated in the front parlor together. "You are back a heap sooner than I expected. What did she tell you?"

· "Nothing. I did not see her. She has gone to bed with a severe headache. But she left a short message for me with Monsieur Le Grange to the effect that the reason why she would not sail by the Kron Prinz was that there was a party going by that steamer with whom she did not wish to travel," answered Lilith.

"Now, did ever any soul hear the like of that?" exclaimed Mrs. Downie. "If that doesn't cap all the

whims I ever heard of in all the days of my life!
But I ought'nt to say anything agin' her, I oughtn't
indeed, for she's a mighty good lady and a charitable
one, and she give me such a heap of money for the
poor street children."

Lilith saw no more of Madame Von Bruyin until
Saturday morning, when the baroness called in her
carriage to pick up her companion on her way to the
steamer.

Madame got out of her coach and went into the
house for the purpose of bidding. good-bye to Mrs.
Downie, whom she found crying over Lilith.

"You'll be good to the child, madame! I know
you will be good to her! I believe, I hope, I trust
you will," said Aunt Sophie, a little inconsistently,
as, after reiterated leave-taking, she resigned Lilith
into the charge of the baroness.

"Have no fear. She shall be happy, if I can make
her so," said the lady. And then, with a sudden
impulse of kindness, she added the question:

"Would you not like to go down to the ship and
see us off? Come with us—do! And the same carriage can bring you back to your own door."

"Oh, thank you, yes. Indeed, indeed, I would.
And I won't be a minute in getting on my things,"
said the grateful old lady, as she hurried from the
room.

In a very few moments she reappeared with her
mashed black silk bonnet, rusty black Canton crape
shawl, and thread gloves.

The three went out to the carriage, in which the
old Frenchman had remained seated. When they appeared he got out, politely saluted the party, handed
them into their seats, and then followed them.

The four persons just comfortably filled the carriage. Madame's maid and footman followed in au-

other carriage, having charge of their lady's lighter luggage.

And so they started to drive down the avenue to the ferry by which they were to cross to Hoboken, from which point the steamer was to sail.

Arrived at the pier on the other side, they found their ship, and in and about it a crowd, mostly composed of foreigners, commercial travelers, returning German emigrants, and a few summer tourists.

Aunt Sophie accompanied her friends on board the steamer, and became an interested and sympathetic spectator of the busy and affecting scene around her. Some of the leave-takings touched her tender heart even to tears, and made her think of the happy land where there would be "no more sorrow nor crying," and she kept on fortifying her mind by repeating over and over to herself the lines of her hymn:

> "Oh, that will be joyful!
> Joyful, joyful, joyful!
> Oh, that will be joyful
> To meet, to part no more!
> To meet to part no more,
> On Canaan's happy shore,
> Where we shall meet
> At Jesus' feet,
> And meet to part no more!"

Tears were in her tender eyes while the music of the simple hymn was sounding through her spirit.

Farewells were falling from faltering lips and failing hearts all around her. And in a saloon not far off a party of Germans were celebrating their embarkation by drinking lager and singing songs, in which Fatherland was the most frequent word and the chorus.

But Aunt Sophie heard none of this. She was in a dream.

She was aroused by the gentle voice of Lilith in her ear, saying:

"Aunt Sophie, the baroness says you have just time to bid us good-bye and get comfortably back to the pier. Monsieur Le Grange is waiting here to take you to the carriage, after which he will barely have time to return to us before the plank is drawn. Dear Aunt Sophie, the moment has come. Bid me good-bye and give me your blessing."

Mrs. Downie caught Lilith to her breast, burst into tears and sobbed aloud.

Lilith kissed her repeatedly, reiterating all the promises she had ever made, never to forget her, always to love her, often to write to her, and soon as possible to return.

"Madame, I must have the honor, if you please," said Monsieur Le Grange, with kindly firmness, as he drew the arm of the little old lady within his own and led her off to the gang plank, over which a sad procession was passing to the pier.

She had not even remembered to take leave of the baroness.

In five minutes Monsieur Le Grange returned to the deck, rejoined Madame Von Bruyin's party and reported:

"Madame Downie has screened herself on the cushions of the carriage. She repeats to herself some consoling office of her religion. She——"

But the good secretary's voice was drowned in the loud report of the farewell gun.

And the next minute the Kaiser Wilhelm stood out to sea.

It was two hours later. Most of the passengers had gone below, either to arrange their berths, or to guard against the first approaches of sea-sickness.

Madame Von Bruyin and her young companion sat well forward on the deck and quite out of hearing of any fellow-voyager. They had been silently gazing out to sea for a few minutes, when the baroness suddenly turned to her companion and said:

"I presume Monsieur Le Grange gave you my message that evening when you came to the hotel and found me too ill to keep my appointment?"

"Yes, madame."

"And he told you my reason for changing steamers?"

"Yes, madame, very briefly, to the effect that there was a party on board the Kron Prinz with whom you did not wish to travel."

"Yes, that was my short message; but he also added, if he reported me aright, that I woulld explain further when we should meet."

"He told me that, madame."

"Well, my dear, I suppose you could never be able to guess who it was from whom I shrank on the Kron Prinz."

"No, I am sure I could not. I have known so very few of your acquaintances, madame."

"Yet of this especial acquaintance I have spoken to you more than once. Surely now you can guess who it is that has gone before us to Europe in the Kron Prinz, can you not?"

"No, madame; unless—unless it was Prince Carl of Altenburg——"

"Prince Carl? Well, you know, of course, he was a bore, and worried me not a little; but I should not have changed my steamer on his account, even if he had been on board the Kron Prinz, which he was not. No, you must try again."

"I am sure I cannot guess, madame," said Lilith, with a smile, but with no interest in the question.

"Then I must tell you," said the lady; and dropping her voice, she added: "Who should it be but my old lover, Mr. Tudor Hereward, who has just been appointed Secretary of Legation to the Court of ——."

Lilith grew cold as death, but did not reply.

The baroness, too full of the subject, and of her own possible fortunes in connection with it, failed to notice her companion's silence, and went on eagerly to say:

"Yes, I first saw the announcement of his appointment, and of his intended voyage on the Kron Prinz, in the *Pursuivant* of Tuesday morning. And I saw something more in connection with his history that surprised me very much—something that seemed to render it indelicate, embarrassing, and even improper for me to make this sea voyage in his company. But we shall be sure to meet on the other side. And that meeting will probably decide our destinies. For now, my dear, we are both free!"

CHAPTER XIII

LILITH REVEALS HERSELF

There was a time when meadow, grove and spring
  The earth and every common sight,
    To her did seem
  Appareled in celestial light,
    The glory and the freshness of a dream.
It is not now as it hath been before;
  Turn wheresoe'er she may,
    By night or day,
The things that she hath seen she now can see no more.
    Waters on a starry night,
    Sunshine is a glorious birth,
    Yet she knows, where'er she goes,
That there hath passed away a glory from the earth.
                   Wordsworth.

" 'That meeting may decide' your 'destinies!' How?" inquired Lilith, in a low, steady tone, which it required all her powers of self-control to regulate.

"Oh, my child, did you never hear the homely old adage concerning lovers—that 'old coals are soon kindled?' We—Tudor Hereward and Leda Von Bruyin—have only to meet to come to a good understanding. My dear, we love one another. That is the reason why, under present circumstances, I did not choose to cross the ocean in the same steamer with him. Nor do I wish to meet him for some months yet. We could not, under any circumstances, unite our destinies in less than twelve or eighteen months, you know," said the baroness, speaking with much self-complacence.

" 'Unite your destinies?' " repeated Lilith, in the same low tone.

"Why, yes! Don't you understand? Why, marry, of course! Mr. Hereward and myself understand each other at heart, I feel sure, although we parted in mutual displeasure, and have never written or spoken to each other since."

"But—his—wife?" queried Lilith, in a low, hesitating voice.

"Oh, well, his wife! I am sorry for her, poor child! Really sorry for her! And he, too, must be sorry that she met such an awful fate," said the baroness, pausing and falling into thought.

"What fate did she meet?" inquird Lilith, in the same constrained, low monotone.

"Why, don't you know? Did not I tell you? Oh, no! I believe I did not. I said that we were both free, however, and you must have understood what that meant."

"No, I did not."

"It meant, of course, that his wife was dead, as

well as my husband—the two events setting us both free to marry again."

"His wife—dead! Tudor Hereward's wife—dead! Madame, what reason have you for supposing so?" demanded Lilith, in a low but firm tone.

"I do not wonder that you are surprised and incredulous! It is so strange that the young wife, with perhaps seventy years of life before her, should have been cut off by accident so soon; but strange things do happen in this uncertain old world of ours! And, my dear, it is true—Tudor Hereward's wife is dead."

"Dead? Yes, in some sense of the word, she is dead, I suppose," muttered Lilith to herself. Then slightly raising her voice she inquired: "Are you sure that she is dead, madame?"

"As sure as I can be of anything in this world. I knew nothing about it until I read what seemed to be a résumé of the whole story in the *Pursuivant*. Strange how we sometimes read and forget things without having the slightest idea of their significance to us! Some weeks ago I read in the papers that the body of an unknown young woman had been found in the woods on Cave Creek, near Frosthill in West Virginia. I read it without the faintest idea that I, or any one connected with me, could have any interest in that fact. And I had forgotten all about it until I read in the *Pursuivant* of Tuesday the announcement of Tudor Hereward's appointment as Secretary of Legation to the Court of ——, and the theory that he had only accepted the appointment in order to seek, by serving his country in foreign lands, some benefit to his health, broken down by grief for the tragic fate of his young wife."

"Merciful Heaven!" breathed Lilith to herself.

"And then, my dear," continued the baroness, unconscious of the interruption, "the whole story was gathered up and rehearsed—how young Mrs. Here-

ward was missing from her home on the night of the
21st of March, and how no trace of her could be found
until about the middle of April, when a body, much
decomposed, was discovered in the woods on the banks
of Cave Creek, which, after much investigation, con-
tradictory evidence and dispute, was proved beyond
all possibility of doubt to be that of Tudor Hereward's
young wife."

"How very strange!" muttered Lilith.

"Yes—very strange. It must have given Mr. Hereward a great shock, even though he never loved the
poor, inane young creature."

"No; of course, he never loved her!" sighed Lilith.

"How could he love her? He loved me—madly,
passionately, idolatrously—at the very time that he
married her. Why, I had rejected him only a few
hours before he proposed to her! And oh! what a
fool she must have been to have accepted a man who
had never wooed her—accepted him at his very first
word! I am sorry for the poor thing, but you must
acknowledge that she was a great idiot, and in no way
a fit and proper wife for Tudor Hereward."

"I do acknowledge it; but—but perhaps she loved
him," meekly suggested Lilith.

"That does not excuse her for snatching at a man's
first offer."

"But do you think it was quite right in him to ask
a girl to be his wife when he could not love her at
all?"

"No, indeed; I do not. I think he did her a most
grievous wrong. I told him so in Washington when
he announced his marriage to me. But, then, my dear,
he was half mad with rage, jealousy and disappointment. He married her to be revenged upon me—nothing more."

"It was a pity for the poor, unloved wife!" breathed
Lilith.

"Indeed it was—poor child. And no doubt he re-
pents the wrong he did her, now that she has met
so cruel a fate—robbed and murdered by tramps, it
is supposed, while she was on her way to relieve the
wants of a sick and destitute neighbor. Remorse is
harder to bear than sorrow, and no doubt it is remorse for the wrongs he had done her, and not sorrow
for the loss of the wife whom he never loved, that
is breaking down his health. However, he will get
over it in time," said the lady, complacently.

"And—you expect—some day—to bestow on him
—your hand in marriage?" slowly questioned Lilith.

"Yes, my dear; I mean to do him that justice—to
give him that consolation. We are both so young
yet. He is not thirty, I am but a little more than
twenty years of age. We have a long life before us,
in which I shall do all that in me lies to make him
forget his early disappointments and sorrows; to make
him as completely blessed and happy as woman can
make man," said the baroness, with more depth of
feeling in her thrilling tones than Lilith had ever de-
tected there before.

A dead silence followed these last words. Then
at length Lilith spoke in a low, firm, steady voice:

"Madame, you must not dream of your future life
in connection with that of Tudor Hereward."

"What! Why must I not? Whatever do you mean?
Why, I ask you?" demanded the surprised baroness.

"Because it would be a great sin."

"Sin! Why a sin?"

"Because Tudor Hereward's wife still lives," replied
Lilith, in a voice of such unnatural, mechanical calmness that it did not seem to come from living lips.

"Tudor Hereward's wife still lives?" demanded the
baroness, in slow, questioning, incredulous tones.
"What can you know about it? Her dead body was
found—was identified; what, then, do you mean by

saying that she still lives? And what can you know about it, in any case?"

"Madame, I do not dispute that some woman's dead body was found near her dwelling. I know not whose it was; but I do know that it was not Tudor Hereward's wife's."

"How dare you say so! How can you know anything about the matter?" demanded the baroness, almost indignantly.

"Because, madame—oh, forgive me—because—I—I am Mr. Hereward's—most unhappy wife!" answered Lilith, dropping her head in her hands with a low, heart-breaking moan.

There was a dead silence between the two for a few minutes.

The baroness was the first to speak.

"You? You the wife of Tudor Hereward? Impossible!" she muttered, glaring down on the little bowed head.

Lilith's bosom heaved with a silent sob; but she did not reply.

"You the wife of Mr. Tudor Hereward? I say it is impossible!" repeated Madame Von Bruyin.

"I would to Heaven that it were impossible," moaned Lilith.

"It cannot be true!" reiterated the baroness.

"I call Heaven to witness that it is true, madame. I am very sorry—I beg you to forgive me—I should never have told you, madame, but to save you from vain and sinful hopes and dreams. Indeed, I am very sorry, and I beg you to forgive me."

"You are, then, the child-wife whom Tudor Hereward married in haste and in rage to be revenged on me?" sternly demanded the baroness.

Lilith, with her face still buried in her hands, answered by a nod and a silent sob.

"You seem, then, to have entered my service under false pretences?" sneered the lady.

"No, madame," gently replied Lilith, "under no false pretences. Under reserve, if you please, under reticence in regard to my past life, but under no false pretences."

"You entered my service as a widow."

"Pardon me, madame, I never told you that I was a widow. I signed my name to my letters, Elizabeth Wyvil. When we met you called me Miss Wyvil. I told you that I was not 'Miss' Wyvil. You then took it for granted that I was Mrs. and a widow—as, indeed, I was in fate, if not in law. Remember, dear madame, that I gave you my college testimonials as references, and told you that the good women who allowed me to refer to them—I mean Mrs. Ponsonby, of Baltimore, and Mrs. Downie, of New York—really knew very little of me, but had taken me up in faith and charity."

"But why did you call yourself Mrs. Wyvil, and allow yourself to be considered as a widow, when your name was Hereward?" demanded the lady.

"Because my husband, on the day that he discarded me, forbade me to use his family name; and in obedience to him I dropped it, retaining only my own maiden name—Elizabeth Wyvil. I could not explain this fact to you without accusing my husband. Nor should I explain now but to prevent a great evil," said Lilith.

Again silence fell between them, which Lilith was the first to break:

"You never once questioned me as to my state, madame. If you had asked me plainly, 'Are you a widow?' I must have told you that I was not except in fate. But you took it for granted that because I was not 'Miss' Wyvil I must be a widow."

"Yes, you are right. It was my own assumption," said the baroness.

"I am very sorry that I have been with you in a mistaken position. I am ready to make any amends in my power; ready even to leave your service at this moment, if it be your wish that I should do so."

"This moment! Why, you are out at sea and will have no opportunity to leave until we reach Havre."

"I remember that, madame; but if you wish to part with me, I can leave you without leaving the ship. I can refund my passage money, and end our connection now and here."

"And what would you do then?"

"As soon as we reach Havre take passage in the first ship back to New York, and return to Mrs. Downie."

"Does she know your true story?"

"No; she knows me only as Elizabeth Wyvil. And by that name only must I be known, since my husband has forbidden me to use his."

"My dear, I do not wish to part with you. But tell me, since you have told me the fact, why did your husband part with you?"

"Madame, you yourself gave the reason. I was not 'fit' to be his wife," said Lilith, mournfully.

"My dear, I should never have said that if I had known you," replied the baroness, who, notwithstanding her own disappointed love for Tudor Hereward, still felt her heart drawn in pity towards his young discarded wife—the youthful stranger to whom she had been so strongly attracted at first sight, and whom in after intercourse she had grown to love.

"But I am surprised that you, who are so different from the girl whom I had imagined as Hereward's hastily married wife—you who are gifted with rare intelligence and sensibility—should have condescended to marry him at such very short notice. How was it?" gently inquired the baroness.

The answer came low and soft:

"Because I loved him, and believed he loved me."

"You believed he loved you. Had he ever told you so?" demanded the lady.

"No, never. Tudor Hereward never spoke an untruth."

"Then what reason, in the name of Heaven, had you for thinking that he loved you?"

"Because he asked me to become his wife. Of course I never once imagined that he could have any other motive than affection for wishing to marry me?"

"But did not the suddenness of the proposal—for an immediate marriage, too—awaken your suspicions?"

"No; for it was his dying father's wish to see us married by his bedside before he should pass away."

"Oh! That puts quite a new face upon the whole proceeding. Poor child! To please that dying father you consented to marry that son at a moment's notice."

"No, madame; no. It was, as I said, because I loved Tudor Hereward, and believed he loved me, that I consented. Otherwise I should never have done so, even to satisfy the beloved, dying father, though I would willingly have died to redeem his life, had that been possible," earnestly answered Lilith.

"Ah, well! You loved him, and I suppose he knew it. That redeems the affair from utter abomination. But perhaps you do not like to speak of your short union with Mr. Hereward?"

"I do not shrink from speaking of it, nor do I break any faith in speaking of him, for, madame, we are parted more effectually than even death can part those who love each other."

"But you love him?"

Lilith answered by a deep, silent sob as she dropped her face into her hands.

"And you are so young! Only seventeen! How long have you loved this man, my dear?" compassionately inquired the lady.

"How long? As long as I have lived, I think. I do not remember the time when I did not love Tudor Hereward as I love my Lord. It was my religion to love him. I was brought up to worship God, and to adore Tudor Hereward. Under the Almighty, he was my lord, my law-giver. This love was my life," murmured Lilith, in a low, thrilling, pathetic voice.

"Who trained you to this idolatry?"

"His father—my foster-father."

Again silence fell between the two.

At length the baroness inquired:

"My dear, will you tell me how you came to be the foster-daughter of the late Major Hereward? But do not do so if you would rather not."

"I have no objection," answered Lilith.

And in a few brief words she told the story of her adoption as it is known to the reader.

"I am half inclined to retract all that I have said of Tudor Hereward. It may be that revenge did not enter into his scheme of marrying a child whom he did not love. It may be that he was actuated solely by the wish to please his father and to pay a sacred debt," said the baroness.

"Yes, to pay a sacred debt. That is what they called it—a sacred debt. Ah! would to Heaven I had died with my mother rather than lived to be the creditor of that fatal debt! Heaven knows how soon I would have absolved both father and son from its responsibility had I known it was only for that cause I was to be married," said Lilith, with a sigh so heavy that it moved the pity of the lady, who took the girl's hand and held it kindly as she said:

"I do suppose that a marriage contracted under such circumstances must, sooner or later, end just as yours has. And, my poor child, since it was doomed to end so, it is better that it should sooner than later. Yet—I cannot imagine that you could have given any provocation for an act so extreme as his repudiation of you; and I feel deeply interested to know just what precipitated the event."

"Dear madame, I can only tell you that it was a misapprehension on his part, which, could he have loved and trusted me, need not have ended in the fatal quarrel that has separated us forever. You understand now. I need not go into the painful details of that scene."

"No, you need not. And so you left your home secretly?"

"Oh, no, not secretly. For when at last he told me that he had never loved me; that he had only married me to please his father; that he should go away from his home and never return while I—desecrated—the house with my presence, then I answered that I must not be the means of driving him from his ancestral home; that I must depart"

"Heavens! What did he say to that?"

"With a look full of scorn and wrath, he bade me quit his sight. I left the room, went to my chamber and prepared for my journey. I went away that night, leaving a farewell letter on my dressing-bureau."

"And no one saw you go?"

"No one. It was late on a winter night, and I went forth alone."

"Poor child! And this accounts for the story of your mysterious disappearance and supposed death."

"Yes, I presume so. They must have believed that I came to my death after leaving the house."

"And he believes that you are dead! And he suffers from remorse, if not from grief. Well, we shall find him on the other side. Shall we make your exist-ence known to him?"

"I do not know, madame. I must think and pray over that question. But even if he be assured that I do still live, he must not be annoyed by the sight of my face. Oh! madame, though I long with all my soul to see him again, to hear his voice once more, yet, yet, I shrink from the ordeal as from fire!" said Lilith.

"I can well believe that. I am glad I did not tell you my news before we sailed. If I had done so, you would not perhaps have come with me."

"No," said Lilith.

Silence fell between the two women, and lasted until the bell rang for luncheon, for which neither of them felt the least desire.

It was an excuse for moving, however—something to do—and Madame Von Bruyin arose and offered her arm to her slighter companion and the two went down to the saloon together. It was about two o'clock. They were well out at sea now and the waves were rather high; the ship was rolling uncomfortably for those who had not found their sea legs and their sea stomachs.

Neither Madame Von Bruyin nor Lilith as yet suf-fered from the motion.

After lunch, however, each retired alone to her state-room.

The baroness threw herself into her berth and gave way to the tide of shame, grief and indignation which it had required all her pride, conscience and self-con-trol to restrain while she was in the presence of Tudor Hereward's young wife.

She had been strangely attracted to Lilith from the first meeting with her, and she had grown to love the girl with the fond, protecting love of an elder sister. She had given Lilith her confidence, revealed her inmost heart, told her love-story—even her love for Tudor Hereward to Tudor Hereward's unknown wife! What a mortification in the thought that she had done so! Yet, there was a selfish comfort, which she blamed herself for taking, in the reflection that it was to the unloved and discarded wife that she had told this story.

She had within the past few days had her heart's deepest affections raised from despair to something near absolute certainty. "Her hopes soared up like fire!" And in the exaltation of her spirits she had called on Lilith to share her joy and to congratulate her—only to have them all extinguished by the damper of the girl's communication—"Tudor Hereward's wife still lives . . . I am Tudor Hereward's most unhappy wife!"

How all her soul had risen up in defiance and contradiction of that statement until its truth was pressed in upon her consciousness. And then, all her sense of justice, all her powers of self-command were required to pass calmly through the ordeal of the interview that ensued. She had passed through it successfully. She had so mastered her pain and repressed her heart that she now felt sure Hereward's young wife regarded Leda Von Bruyin's love for him as the mere passing fancy of a wealthy woman of the world, soon to be forgotten in the change of travel or the whirl of society. She felt no jealousy of this despised and discarded wife, as she might have felt had Lilith been the beloved, honored and cherished companion of her husband; on the contrary, she felt pity, affection and sympathy for the poor, lonely and dependent child.

But her spirit blazed out in fierce anger of Tudor Hereward's whole course of conduct toward them both, so that she was very unjust to him.

"He has ruined two lives by his arrogant recklessness and precipitation. He loved me; he never loved that poor girl. He loved me, and he ought to have waited, in hope and faith, as long as I continued unmarried. He ought not to have rushed into matrimony with that young creature whom he never loved, and so made her miserable and put an insurmountable obstacle between himself and me! Or—having married her, he should have cherished her and not discarded her.

"No, Tudor Hereward," she continued to herself, "you are no longer the chevalier sans peur et sans reproche, that I once believed you! And—if I suffer now, it is not that I love you still, but that my love is dying hard—very, very hard!"

"But I will take a queenly revenge upon you, my master! A most noble and royal revenge. This child-wife whom you have discarded shall be to me as the dearest little sister. She is already beautiful, elegant and graceful by nature. She is cultivated, refined and accomplished by education; all she needs is intercourse with the highest European circles to give her the tone and manner of the most cultured society. And that she shall have. I will introduce her, not as my salaried companion—though she shall have her salary and much more than her salary—but as my own adopted sister. And when you see her again, Tudor Hereward, you will not be likely to despise her.

"And oh!" she passionately broke forth, "that I had the power to annihilate the very fragments of that broken marriage tie and the very memory of it, in her mind, and give her, all perfect as I shall make her, into the hands of some nobler husband! But no! that would not be a worthy revenge.

"To give her back, a pearl above price, to you, perhaps! Can I do that? Can I conquer myself so entirely? That would be a magnanimous revenge."

So ran the thoughts of the petted beauty, rioting through a mind governed rather by feeling than by reason, yet with much more of good than evil in it.

Meanwhile, Lilith, lying on the narrow sofa in her state-room, gave way to one hearty fit of crying, and then wiped her eyes, and began to try to understand her position and her duty.

She was not jealous of the handsome baroness, either. She remembered all her husband had told her of his first fancy, of how harshly he had come to judge her, and she fully believed that Madame Von Bruyin deceived herself in imagining that Tudor Hereward still continued to love her, or to entertain other feelings than disapprobation and dislike towards her.

Lilith now knew, from her intimate relations with the baroness, that Mr. Hereward had greatly misjudged her; that she was not, and never had been, the heartless coquette he had termed her; but that, in spite of her training, she was a warm-hearted, generous and conscientious woman.

But the question now before Lilith was—whether she should continue with the baroness, and run the risk of meeting Hereward in the court circle of the city to which they were going, or whether she should, on reaching Havre, take the first homeward-bound steamer and return to New York and to the safe protection of Aunt Sophie's humble roof.

And though Lilith thought over this question and prayed over it, yet she had come to no decision when there came a rap, followed by the entrance of Lisette, the lady's maid, who said:

"Madame has sent me to say that it is time for dinner, and to see if I can assist you, madame."

"Thank you, no. I will be ready in a few minutes," replied Lilith, rising from her sofa, and beginning to smooth down her dress and arrange her hair.

She soon completed her very simple toilet and went out into the cabin, where she found the baroness waiting for her.

The lady looked pale and grave, but otherwise as usual. No one could have judged from her manner the dread ordeal through which she was passing.

She looked searchingly into Lilith's face, and saw there the traces of emotion but recently overcome. She smiled softly, as she drew the girl's arm within her own and whispered:

"We do not either of us look quite well, dear; but n'importe—the fault will be laid upon the sea! On land, all our feminine troubles, for which we do not wish to account, we explain by a headache. At sea, all grievances of soul or body may be put down to sea-sickness. Is a woman pale from vexation or disappointment? She is only sea-sick. Is a man unable to leave his berth in the morning, from having had too much champagne over night? He is very sea-sick, poor wretch! Come! let us go into the saloon."

There were very few people at the tables, and so Madame Von Bruyin and her companion had a large share of attention from the stewards. Yet they could receive but little benefit from the sumptuous fare laid before them, and they soon left the table for the upper deck, where they sat late into the June night, watching the clear, star-lit heavens above and the boundless expanse of ocean below.

At eleven they retired to their berths.

And so ended the first day at sea.

CHAPTER XIV.

LILITH'S METAMORPHOSIS

THE run of the Kaiser Wilhelm was an almost ideal voyage. After the first few hours, winds and waves subsided.

On Sunday morning the voyagers arose to find themselves borne steadily onward over a summer sea, under a sunny sky, freshened by a gentle breeze.

As this day was, so were all the succeeding days of the voyage.

Only twice it rained, and then only in the night, so that all the mornings were clear and fair.

Lilith was young, fresh and sensitive and so, notwithstanding all her past griefs, disappointments and humiliations, she enjoyed the voyage.

The baroness was very kind to her young companion, and very delicate in making the gradual change she had determined upon in her case. She never said to the young creature in so many words: "From this time you are my little sister;" but she treated her with the free and fond affection due to such a relationship. She never asked Lilith to perform the slightest service for her; but, on the contrary, very often offered attentions to the girl—wrapping her shawl around her when they were going up on deck, and showing her all the solicitous tenderness of an affectionate relative.

Lilith was very grateful for all this kindness; nor did its excess embarrass her in the least degree. She had been used to the greatest care and the tenderest love all her young days until the brief episode of her married life; and she had no experience to teach her that the baroness' treatment of her was not the treatment usually bestowed by a lady upon her salaried companion. So she accepted all the favors and all the attentions of the great lady with gratitude and enjoyment.

Their fellow-voyagers had not the least idea that these two young ladies stood in the relations of employer and employed towards each other, but believed them to be very young widowed sisters or dear friends.

There happened to be on board not one of Madame Von Bruyin's own circle who was acquainted with her family history and knew that she had no sisters.

The baroness happened to come on deck one morning with Lilith.

She sat down near a lady, who, after exchanging salutations with the new-comer, said, politely:

"I hope, madame, that your dear sister is not indisposed this morning, this fine, fine morning, that she is not on deck."

"Thank you, she is quite well, only a trifle late in rising; but Mrs. Wyvil is not my sister except in affection; though indeed there are few sisters so strongly attached to each other as we are. Circumstances have brought this friendly union about. We are both orphans, without sister or brother; both widows without children; we have, in fact, no family ties whatever. We are fast friends who have no one but each other," Madame Von Bruyin explained, speaking purposely so to one whom she knew to be one of the busiest gossips among all the ladies of the first cabin.

After this there was much talk about the "romantic friendship" existing between the two beautiful young widows. This talk found its way from the ladies' cabin to the gentlemen's saloon, where the status of the two lovely widows was often canvassed. Both were acknowledged to be "beautiful exceedingly," and yet so different in style that there could be no comparison between them—one a tall and stately blonde, the other a petite and graceful brunette; so that they were relatively called Juno and Psyche. Both were supposed to be enormously rich—great chances for "elegant but impecunious" fortune-hunters. And more than one adventurer who could not manage to approach the hedged-in royalty on ship-board, determined to keep track of the beauties in hopes of golden opportunities after they should have landed on the other side.

Meanwhile Madame Von Bruyin and Lilith, unconscious of the buzz of gossip, criticism and speculation going on around them in cabin and saloon, kept on the even tenor of their way, until one fine morning near the middle of June they awoke to find themselves at Havre. Their ship had arrived in the night while they slept.

Lilith started up to look through the port-hole of her state-room, but she could see nothing but the hulk of another great steamer that lay close alongside.

She dressed herself with eager, childish haste to go upon deck and look upon the shores of the old world, so new to her, and which she had so longed to see.

Such first sights are often a surprise and a disappointment to the young traveler. They expect to see something very new and very strange, instead of which they see what seem to be very familiar objects—all sea-port towns are at first view so very much alike in their general appearance.

When Lilith hurriedly dressed herself, and without waiting for Madame Von Bruyin, hastened up on deck, and looked around her, she saw what, as it seemed to her, she must have seen a hundred times before—a harbor with a forest of shipping, docks crowded with men, women and children, horses, mules, carts and vans, and laden with bales, boxes, barrels and bundles of merchandise; dingy warehouses rising to the sky, with dusty windows and many ropes and pulleys reaching from roof to basement; beyond these the crowded streets of the city.

"Why, but for that old tower in the distance, and those old churches, this might be New York or Baltimore," said Lilith, unconscious of having spoken out.

"Yes, my dear, at a very casual and superficial glance; but wait until we get into the town. Then I will show you some antiquities of the time of Louis XI., when Havre was but a little fishing-hamlet and never dreamed of becoming the great sea-port that it now is," said the baroness, who had come quietly up to the side of her young friend.

"Ah! but it is not beautiful to look upon from this point," said Lilith.

"What sea-port town is? But it is interesting away from the docks—though I can well believe that the ships, docks and warehouses are decidedly the most interesting portion of the town to those busy business men whom we see in the crowd there. But, as I said, wait until we land and see the old city. And remember that beyond the city spread

'Thy corn-fields green and sunny vines,
Oh, pleasant land of France.'

I always enjoy the railway ride from Havre to Paris. We will take that ride to-morrow, little beauty. To-day we will do Havre."

"But, madame, I was thinking, as I have before hinted to you, of returning to New York by the first homeward bound steamer," said Lilith, deprecatingly.

The baroness turned suddenly around and stared at her little friend for a moment, and then exclaimed:

"You must never think of doing such a thing! Why have you ever thought of it?"

"Because you are going in the course of your travels

to the very city and court where you will be sure to meet—Mr. Hereward," said Lilith, hesitating over the name. "And I should not like to seem to be following him, after all that has passed," she added.

"Nonsense, my dear! We may make the tour of the continent without going to that city. Or even if we go there, we may see everything worth seeing without meeting that man."

"But——"

"I will hear no 'but,' my dear. You must not leave me. You engaged to stay with me for twelve months, unless our engagement should be annulled by mutual consent. Now, I do not consent to any such thing, my dear; and you, I know, are too honest and honorable to break a contract. There has been quite enough of that sort of thing in our lives, at least in yours, without a new example. But there! we will not discuss this matter further until we get to our hotel. See! the plank has been laid and the people are beginning to go on shore. Ah! Monsieur Le Grange, will you be so good as to send Felix on shore to engage two carriages? I shall then ask you to attend Mrs. Wyvil and myself to the Hotel de l'Europe, where you will please engage rooms for us," said the baroness, turning to her private secretary, who had just stepped up.

The polite old gentleman bowed and bowed and went away to perform his commission.

"We will go down and put on our wraps, my dear. You need not take the trouble to pack or to remove anything. I will leave Lisette in charge of our rooms to do all that. Felix can see our trunks through the Custom House, and then come on with Lisette and all the other trumpery to the hotel."

Lilith followed her friend's advice and soon joined her in the cabin, dressed for landing.

They went up on deck, and while they stood wait-

ing for the return of Monsieur Le Grange they ex-
changed good-byes with several fellow-voyagers who
were leaving the ship for various points.

At length Monsieur Le Grange came up, bowing.

"I have procured a very comfortable carriage which
awaits madame, and I have sent Felix on to the Hotel
de l'Europe to secure a suite of rooms that they may
be ready for madame, that she may not be kept waiting."

"Thank you, monsieur; you have been very prompt,"
said the baroness, graciously.

"Will madame now proceed to the carriage?" for-
mally inquired the precise old gentleman.

"If you please, monsieur. And will you do me the
favor to give your arm to Mrs. Wyvil?" inquired the
baroness, according to her usual custom, "in honor
preferring" her protégée, to herself.

"I will with pleasure do myself that honor,
madame," said the courtly old gentleman, first with
a deep bow to his patroness and then with another
to her protégée, as he offered the latter his arm.

"I have left everything here in charge of Felix and
Lisette, monsieur. They will follow in the second
carriage, as soon as our luggage can be got through,
to that you need take no trouble at all," the baroness
explained, as they left the steamer.

The old secretary then put both ladies into the carriage, seated himself beside them, and gave the order:

"To the Hotel de l'Europe."

A few moments' drive through the narrow streets
brought them up to the fine hotel.

Their rooms were ready, so that there was but
little delay before they found themselves in possession of them—handsome rooms they were, on the
second floor, fronting the street, very elegantly furnished—"chiefly with gilded mirrors," as the baroness
laughingly observed. But there were also luxurious

lounges and reclining chairs, downy cushions and hassocks, and soft rugs, graceful draperies before doors
as well as before windows, and, in fact, all the refine-
ments of modern upholstery, better understood by the
French than by any other people.

Monsieur Le Grange had ordered the breakfast,
which was soon served in madame's small salon.

The two ladies had just time to lay off their bonnets and wraps, before it was placed on the table,
served in silver and Sevres china by the most ob-
sequious of garçons. The dainty new dishes, the delicate rolls, the exquisite coffee, and the rare light wines
of the French breakfast, were all novelties in the experience of Lilith, and greatly enjoyed by her.

When the breakfast was over, the two ladies put
on their bonnets, and took the carriage that had been
engaged by Monsieur Le Grange, and, with him for
their cicerone, drove around the city to whatever they
considered worth looking at.

They visited the old churches of Notre Dame and
St. Francis, and the ancient tower of Franart. They
drove out to the picturesque suburbs of Ingouville
and Graville l'Heure, lunched at the little café in the
last mentioned place, and finally returned to their
hotel in time for late dinner.

That evening, after Monsieur Le Grange had bidden
them good-night, Madame Von Bruyin and Lilith had
a final talk on the question of her—Lilith—returning
to New York or traveling over Europe with the
baroness.

The prospect of varied travel in company with her
charming friend had great attractions for Lilith, certainly, so that when the baroness put it to her heart
and conscience not to break the compact she had made
with so fond a friend, Lilith not only yielded the point
and consented to remain with the baroness, but she
did so with evident pleasure.

Madame Von Bruyin kissed her ardently to seal the bargain, and they retired to bed in their adjoining alcoves.

Early the next morning the whole party commenced their continental tour by taking the railway train to Paris.

CHAPTER XV

WORLD-WEARY

> The memory of things precious keepeth warm
> The heart that once did hold them. They are poor
> That have lost nothing; they are poorer far
> Who, losing, have forgotten; they most poor
> Of all who lose and wish they might forget.
> For life is one, and in its warp and woof
> There runs a thread of gold that glitters fair,
> And sometimes in the pattern shows most sweet
> Where there are sombre colors. This thread of gold
> We would not have it tarnish; let us turn
> Oft and look back upon the wondrous web,
> And when it shineth sometimes we shall know
> That memory is possession. *Jean Ingelow.*

THE Baroness Von Bruyin and her suite reached Paris about the middle of June.

They went first to the Splendide Hotel, Place de l'Opéra, at which Monsieur Le Grange had secured, by telegraph, a handsome suite of apartments.

But they remained there only for a few days, until a suitable house was procured on the Champs Elysées to wich they immediately removed.

Madame Von Bruyin was supposed, on account of her recent widowhood, not to go into the gay world; yet, somehow or other, as soon as she was settled in

her magnificent "hotel," she managed to see much
of society, or what was left of society in the French
capital; for at this season the gay birds of passage
in the fashionable world were already pluming their
wings for flight to sea-side or mountain range for the
summer. Yet enough still remained to make life gay
in the gayest city of Christendom.

And though Madame Von Bruyin went to no balls
or large public receptions, yet she saw a great deal
of company both at home and abroad. And Lilith
was always by her side, not as her salaried companion, but as her friend and equal.

The court had not left Paris, and it was through
Madame Von Bruyin that Lilith obtained her first
entrée into the "charmed" circle of Tuileries. And
no less from her freshness, her piquancy and simplicity than from her rare beauty, la belle Virgin-
ienne became the fashion, just when the season was
wearing to its close and wanted a new sensation.

Somehow also the impression had got abroad that
Madame Wyvil was a very wealthy woman—the
daughter of some New York merchant prince and the
widow of some California mine king.

Who was responsible for starting the story is not
certainly known; but it is undeniable that Madame
Von Bruyin chuckled a great deal over the hallucination, when she saw Lilith sought, followed, flattered
and fawned upon by impoverished nobles and impecunious princes.

Lilith knew nothing of the romances in circulation
concerning her vast riches. The adulation she received both pleased and pained her. No beautiful
girl of seventeen could be quite insensible or indifferent to the homage of the world; homage that she
innocently supposed was paid to herself, rather than
to her imaginary wealth; but when she remembered
her position, she felt that she would gladly give all,

all this worship for one kind word, or glance, from her alienated husband—

"Coldly she turns from their praise and weeps,
For her heart 'at his feet' is lying."

She was often glad to get away from those court circles—though they were never gay scenes—to escape from everybody, even from her kindest friend, Madame Von Bruyin—lock herself up in her room at night, and there in solitude and darkness forget or ignore the cruel sentence that had banished her from her beloved husband and her dear home; bridge over the painful scenes that had marred the last weeks of their wedded life and go back and live over again in memory and imagination the brief, bright days of their harmony and happiness, and recall the few precious words of affection or approbation Tudor Hereward had ever addressed to her.

How fondly, how vividly—lying with her eyes closed and her fingers laid upon her eyelids as if the better to shut out the real world and the present time—how fondly and how vividly she recalled that day when she sat all day long over the writing-table in their room at the hotel, so busy at work for him, so happy, ah! so happy to be of use to him, answering piles of letters that he had marked for her, copying the crabbed manuscript for his speech, looking out authorities for his reference.

And when evening came and he returned from the Capitol, and sank wearily into his easy-chair at the table and slowly examined her work, and finally said:

"You have performed your task only too well. . . . Your day's work has saved me from a night's work, my little lady love." And he kissed her.

It was a precious memory.

How happy she was that day! How very, very happy!

Again and again, through the power of memory and imagination, in the silence and solitude of night, she recalled and lived over that day—and one or two other days embalmed in her mind.

All these few happy days belonged to the month of February—the most sunshiny month of her year, midwinter though it might have been to everybody else.

During all the remainder of the season in Paris it required all Lilith's tact to avoid receiving a direct proposal of marriage from one or another of her fortune-hunting adorers.

At length she almost offended Madame Von Bruyin by declining to go into company at all.

"They take me for 'a widow indeed,' madame, and it becomes very embarrassing," she pleaded.

"Well, but, petite, we cannot explain; so what is to be done?" inquired the baroness, laughing at the absurdity of Lilith's dilemma.

"I do not know, unless I avoid society. I might stay home when you go out, and keep my room when you have company here," replied the girl.

"But I cannot consent to any such isolation on your part. It would not be good for your health of mind or body. Come, my dear, cheer up! Endure the homage of the world for a few days longer—only for a few days, petite, and then it will be over. Paris will be empty, and we ourselves will be inhaling the mountain air of Switzerland," laughed the lady.

And Lilith, having no alternative, endured the tortures of her false position until the fashionable world had fled from town.

The baroness and her companion lingered a little behind the others, in order that Madame Von Bruyin might show Lilith all those places of interest which a newcomer must see, but which had hitherto been neglected for other and more social pastimes.

It was, then, near the end of July when they left Paris for Switzerland.

They spent the months of August, September and October in traveling over the north of Europe, halting at no point for more than three or four days.

In November they went to Rome, and sojourned in the "Eternal City" until the first of January, when they returned to Paris, where the Baroness Von Bruyin, having laid aside her first mourning, plunged into all the gayeties of the capital, taking her young companion with her.

Everywhere they were very much admired. They could not possibly be rivals, even when constantly seen together. They were both so beautiful, yet their style was so dissimilar, so well contrasted, that they actually enhanced each other's attractions.

Lilith was no longer in danger of receiving embarrassing proposals of marriage. The same mysterious agent which had started the report of her fabulous wealth was most probably responsible for another report, to the effect that the beautiful young widow was about to bestow her hand and fortune upon an eminent American statesman, to whom she had been for many months engaged. But she was none the less admired because she was inaccessible.

In February, however, the restless baroness, with all her party, crossed the channel, and went to London, to be in time to see the pageant of the queen's opening of Parliament.

Madame Von Bruyin, through her friends, obtained admission for herself and protégée to the peeress' gallery in the House of Lords, and from that vantage point witnessed the imposing ceremony.

But in all the solemn magnificence of the scene Lilith seemed to see only the queen, and through the queen only the almost peerless woman, wife and mother, and as Lilith gazed she sank into a dream of Victoria's life.

Later on in the season our country-girl from West Virginia saw the majesty of England once again.

It was on the occasion of the first drawing-room of the season at Buckingham Palace, when Madame Von Bruyin and her protégée were presented by the wife of the German Ambassador.

After this presentation, the baroness, who had taken a handsome furnished house on Westbourne Terrace, and whose year of mourning had expired, issued invitations for a large party, which she wished to make the most brilliant of the season.

The baroness had passed two seasons in London. The first as a débutante with her father, and a German princess as a chaperone; the second as a bride, with her newly married husband; and now in her third season she entered society as a young, handsome and wealthy widow, with a very extensive acquaintance.

She issued over five hundred invitations to her ball, and these included many of the most distinguished persons of the age, celebrities of high rank, of worldwide scientific, literary, diplomatic or military renown, the beauties and geniuses of the hour, and so forth.

The ball was to be a great success.

Lilith strongly objected to being present—pleaded earnestly to be relieved from attending it.

"Dear madame, I feel as if, in my circumstances, I ought to live in strict retirement. I am not Mrs. Wyvil. I am not a widow. I am Tudor Hereward's repudiated wife. When I find myself in a ball-room or in a drawing-room, surrounded by people who seem anxious to do me honor—I feel—oh, I feel just as if I were only a fraud, a humbug, an impostor, an adventuress. And, oh! I feel so deeply ashamed of myself and my false position! So humiliated and degraded! I feel this even more deeply in these

English drawing-rooms than I did in the Parisian salons. Oh, dear madame, pray do not insist on my presence at your ball!" she prayed.

"Lilith, you are the most morbid creature I ever met with in all the days of my life. You would like to shut yourself up in a convent, I suppose, just because that hateful man, after marrying you to be revenged on me, has thrown you off to please himself!" exclaimed Leda Von Bruyin.

"Pray do not speak of Mr. Hereward in that way," said the loyal young wife.

"I will speak of him as he deserves. I am beginning to hate that man. Yes, and to hate myself for ever having imagined that I liked him."

"Oh, Madame Von Bruyin!"

"It is true. The more I see of the world, the longer I live, the more experience I gain, the more heartily I dislike that man, and dislike myself for ever having fancied that I liked him," exclaimed the baroness.

"I am very sorry you feel so," said Lilith.

"Sorry! Sorry that I have ceased to be in love with your husband, Lilith? Well, you are an oddity!"

"Oh, no, not sorry for that! Glad—thankful for that! But very sorry that you cannot feel friendly towards him!"

"Bah! what a baby you are! He himself once quoted this line to me:

'Friendship sometimes turns to love,
But love to friendship, never!'

And it does not! It dies out in indifference, or it turns to hate and scorn, and self-scorn as well!"

"Ah, madame——" commenced Lilith.

"'Ah, madame,'" mocked the baroness. "Look here, my dear, I have known, and I thank Heaven that I have known one unselfish man who loved without self-love! And he was Nicholas Von Bruyin. And the more I see of other men, the more I love and honor him. Mr. Hereward certainly suffers in that comparison. But to return to the subject of the ball, Lilith, my dear, I really cannot consent to your absenting yourself."

"But, madame——"

"But, nonsense! If you are in a false position it it not one of your choosing. Your husband has forced you into it. If you are called Mrs. Wyvil, it is because your husband has forbidden you to bear his name, and you are so meek as to obey him. And if you seem to be a widow, it is because he has made you one in fate if not in law. But you shall not 'wear the willow' for his undeserving sake! You shall enjoy life as your youth and beauty entitle you to do. And I will protect you in this. Do not fear to be embarrassed by any more proposals of marriage. That embarrassment is forestalled. You are understood to be engaged to an American statesman of high rank. And that is also true, is it not? You do consider yourself most solemnly engaged, yes, most solemnly and eternally engaged, to that man, notwithstanding his repudiation of you, do you not?"

"Yes, madame! But I wish you would not call Mr. Hereward 'that man,'" said Lilith.

"Very well! Since you object, I will call him this man! And while we are objecting, let me tell you that I object to your calling me 'madame,' as if I were somebody's aunt or grandmother! I am only about three years older than you are. And I call you 'Lilith,' do you observe? And my name is Leda; though I am likely to forget it, for since my father and my husband died there is no human being in the world left to call me Leda, unless my chosen friend and sister will do so," said Madame Von Bruyin, with a touch of pathos in her tone.

"I will go to your ball, Leda," said Lilith, conceding both points in her gentle answer.

The ball was to be a great success, and it was a great success.

Lilith was exposed to another complication. She was in danger of being "taken up" by a certain distinguished clique, patronized by a certain august personage, and being turned into a "professional beauty."

And the baroness made the conquest of an Italian prince, of about her own age, of much grace, beauty and accomplishments; of—what is much rarer in continental princes—great wealth also, and of a family who claimed to read their title clear through all the centuries of recorded history, back into the age of fable and chaos, where all things are void or misty.

Prince Otto Gherardini as a matter of detail.

This fascinating young Florentine was in personal appearance and temperament so diametrically antagonistic to the charming baroness that they were inevitably destined to be attracted to each other, as positive and negative in electricity.

Therefore it followed that at their very first meeting the dark, graceful, fiery Italian youth became desperately enamored of the fair, stately, serene German lady.

After the ball, the baroness and her protégée were inundated with invitations to all sorts of entertainments, so that had they accepted every one, between garden parties, morning concerts, five o'clock teas, dinner parties and balls, they would have had scarcely an hour to call their own.

Lilith, with her saddened heart, sank from all these social excitements and dissipations, yet, being irresistibly borne on by the imperious will of the baroness, she was drawn into the maelstrom.

Gherardini, with Italian subtlety, contrived to meet the baroness everywhere, so that gossip soon counected their names, and the world looked forward to the announcement of their betrothal.

The baroness laughed at him, as a boy, behind his back, but treated him as a prince before his face.

Lilith secretly hoped that they might marry, and be happy, so that she herself might be at liberty to return to New York and rest in Aunt Sophie's quiet though humble home.

So the London season drew to its close. The announcement of the marriage of Prince Otto Gherardini with the Baroness Von Bruyin, arranged to come off early in the ensuing year, appeared in the *Court Journal*, and in the society columns of other London papers. It took no one by surprise, not even Lilith.

Madame Von Bruyin and her suite left London for a short tour in Wales and Cornwall, and spent a few pleasant and healthful weeks in leisurely travel through that beautiful, picturesque and legendary land.

In September they halted, and took lodgings at a farm-house near the mountain village of Llandorf.

There they settled down for a brief period to enjoy the simple country life of the neighborhood.

Lilith, world-weary and heart-sick, felt the benign and soothing influence of nature around her, and resigned herself to rest—if rest might be granted her.

It was now eighteen months since she had been driven from her home. In all this time she had never once heard from her husband, and only once had she heard of him; and that was when she learned from Madame Von Bruyin that Mr. Hereward had been appointed Secretary of Legation to the Court of ——. Since that day, fifteen months ago, no sign of his existence had appeared to her. In vain she searched all the insular and continental papers. His name never by any chance appeared in any paper.

Did Lilith resign all hope of ever hearing of him, seeing him, being reconciled to him again?

Ah, no! Though hope was only torture now, she could not help but entertain it. A thousand times she had said to herself:

"There is not the slightest possibility of such happiness for me. I am dead to my husband! Yes, I am dead to him, as I could never have been had only a natural death divided us, and not a spiritual one. I shall never meet him again, neither in this life nor the life to come."

But though she continually said this to herself, and though she tried to school her heart to believe it, yet, yet, she could not resign hope, for "While there is life there is hope"—"Hope springs eternal in the human breast." And so, though hope was anguish, she could not give it up.

One lovely day, near the last of September, Lilith was sitting alone in the little parlor of their lodgings. She had drawn her chair to the window to sit and enjoy the fine view of mountain, lake and wood stretched out before her.

The breakfast table was set, but Madame Von Bruyin, who was a late riser, had not come down.

While Lilith sat there gazing from the window, and waiting for her patroness, the old postman for that neighborhood came up the garden walk, and seeing her at the window, nodded pleasantly, and stopped to deliver his mail.

He laid a pile of letters and papers on the sill, nodded and smiled again, and turned away.

Lilith looked over the superscriptions of the letters. They were all for Madame Von Bruyin, Monsieur Le Grange, the lady's maid or the footman. There was not one for Lilith. Nor was she disappointed. There seldom was a letter for her, so she did not expect one.

She placed the letters on the breakfast table, and turned to look at the papers.

She took up the *Times* first, of course, and she turned first to the foreign and diplomatic news, hoping against hope—as she had done a thousand times before—that she might see her husband's name, if it were only a line in the list of guests at some State dinner, or in any casual event.

But no! There was nothing! She was again disappointed, as she had been a thousand times before.

Wearily, drearily her sad eyes wandered over the paper, indifferent now to anything she might find there.

Yet—great Heaven! What was this? Not the name of Tudor Hereward! No; but the answer to a daily, nightly agonized prayer to Almighty God! —or so it seemed to Lilith's amazed vision. Daily and nightly, in her morning and evening worship, for the last two years, Lilith had prayed:

"Have mercy, oh, Father, upon all poor prisoners and captives; upon all miserable criminals and convicts; bringing the guilty to a profound contrition, to pardon and to peace; bringing the innocent to a full vindication, deliverance and salvation."

And these words, upon which her wandering eyes became fixed in astonishment, seemed the answer to that prayer.

CHAPTER XVI

"A FULL VINDICATION"

Such was the heading of the article that riveted the attention of Lilith and that read as follows:

"A deplorable instance of the conviction of an innocent man, under false circumstantial evidence, of

a crime that first consigned him to the scaffold, and
afterward, by the commutation of his sentence, sent
him to penal servitude for life, has lately come to
light. Many of our readers will remember the case of
John Weston, the young man who was convicted,
eighteen years ago, of the robbery of the mail coach
running between Orton and Stockbridge, Yorkshire,
and the murder of a passenger. The young prisoner
declared his innocence to the last, but through the
overwhelming circumstantial evidence he was convicted and condemned to death. Great efforts were
made in his behalf, and finally, upon account of his
youth and previous good character, his sentence was
commuted to transportation, with penal servitude for
life. He was sent to Tasmania, where it is believed he
died soon after his arrival at Port Arthur.

"But that John Weston was entirely guiltless of
the crime for which he suffered is made quite clear
by the ante-mortem confession of a convict named
Thomas Estel, who died yesterday in the infirmary
of Portland prison.

"This man, convicted of forgery one year ago, was
almost immediately after his commitment to Portland discovered to be in a consumption, and assigned
to the infirmary, where, after languishing for nearly
twelve months, he died yesterday.

"His ante-mortem confession, made in the presence of the prison chaplain, the governor of the jail,
and a justice of the peace, is as follows:

"I, Thomas Estel, of the city of Carlisle, being
sound of mind, though very infirm of body, and believing myself to be about to appear before the
tribunal of my Eternal Judge to give an account of
the deeds done in the flesh, do now make this my
last statement and confession, concerning a crime
committed on the Orton and Stockbridge road, on
the night of November the 13th, 18—, the robbery of

the mail coach and the murder of a passenger at that time and place.

"And these were the circumstances under which the deed was done:

"There was a young gentleman of the West Riding, a little wildish in his ways—young Mr. James Hawkhurst, nephew and heir to Squire Hawkhurst, of Hawkhurst.

"This uncle had made a will, disinheriting him, leaving all his property to hospitals, which he had no right to do, seeing that, although the estates were not entailed, yet they were the Hawkhurst family estates, and should have gone to the heir-at-law, young James Hawkhurst.

"This wicked will was understood to be in the hands of the family solicitor, one John Keitch, of Carlisle.

"Old Squire Hawkhurst lay dying at Hawkhurst Hall, and the vicar wrote to the solicitor to come down to the Hall, and to bring the will along with him.

"The solicitor wrote back that he should come down by the late train to Stockbridge and arrive by the mail-coach at Orton on the night of that 13th day of November.

"Now, the disinherited heir, young Mr. James, was drinking with a lot of us wild young blades at the Tawny Lion public house at Orton. And he told us all about it. We talked about the injustice of the old squire in having robbed young Mr. James of his inheritance in order to give it to hospitals. And we argued this way: that as the squire had not made the fortune himself, but had received the estate from a long line of forefathers, so it was his bounden duty, in common honesty, to pass it along to their descendants, and that if it were not for the existence of that wicked will, the last of the line, the young squire, would enjoy his own, because he was next of kin, and heir-at-law.

"We all loved the young squire, because he made himself one of us and had no pride, and we knew that was the chief reason why the old squire disinherited him. So he was in a measure suffering for us.

"After a little while Mr. James left us, but we all kept drinking and arguing and getting ourselves up more and more into a mad excitement, until one of us—I do not remember now which it really was—proposed that we should all go in a body and stop the coach that ran between Stockbridge railway station and Orton, and take that will away from the lawyer and destroy it, so that our young squire might enjoy his own.

"We were all mad drunk, or we would have remembered that our proposed adventure was really highway robbery—a felony punishable, it might be, with transportation for life—instead of being the brave, heroic exploit we in our madness believed it to be.

"We, five in number—no matter who the others were—I confess only my own part—procured masks and fire-arms, and on the night in question we started out on our adventure.

"On the road we met young Joseph Wyvil, who had just come from Scotland, to which he had run away to marry his sweetheart. He did not belong to our part of the world, though he was known to most of us. He was a wild one, up to any sort of fun, ready for any sort of frolic, but not bad.

"He gave us good e'en, and asked us, 'Where away?' And we told him we were going on a glorious lark, and asked him to come along with us, but we would not tell him, no, nor give him a hint of what our adventure was to be.

"First he said he could not, that 'Lil'—that was his wife—was expecting him; but at last he consented.

"I do think it was curiosity more than anything else that made him join us! Poor fellow! I have had many a heartache for him. He kept on asking us in his smiling way where we were going? What we were going to do?

"But we only laughed and told him to come and see. And his curiosity was worked up to such a high pitch that he did come to see.

"We reached at last a favorable part of the road for our enterprise. Not one of us thought it would end as badly as it did. We only wanted to destroy the wicked old squire's will.

"We got to the place where we meant to stop the coach.

"It was where the road went down into a deep-wooded hollow. There were thick, heavy woods on each side. It was as dark as pitch.

"We halted and stretched a strong thick rope, three times doubled, across the road, tying the opposite ends to the trunks of trees.

"And then we waited for the coach.

"That poor Joe Wyvil kept on asking us what we were up to.

"And we telling him to wait and see.

"And his curiosity was so intense that he did wait and see, though all the time he kept blaming himself and saying that 'Lil' would be looking for him and wondering why he did not come.

"Ah, poor boy! And poor girl! He never went back to 'Lil.' 'Lil' was doomed to look and wonder, and wonder in vain. He waited to see what we were up to. Waited to his own ruin.

"Ah, yes! the fate of that poor, rollicking, good-natured young Joe has set heavier on my conscience than the death of that old scoundrel of a lawyer;

for his death was an accident, after all, though, as it occurred while we were trying to get at the wicked will, it was construed murder.

"We waited there for the coach longer than we expected to have done. It was behind time. I asked in a whisper if anybody had a watch.

"Joe said that he had one. He took it out, and I struck a match and looked at the hour. It had gone eleven. Joe started up and said he must go, or 'Lii' would think 'he was never coming home.' Seems to me we sometimes utter prophecies unawares.

"Joe was really going that time, but almost at the same moment the sound of wheels was heard and the light of the lantern was seen.

"Several of us spoke out at once, telling him to sit down quietly and wait five minutes and then he might go. He dropped down again on his seat beside the road.

"The coach came on very fast, as if to make up for lost time, the light of the lantern shining like two fiery eyes through the darkness of the night in the narrow, wooded road.

"On it came at full speed, the leaders stepping high, until suddenly they struck the barrier of ropes we had stretched across the road, reared, plunged, overturned the coach, extinguished the lanterns, and all was instant confusion, men swearing, women shrieking, horses struggling.

"This was much worse than we had intended. We wished to stop the coach and get the wicked will, not to upset it at the risk of the passengers' lives.

"We immediately surrounded the wreck.

"I struck a match, and keeping the black crape well over my face, leaving only one eye uncovered, I peered into face after face of the fallen passengers, until I found my man, the lawyer from Carlisle, with the old squire's wicked will in his possession.

" 'Hand out that beastly will and you shall not be hurt; but if you don't——'

"He instantly drew a pistol, aimed it at my head and cocked it.

"I struck the weapon up with a swift stroke of my hand.

"Heaven knows I never meant to harm the man, but the pistol went off, and he fell, shot through the brain, as I afterwards learned. I did not know it then. I was mad with drink, I repeat, and what little mental power I had left was occupied with the will. I got it! It was safe in my hands. I hid it in my bosom.

"I hardly noted the increased confusion that was all around me, until one of my companions took me by the arm and whispered, hurriedly:

" 'Are you dead? What's the matter with you? There's murder done! The posse is upon us! Run!'

"It was true. The terrible noise had been heard even from that lonely road, the alarm had been given, and the constabulary force of the neighborhood, with all the stragglers that could be picked up at that hour, were coming.

"We made off into the thick woods that bordered the road, and made good our escape into the woods that bordered the road on either side—every one of us, except that poor boy who had nothing to do with the crime.

"I got off to America; for being the most deeply in for it, I knew I must put the broad ocean between me and my native land.

"I led a wandering life over there—that of honest work sometimes, that of doubtful speculation often; was a billiard marker in Chicago, a bar-tender in San Francisco, a digger in the silver mines of Colorado.

"It was years before I heard what had become of

my comrades in that fatal night's adventure. I feared
that some of them had been caught, tried and sent
to penal servitude; but I never once imagined that
any harm could have come to young Wyvil, who was
not in it at all, and only happened to be in our company by accident, and somewhat against his will, and
in total ignorance of our intention to stop the coach
that night.

"But one day, about seven years after I had left
England, and while I was in Colorado, I fell in with
an old neighbor from Orton. He, too, had come to
seek his fortunes in the new world and had drifted
out to the silver mines.

"It was the first home-face I had seen since I had
left the country. It was a great meeting, I can tell
you. I scrutinized Stone's face to see if he suspected
me of complicity in that highway robbery and murder, and I was satisfied that he did not.

"I asked after old friends and acquaintances—
parents or near relatives I had none to inquire of.

"He told me of this, that, or the other person,
married, dead, emigrated, or remaining as before.

"Finally I asked, in turn, about the comrades who
had been with me on that fatal night, and learned to
my astonishment that they were living and prosper-
ing on their small farms on the great Hawkhurst
estate. It was therefore evident that they had never
been suspected.

"His mention of the Hawkhurst estate led me on
to inquire who ruled at Hawkhurst now.

"He replied that the young squire did, of course;
that no will had been found and Mr. James had entered into possession as next of kin and heir-at-law,
and everybody was satisfied.

"So far our mad adventure had been successful, at
least. The heir enjoyed his own and no great harm
had been done, except the accidental death of that

old scoundrel, so far as I knew then. And I might have remained in that happy belief if it had not been for my next question.

"I asked him if anything had ever been found out concerning the parties who had stopped the mail coach that dark November night.

"He said that the robbery was believed to have been committed by the pit men, who were on a strike, and known to be a most lawless set, fit for any sort of violence; but though several of them had been arrested on suspicion, nothing could be proved, and they had to be released. And as for young Joe, he was game to the last.

"Young Joe! The name went through my heart like a sword! I trembled when I asked Stone if he meant Joe Wyvil, and what he had to do with the affair.

"And then he told me all the terrible truth! that young Wyvil had been the only one of all the gang who had stopped the mail-coach to be arrested. That the roughs had escaped into the woods, but that he had been taken 'red-handed' on the spot where the lawyer fell.

"I inquired what explanation the unhappy boy had given of his presence there.

"The man told me that he had given no satisfactory account of himself whatever—that he had most earnestly asserted his innocence, and his appearance on the scene of the murder as a mere accident, owing to his having met a party bent on a 'spree,' and joined them. He was game to the very last.

"With a great sinking of the heart, I next inquired of Stone what had been the fate of young Wyvil, and I dreaded to hear his answer as if it had been a sentence of death. And, indeed, in one respect it was a sentence of death.

"He told me that the youth had been tried for

murder, but not under the name of Wyvil. The name he had given was that of John Weston, and as there was nobody to contradict him, he being but a stranger to most people in the neighborhood, as John Weston he was convicted and condemned to death. But on account of his being a mere boy, with nothing against him before that, and on some other account, his sentence was commuted to transportation and penal servitude for life, and that he had been shot dead while trying to make his escape, or so it was reported.

"So of the crime in which five men had been implicated no one had been suspected, and no one punished but the innocent boy who knew nothing about it.

"Finally I asked Stone what had become of 'Lil,' the poor boy's wife.

"He informed me that her brother, another Joseph Wyvil and a cousin of the prisoner, had come and taken her away, and it was reported that he had taken her to America.

"This was all my old neighbor had to tell me. And soon after, the fortunes of war—in the mines—separated us, he going farther up the country.

"We never met again.

"About two years ago my health began to fail. I was attacked with this disease of the lungs that had carried off both my parents before they had reached their fortieth year (consumptives ought never to marry —each other, anyway). I knew I did not need the doctor to tell me the truth, and so I did not tempt him to tell me a pious, professional lie. I knew by family experience that I was booked for the last journey, and just about how long it might be.

"I was seized with a homesick longing to see once more the English village in which I was born and brought up, and where my old friends lived, if any remained.

"So, about eighteen months ago, I sailed for England in one of the fast-sailing ocean steamers. And when we landed in Liverpool I took the first express train for Carlisle, got out at the Stockbridge station and took the same coach, or one exactly like the same coach, that I and my reckless companions had helped to wreck, that fatal 13th of November, seventeen years before. I went over the same road at the same hour, and put up at the Tawny Lion, where the coach stopped, and where we, reckless young roughs, had laid the plan to recover the wicked will which had ended in such a tragedy.

"But, oh! the changes in seventeen years! The Tawny Lion had passed into strangers' hands. Very few of my old friends were left. I went to see the young squire at Hawkhurst. Quite a middle-aged squire now, a sedate magistrate and sub-lieutenant of the county; married and surrounded by a large family of sons and daughters. He was very glad to see me, although he could never have suspected that it was to my hand he owed the destruction of that will which left him to inherit his own, as next of kin and heir-at-law.

"I did not stay at Orton long. I went up to London; and there, as you know, I was soon arrested for forgery, tried, convicted, and sentenced to penal servitude.

"But, gentlemen, as I maintained during my trial, I maintain here, on my death-bed, I never committed that forgery. What call had I to forge a check for a miserable five-pound note, when I had a plenty of money made in the mines?

"No; as I told the judge and jury—though they would not believe me—I now tell you with my parting breath, I cashed that check to accommodate a gentleman who was a guest in the same hotel with myself. I gave him five sovereigns for his forged check, not suspecting it to be forged, and in a day or two after presented it at the bank for payment, and was nabbed.

"Though I told my tale, I was not for a moment believed. No gentleman answering to his description could be found. I was the scapegoat, and here I am. Not so badly off. Not worse than I should be in a hospital. I have not done a day's penal servitude, but have had my long illness and slow passage to the grave soothed and cared for by physician and chaplain.

"I never meant to be wicked; but when I think of the fate to which I brought young Joe Wyvil I feel as if I were much better off than I deserve to be, even though dying in a prison infirmary.

"I thank the officers of this prison, and especially I thank the chaplain and the doctor for their great goodness to me; and I pray the Lord to forgive the sins of my youth.   THOMAS ESTEL."

Thus ended the dying man's confession, which was duly sworn to, witnessed, signed and sealed.

A few lines at the end of the article testified, on the authority of the prison officers, to the uniformly exemplary conduct of Estel while in confinement, his patience under long and painful illness, his humility, resignation and gratitude for the least favors.

CHAPTER XVII

COMING TO A CRISIS

Look forward what's to come, and back what's past;
Thy life will be with praise and prudence graced;
What loss or gain may follow thou mayst guess;
Then wilt thou be secure of the success.
For on their life no grievous burden lies
Who are well natured, temperate and wise;
But an inhuman and ill-tempered mind
Not any easy part in life can find.
Lords of the world have but of life their lease,
And this, too, if the lessor please, must cease.
The youngest, in the morning, are not sure
That till the night their life they can secure.

Sir I. Denham.

AFTER reading that strange confession, Lilith sat in a trance of delight so rapt that in it she forgot every source of trouble to herself.

Now the guiltless was vindicated. Now the secret that had weighed her young life almost down to death might be told. Now the sorely persecuted yet withal light-hearted and joyous exile and wanderer might return to his own a free and justified man.

· But where was he?

Lilith did not know. She could not even conjecture. He might not be living. He was young, indeed, but life is uncertain at all ages, and his was a very careless and adventurous life.

It was now more than eighteen months since Lilith had heard from him.

On that fatal March 21st, when her husband had driven her away, she had received a letter from the wanderer, saying that he was en route for Chicago, and appointing the Personal column of the *Pursuivant* as the medium of their correspondence.

But after having been banished by her husband
on account of this very wanderer, whose sacred claim
on her he could not understand, Lilith had conscien-
tiously abstained from using the Personal column of
the *Pursuivant* for opening any communication with
the banned exile.

Indeed, as it will be remembered, Lilith had never
sought intercourse by letter or otherwise with the
mysterious stranger who laid so much stress upon
his natural right to her duty. In every case it was
he who had sought her, often to her great peril, and
always to her distressing embarrassment.

But, though Lilith had abstained from all attempts
to open a correspondence with him, yet she had
regularly searched the papers for any possible news
of the poor stroller, but without success.

At first she had wondered much at his utter silence,
but since hearing the report of her own death she
understood that silence; she knew that he believed
in the truth of that report. Yet still she had not
sought to communicate with him, even for the purpose of announcing her continued existence, though
she knew what joy such news must bring to his lonely
heart. Her fidelity to the husband who had repudiated
her was so perfect!

Yet now that the fugitive from justice (or from
injustice) was fully vindicated—now that the secret
might be told, the mystery cleared up—she must seek
to communicate with the wanderer, and immediately.

Two courses were very urgent—the first to get that
published confession into the hands of the wanderer;
the second to get an interview with her husband.
Yet, no! She dared not seek the latter. If it had
only been the fatal secret which had parted them,
then, indeed, she might have written to him or sought
his presence, and said:

"The mystery that raised a cloud between us has

been cleared away, and I shall be justified in your
sight."

But it was not only the secret which had divided
them.

It was his antipathy to her—his incurable antipathy
—expressed in his words—bitter, burning words—
that had branded thmselves upon her soul:

"I never loved you. I married you only to please
my dying father. . . . In a few hours I shall leave
this house, never to return while you desecrate it with
your presence."

No! In the face of such a sentence she could not
seek to see Tudor Hereward. All womanly delicacy
forbade the step.

But she must bring this published, vindicatory confession to the attention of the exile, who had for
more than eighteen years lived under a false charge
and false conviction, an outcast from society, a wanderer over the face of the earth.

Lilith roused from her trance and acted promptly.

She cut the slip containing the confession from the
paper, and then sat down at the little side table on
which her traveling portfolio lay, and wrote this personal for the *Pursuivant:*

"MAZEPPA—J. W.—J. W.—A. A.—A. M. L. Z.—
Send your address to E. W. H., Poste Restante, Paris,
Search *Pursuivant* for news."

Having written this, she took another sheet of
paper, and wrote a letter to the editor of the *Pursuivant*, inclosing the slip of paper containing the confession of Thomas Estel, and asking him, in the name
of justice and humanity, to give it a place in his
columns; or if he thought it a matter of not sufficient
interest for the reading public, at least to put its
purport in a few lines that might meet the eyes of
an unhappy fugitive, suffering under the blight of

a false conviction. She enclosed the whole in one envelope, but did not seal it, for it was necessary that she should get a letter of credit to send with it to pay for the advertisement.

She had scarcely finished her work when the baroness entered the parlor.

"Writing so early in the morning, mignonne? The mail must have brought you important news," said the lady, as she sank languidly into an easy chair.

"It has, madame! News that will oblige me to go to Chester to-day, if you can spare me," said Lilith.

"Why, of course. I must spare you, petite, if you have affairs. You can take Monsieur Le Grange to escort you, if you please," said the baroness, kindly.

"If monsieur would be so good I should be very grateful," began Lilith.

"Bonjour, mesdames! In what manner can I be so happy as to serve you?" inquired the gallant old Frenchman, who entered at this point of the conversation.

"Mrs. Wyvil has business in Chester to-day, and would be glad of your escort, if you could find it convenient to attend her," said Madame Von Bruyin.

"I shall find myself most happy, most honored," replied Monsieur Le Grange, with a bow.

"Touch the bell, if you please, monsieur; it is within your reach," said the baroness.

The Frenchman rang, and breakfast was immediately served.

A messenger was dispatched to bring a carriage from the "Llewellyn Arms," the only hotel in the village.

And as soon as the morning meal was over Lilith prepared for her journey.

Madame Von Bruyin was not without her share of feminine curiosity; but she refrained from asking questions, and occupied herself with opening and read-

ing her letters—there were seven from her princely
lover, and one from an eminent Paris man-milliner or
ladies' tailor, whichever you please, with whom she
was in correspondence on the subject of her trousseau.

Lilith and Monsieur Le Grange appeared in the
parlor equipped for their journey at the same moment
that the fly from the hotel drew up at the door.

"I shall return as soon as possible, madame, and I
hope our absence will not inconvenience you," said
Lilith.

"Enjoy yourselves, mes enfans!" said the baroness,
gayly. "I shall occupy myself with answering letters."

The two travelers took leave and departed on their
journey.

Llandorf was distant five miles from the nearest
railway station; and it took the one-horse fly from
the Llewellyn Arms a full hour to get there. Fortunately, they were in time for the eleven o'clock express.

Monsieur Le Grange made a bargain with the fly
to meet them again on the arrival of the seven o'clock
train, and then took tickets and put his companion
into a coupé, which he shared with her.

A two hours' rapid ride through the most picturesque part of Wales brought them into the ancient city
of Chester.

At Lilith's request, they went first to the Bank of
Wales, where she obtained her bill of exchange,
which she enclosed with her letter, advertisement,
and so on, in the large envelope, directed to the editor of the *Pursuivant*. This done, they went to the
post-office, posted the letter and then drove to the
Grosvenor Hotel, where they took lunch.

At five o'clock they took the express train back to
the station, where on their arrival they found the fly
from the Llewellyn Arms waiting for them.

In another hour they had reached the farm-house

where it pleased the Baroness Von Bruyin to rusticate for a season.

The lady, who affected rural hours, had dined early, and was waiting tea for them.

She asked no questions, though still very curious to know what was the nature of that business which had taken her young friend off so suddenly.

Lilith, totally unconscious of madame's silent curiosity, gave no sign.

After tea the professor read to the two ladies for some hours. Then the party separated and retired to rest.

Lilith, having done all that lay in her power to do, under the circumstances, impatiently waited for results.

Weeks passed away, and the baroness began to weary of the rural life that at first had pleased her so much.

It was now late in October, and the weather was growing cool. Pony rides among the mountains and rowings on the lake were not such delightful recreations as she had found them earlier in the season.

In a word, Madame Von Bruyin was tired of Llandorf, and longing for Paris—weary of the world of nature, and sighing for the world of society.

One morning she suddenly announced her intentions:

"We will go to Paris on the first of November. A proper trousseau cannot be arranged entirely by correspondence. If we get settled by the first week we shall have a clear month before the gay season begins. What do you say, mignonne?"

"I am ready, madame," answered Lilith, so cheerfully that the lady could not doubt the sincerity of the girl's assent. Lilith was also anxious to be in the French capital in time for any answer that might come to her advertisement for the wanderer, whom she had notified to address all communications for her to the Poste Restante, Paris.

Monsieur Le Grange, who added to his duties of secretary those of courier and general utility, was instructed to make immediate preparations for their journey.

On the thirty-first of October, being All-Hallow Eve, the party left Llandorf for Southampton, and on the evening of the first of November they reached Paris.

Madame Von Bruyin's house on the Champs Elysées had been put in order for her reception, in obedience to a telegram from Monsieur Le Grange, so that the travelers at once found themselves at home in comfortable and luxurious quarters.

The day after their arrival Lilith went to the post-office to inquire if any letters had arrived directed to E. W. H.

She received an answer that there were none.

Disappointed, she returned home, and spent the remainder of the day in driving about with Madame Von Bruyin among the most fashionable shops.

The woman of vast wealth displayed, perhaps, more extravagance than taste in the selection of her costumes. She carried in her hand a slip cut from a newspaper, describing at great length, and very minutely, the dresses and jewels of some "royal highness," who had just married an imperial prince, and she was resolved to have fac-similes of each dress, with additional dresses of, if possible, still more beautiful styles and more expensive materials.

Her interviews with Worth, Pingen and other "celebrated" man-milliners or ladies' tailors (as you please) occupied her the whole day, so that late in the evening she returned with Lilith, almost exhausted with fatigue.

As that day passed, so passed many others.

Lilith, on going early in the morning to the post-office to inquire for letters directed to E. W. H., would meet nothing but heart-wearying disappointment, and on returning home would be required to attend Madame Von Bruyin on her round among jewelers, milliners and modistes.

Madame Von Bruyin, with the most amiable intentions, embarrassed Lilith very much by forcing upon her costly presents in jewelry, Indian shawls, dress patterns, and so forth; for how could the wealthy and good-natured baroness make such magnificent purchases for herself, and before the eyes of her pretty young companion, and not give her beautiful adornings? And though Lilith shrank from these offerings, and declared that such splendors were not suited to her condition, the baroness persisted in pressing them upon her, declaring that they were all most peculiarly fitted for her, having been designed and manufactured to adorn youth and beauty just such as hers.

As day after day passed with the disappointment of the morning, and the wearying round of the afternoon, Lilith grew heart-sick and brain-sick over it all. The splendors of the preparations for the approaching wedding were in such dissonance to her anxious and despairing mood that, young and beautiful as she was, she began to take a strong distaste to finery, and to wish herself among the plain Methodists of Aunt Sophie's humble boarding-house.

Lilith longed for sobriety and repose, while her life seemed to pass in whirlwind and lightning.

She had formed her resolution, however, and it was this:

If she should hear from the wanderer she would send him to Mr. Hereward to divulge his secret, now no longer needing to be kept, to justify her conduct, and leave it to her husband to seek her if it should please him to do so.

Or—if she should hear nothing from the wanderer up to the time of Madame Von Bruyin's marriage, she would, on that occasion, only wait until the bride and bridegroom should have left Paris, and then she would run down to Havre by rail and take the first homeward-bound steamer to New York.

Sometimes she wondered why the baroness never seemed to take any interest or to care to ask any questions in regard to her young companion's future plans. But she supposed that Madame Von Bruyin was too much absorbed in her own interesting prospects to think of anybody else's.

In this supposition, however, Lilith did her friend but scant justice.

The baroness—in her secret heart—had quite settled the question of her companion's future, and had no suspicion that Lilith would raise any objection to her plan or that it was even necessary at present to allude to it.

The day of explanation soon came, however.

It was Sunday. They could not go out shopping. They attended church in the forenoon, and, after an early dinner, lounged about in Madame Von Bruyin's boudoir. Letters had been left for the baroness on the previous day, but she had returned from her shopping too tired to examine any of them except those addressed in the handwriting of the prince, her betrothed, which she had read with avidity; the others she had pushed aside until a more convenient season.

Now, on this Sabbath afternoon, her languid eyes fell upon the little heap of letters still lying upon her writing-table.

"Nothing more interesting than circulars from tradespeople, I fancy," she said, as she lazily picked them up and passed them through her fingers as if they had been a pack of playing cards.

"Ah! but here is one for you, petite, directed to my care! I am sorry I did not find it yesterday, when I should have given it to you. It bears the New York postmark, and is perhaps from the good Aunt Sophie, who is, I believe, your only correspondent in the world. Is it not so?" said the baroness, as she held the letter out to Lilith, who came eagerly forward to claim it.

Yes, it was from Aunt Sophie.

And while Madame Von Bruyin opened and glanced over her own hitherto neglected correspondence, Lilith opened and read Aunt Sophie's simple epistle:

"NEW YORK, October 21, 18—.

"MY DARLING CHILD:—I take this favorable opportunity to rite to you to inform you that we are all in good helth, thanks be to the gracious Lord, and hoping that this letter may find you and the barreness enjoying the same rich blessing.

"My dear child, I have not received any letter from you sence I rote to you last September, which I think my letter must of miscarryed or else the ship must of been shiprecked. Oh, do rite to me and tell me how you are and when you are coming home, for you know this is your home, my darling child and honey. There is an interesting young man here, who have taken Mr. More's room which he left when he got married, you know, and he is a very hopeful young man, indeed, which I hope he will make a powerful minister some of these days, though he says he is not worthy to black a Christian minister's boots. He saw your photograf on the mantlepiece one day and took such an interest into it and read the dedercation on the back, where you know you rote To my dear Aunt Sophie, from her loving child, and he asked

me most a hundred questions about you and I tolde
him all I knowd. He is a Perfeck Gentleman and his
name is a Mister Ansolong. I dont know as I spell
it rite because I never saw it rote but thats the way
it sounds. Well honey we are all going on very much
in the same way as when you left. Mrs. Farquier I
think is agoing to be married to Elder perkins of our
church. I don't holde with second marriages myself,
but everybody must walk accordin' to their own lites.
Brother More has done a good work for the Lord
and brought a menny wandering sheepe into the fold.
But you know his term with us will soon be out and
I hope and pray as the Conference will send him
back to us but after all we mussent lean too much
on the Arm of flesh knowing who is Our Helper.
I do wish as that dear Mister Ansolong would enter
the ministry. What a preacher he would make! He
reads the Bible like an Angel! It is enough to make
one Cry to hear him. But he says he has not studied
and I tell him that Peter and John and James and
their bretheren never studied because there want any
collidges in their days but he up and put it to me
that John and James and they had the best of all
teaching in the pursonal presence and example and
instruction of Our Saviour. And there he got the
better of me which only makes me feel surer what a
powerful preacher he would be if he only had the
Holy Spirit. But there, my darling child, I am running on until this shete of paper though it is foolscap
is almost full—so I must finish, with praying that the
Lord will bless you. Give my Love to the dear barreness and tell her the money she giv me to spend
on the poor Street children is doing a good work and
Brother More is drawing up a Report to send her,
with the names and histories of the children Beni-
fitted. So no more at present from your Affectionate
Friend   SOPHIE DOWNIE."

Lilith read this letter with a joy scarcely less profound and grateful than that with which she had read the vindicatory confession of the convict, Thomas Estel.

Ancillon was still living; he had not fallen a victim to any deadly fever of the South, or to the knife of any border ruffian of the West; he had not perished in any railroad collision or steamboat explosion; and these were the only perils which, in Lilith's opinion, could end a life so young and sound as his was. He still lived, and in his adventurous or drifting life had drifted into the calm haven of Aunt Sophie's home.

It was very curious that he should have done so, Lilith thought; but, then, experience shows us many curious coincidences in life.

She wondered whether he had seen her advertisement in the *Pursuivant*, or whether, since he had given her up for dead, he had not ceased to search the Personal column, which was to have been their medium of communication when far distant from each other. But even if he had neglected that particular column in which her one advertisement was a standing item, still he must have read other portions of the paper, and so must have seen the account of the convict's ante-mortem confession, which cleared John Weston from all complicity in the crime for which he—John Weston—alone had suffered; and yet, perhaps, he might have missed that one paper, or even in reading it, he might have overlooked that one article, so full of importance to him.

At all events it appeared that he had not seen either the standing advertisement in the Personal column or the copied account of Thomas Estel's ante-mortem confession.

He was still lingering at Mrs. Downie's quiet house in New York City. And Lilith's joy and gratitude at having a sure clew to the wanderer was so great as to exceed her surprise and wonder at the manner in which it was recovered.

She determined to write by the first mail to Mrs. Downie and to Alfred Ancillon.

So absorbed was she in the subject of her thoughts that she did not perceive that Madame Von Bruyin had been watching her attentively for some moments, until at length that lady spoke.

"Lilith," she said, "you must have received some very happy surprise in your letter, to judge by the rapt delight of your face."

"I have," replied the young creature, in a joyous tone. "I have received news of a long absent and very dear relative, from whom I had not heard for nearly two years. I had feared he was dead; but he is living, in good health, at Aunt Sophie's house."

"Ah! I congratulate you, my dear. So this letter is from Aunt Sophie, as I supposed. How is the dear woman?" sympathetically inquired the baroness.

"Well as ever, thank Heaven, always well. She sends you messages of love and gratitude. Would you like to see her letter?" said Lilith, holding out the paper.

"No, dear; I have seen letters enough for one evening. That good Aunt Sophie! There she is, always confined to one narrow round of duties. I wonder if she would not like to see more of the world? Could not she come out to us, if I were to send her an excursion ticket? Could not she leave the quiet, well-ordered little household in the hands of one of those matronly widows who, having lived so long with her, seem to be of the same family? What a delight it would be to show her Paris! What do you think, Lilith?"

"It would indeed be most delightful! And, indeed, although it does not seem so at first view, I think it would be quite practicable. Aunt Sophie is such a brave, enterprising little woman. I even think she need not cross alone. I think Mr. Ancillon, my relative, may be coming over on business and may bring her."

"Enchanting! And they can both stay here and take care of you while Gherardini and myself are on our wedding tour. Ridiculous etiquette, a wedding tour."

"But, madame," said Lilith, in a tone of surprise, "do you really wish to keep me on after your marriage?"

"I wish, and with your consent I intend, to hold you, as a dear sister, under my immediate protection as long as we both shall live, or until you shall be claimed by Tudor Hereward, in the case of his repentance, or by some better man in case of Hereward's death."

"But, madame——"

"There, there, mignonne, do not let us dispute tonight. It is time to go to bed. Write to-morrow to your friend Mrs. Downie, and invite her here in my name. To be present here at my marriage. And to take care of you during my absence. Put the last-mentioned reason strongly, as—to be of use would be a great inducement to that dear, unselfish soul! There are people, Lilith, who must be convinced that they are doing something of utility for somebody else before they can be persuaded to enjoy themselves. Convince this dear Aunt Sophie that you will need her, and she will come over and enjoy sightseeing in Paris with all the zest of youth. I will get Le Grange to see about the ticket to-morrow, so that you can inclose it in your letter."

"But suppose, after all, she should not come? The ticket will be lost," said Lilith.

"Well, the steamship company will gain. That is

all," replied the baroness, rising and putting her fair
hand over her lips to conceal a yawn.

At this unmistakable sign of weariness, Lilith took
the hint and rang the bell for the servants to close
up the apartments.

In a few minutes the friends had retired.

CHAPTER XVIII

SURPRISE ON SURPRISE

THAT letter and that ticket were destined never to
be sent!

The next morning, while Madame Von Bruyin,
Lilith Hereward, and Monsieur Le Grange were seated
at breakfast together, a card was brought in on a
silver waiter and offered to Lilith.

She picked it up and read:

SEÑOR ZUNIGA.

And underneath, in brackets, the lightly-penciled
name of Alfred Ancillon.

Lilith could scarcely suppress a cry as she started
to her feet.

"What is the matter?" inquired the baroness.

"My relative from New York has arrived!" joyfully exclaimed Lilith.

"Indeed! I congratulate you. Go to him at once,
my dear," said the baroness, cordially. Then turning
to the page, she inquired:

"Where have you shown the gentleman, Henri?"

"Into the small salon, madame," replied the lad.

"Quite right. Attend Madame Wyvil thither. Go,
my dear. Do not keep your friend a moment waiting," said the baroness, sympathetically.

Lilith left the room, attended by the page, and

crossed the hall to enter the small salon overlooking the Champs d'Elysées.

The young page opened the door for her to pass in, and then closed it and retired.

Mr. Alfred Ancillon, or Señor Zuniga, stood in the middle of the bright room, looking the image of glorious, immortal youth.

He came eagerly forward and opened his arms.

Lilith fell upon his bosom in a passion of joyous sobs and tears.

He embraced her warmly, straining her to his heart, pressing kisses on her face, before either of them spoke a syllable.

Their first utterances were almost incoherent in their gladness.

"Oh, thank Heaven that you still live!"

"Thanks be to the Lord that I find you safe, my darling child!"

"At last! Oh, at last you are vindicated!"

"Restored to life, almost from the grave. Oh! my child!"

"By what happy chance did you drift into Aunt Sophie's house?"

"I will tell you presently, my dear, for——"

"And how is dear Aunt Sophie?"

"You must judge for yourself, darling! Look up! There—there she is!"

Lilith lifted herself from the señor's breast and turned her head to see a round, black bundle of a little old woman, on the bottom of an easy-chair, unroll itself and come towards her in the form of Mrs. Downie.

Yes, it was indeed Aunt Sophie! There was the same soft, round form, the same careless though clean black gown and shawl, the same little mashed black silk bonnet, the same smiling, babyish old face, with its fair skin, blue eyes and rumpled gray hair. It

was dear Aunt Sophie in person, wonderful as the fact
appeared.

With a half-suppressed cry of joy Lilith ran to her,
caught her in her arms and covered her face with
kisses, while Aunt Sophie cried quietly without speaking a word.

Presently Lilith led her to a seat on the sofa and
sat down beside her, holding her hand, gazing into
her sweet old face, and uttering her delight in fragmentary words.

"How comes it that I have the joy of seeing you?
It was only yesterday evening that I got your dear
letter. This very day I was going to write to you
to come here to us. Was not that strange? But
you always anticipated my wishes, did you not? But
what happy inspiration, what angel sent you here?"

"Why, it was him," replied Aunt Sophie, simply,
pointing to the señor. "He fetched me. I believe
he could persuade anybody in this world to do anything he wanted. And all in such a hurry, too! I
never made up my mind so quick in all my life before; and never shall in all my life again. I declare
I was on board of the ship before I well knowed what
I was doing."

The Señor Zuniga broke into one of Alfred Ancillon's joyous bursts of laughter as he explained:

"If I had given her time to reflect she might have
hesitated to come. If I had not hurried her out of
her senses I could not have brought her. Hear! I
saw your advertisement in the Personal column of
the *Pursuivant*, by chance, just thirteen days ago. I
saw that it had been in for some weeks, though I had
not observed it. This was on Tuesday. I reflected
that I could go to you in person as quickly as I could
communicate with you by letter, so I made up my
mind to sail the next day by the City of Paris. The
steamers from America to Europe are not crowded

at this season, whatever the steamers from Europe
to America may be. I went to the agent's office, feeling sure of getting berths, and I got them. I got
two tickets, one for myself and one for Aunt Sophie,
for I felt sure of persuading her to accompany
me——"

"He could persuade any mortal man or woman to
do anything he wanted them to do," put in the old
lady.

"Well, you may call it whim, eccentricity or inspiration, but I felt a great desire to take Mrs. Downie
with me, and I was resolved to gratify that desire."

"Yes, he did," again put in Aunt Sophie. "He come
right in the kitchen, where I was sitting down with
a blue check apron on, paring apples to make pies
for dinner; for, my dear, he went all over the house
like a tame kitten; and he says to me all of a sudden:

" 'I want you to let the house take care of itself
and go to Europe with me to-morrow morning to see
your favorite' (that was you, my dear).

"And I declare I was so startled I give a jump
and let the pan fall, and the apples rolled all over
the kitchen floor. Asking me all in a minute to go
to Europe with him to-morrow as if it had been going
to Harlem or Brooklyn!"

Again the irrepressible laughter of the señor burst
forth as he said:

"Well, you are not sorry you came?"

"Oh, no! But, goodness, child, think of it! I, who
had lived nigh seventy years in this world without
ever going more than fifty miles from home, and that
only once in my life, to be asked all of a sudden to
go to Europe next day!"

"It was startling!" said Lilith, smiling.

"Startling! And then to hear him talk. Why, to
hear him you would think to go from New York to

Havre was no more than to row across a river. Then
he got my boarders on his side. I think they thought
it was fun. And they all got me in such a whirl
that I hardly knowed whether I was awake or asleep.
And before I rightly knowed what I was about I was
on the steamer and out of sight of land!"

"I hope you left them all well at your house," said
Lilith.

"Oh, yes, honey, all mons'ous well. Mrs. Farquier
is going to be married to Elder Perkins, of our church.
I believe I told you in my letter."

"Yes, you did."

"Well, child, he is rich—awful rich. And they
are to be married next spring. He is a building of
a fine new house way up town, facing on the Park,
and soon as it's finished and furnished they're going
to be married and move right in. She's giv' up her
employment, and hasn't got much to do; so she offered
if I would only go along of this young gentleman
to Europe, how she would keep house for me until I
come back. She is a dear, good woman and deserves
all the prosperity she will have."

"So you need have no anxious cares about the
house," said Lilith.

"No, honey. And I expect I shall feel right down
well satisfied, once I get settled. But I was that
whirled around before I started that I hardly knowed
what I was doing of, or even who I was. Now what
do you think? When I opened my trunk to get out
a change of clothes, what do you think I found out!"

"I do not know," said Lilith, smiling.

"Well, I found that I had left behind my Sunday
gown—that black silk gown as I have worn to church
more years than I remember."

"That was unlucky; but never mind; you must have
a new one. Silk is cheap in Paris."

"Yes, honey, but that is not the worst of it. Instead of my own Sunday gown, what do you think I had packed away in my trunk?"

"A common gown?"

"No, child! But poor, dear, young Brother Burney's best black trousers, as I had taken out'n his room that very morning to clean for him, with benzine. And what he'll do for a decent pair to wear to church, I don't know; for he's only got one more pair, and they are patched awful, so as when the wind blows—well, I have to pin the flaps of his coat together. 'Deed I am mons'ous sorry I took his trousers. I hope he will never s'picion as I pawned 'em or anything."

"Of course he won't. But who is Brother Burney?" inquired Lilith.

"Oh, a hopeful young brother as is studying for the ministry. He has got the little teenty room at the end of the passage in the third story. And I reckon he's very poor. Ah me! I am sorry about them there trousers."

Here Lilith bent and whispered to Aunt Sophie: "We could send him, anonymously, a letter of credit for fifty or a hundred dollars, to get him a complete outfit."

"Could we, now? Without letting him know where it comes from? Without hurting his feelings? For it's very hard to be beholden, you know. Hard for a gentleman, let alone how poor he may be."

"We can fix it, Aunt Sophie; a letter shall go out to him this very day. And now I want you to come into my room and take off your bonnet. You will, I am sure, excuse us," said Lilith, turning with a smile to the señor.

"I will go back to the hotel, where I have some business to attend to. I will call later to pay my respects to Madame Von Bruyin," said Zuniga, as he arose and prepared to leave.

"But—hadn't I better be going, too? The baroness might think I was intruding," said Aunt Sophie, uneasily.

"Indeed she will not! She will be rejoiced to see you. She commissioned me to write to you, and urge you to come over to us."

"She did?" cried Aunt Sophie, in amazement.

"Indeed she did! I was to have written to you this very day, as I told you. Come, now, into my room and take off your bonnet and consider yourself quite at home; for I know the baroness will not allow you to return to the hotel," said Lilith.

"I will bid you good-morning," said the señor, bowing.

"Stay—one moment! Will you now release me from my promise? May I now tell the secret?" demanded Lilith, in an eager whisper.

"Yes! You might have given it to the winds, had you chosen, on the day that you read Estel's confession. You might have known then that it would be quite safe to do so."

"Yes, but I had not then been released from my promise."

"That, my child, shows a morbid conscientiousness in you. You were morally released from the moment that I was vindicated. Good-morning, my brave girl! I will see you later! By the way, though—where is your husband?" he suddenly stopped to ask.

"Still at the Court of ——, I think, where he has been Secretary of Legation for nearly two years."

"Do you ever hear from him?".

"Never."

"Does he know that you are living?"

"I think not."

"Then I exonerate him. I have a great deal to say to you, my darling, which I must defer for the present. Good-morning again."

And the señor bowed himself out.

Lilith took Aunt Sophie's hand and led her across the hall to a beautiful chamber with an alcove.

She gave the good woman a soft easy-chair, and then with her own hands took off her bonnet and her shawl, and made her comfortable.

"Now, have you been to breakfast, Aunt Sophie?"

"Yes, honey, at the hotel! And such a breakfast! Instead of good, wholesome tea and coffee and beefsteak, and buckwheat cakes, there was wine, if you believe me! And oranges, and grapes, and figs, and kickshaws! And I tried to be polite and 'do at Rome as the Romans do,' but la! I tasted the wine, and it tasted for all the world like vinegar and water, and sugar of lead! And I asked, please, mightn't I have a cup of coffee, and the waiter, as they called the gosling, or something like that——"

"Wasn't it the garçon?"

"Yes, gosoon, and he did go soon! He was spry! He asked me, 'Caffynore or caffylay,' and I had a hard time to make him understand that I didn't want no caffy at all, nor any other of their foreign wines, but just coffee, and I did get it at last, just about the splendidest cup of coffee as ever I tasted in all my life. I would have asked the gosling how they made it; but, law! he couldn't understand more'n half I said to him. The ignorance of these foreigners is amazing. A 'Merican child three years old could have understood what I said better than he did. But they know how to make good coffee."

"But you could not breakfast entirely on coffee, Aunt Sophie."

"No, no, honey; but they had good bread, too—excellent bread, and nice fresh butter. And so, you see, I didn't suffer. And they had a number of different sorts of stews, or hashes, I should call them, but the gosling called them awful hard names. They smelt mighty nice, all of 'em, but I was afeard to ventur' on any of 'em. I was afeard of frogs. And that gosling was always a sticking one or other of them stews under my very nose, too."

"Well, Aunt Sophie," you need not be afraid of anything you may find on our table, though we have a French chef."

"A French shay? That may be good to ride in, but what has that got to do with cooking, honey?"

"I should have said a French cook."

"Oh, I see. It was a slip of the tongue."

"Did you have a fine voyage, Aunt Sophie?"

"Splendid."

"And you were not sea-sick?"

"Oh, yes, I was. For two days I was just as sick as if I had taken an old-fashioned dose of calomel and jalap. And I think it did me a heap of good, too, for after I got over it I was that hungry! Indeed, I was so hungry I was ashamed to eat as much as I wanted. And all the rest of the voyage I thought more of eating than of anything else in the world."

"When did you reach Havre?"

"Yesterday; and it so happened as there was a train for Paris in an hour afterwards; so we took that train and came right on, and got here last night. We slept at that hotel, and, if you please to believe me, I had one of the goslings for a chamber-maid. I don't like foreign ways, myself."

"Never mind, dear; you will be more comfortable with us. But now tell me, Aunt Sophie, did you know that the señor was a near relation of mine?"

"What makes you call him the sinner, honey? He's no more of a sinner than the rest of us, I reckon. We are all sinners, for that matter."

"I said señor, Aunt Sophie, which is all the same as if I had said Sir or Mr."

"Oh! Well, I shall never get used to foreign words.

Yes, honey, he did tell me; but not till he had pumped me of every single thing I knowed about you. Then, to account for his curiosity, he told me as you was a very near and dear relative of his'n as he had given up for dead."

"How did he come to board at your house? He is not a minister or a theological student."

"No, honey; but he do look just like a preacher. Don't he, now?"

"Perhaps."

"Well, my sign is always out, you know, and he saw it, and wanting board, he stepped up and rang the bell, like any other applicant. Anyways, that's how he came into the house, and he looked so much like a hopeful young minister of the Gospel that I took him, without once remembering to ask for his references. Afterwards he happened to see your photographs on the mantelpiece, and he took it down and gazed at it, and read your writing, and seemed so upset I didn't know what to make of him. And he asked about one hundred questions about you, and I told him all I knowed. Then he let on as you was a near relation of his'n," said the old lady, as she settled herself comfortably in her chair.

"Thank you, dear Aunt Sophie. And now if you will excuse me for a few moments, I will go and let the baroness know that you are here. She will be delighted," said Lilith, rising, and leaving the room to tell the good news.

CHAPTER XIX

ANCILLON'S REVELATIONS

Doubt is the effect of fear or jealousy,
Two passions which to reason give the lie;
For fear torments and never doth assist;
And jealousy is love lost in a mist.
Both hoodwink truth and play at blind man's buff,
Cry "Here" and "There," seem quite direct enough;
But all the while shift place, making the mind,
As it gets out of breath, despair to find;
Or if at last something it stumbles on,
Perhaps it calls it false, and then 'tis gone.
If true, what's gained? Only just time to see
A breathless play—a game of fantasy
That has no other end than this: that men
Run to be tired, just to sit down again.

Anon.

AUNT SOPHIE, left to herself, got up with a childish curiosity to look around on the elegant chamber to which she had been introduced—the furniture all made of some wood that looked like ivory, and up-holstered in rose satin and white lace.

"Too fine to live in," she said to herself, as she stood before the beautifully draped dressing-table, with its broad and tall mirror filling up all the space between the two front windows, and curtained, like them, with rose silk and white lace, and with its toilet service of Bohemian glass and gold.

She turned from this to the richly festooned alcove, in which stood the luxurious bedstead, and from that view to the inviting chairs and lounges, her wonder and admiration growing with all that she saw.

She was still moving around, when the door opened, and Lilith appeared, ushering in the baroness—Lilith

in her simple black silk dress, and Madame Von
Bruyin in an elegant negligée of pale mauve velvet,
edged with swan's-down.

She advanced to Aunt Sophie with smiling eyes and
outstretched hands, exclaiming brightly:

"My dear Mrs. Downie! I am so rejoiced to see
you! You have come to us so opportunely! How
opportunely you shall soon know. Why, only to-day we
were to write to you and ask you to come. You have
only anticipated our very great desire to see you."

"Indeed you are very good to say so, ma'am, I'm
sure. It was the sinner who made me come, whether
or no; and I was so awful 'fraid I was intruding," said
the child-like old lady, in simple truth, as she placed
both her plump little hands in the warm, welcoming
clasp of her hostess.

"You are looking so well; and Lilith tells me you
had a fine voyage."

"Yes, thank you, ma'am; I had an awful fine voyage, considering the season of the year; and it done
me a heap of good."

"I can see that it has. Sit down now and let us
be comfortable," said the baroness, drawing one of
the luxurious chairs nearer to Aunt Sophie, who
smiled and bowed in a deprecating little way before
she took it.

When they were all seated near what seemed to be
a beautiful vase, but what was in reality the porcelain stove that heated the room, Aunt Sophie broke
out in child-like admiration:

"I never seen a stove like this in all my life before.
I didn't think as they could make stoves out'n anything but iron."

"We don't have them in our own country," said
Lilith. "At least I never saw one."

The baroness smiled, and then changed the subject by asking Aunt Sophie about the health and wel-

fare of her inmates, and the prosperity of her house.
And the old lady answered with simple truth, relat-
ing all about the poor young theological student
whose only pair of Sunday trousers she had inad-
vertently brought away; and all about the coming
marriage of her favorite boarder, Mrs. Farquier, and
Elder Perkins, of their church.

The baroness listened with sympathetic attention,
and after a few more cordial words of congratulation
or of inquiry, the lady said:

"Now, Mrs. Downie, you will please tell me the
name of the hotel you stopped at, so that I may send
and have your effects brought hither."

"The hotel where I stopped, ma'am?" said Aunt
Sophie, with a slightly puzzled air.

"Yes, Mrs. Downie; I wish to know so that I may
send for your trunk."

"Why, it was the same place where the sinner is
stopping!"

"But where is that, my dear friend? What is its
name?" smilingly inquired Madame Von Bruyin.

"The hotel—le' me see, now—what was the name
of that hotel ag'in? The sinner did tell me; but
there! my poor head has been in that whirl ever since
I was snatched away so suddenly and fetched over
here that I declare to man I haven't got no memory
left! I ought to remember that name, too, 'cause
it sounded for all the world like a name in a ballad
or a fairy story, and as if it might 'a' been the palace
of the fairy queen or the enchanted princess. What
was it, ag'in? Oh! I know. It was the Hotel of Love,
on the Rue River. That's what it was. Now ain't
that just like a place in a ballad or a fairy story?"
inquired Aunt Sophie, with a smile. "Just fancy it!
The Hotel of Love on the Rue River!"

The baroness looked helplessly and hopelessly perplexed.

"The Hotel du Louvre, Rue de Rivoli," suggested Lilith, in a low tone.

"Oh, certainly! I see! Touch the bell, if you please, my dear," said Madame Von Bruyin.

Lilith complied, and the baroness gave her instructions to the servant that answered the summons.

"And now, my dear," said the lady, rising to leave the room, "I have some papers to sign, and Monsieur Le Grange is waiting for me. Make our dear guest as comfortable as you can, and here, my dear, give her the choice of the vacant chambers on the other side."

And with a smile and a bow the beautiful hostess left the room.

"Come, Aunt Sophie, and select your bower!" said Lilith, playfully, as she arose.

The simple-hearted widow gathered her belongings and prepared to follow her guide.

Lilith led the old lady across the hall and opened the door of a chamber opposite the one they had just left, and introduced her into the most elegant apartment she had ever seen.

It was upholstered in satin-wood, pale blue velvet embroidered with silver and white lace.

Aunt Sophie hesitated to sit down in her black alpaca gown on any of the elegantly covered chairs, and feared to lay down her black shawl and mashed bonnet anywhere, lest they should soil the delicate draperies.

At length Lilith relieved her funny embarrassment by taking those articles from her hands and hanging them in a handsome armoire, the door of which was one sheet of crystal mirror.

And then the simple old lady looked at the dressing table with its draperies of pale blue velvet and fine white lace, and its accessories of pearl combs and pearl-handled brushes, and gold vases, and

flaçons, and thence to the bed with its costly hangings of the same velvet and lace, in such distressing
embarrassment that Lilith said to her at length:

"Madame Von Bruyin wished me to give you your
choice of all the vacant chambers. If you do not like
this one, I can show you a plainer."

"Oh, yes, please do, honey! This is so awful grand!
I wouldn't dare to sit down on one of these chairs,
and as to lying down in that grand bed—I couldn't
dream of such a thing! And that sounds so ungrate-
ful of me, too, when the baroness is giving me the
best of everything! But, honey, I ain't used to it,
and I couldn't get used to it, and that is the solemn
truth, so I hope you'll excuse me," said the old lady,
in her soft, slow, deprecating tones.

"There is nothing in this world too good for you,
dear Aunt Sophie! There is indeed scarcely anything
good enough for you, we think," said Lilith, as she
took the little black bonnet and shawl from the
armoire in which she had hung them, and led the way
down the corridor to the rear of the building and
opened a door at its extremity, and ushering the guest
into a pretty, bright, fresh chamber, furnished in
curled maple and gay chintz.

"How do you like this room?" inquired Lilith.

"Oh! ever so much better than t'other one! I ain't
afraid of hurting anything here!"

"And you can make yourself quite comfortable?"

"Oh, yes, awful comfortable, honey."

"Your trunks will be here very soon," said Lilith,
as, still acting in her rôle of lady's maid to the visitor,
she hung up Aunt Sophie's bonnet, shawl and hand-
bag in the maple-wood wardrobe.

Then she sat down to "keep company" with the old
lady until her boxes should arrive to give her some
employment.

"I hope you will tell the baroness that I ralely

didn't expect this! I ralely didn't mean to intrude. I only come this morning with the sinner to call and pay my respects to the baroness and see you, honey, and then go back to the Hotel of Love. I never would have presumed to come and set down on you all without an invitation," said Aunt Sophie, in a soft, slow, deprecating tone.

Lilith went and kissed her gently before replying:

"You did not come without an invitation, and a very pressing one. You cannot doubt how pleased Madame Von Bruyin is to see you, or how happy I am to have you here."

"I know you are all awful good to me. I know that," said Aunt Sophie.

A little later on her trunk arrived and was brought up into her room, and Aunt Sophie made the best of her limited wardrobe to dress for dinner.

Simple as any child, she accepted all the aid that Lilith could give her, even obediently submitting to have her unruly hair "fixed," and to wear the pretty little lace cap, fichu and cuffs that Lilith's deft fingers constructed from her own materials.

Aunt Sophie liked herself in this new dress, and did not hesitate to say so.

The dinner that followed soon was served in what was known in the maison as the petit salon. There was no one present but Madame Von Bruyin, Lilith, Mrs. Downie and Monsieur Le Grange, whom Aunt Sophie mistook for a preacher of the gospel, and ever after referred to as the old minister.

Lilith saw no more of Mr. Alfred Ancillon, or Señor Zuniga, during that day.

The next morning, after breakfast, the baroness went out shopping as usual, but excused Lilith from attending her, and took Aunt Sophie instead, "to show her the shops," as she said.

They had not left the house more than half an hour,

when a card was brought to Lilith bearing the name, Señor Zuniga.

And Lilith went down into the small drawing-room to receive him alone.

"Madame Von Bruyin has gone out and has taken Mrs. Downie with her," said Lilith, when their mutual greetings had passed.

"Ah! I am glad! Well as I like the beautiful baroness and the good Aunt Sophie, I can dispense with their society this morning, for I wish to talk with you alone," he said, seating himself by her side on the sofa. "I told you yesterday that I had much to say to you."

"Yes," she replied.

"Hereward, you say, is still at the Court of ——?"

"Yes."

"And yet you have never heard from him?"

"No."

"He does not know that you are living?"

"No."

"Well, neither did I until an accident revealed your continued existence to me. I will tell you all about that by and by. Now I tell you, Lilith, that he must learn the truth."

"Oh, no! no! Do not bring me in any way to his notice," she pleaded, clasping her hands and fixing her eyes upon him in the earnestness of her entreaty.

"But why not, now that you are able to clear up the mystery that separated you?" demanded Zuniga, in astonishment.

"Oh, because he does not love me. He never loved me! He told me so with his own lips," moaned Lilith, wringing her hands.

"No heroics, if you please, child. I get quite enough of them on the stage. I hate them off it. But tell · me, in a matter of fact way, did you really believe him when he said that?"

"Oh, yes! Oh, yes! For he spoke in the most bitter, scornful, insulting manner. He said that he should leave the house, never to return while I desecrated it with my presence. Desecrated it, mind. That was what drove me away, and what will keep me away from him," she wailed, twisting her hands together.

"Pray don't be melodramatic, Lilith, my dear. I am so tired of that sort of thing that I have left the stage forever, I hope. But tell me quietly and sensibly when and under what circumstances Hereward talked such very objectionable nonsense."

"It was on that fatal twenty-first of March when——"

"There you go again. There was nothing fatal about it. However, proceed."

"It was on the twenty-first of March, then, that he came down suddenly to Cloud Cliffs. That letter which you had written to me had fallen into his hands, and he rushed down to Cloud Cliffs, just as I feared he would, in a——"

"Deuce of a rage. Quite natural under the circumstances. Well?"

"He came in just after I had read your last letter, which was even more compromising than your first, and as I was about to drop it into the fire he seized it from me——"

"Very rude of him."

"And he read it."

"Quite so. It was what we should have expected of him. Proceed."

"And then—— But, oh, indeed, I cannot describe the scene that followed."

"You needn't. I can see it all. The fat was in the fire. There was a fiz, a blaze, a conflagration!"

"I cannot blame him for his anger then. The circumstances were so criminating. He demanded an explanation, but I could give him none without betraying your secret, which I was sworn to keep. It ended, as I told you, in his declaring that he did not love me, congratulating himself that he had never fallen into the deep degradation of loving me, and saying that he would leave the house, never to return while I should desecrate it with my presence."

"Very melodramatic, and consequently very nonsensical, as all heroics are off the stage. And you believed him?"

"Yes; for I left the house that night."

"And you still believe him, eh?"

"Yes; for I will never make known my existence to him."

"What a baby you must be, Lilith, to believe all the ravings of a man maddened by jealousy. Why, child! you were no sooner gone than he 'sought you sorrowing' all over the country. A month later the body of a poor, unfortunate young woman who once belonged to our troupe, and was the wife of a man who sometimes acted under my name, was found in the woods in such a state of decomposition that it could not be recognized; but it was dressed in a suit of your clothes, which were readily enough identified by all your servants, so that the sapient coroner's jury who sat upon the remains brought in a verdict that—'Lilith Hereward came to her death by a blow on the back of her head from some blunt instrument held in the hand of some person unknown to the jury.' When Hereward learned this verdict he fell like a slaughtered ox; and he knew no more of life for weeks——"

"Oh!" cried Lilith, involuntarily.

"In the meantime, I, out in California, knew nothing of what was going on in West Virginia until a month after that coroner's inquest—until one day I met with an old copy of the *Pursuivant*, in which I read a full account of your supposed fate. Then, my child, I understood, or thought I understood, what had happened—that your death had been caused, directly or indirectly, by the jealous rage of your husband; and I threw up my engagement and traveled as fast as steam could take me to West Virginia and to the presence of Tudor Hereward. I found him the mere shadow of his former self."

Lilith moaned.

"But I did not pity him in the least! I bitterly upbraided him for having been the cause of your death, as I fully believed him to have been. I am afraid I even became melodramatic over it all, which was very unprofessional off the stage, you know. He never sought to excuse or defend himself. Still I had no mercy on him. I rubbed it into him. To deepen his remorse for his wrong to you, I gave him the secret! What cared I then for any consequences to myself? I gave him the secret!"

"What! You told—you told him—who you were!" exclaimed Lilith.

"No, I did better than that. He might not have believed my word. I told him nothing. But I directed him to the papers in the old trunk for all information and all proof. And then I left him and went to the village hotel and waited for events. But nothing happened, and at last I heard that he had gone to Washington to accept some foreign mission that had been offered him. Then I also left the neighborhood and went to the Southwest. I took no further pains to conceal my identity; yet no evil happened to me. No requisition under the extradition treaty was made for me. But, Lilith, my child, you are cleared from suspicion in the eyes of your husband. He has the secret!"

"Oh, no, he has not!" exclaimed Lilith. "He has not! For those papers to which you referred him

for information were not in the house! I brought
them away with me when I left Cloud Cliffs."

"You brought them away with you!"

"Yes, for I would not leave them there to endanger
you. So, you see, he does not yet know that I am
innocent."

"I am sorry that he did not find the papers. But,
Lilith, my darling, he does know that you are innocent. He came to his senses from the very day in
which he lost you. All that I heard about him in his
own neighborhood proved his profound sorrow at your
loss and his faith in your integrity."

"And yet he told me——"

"Never mind what he told you. He was mad with
jealousy then, and his words must not be remembered.
He loves you, I am sure. He always loved you. I
tell you this—I who know something of human
nature."

"Oh, if I thought so! Oh, if I thought so!"

"Now, now, now, now, don't be stagey! Hereward
loves you devotedly. I was sure of it when I talked
with him of you. It was not only remorse for his
cruel suspicions, but sorrow for your loss, that was
almost driving him mad!"

"He had but little cause for remorse about his suspicions. The circumstances were so criminating."

"And your life and character so vindicating."

"Was it accident that led you to Aunt Sophie's
house?" inquired Lilith at last.

"Yes and no. I will explain. After I had made
a short theatrical tour in the Territories I came East
and to New York. I was so reckless that I did not
care what might become of me. I was on Broadway
one day, when I saw your picture in a photographer's
show-case. I did not then connect it with any idea
that you were still in the land of the living, but
fancied that it was a photograph that might have

been taken for your foster-father, the summer before your marriage when you were on your last trip with him."

"No, it was taken just before I sailed from New York, for Aunt Sophie. She wanted a picture of me, and she took me to a photographer who was a member of her church and for whom one of her lady boarders colored the photographs," Lilith explained.

"So I learned later. Having no picture of you, my darling, and wishing to possess one, I went in to the artist and asked to buy a copy. He told me that he could not sell one without permission from the customer who had had the photograph taken. I told him that the customer and the original of the picture were both dead. At this he stared and said that he guessed not, unless they had died very recently. And then the artist told me that the pictures had been taken by the order of an old lady friend of his own, and of a young girl boarding in her house then, but now away to Europe. Still I had no suspicion that they represented my living Lilith, but believed the likeness to be an accidental one, though so good that I wished to possess a copy. So I requested the artist to give me the address of the customer for whom they had been taken. He very readily obliged me. I went to Mrs. Downie's house the same day. Seeing her sign out, I requested the girl who answered my ring to take my card to her mistress. While I was waiting in the parlor I saw your photograph on the mantelpiece. I took it down and examined it minutely, a faint suspicion coming like hope into my heart that it might be yours after all. I turned to the back and read the inscription, 'To Aunt Sophie, with the love of Lilith,' or something to that effect. My child, I am not given to wild emotion—off the stage—and yet I was so overcome with joy and fear that I dropped upon a chair, and had some trouble to compose myself before the landlady came in. But in that short space of time I had resolved to take board in the house, if possible, in order to find out all about you. So when Aunt Sophie came in I broached the subject of board and lodging, and the good creature consented to receive me."

"Yes, she wrote to me about that," said Lilith.

"But I governed my strong anxiety and refrained from asking her questions about the original of that photograph for a few hours, and then began cautiously to examine her. It is needless to say that I learned all she knew of you."

"Did you return the confidence, and supplement her small knowledge of my antecedents by telling her all you knew of me?" inquired Lilith.

"Only by saying that you were a very near and dear relative of mine."

"So much she herself wrote to me; but she wrote of you as Mr. Ancillon, and yet she speaks of you as Señor Zuniga——"

"Yes. I took board with her as Alfred Ancillon. I did not wish, in the case of my arrest under the extradition treaty, to bring an old and proud name into that connection. And so it was not until after I had seen your advertisement, and searched the files of the *Pursuivant* and discovered my full vindication from that imputed crime, that I determined to resume my own name. When we were once on board the steamer, I told Mrs. Downie that Ancillon was only my professional name, by which I think she understood that I was a literary man writing under that nomme de plume, but that my true name was Zuniga. You look very much astonished, Lilith."

"I am astonished. I have been wondering in a state of the deepest perplexity over that whole matter!" exclaimed Lilith.

"Wondering why I called myself Zuniga?"

"Yes."

"Why, my dear, because of all my names, professional or otherwise, that is the one to which I have the best right."

"Were you—were you, then—were you——"

"The Señor Zuniga of Washington society?"

"Yes."

"Of course I was. You recognized me at first sight, and so also did Hereward, as I saw by your amazed looks, although afterwards you were both persuaded that you were only deceived by a very striking likeness."

"Yes, we were. For we knew you as Mr. Ancillon, and believed the professional announcement that you had gone to California——"

"When my stage name loaned to another member of the troupe alone had gone."

"But believing as we did, how could we imagine you to be identical with Señor Zuniga, the nephew of the P—— minister? Even now I cannot understand it."

"But you will when I tell you the whole of my story, Lilith."

"And you acted your part so well! When you were introduced to us you looked so sublimely indifferent and unconscious of ever having seen us before. And, besides, though you looked so nearly identical with Alfred Ancillon, there were really striking points of dissimilarity."

Señor Zuniga broke into one of his wild laughs, and then said :

"Exactly! Precisely! There were striking points of dissimilarity. When I dropped my stage name and character, and took up my real ones, I made no coarse disguise of other colored hair or complexion. Not at all. I just gave the ends of my very peculiar and characteristic eyebrows a quarter of an inch's twist upward instead of downward, with the aid of a camel's hair brush and a little Indian ink, and the ends of my mustache a corresponding droop downward instead of upward, and the character of my countenance and expression was changed. This, with my 'sublime unconsciousness' of which you spoke, your prepossessed idea that I had gone to California, en route for Australia, together with the utter improbability that Alfred Ancillon, the strolling player, should have anything in common with Señor Zuniga, the nephew of the P—— minister, completed the illusion."

"It did, indeed."

"And so, my child, as Señor Zuniga, I enjoyed opportunities of conversing with you such as I should never have been permitted to do as Alfred Ancillon."

"But now you are forever Zuniga?"

"Yes, forever Zuniga."

"And as the baroness may return before you leave, I must present you to her—by what name?"

"By my true name, of course. By the only name —now that my character is cleared from the faintest shadow of reproach—by which I shall henceforth be known—Zuniga."

They talked on for an hour longer, asking and answering questions, but Zuniga was reticent about one matter—his right to the name he claimed.

"I will tell you later, Lilith," was all the explanation that he would give of his reserve.

While they were still talking, the door of the drawing-room swung open and the baroness, accompanied by Aunt Sophie, entered the room.

Lilith and her visitor arose to receive them.

"Madame Von Bruyin," said Lilith, addressing her patroness with a slight gesture of her hand towards her visitor, "please permit me to present to you the Señor Zuniga, my father."

The gentleman bowed profoundly; the lady graciously, saying:

"I am glad to see you, señor. Your daughter is a dear young friend of mine. Pray resume your seat. I hope that you will favor us with your company at luncheon."

"I thank you, madame, I shall be very happy," replied the señor, with another bow.

But there was one figure in the group that stood transfixed, staring with eyes and mouth wide open, then muttering:

"Why—why—why—I didn't know—why—why— why——"

But she could get no further.

Lilith went and put her arms around the old lady's neck, and murmured, softly:

"Yes, Aunt Sophie, he is my dear father. I will tell you all about it by and by."

"But—how come he, the sinner, to be your father?" inquired the dazed old lady.

Lilith laughed, and answered:

"I suppose because he married my mother."

The luncheon bell rang, and the baroness requested Señor Zuniga to give his arm to Mrs. Downie.

At this moment Monsieur Le Grange joined the group and was informally introduced to the Señor Zuniga.

The whole party then moved to the small salon, where the luncheon table was spread, and where Madame Von Bruyin's liveried servants were in attendance.

The light meal passed off very pleasantly—the señor being more than usually brilliant in sparkling wit and anecdote.

Soon after their return to the drawing-room Zuniga

took leave, pleading that he had to run down to Calais that night to catch the earliest boat to Dover, but that he hoped to be in Paris again within a few days.

As soon as he was gone the baroness was eloquent in his praise. She commended his dark beauty, grace, elegance of person, his brilliancy in conversation and so forth.

CHAPTER XX

UNEXPECTED MEETING AT A WEDDING

WITHIN a week from the day of his departure the Señor Zuniga returned to Paris.

He found such favor in the eyes of the baroness, that he became an habitué of the house.

They were, indeed, often closeted together in long interviews that set Aunt Sophie and Lilith to speculating.

"I think it is something about you, honey. Indeed, I feel sure of it!" said the old lady to her young favorite; and in fact she was right, as the event proved.

Aunt Sophie herself had grown to be more and more of a favorite with every member of the family.

The baroness, without consulting her companion, had put the old lady in possession of much of Lilith's history that had hitherto been kept from her.

Madame Von Bruyin had also explained to Mrs. Downie that she should remain at the house as companion and protectress to Lilith while the soon-to-be-wedded couple should be on their wedding tour.

And Aunt Sophie, with many deprecating sighs and self-disparaging disclaimers, had finally consented to do so.

"And while we are gone, Monsieur Le Grange and

Lilith can show you all the wonders of Paris and its environs," Madame Von Bruyin added, as an inducement or a consolation.

"I am sure I have already seen more than I ever expected to see in all the days of my life," said the old lady, with simple candor.

Preparations for the marriage went steadily on.

Paris was beginning to fill with fashionables, returning from the sea-shore or mountain height. The wedding cards were out. Some of the most unique jewels and costumes prepared for the occasion were on exhibition in the show-cases of the most recherché bazaars.

The public journals were sparkling with descriptions of the costly presents in course of preparation.

The Prince Gherardini had arrived in town and taken apartments at the Grand Hotel du Louvre.

The princely wedding was to be the opening event of the season.

The two sisters of the prince, the Princesses Bianca and Julietta, were to be the first and second bridesmaids, and six young ladies, selected from the most noble families of the French capital, were to complete the bridal retinue.

On Monday of the last week in November, a small party collected in the little salon of the maison to witness the signing of the marriage contract.

This party consisted of the Baroness Von Bruyin, Monsieur Le Grange, Lilith Hereward, Señor Zuniga and Mrs. Downie, on the part of the bride elect, and Prince Gherardini, the Princesses Bianca and Julietta, and the Marquis Orsini, on the part of the bridegroom.

Besides these there were two notaries public with their clerks.

On this occasion the baroness was richly dressed

in a Mazarin blue velvet, trained, and trimmed with ermine, and ornaments of pearls and sapphire.

The two young princesses wore white satin embroidered with rosebuds.

Lilith, ruby velvet, point lace and pearls.

Aunt Sophie, black satin, with white lace shawl and white lace cap—all presents from the baroness.

The gentlemen wore the conventional black swallow-tail coat, black vest and black trousers, with white neck-tie and white gloves.

When the contract was signed the whole party adjourned to the dining-salon, where a rich and rare repast was spread for their refreshment.

And after this they separated amid hearty congratulations.

The next day, Tuesday, the same party met at the Mairie, where the civil ceremony, which the French law requires, was duly observed.

But the grand pageant of the ecclesiastical rites came off at the Church of St. Genevieve about noon on Thursday.

At an early hour of the forenoon the church was crowded with the nobility, fashion and beauty of Paris.

The Archbishop of ——, attended by two bishops, all in their sacred vestments, were in readiness to officiate.

At half-past eleven the bridal train entered the church.

First came the bride, leaning on the arm of her old friend, the Duc de L——. She was, of course, the observed of all observers. She wore a trained dress of white Genoa velvet, richly embroidered with seed pearls and trimmed with marabout feathers. Being a widow, she wore no orange blossoms; but her golden tresses were crowned with a diadem of pearls and diamonds in three bands, while down on the graceful neck floated a tuft of marabout feathers and over all the sumptuous costume flowed a rich old cardinal point lace vail. Pearl and diamond necklace in a dozen graded festoons encircled her fair neck and lay upon her white bosom. Pearl and diamond bracelets clasped the lovely arms. Kid gloves, embroidered with small pearls, and trimmed with point lace, covered the slender yet plump hands. White boots to match the gloves encased the shapely feet. In her hand she carried a bouquet of rare white exotics.

Behind her followed eight bridesmaids, in thread lace dresses, looped with rosebuds, over white silk skirts; white gloves, wreaths and bouquets of white rosebuds.

Lilith wore a trained dress of ivory-white brocade satin, trimmed with duchess lace; pearl necklace and bracelets on her pretty neck and arms, and a pearl bandeau in her dark hair.

Aunt Sophie was very grand in a black flowered satin, a black velvet dolman, and a black plush bonnet —all the gifts forced upon her acceptance by the baroness. The bridegroom, with his attendants, came out of the vestry as the bride's party filed up the aisle to the music of Mendelssohn's wedding march.

The two parties met at the altar and kneeled upon the hassocks prepared for them.

. The music ceased, and the ceremony began. It was rather more lengthy, stately and solemn than such rites usually are. But at last it was over; the benediction was pronounced; the register was signed and witnessed; intimate friends crowded around the newly-married pair with congratulations more or less sincere.

It was one o'clock before the bridal cortège and the wedding congregation entered their carriages and dispersed, to meet again at four o'clock at the reception to be held at the home of the bride.

At the hour fixed the guests began to arrive, and soon all the reception-rooms were filled with one of the most brilliant crowds that had ever assembled in Paris salons.

The whole house, profusely decorated with the rarest flowers, was thrown open to the guests.

One room of the suite was given up to the exhibition of the wedding presents; tables arranged around the walls and set here and there through the room, were laden with the richest, rarest and most beautiful products of modern art and science in manufactures. Jewels that seemed poems; watches that seemed vital; India shawls that were perfect studies of finest workmanship; services of gold, pearl, porcelain of wonderful grace and elegance in form; laces and embroideries of marvelous pattern and design; dress fabrics of velvet, satin, silk, crêpe, gauze, and so forth, that seemed woven for the wearing of goddesses and fairies rather than for clothing any woman of mere flesh and blood.

This room possessed a great charm for lady guests, who crowded it during the whole two hours of the reception.

Another room was elegantly fitted up for refreshments, that were laid upon many small tables, with services of pure gold and fine porcelain, and attended by servants out of livery who wore the evening dress of gentlemen, varied only by white satin vests, kid gloves and fragrant boutonnières.

Here the greatest skill of the best caterer in Paris had been expended in the many tempting delicacies of the table; and the rarest wines of the southern vineyards added their serpent charm to the feast.

This room found greatest favor from the elder ladies and the gentlemen.

But, after all, the most charming apartment of the many that were thrown open was that in which the bride and groom, the Prince and Princess Gherardini, received their guests.

They stood together near the door. Behind the princess were grouped her eight lovely bridesmaids, and near them sat Aunt Sophie, trying to keep herself out of sight, but enjoying the scene with all the zest of the youngest girl there. On the left of the princess stood Lilith, looking, every one said, the loveliest woman present. She still wore the rich but simple dress of ivory white brocade, and the ornaments of pearl on her bosom, on her arms and in her black hair; and now her cheeks and lips were flushed, and her eyes were brilliant with sympathetic excitement. Lilith, however, had acquired all the ease and grace of the bon ton, so that her animation only added glow and sparkle to her lovely face, and left her form and manner in perfect repose.

The baroness—I beg her pardon—the newly-wedded princess took care to present every one who approached the group to her friend, "Mrs. Wyvil." And every one went away to talk of the beautiful creature. Some to ask others who this lovely Mrs. Wyvil could be; and to be told that she was a very wealthy young American widow, who had made a great sensation during the last season, but who was understood to be on the eve of marriage with some distinguished American statesman, whose name had escaped the memory of the latter, and so forth.

The princess perceived and enjoyed the triumph of her young protégée, even in the midst of her own bridal ovation; and occasionally a humorous smile curled her beautiful lips and lighted her blue eyes, as if she was enjoying in anticipation some rare, good jest; and semi-occasionally, as it were, she slightly craned her graceful neck and tried to look through the nearer crowd and beyond towards the approaching one.

"For whom are you watching, madame?" inquired the prince, in a low voice, as soon as he got an opportunity to speak to his bride.

"Oh, for an old friend of mine whom I particularly pressed to come to us to-day," replied the princess. "And there he is, slowly working his way through this human thicket," she added, as her eyes lighted up with animation.

The prince looked, but there were so many gentlemen approaching from the same direction that he could not distinguish the especial person of whom the lady spoke.

Meanwhile the stranger in question came on, not pushing his way, but rather tacking, like a craft sailing against wind and tide, and suffering himself to be driven this way and that, but always slowly nearing "port."

As he came on, the topic of the hour, the praises of the new beauty—the lovely Mrs. Wyvil—met his ears from all sides—her grace, her wit, her genius, her elegance, her accomplishments were the theme of the salon.

"Wyvil!" he said to himself—"Wyvil! the name is certainly not a common one! Who can she be, I wonder? An American, too! I must see this belle."

The princess, still watching the approach of the stranger, turned to Lilith for an instant and said:

"My love, I wish you would speak to dear Aunt Sophie. There she sits, hiding behind you, quite neglected."

Lilith at once turned around and opened a conversation with the good old lady by asking:

"What do you think of all this?"

"Oh, honey, I'm half scared and half delighted, you know. 'Pears to me I don't know whether I'm in a dream of heaven!" replied the dazed and delighted old lady.

Meanwhile the stranger came up to the bridal group, bowed low before the princess, bowed to the prince, and then spoke the required words of congratulation, and was about to pass on and give place to others who were pressing forward to pay their respects when the princess, laying a light, detaining hand upon his arm, said:

"Pardon. One moment, if you please. I wish to introduce you to a fair compatriot of yours."

"I thank your highness. I shall be most happy," replied the new-comer.

"Lilith, my love," said the princess, in a low voice, to the young lady behind her.

Lilith turned at once.

"Mrs. Wyvil, my dear, permit me to present to you Mr. Tudor Hereward, American Chargé d'Affaires to our Court."

CHAPTER XXI

THAT STARTLING INTRODUCTION

Each in the other can descry
The tone constrained, the altered eye;
They know that each to each can seem
    No longer as of yore;
And yet, while thus estranged, I deem
    Each loves the other more.
Hers is, perhaps, the saddest heart;
His the more forced and painful part;
And troubled now becomes, perforce,
The inevitable intercourse,
    So easy heretofore.

Southey.

A SLIGHT start from Tudor Hereward, and a sudden paleness of Lilith's face, were the only signs of the shock that both had sustained in this unexpected encounter; and even these had been seen by no one except the watchful princess, who had planned the meeting and studied its effect.

Hereward bowed as to any other lady.

Lilith courtesied.

Both grew paler. Neither spoke. The strain was becoming unbearable. Besides, Hereward was stopping the way.

The princess pitied them; and then she became frightened for the result of her own coup-de-théâtre. Should Hereward "lose his head," or Lilith faint, or should they in any other manner bring "admired disorder" into the serene repose of this patrician drawing-room? For nature, when hard pressed, does sometimes break through all the elegant little barriers of convenances and assert itself.

All this flashed through the mind of the princess in a very few seconds, and then—always equal to the occasion—she turned with perfect ease to her latest guest, and said:

"Mr. Hereward, the rooms are close, and Mrs. Wyvil is faint; will you give her the support of you arm to my boudoir? She will show you the way."

Hereward bowed, drew his wife's arm within his own, and led her from the salon by the shortest way indicated only by a gesture from Lilith.

They entered the elegant boudoir, with its walls of fluted white satin, and its furniture and draperies of white satin flowered with gold, and its innumerable treasures of beauty and of art; but they saw none of these things. They might have been in a West Virginia hut, for all consciousness they had of these splendors.

As soon as they entered the room—which had no other occupant—Lilith, sliding from her hold on Hereward's arm, dropped into the nearest chair, as if no longer able to stand.

Hereward bent over her.

No word had passed between them as yet.

"Lilith!" he said, at length.

"Tudor!" she murmured in reply.

"Lilith, is this real? Can this wonder be real, or is it only a phantasm of fever, such as I have often had since I lost you! Oh, Lilith! if this be real, come to me—come to me! Come to me, my own, and let me clasp you to my heart!" he pleaded, holding out his arms.

"Tudor—do you care for me—now?" she inquired, in low and broken tones.

"Do I care for you? Oh, Lilith! so much, so much that your loss has almost destroyed my life! Oh, my love! Oh, my darling. Why, why did you ever leave me? Why, Lilith, why?" he pleaded, earnestly.

"Because," she murmured very low—"because you told me that you had never loved me; you said that you had married me only to please your dying father; you bade me leave your presence, and you added that in a few days you should leave the house, never to return to it while I should desecrate it with my presence."

"I! Did I ever utter such words as those to you —to my wife?" exclaimed Hereward, as soon as he had recovered from the shock of hearing them repeated to him.

"Indeed you did, Tudor. They were stamped— burned—too deeply into my memory ever to be forgotten. I do not give them back to you now in reproach, but only in reply to your question as to why I left you. You see now that I had no alternative. I answered you at the time that I must not be the means of banishing you from your patrimonial home; that since one or the other must go, I myself should leave, and leave you in peaceable possession of your home. Something like this I said to you then, Tudor;

but you bade me begone, and—I obeyed you. That was all," she concluded, in a low, gentle tone.

"I was mad—mad! Not one word that I uttered then was true or rational! Oh, Lilith, I am no more responsible for the words and actions of that hour than is the veriest maniac for his ravings!" he pleaded, sinking over and leaning heavily on the back of the chair that supported her slight frame.

"I know, Tudor," she said, in a humble, deprecating tone—"I know, and I do not criticise you. How could I? The circumstances that surrounded me seemed criminating enough to destroy the faith of the most confiding husband in the world, though he were married to the most faithful wife!"

"And yet they should not have touched my faith in you; the child brought up in my father's house, the child not only loved, but esteemed and honored by my father, and not by him only, but by all his friends and neighbors! No, Lilith, even those surrounding circumstances, though you could not explain them, should never have touched my faith in you! would never have done so, but that I was mad— mad with jealousy! Yes, I confess it. Lilith, can you forgive me for that causeless, injurious jealousy?" he pleaded, bending over her.

"Oh, Tudor! If there were anything to forgive, it was forgiven on that very night in which we parted."

"Ah! why did you go, my Lilith? Why did you let words of frenzy drive you away? Could not you, my gentle child, have been patient with a madman for a little while? Why act upon reproaches that you knew to be undeserved and altogether unreasonable?"

"I knew they were undeserved, but I thought they were very reasonable, under all the circumstances. Oh, Tudor, it was not your reproaches, not your anger, that drove me away from you! I could have borne them and waited for time to vindicate me, to justify me in your sight. No, Tudor, it was not anger nor reproach that drove me away."

"What was it, then?"

"I told you; but you have forgotten it, or misunderstood. Tudor, I had to go. I had no choice. You told me that you did not love me; that you had never loved me, and said that you would go away and never come back while I stayed in the house. But you 'never loved' me. These were the words that drove me from you."

"The words of a maniac!"

"Did you find my farewell letter, left on your bureau, Tudor?"

"Yes—I did."

"Do you remember its contents?"

"Yes. When I think of it I can recall every word. That letter is stamped upon my memory, Lilith, as you say my sentence of banishment is upon yours."

"Then, Tudor, will you now recall what I said on bidding you good-bye? It was something like this —though I cannot recall the precise words—I told you that though I should not trouble you by my presence, or my letters, yet neither should I take any pains to hide myself from you. I told you that if the time should ever come when, after revising your judgment of me, you should see reason to retract your charges against me, and should ask me to return to you, I would return and would be all to you in the future that I had been in the past. Do you remember reading that in my farewell letter, Tudor?"

"Yes, yes! I do, I do! And oh, my child, I do retract all the cruel charges that Satan and false shows ever goaded me to make. I believe you to be as pure in mind and heart and life as any angel that stands before the Throne," he said, bending over her chair.

"Thank Heaven!" she fervently breathed.

"And you forgive me, Lilith?"

"I have more cause to ask forgiveness than to extend it," she answered, humbly.

"No, no!" he exclaimed, deprecatingly.

"Tudor," she said, "you say that you esteem me— that you trust me; and I thank Heaven for that! But —Tudor—do you love me?" she inquired, in a low, thrilling, pathetic tone.

"I love you more than my own life, so help me Heaven!" replied Hereward, in such tones of impassioned earnestness that no one who heard them could have doubted their truth.

Lilith arose and turned, fronting him, and said:

"Then, Tudor, take me, for I am yours, yours entirely—spirit, soul and frame! I say now, as I said once before, there is not, there never was—a pulse in my heart that is not true to you."

These last words were breathed out upon his bosom, to which he had gathered her.

Presently they sat down, he holding her hand within his own, and gazing with infinite content into her beautiful face.

CHAPTER XXII

LOVE'S OVATION

"You have the victory, my own!" he said at last, with a droll smile. "You have triumphed!"

"How triumphed?" inquired Lilith.

"You have drawn me to your side, you have brought me to retract, and yet you have not told me your secret!"

"No! I have not, indeed; but——"

"Nor has any one else told me, nor do I even surmise its nature; in a word, Lilith, I know no more of that mystery now than I knew on that dreadful day when it parted us! And yet I am here beside you, repudiating all my own injurious doubts and suspicions, taking you in perfect love and perfect trust."

"Oh, thank Heaven that you can so take me!" exclaimed Lilith, fervently.

"And now I do not even ask you for your secret."

"Oh, but I can tell you now! I am free to tell you now——"

"But I do not even care to hear it! I do not even ask you by

'What conjuration and what mighty magic'

you, my little country girl, are here in Paris, arrayed and lodged in royal magnificence, and gracing more than any other lady in it the salon of Madame la Princesse Gherardini. I am so perfectly satisfied for the present just to have you by my side."

"I bless you for your faith and your forbearance, Tudor! But—I can tell you the secret of Monsieur Ancillon's correspondence with me in one single word. He is my—father!"

"Your father, Lilith! Ancillon your father!"

"Yes, though I never knew it until after we were married."

"Ancillon your father! Incredible! Are you sure of that?"

"Quite sure."

"How did you discover the fact? Did he tell you?"

"I first discovered it by the packet of old letters and papers put away in that trunk which was the sole legacy of my dear mother to me."

"Ah! Ah! Ancillon himself, when he came to me once at Cloud Cliffs, referred me to those documents; but when I had the trunk broken open and searched, the papers were gone!"

"I had brought them away for safe keeping. They were too important to be left."

"I understand now! I understand. But, Lilith! We all thought your parentage was so well known that there could be no mistake about it! Your father and mother lived at Seawood. Your father was drowned in saving my life. Your mother died of the shock the very day of your birth. How, then, is it possible that this man can claim to be your father?"

"Oh, Tudor, it is a long and sad story. There is no time to tell it to you now; but this much I can tell: Joseph Wyvil and Elizabeth, who lived such a secluded life at Seawood that their neighbors knew little or nothing of them except that they belonged to the village church, and led quiet, industrious and blameless lives—were not husband and wife as people took them to be—but a devoted brother and a most unfortunate young sister, who had lost her husband by a fate much worse than death. More than this I cannot tell you now. Both died too suddenly to confide the secret to any one. So I was registered as the child of Joseph and Elizabeth Wyvil, when in fact I was the child of Alphonzo and Elizabeth Zuniga!"

"Zuniga!"

"Yes."

"Then Ancillon is a relative of that young Spaniard we met in Washington who looked so much like him?"

"He was the same. Ancillon and Zuniga were one. Ancillon was his professional name, Zuniga was his family name."

"A very strange story, Lilith."

"My father will give you every particular as soon as your convenience permits him to do so. And I shall furnish the documents that shall prove the truth of his story."

"How is it, my child, that you could not at the very first have told me that Ancillon was your father?

That you are now at liberty to tell that secret which cost you so much to keep a year ago?"

"Because I am now in possession of the sequel to the secret, without which I could never have told the secret. But you shall know all from my father. I think, also, I ought to tell you how I happen to be in Paris with the Princess Gherardini. I can do so in a very few words. When I left home I went to New York, found a home with a good Christian, motherly woman, the widow of a clergyman. After waiting many weeks to hear from you, without success, I answered a lady's advertisement for a traveling companion, and was so fortunate as to be accepted and to enter the household of the Baroness Von Bruyin, now, since morning, the Princess, Gherardini. I did not know that she was your first love. In telling me the story you had not told me any names. She grew to love me. I know not why——"

"Why does every one love you, child?"

"Ah, I don't know that every one does! I don't even think that many do. Madame Von Bruyin has always treated me with the distinction of an honored guest and the affection of a beloved sister. You saw me in her immediate circle to-day. That has always been my place."

"She is a much nobler and more generous woman than I had ever supposed her to be."

"Oh, she is indeed! But, Tudor! Tell me how you came to be here at this wedding reception, when I supposed you to be at the Court of ——?"

"My love, I received a pressing letter from the baroness, not only inviting but commanding, exhorting and entreating me to come; going through all the variations of the potential mood to compel me to come. In short, darling, it was such a letter as could not be gainsayed. I obeyed, thinking that the lady only wanted an opportunity to say—Hail! and Farewell!

to an old friend. I came and found my lost treasure! And now I know her motive was to restore that treasure to my possession. And I thank and bless her for it."

"Amen and amen!" breathed Lilith.

"But, dearest dear! She introduced you as Mrs. Wyvil! How was that?"

"Oh, Tudor, I dreamed that some one in a high, delirious fever had told me that I must never call myself by the name of Hereward again, and I was so foolish as to take the sick man at his word."

"I remember! I remember! Oh, Lilith! How much you have to forgive!"

"I have nothing to forgive! nothing! I am just as happy as a lark!"

"My darling, since you entered Madame Von Bruyin's family under the name of Wyvil, how could she have known or guessed that you were my wife?"

Lilith paused and reflected, and then she answered:

"I am not pledged to secrecy in this matter; yet, if you were not my husband, and if I were not fully resolved never to have a secret, either of my own or of any one else's, from you, I should not tell you this; for women should not betray women, especially to the common enemy; but I know you are not vain, Tudor, and you are generous."

"Now, if you object——"

"I do not object—I insist on telling you."

"Go on, then."

"You know she was your first love——"

"My first—and last—hallucination! You, Lilith, were my first and enduring love," amended Hereward.

"Oh! thank Heaven!" breathed the young wife, almost inaudibly; then she said:

"You were not quite just to her, Tudor. The old baron whom she married was more of a father than a husband to her; he doted on her from her infancy.

She was the only creature in the world that he loved
—except her father."

"She told me that."

"He engaged himself to her that he might give her
a title and leave her his fortune."

"She did not need his fortune. She was the heiress
of great wealth."

"I know, but still he wished to leave his darling
all he possessed."

"He might have done that without marrying her."

"Yes, but he wished also to give her his title; the
title which—they said—he meant to ask of the emperor, in lieu of the payment of many millions loaned
by him during the war. He wished to ennoble his
pet."

"Well, love? What has all this got to do with your
telling the baroness your story?" inquired Hereward,
with a smile.

"Everything! You shall hear. This old man, who
loved without self-love, discovered that his fair betrothed was very unhappy, and pressed her for the
reason. That she should have a sorrow that he could
not comfort, with all his wealth and power, seemed
as wonderful as it was insupportable! He pressed
her for her confidence, and she gave it to him—told
him—well, she told him, in effect, that she would
rather marry Mr. Tudor Hereward than Herr Bruyin.
And he released her from her engagement to himself, and promised to win over her father to consent
to her marriage with you. When you returned to
Washington, she sought you out and offered the hand
that she had once refused. But you, being then
married, could not accept it. Tudor! were you sorry?"

"I am not sorry now, dearest, at all events," he
answered, drawing the little figure closer to his side.

"Of course, sorrow, disappointment and humiliation preyed upon the spoiled beauty. Your marriage

with me was announced, and Herr Bruyin, who was still watching over his darling, knew then the three-fold cause of her anguish. He went to her and reminded her that their marriage had been announced some weeks before, and that the announcement had not been contradicted, and he proposed to her to let their betrothal stand; to marry at the appointed time; to go with him to Europe; and, in the grand tour and at the great capitals, where she would be welcomed and fêted, to forget the disappointments she had experienced here. She followed his counsel, and they were married and went abroad. I tell you this, Tudor, that you may be just to her; for now you see that she was not a double-dealer; she was not deceitful; she was perfectly frank with you and with her old betrothed, from first to last."

"Then I have wronged her in my judgment. And it begins to seem to me that I am rather given to wronging people, eh, Lilith?"

"No, you are not. You have been misled by false appearances, which were nobody's fault."

"You, at least, are very charitable, Lilith. But go on, dear."

"You know, I suppose, that Herr Bruyin received his title soon after his arrival in his native city, and that he survived the event but a few months, and that Herr Von Kirschberg died about the same time?"

"Yes, I heard that."

"Madame Von Bruyin, bereft of husband and father, returned to New York early in April. In May she advertised for a companion. I applied for the situation, pleased madame, and was accepted, as I told you. She knew me only as Mrs. Wyvil and believed me to be a widow. She grew very fond of me——"

"Very naturally."

"We were to sail by the Kron Prinz on the first of June."

"Why, I sailed on the Kron Prinz, on the first of June!" Hereward interrupted.

"Exactly. And that was the very reason why we did not. And now comes the crisis of my story—the reason why I was compelled to discover my real name and position to Madame the Baroness. She had seen the account of your appointment as Secretary of Legation, coupled with the theory that you had accepted the post mainly for the sake of serving the country in a place far removed from the spot associated with the tragic death of your wife——"

"'Young and lovely wife,' I think they put it, Lilith," said Hereward, with a droll smile. "Well, it was true, so far as I know. My health had broken down under the heavy blow of your loss and your supposed death, Lilith. And when I was convalescent I eagerly snatched at the opportunity of leaving a home that had become hateful to me, and of seeking distraction, not consolation, not forgetfulness, in new scenes and new duties. And madame saw my name in the published list of passengers, I suppose?"

"Yes; curiosity, a very natural curiosity, led her to read the list of cabin passengers by the Kron Prinz, to see who were to be our fellow-passengers, and she saw your name there. In another part of the paper she had seen the account of your voyage and its causes, of which I have just told you. But, Tudor, she did not tell me all this until we were out at sea. On that day when she sent for me she gave me, as I said, only an outline of her reasons. She told me that there was a party going out by the Kron Prinz with whom she did not choose to travel."

"A very proper decision, under the very peculiar circumstances. But what has that got to do——"

"I am rapidly coming to that, Tudor. After we had sailed, when the pilot left us and we were far out of sight of land, Madame Von Bruyin gave me her whole confidence. She told me the story of her early betrothal with an old millionaire; and of her first love —or fancied love—into which her inexperienced heart had betrayed her. She told me everything just as I have told it to you."

"And as I had told you, months before," put in Hereward.

"Yes; but you gave me the facts from your point of view, and she gave them to me from her own. And hers was the true view, Tudor."

"Yes, I acknowledge that."

"She said that in her position and in yours—both so recently bereaved—she could not possibly think of crossing the ocean in the same ship with you. And then, Tudor, she added an explanation that made my hair stand on end—so to speak."

"Ah! what was that which could have straightened these pretty, rippling locks and made them stand erect 'like quills upon the fretful porcupine?' " gayly inquired Hereward, as he passed his hand fondly over her little curly black head.

"She told me that in a few months you (she and yourself) would probably meet in ——. And, in short, that—both being free to form new ties—the old interest in each other would be revived; that after the year of mourning had been past, you two would, of course, marry, and that she should do everything in her power to atone to you for all the disappointment she had caused you, and to make your life happy! Was not that enough to make my hair bristle up on end—to hear another woman tell me to my face that she was going to marry my husband and live happy all the rest of their lives?"

Hereward broke into a merry laugh.

"You know, I could not let her go on dreaming that dream. I told her she must not think of such a thing. And when, being very much astonished at my assurance, she asked me why she must not, I told her because it would be a deadly sin, for that Mr. Hereward's wife was still living. And when she pressed to know why I thought so, I had to tell her, because I myself was that wife, supposed to be dead. Well, then, of course, it was necessary to tell her the cause of our parting—that it was a bitter misunderstanding growing out of circumstances which placed me in a false light. I spoke only in general terms; and because I could not go into details I offered to cancel our contract and leave her as soon as we should land at Havre."

"And what would you have done, then, as 'a stranger in a strange land,' Lilith? Would you have come on to me?" inquired Hereward.

"Uncalled, and after all that had passed? Oh, no! I could not have done that. I should have taken the first steamer back to New York and returned to Aunt Sophie."

"Aunt Sophie?"

"Mrs. Downie, the clergyman's widow, with whom I had lived in New York. But Madame Von Bruyin would not consent to cancel our contract. She insisted that I should remain with her. She was very good about it all. Indeed, she treated me with more than even her usual kindness, and from that hour I became to her as a beloved and cherished sister. I think she got over her sentimental fancy for you, for I think it was nothing more than that."

"Probably not," said Hereward, with a smile.

"And when the 'Fairy Prince' appeared in the form of Gherardini, I think the beauteous lady discovered that she had never really been in love in all her life before," added Lilith, archly.

"I am very glad to hear it. No heartier congratulations were ever offered to any bride than were mine to the newly married princess to-day," said Hereward.

"And, by the way," suggested Lilith, "the bridal pair are to leave for Marseilles, en route for Rome, at five o'clock, and it must be near that hour now. Will you return to the drawing-room or remain and await me here?"

"I will go with you," said Hereward, as he arose and offered Lilith his arm.

CHAPTER XXIII

HAPPY HOURS

THEY went back to the salon, which was now nearly empty. Only a few late-comers were present, and they were taking leave of the newly wedded pair.

When these had withdrawn from the room, Hereward led Lilith up to the receiving circle, and addressing the bride, said:

"Madame, I have to add to my congratulations the most heartfelt and grateful acknowledgments. Words cannot thank you for the boon you have given me in the resoration of this lost treasure."

"Let us hope, Mr. Hereward, that you will in the future guard that treasure too carefully ever to—mislay it again," archly replied the princess.

Hereward bowed deprecatingly.

"You remain in Paris some time, I hope?"

"I have a month's respite from official duties, madame."

"Then you will, perhaps, kindly permit me to place this house at your disposal during your stay. Mrs. Hereward had already arranged to remain here during my absence. To change that plan at this late hour would not be easy. So, if it would not inconvenience you to take up your quarters here for a season, you would oblige me very much by doing so," said the princess.

"Madame, it is certainly my wife and myself who are obliged in this matter. We feel your kindness, and thank you very sincerely," replied Hereward.

"And now, Lilith, dear little sister, will you go with me to my room? It is time to dress for the journey," said the princess, drawing the arm of her young friend within her own, bowing to the circle, and sailing out of the salon.

When the two friends reached madame's sumptuous dressing-room they found the lady's maid waiting with the traveling suit of mouse-colored velvet, plush hat, and marabout plumes of the same shade, and silver fox fur cloak and muff, all laid ready for her mistress.

"Madame," said Lilith, "I have to thank you for the happiness of my life, though thanks can ill express all I feel."

"Ah, bah, ma chère! I had planned this meeting long ago. But, indeed, I was able to bring it about even under better auspices than I had hoped. The 'sinner,' as Aunt Sophie calls Zuniga, helped me. I shall find you here when I return four weeks hence, I hope?"

"Yes, madame. You will reside in Paris, then, always?"

"Oh, no. Only during the season. We shall reside principally in the Gherardini Castle, among the Apennines, an old ancestral stronghold, which half charms, half frightens me; but I shall know more about it when I see it. And some day, Lilith, you will come and spend a summer with us there, and help to lighten the gloom."

"I thank you very much. I think that I should like it extremely," answered the younger lady.

The princess' rich but plain toilet was soon finished, and she went below, accompanied by Lilith.

The prince was waiting for her in the lower hall, where all her household had gathered to bid the newly married pair good-bye.

Aunt Sophie stood there, leaning on the arm of the gallant old professor, and quietly smiling and weeping—the soft-hearted creature smiled and wept a little at every wedding.

The domestics were gathered behind.

The prince and princess took a kindly leave of all, and a most affectionate one of Aunt Sophie and Monsieur Le Grange.

So, followed by the good wishes of their friends, they left the maison.

Not until the assembled household had seen the traveling carriage roll out of the court-yard gate did they separate and disperse to their several quarters.

"I must go and see to those valuable wedding presents being locked carefully away. Indeed, I think I shall finally send them to the valts of the bank. Will madame graciously excuse me?" inquired the polite Monsieur Le Grange, as he led Mrs. Downie to the little salon.

"Oh, yes, sir. Please go look after all that gold and silver and jewels at once. It is an awful temptation to leave in the way of servants—awful. And so many strange waiters in the house, too!" said Mrs. Downie, as she sank into a seat.

"Aunt Sophie," said Lilith, approaching on the arm of Tudor, "this is Mr. Hereward, my husband. And this lady, sir, is Mrs. Downie, who has been so kind to me ever since I made her acquaintance."

"I am very glad to know you, madame, and very grateful for all your goodness to my wife, in the days of her adversity," said Hereward, taking the old lady's little offered hand.

"Thanky, sir; I am happy, very, to see you; but as for my being good to her, it's all even, I reckon. I wasn't one bit better to her than she was to me, all the time," said Mrs. Downie.

"You were like a mother to me, always," warmly replied Lilith.

"Well, then, and wa'n't you all the same as an own dear daughter to me? That she was, Mr. Hereward. But, honey, I never knowed you had a husband, or a father either, till this very afternoon. While you were out of the room with Mr. Hereward the 'sinner' come in to pay his respects to the bride and groom, and then stood with me, behind the grandees, and told me all about it—how you was his daughter and Mr. Hereward's wife! Of course, naturally I knowed you must have been somebody's daughter, honey; but the idea of you being anybody's wife! Why, I didn't know you was married!" exclaimed the old lady, in comic wonder.

"Aunt Sophie, will you forgive me for not telling you anything about my father or my husband? And for all the secrets that I have kept from you, who was like a mother to me?" inquired Lilith, tenderly taking her old friend's hand.

"Lor', honey, what call have I got to forgive you? Forgive you for what? For keeping of your father's and your husband's secrets? Why, child, you hadn't any right to tell other people's secrets. I reckon you had none of your own; though most people do have some secrets. Lor'! everybody can't tell everything in the world to everybody else, I reckon. 'Twouldn't do, anyways. So don't say no more about that, my dear."

"You are very sweet, Aunt Sophie."

"Oh, no, I ain't, honey."

"I used to think, sometimes, that you looked at me as if you suspected that I was not all I seemed to be."

"No, honey; that wasn't it. I couldn't help seeing that you had had great troubles—very great troubles for one so young—and I used to look at you and wonder what in this world they could be. But all the time I know'd very well—I know'd 'way down deep in my heart—that you was good and true, and didn't deserve to be so afflicted. And now it is proved as you didn't. The 'sinner' told me all about it—every bit—and I reckon I know more than you do, now, honey; because the 'sinner' said that to-morrow he meant to come to the house and tell you and Mr. Hereward all that he had told yesterday to the baroness, and to-day to me. So, of course, you see, you have got to hear something you don't yet know."

"He told the baroness!" exclaimed Lilith, while Hereward listened attentively.

"Yes, yesterday; and me to-day."

"Where is Zuniga now?" inquired Hereward.

"Gone back to the Hotel of Love, on the Rue River."

"Where?" inquired Hereward, looking to Lilith for an explanation.

"Hotel du Louvre, Rue de Rivoli," said Lilith, adding: "Aunt Sophie has not yet become accustomed to foreign words."

"No, honey; and I never shall, neither—never! Now, everybody here calls the nicest man that I know the 'sinner,' as if he was the only sinner in the world. Why, we are all sinners, for that matter. And then Mrs. Hereward here——"

"Lilith! Lilith! dear Aunt Sophie."

"May I, honey? Well, anyhow, she told me how 'sinner' meant Sir and Mr. in the foreign language. Now, if all the Sirs and Mr.'s in foreign lands are so wicked and so barefaced as to call themselves and each other sinners, in that defiant manner, to their very faces, I say it don't speak well for foreign lands, and the sooner we get back to New York and Brother More's ministry the better."

"I quite agree with you, Mrs. Downie," said Hereward, laughing.

"And them waiters at the Hotel of—no; I mean the Hotel do Love—which I thought they called them goslings, but she says they were 'go-soons,' and that name fitted them young mounseers right well, 'cause the spry way they did fly around was enough to make one's head giddy. But there! I reckon as I am letting my tongue run before my wit."

"Oh, now, Aunt Sophie, you shall not say such wicked things about yourself. But tell me, did my father leave no message for us?"

"Yes, honey. He asked me to tell you that he would be here airly to-morrow morning. And I reckon as that don't mean seven or eight o'clock, as it would with us, but more likely half-past eleven or a quarter to twelve. He said he wouldn't interrupt you this first evening of your meeting. The 'sinner' is right-down considerate—for a sinner. And I must not intrude longer, neither," said Aunt Sophie, rising to leave the small salon in which this interview had taken place.

Both Hereward and Lilith protested against her going, but she said:

"Children, I have to see the remnants of the wedding feast gathered into hampers, and tied up and sent out to be distributed to the poor. And I reckon there will be a great many more than 'twelve baskets full.' The wine and fruit and potted things is to be sent to the Hope-it-all of Sand Marree, or some such name. Antoine knows. But the baroness wanted me to see to it, to keep temptation out of the way of the weak. You'll excuse me now?"

"Yes, Aunt Sophie, since you must go," said Lilith.

"And I'll send your tea up into this room, so you

can have it all to yourselves tater-tater, as these funny foreigners say of two together, though what they mean by it I don't know, unless it is potatoes, which they do know how to cook—I will say that for them—though why potatoes in this case nobody but a foreigner could tell. Well, oh river! that means good-bye, or something of that sort. I knw the moun-seers often say it when they go 'way."

So speaking, half to her friends, half to herself, in her soft, slow tones, Aunt Sophie passed out of the room.

Tea was soon served to the reunited and really happy pair, and as this refreshment was prepared under the immediate supervision of Aunt Sophie (who declared that though the mounseers and gosoons were great on coffee, they could not begin to make a decent cup of tea), it was really as good as they could have obtained in their own home.

The evening of that exciting day was spent very quietly.

The wearied household retired early and slept until late in the morning.

Tudor Hereward, Aunt Sophie and Monsieur Le Grange sat down to breakfast at ten o'clock.

They were still at the table when Señor Zuniga's card was brought and laid before Mr. Hereward.

Lilith and Tudor arose at once and passed out to the little salon where the visitor was waiting for them.

Zuniga stood in the middle of the room. He wore an elegant morning suit of dark olive; his long, curling black hair was carefully dressed; his gypsy face full of droll humor. He looked more like a rollicking boy than ever.

He advanced towards Lilith, took her in his arms and kissed her fondly.

Then releasing her he held out his hand to Hereward, shouting, joyously:

"How are you, my dear son?

> 'It gives me wonder, great as my delight,
> To see you here before me, oh! my soul's joy!' "

"I am very glad to meet you, Señor Zuniga," began Hereward, in his stately manner.

"Father, my son! Call me father!

> 'Mislike me not for my complexion.' "

"Will you take this seat, dear?" inquired Lilith, drawing forth one of the most comfortable chairs in the room.

When they had all sat down, Hereward once more said:

"I am really happy to see you, señor, and to have this unpleasant family mystery, which has caused us so much trouble, finally cleared up."

"So am I! So is Lilith! So are we all! Or, rather, so we shall be when it is cleared up! But it is not cleared up yet by a long shot! And so you shall soon find.

> 'Lend me your ears!'   .   .   .
> 'I could a tale unfold, whose lightest word
> Would harrow up thy soul!!'
>   'Then shall you hear
> Of moving accidents by flood and field,
> Of being taken by the insolent foe
> And sold to slavery!'

Are you ready to listen?" inquired the señor, as he threw himself back in his chair.

"We are very anxious to hear," said Lilith.

"Very well, then," replied Señor Zuniga.

And he began his story.

CHAPTER XXIV

THE STORY OF A WILD LIFE

Listen, how still waiting, dreaming
  Of some wild, heroic life,
How the young heart, all unconscious,
  Had really entered on the strife.

Now that I can reason calmly,
  And look clearly back again,
I can see the brightest meaning
  Threading each dark, torturing pain.

How the strong resolve was broken,
  Why rash hope and foolish fear,
And the prayers which God in pity
  Still refused to grant or hear.

                                  Anon.

IT was a picturesque group gathered around that
table—Zuniga, Hereward and Lilith.

Zuniga, with his slight, elegant and graceful form,
his dark complexion—darker still with his luxuriant
black curls—fine black eyes, shadowed with black
eyelashes, and arched by black eyebrows, and his
perfect features, the beautiful mouth not hidden by
the twirled moustache divided on the upper lip.
Zuniga, with his laughing, reckless, boyish air,
seemed the youngest of the group of whom he was
the father—or at least the younger of the two men.

Hereward, with his tall and stately figure, his noble
head, blonde complexion, severe classic profile, and
steel-blue eyes, and with his grave and dignified de-
meanor, seemed, certainly, the elder of the two.

Lilith, in her simple and elegant morning dress of
white foulard silk, which well became her lovely
brunette beauty, sat between them, but nearer to the
Señor Zuniga.

Had any stranger been told that here sat a married pair and a father, and had been required to tell "which was which," he would certainly have pointed out Hereward as the father, and the two others as the son and daughter.

Their relative ages were as follows: Zuniga was thirty-eight, Hereward twenty-nine, and Lilith nineteen.

Zuniga began his story in his usual eccentric manner:

"Esteemed son-in-law and beloved daughter! That little personal pronoun, in the first person singular, nominative case, is such a very obtrusive person, that it should be suppressed on every possible occasion. This autobiography, or fragment of autobiography, then, shall be delivered in the third person, with your consent. What do you say?"

Zuniga paused for a reply.

"As you like, señor," gravely responded Hereward.

"Yes, do, please," assented Lilith.

Zuniga proceeded:

"About thirty-five years ago—— Now don't throw yourself back in your chair with such a look of anticipated weariness, Hereward. Have more respect for your venerable father-in-law, and set a better example to my daughter, or I shall 'set' a mother-in-law over your head, or, rather, a step-mother-in-law, which must be a combination of domestic autocracy. Besides, the story is not so long as the time.

"Well, about thirty-five years ago, the good ship Polly Ann, of Glasgow, Swift, master, bound for New York, when about half way across, sighted a nondescript object, which, on nearer view and closer inspection, proved to be a raft, on which languished a half-dead shipwrecked sailor, and a three-quarters dead shipwrecked child.

"The victims were rescued, taken on board the Polly Ann, and restored by such simple and efficacious treatment as was familiar to the skipper and his crew as specifics 'for such cases made and provided.'

"The sailor was a man of about fifty winters; the child, a boy of three summers—though why the winters should always be enumerated for the old, and the summers for the young, is more than I can understand, since both young and old have an equal distribution of summers and winters in their years. But this is a digression.

"As soon as the sailor was able to give an account of himself and his fellow-sufferers, we learned that they were the survivors of the ship Falcon, Captain Pentecost, homeward bound from Havana to Liverpool, and foundered in the late equinoctial storm, when in latitude this and that, and longitude so and so; never mind the figures, they are forgotten long ago, even if they were ever exactly known, which is doubtful.

"The crew and passengers of the wrecked ship had left it in two boats and on a raft. The captain had taken command of the first boat, the first mate of the second boat, and the second mate of the raft.

"The sailor could give no account of the fate of either boat after they had left the wreck.

"On the raft besides himself, Zebedee Wyvil, second mate of the Falcon, who was in command, there were seven common seamen and three passengers; these passengers being Señor Don Alphonzo Zuniga and his wife and child.

"A sad story could be told of the long sufferings and terrible deaths of these shipwrecked victims, but it would not only be quite useless, but altogether too heart-rending. Besides which, tragedy is both unpleasant and unprofitable, except to the performers on the stage, with an audience of two thousand persons, averaging a dollar a head.

"In brief, all the passengers on the raft perished

from want and exposure, except the sailor, whose strong vitality sustained him, and the child, for whose sake all had denied themselves from the beginning.

"You may be sure that the captain and the crew of the Polly Ann were very much interested in the story of the shipwrecked sailor and the child. The captain gave Zebedee Wyvil a berth as soon as he was able to handle a rope; and one and another talked of adopting the little Spanish waif. But Zebedee Wyvil informed all and sundry that the child was his own treasure trove, and that he should keep it until it should be claimed by those, if any such lived, who should have a better right to it than himself.

"Certainly no one on the Polly Ann ventured after that to dispute Wyvil's possession of the little Zuniga.

"In due time the Polly Ann reached New York, discharged her cargo of linen, tartan, Paisley shawls, and so forth; loaded with another cargo of tobacco and cotton, and cleared for Glasgow, Zebedee Wyvil going as third mate, and taking with him his treasure trove, to which arrangement no one, under the circumstances, objected.

"In due time also the Polly Ann reached Glasgow, and there Mate Wyvil, who had only engaged for the homeward voyage, left the ship, taking his little Spanish boy with him.

"Zebedee Wyvil was a bachelor; and he was the main support of his sister-in-law, the widow of his younger brother, Andrew, and of her two children, Joseph and Elizabeth, who lived at Stockton, a small village in the West Riding of Yorkshire.

"Zebedee Wyvil, when on shore, always made his home with this sister-in-law.

"Now, on leaving his ship, he resolved to take the Spanish child with him to Stockton, and place him under the care of this sister-in-law.

"But first he bethought him of having the boy christened, lest that necessary ceremony had not already been performed.

"So he took the lad to St. John's Church in Glasgow and had him christened Joseph Wyvil, in honor of his—Zebedee's—own father.

"Then he carried the child to his own home and presented him to his sister-in-law.

"The widow and her children received the sailor and the orphan boy with great kindness; but when his name was given—

"'Joseph Wyvil!' exclaimed the widow. 'Why, what in the name of sense put you on giving the bairn that name?'

"'It was the name of my old feyther, as good a man as ever lived,' retorted Zebedee.

"'But it is the name of my own lad!'

"'So it be! I had forgot that same.'

"'And now if the bairn bides wi' us there'll be two Joseph Wyvils in the one house.'

"'Well, then, and there cannot be too many Joseph Wyvils anywhere, if they be one and all as good as the first of the name! And, moreover, to distinguish the lads apart, we may even call the elder Joseph, and the younger Joe,' concluded Zebedee.

"And as he carried the purse, his will was law in that little household, and so the point was settled. His nephew was known as Joseph Wyvil, and his little treasure trove as Joe.

"Joseph was a fine, strong, red-haired and freckle-faced youth of ten, Joe an ugly little black-a-vizzed monkey of four, and Elizabeth, or 'Lil,' a pretty baby of two years.

"Uncle Zeb left all his pay with his sister and shipped for another long voyage.

"The three children were brought up together and in due time sent to school.

"Joe, as the adopted son of Uncle Zeb, was taught to call the Widow Wyvil 'Aunt,' and her children each 'Cousin.'

"Years went by with but little of incident to the humble household, except in the periodical home-coming and sea-going of Uncle Zeb.

"When Joseph Wyvil, the widow's son, was fifteen years of age, he was taken from school and apprenticed to a house carpenter, and in time he became a very skilful workman.

"When Joe was about twelve years old he was placed in a collegiate school by his adopted father, whose ambition it was to get his son in the naval academy.

"He remained in that school for three years, during which time two members of the small family passed away—Zebedee Wyvil died of yellow fever, while his ship was in port in Havana; and Susan Wyvil succumbed to pulmonary consumption, in her cottage home at Stockton.

"At the end of the third year Joe left the collegiate school. Not that his preparatory course was finished, and not that he wished to leave, but because the quarterly payments for his board and tuition had ceased with his adopted father's life.

"And though the masters, knowing the case and the circumstances, would have kept him longer, the pride of this son of the hidalgoes would not suffer him to receive the favor.

"You may object that he had already received favors from humbler people, in having been adopted and cared for by the mate of the Falcon. Ah, but that was so different! Old Zebedee Wyvil had seemed like his own father. He had known no other.

"Well, he left the college, and went home to Stockton, to those who seemed like his own people, poor as they were, since they were all he had left.

"He found his cousins, as he called them, still living together, and occupying the old cottage.

"Joseph was now a fine young man of twenty-one, doing a thriving business at his trade, and making a very comfortable home for his young sister Lil, a lovely girl of thirteen, who kept house for him, and to whom he was devotedly attached—yes, so devotedly attached that friends and neighbors all said Joseph Wyvil would never take a wife while that beloved sister remained unmarried and in his home.

"This sister and brother received poor Joe with the most affectionate welcome, making him feel perfectly at home and at ease.

"In return for all this kindness the dark and swarthy descendant of the Castilians fell desperately in love with the fair-skinned, blue-eyed and flaxen-haired child of the Saxons. He made such ardent and persistent love to the little maid that Lil grew frightened and fled his company, yet never complained of him to her big brother—the little angel! I mean she—Lil—was the little angel, you will all please to understand, and not the big brother, though he was a good fellow enough.

"Ah, well, after Lil repulsed and fled from him, and shunned him altogether as if he had been the horned and hoofed demon himself, he grew desperate and went off to sea.

"Being fairly well educated, and having permission to refer to his college masters, he got a good berth from the first, as captain's clerk in an East India merchantman.

"For some months all went well enough, and Joe 'won golden opinions from all sorts of' officers and men. But being a wild, reckless, impulsive, rollicking sort of a little devil, he soon began to get into all manner of troubles, though he always contrived to get out of them again, falling like a cat on his feet.

"During all this time he kept up an irregular correspondence with his cousin Joseph, freely confessing all his peccadilloes, but stipulating that no one was to tell Lil.

"After a three years' voyage all around the world, Joe came home, and went straight to the dear old cottage at Stockton.

"He found the house and garden enlarged and improved in proportion to Joseph Wyvil's increased prosperity.

"Joe was now a sun-burned sailor boy of eighteen, much darker and very much more of a dare-devil than ever.

"Lil was sixteen, and more beautiful than before. She was still the idol of her brother, for whom she kept house, and who—for his dear sister's sake, as it was said—remained unmarried and unengaged.

"The brother and sister received their sailor cousin with all their old confiding affection. Lil had forgiven his presumption and forgotten her fears of him.

"But, ah! poor Joe! His passion for this 'fair one with golden locks' was rekindled into such a fierce flame that nothing on earth seemed strong enough to resist it.

"It was her love or somebody's life!

"He demanded to marry Lil right off.

"But her brother opposed such precipitate measures; urged that both parties were much too young to dream of marriage, Joe being eighteen, and Lil but sixteen. Why, he said that he, himself, Joseph Wyvil, his elder by six years, did not yet contemplate matrimony. Besides, he could, in any case, give his sister a comfortable home yet for many years, or even for her whole life, while Joe had no home to take her to, and had still his own way to make in the world.

"In answer to all this, Joe, with the modest assurance—or shall we say consummate impudence?—of his nature, proposed that he should immediately marry Lil and that they should continue to live on at the cottage until he should have to go to sea again, when he would leave his wife as heretofore in her old home under the protection of her brother.

"Naturally enough, Mr. Wyvil did not see the excellence of this arrangement in quite so strong and vivid a light as did Joe and even Lil.

"After laughing a little at the ingenuous proposal, he reverted to his first argument, that both were too young, foolish and impecunious to be married—adding that a boy of eighteen and a girl of sixteen, who talked of such a proceeding, should be locked up for a calendar month on a depleting diet of bread and water.

"Whereupon the Spanish lad eagerly declared that as for himself he would most joyfully submit to the terms, bread, water, imprisonment and everything else that might be required to purchase the indulgence, if only Joseph would be so good as to lock him and his sweetheart up in the same room.

"For all answer to that suggestion, Mr. Wyvil informed the ardent lover that he was a lunatic and should be sent to a mad-house.

"Opposition only added fuel to the flame of Joe's passion. Mr. Wyvil did not understand the difference between the dark blood and the bright when he contemptuously characterized that passion as puppy love.

"Mr. Wyvil went off to his work. He was finishing the interior of a church at that time. Joe raved and Lil cried. And then they took their fate into their own hands. They resolved to run away and get married! Or rather to sneak away.

"Late that night, when honest Joseph Wyvil was in bed and asleep, Joe and Lil, in traveling rig, and with a couple of small valises, in which all their worldly goods were packed, and which were gallantly carried by the gentleman, who balanced them one in each brown hand, Joe and Lil sneaked out of the back door, and under cover of the darkness, trudged on to the railway station, where they took the 12.30 train to Scotland.

"They left the train the next morning only to hasten to the nearest minister's house to get married. As soon as the ceremony was concluded and they had got a bit of breakfast at the counter of the railway station, standing up at it, uncomfortably, to drink weak and lukewarm coffee and eat stale sandwiches, they took the next train back to England.

"But not daring to face Joseph Wyvil in the first hours of his 'roused wrath,' they shunned the neighborhood of Stockton and stopped at a little Yorkshire village of Orton, not far from the city of Carlisle.

"They took lodgings at a pretty, picturesque little farm-house called Hayhurst, from which retreat they both wrote a mutual penitent letter to Joseph Wyvil, expressing profound sorrow for having disobeyed and offended so dear and good a brother, but declaring that they could not do otherwise, as, though he had forbidden them to think of marriage, they loved each other so much that they must either marry or die, and they ended by imploring his forgiveness, and signing themselves his devoted, obedient, loving brother and sister, Lil and Joe.

"Both Joe and Lil thought this letter so very touching, eloquent, pathetic and convincing that it must bring Mr. Wyvil hurrying to them in person with open arms and fervent blessings.

"And they waited for some such happy result.

"But no Mr. Wyvil came to greet their longing eyes. And no letter came in answer to theirs.

"Every day Joe went to the village post-office, but found nothing for them.

"A fortnight passed in this suspense, and then Joe suggested that their letter might have miscarried, and so they sat down together and indited a second letter, more penitent, more pathetic, more eloquent and convincing than the first. Joe posted it with his own hands, and they both waited confidently for some happy result.

"None came. Another fortnight passed, and then Joe grew angry and Lil anxious.

" 'If a man is not satisfied with repentance and confession he is no Christian,' said Joe.

" 'But we don't repent, and we only confess what is already known; and perhaps Joseph is sick,' suggested Lil.

"Then Joe wrote a confidential letter to a mutual friend in Stockton, making inquiries concerning Mr. Joseph Wyvil. In due time he received an answer, stating that Mr. Wyvil was well and prosperous, but so very deeply offended by the runaway marriage that he would not permit his sister's or his cousin's name to be mentioned in his presence. The writer concluded his letter in some such words as these:

" 'Give him time and he will come around. He is too good-hearted a man and too fond of his sister, and even of you, to hold out against you both much longer.'

"Lil cried a good deal over this, but Joe encouraged her, and so did their landlady, Mrs. Claxton, who had taken a great fancy to the young pair.

"Fortunately, Joe had thirty pounds saved up from his three years' pay as captain's clerk, and so there was no fear of immediate embarrassment.

"Lil, led on by the landlady, interested herself in farm life, in the dairy and in the poultry yard. She was pleased to be permitted to help to skim the milk, or to churn the butter, or to look after the newly hatched, pretty little fluffy chickens and ducklings; and though she often heaved a sigh at the thought of her brother, it soon passed away, leaving no trace behind.

"Joe was more to be pitied. He was in more danger from his idle and objectless life of the present moment. He went daily to the village, and what was worse, he went nightly to the Tawny Lion, the village ale-house, where he formed acquaintance with the young farmers and mechanics of the neighborhood, all tenants of Squire Hawkhurst, of Hawkhurst Hall.

CHAPTER XXV

A FATAL SNARE

"Just now the whole neighborhood was excited over the situation at the Hall. Young Mr. James Hawkhurst, nephew and heir of Squire Hawkhurst, was a sort of Prince Hal, in his way, and had by his wild life and free manners at the same time won the love of all his young tenants, whose boon companion at the ale-house he frequently became, and the indignation of his uncle, who threatened to disinherit him.

"This, the gossips of the village said, the squire had the legal power to do, since the estate was not entailed; but they also urged that the squire had no moral right to rob his heir of that land which he should justly inherit, not only from his immediate progenitor, but from the long line of ancestors who had gone before him.

"This was the view taken by all the youthful tenants and boon companions of the young squire.

"At every evening gathering in the tap-room of the Tawny Lion, Joe heard this matter discussed, and naturally he took sides with the young squire and his followers.

"At length, when Joe and Lil had been in the neighborhood for about five weeks, a crisis came in the affairs of the Hall.

"It was understood that a very violent scene had ensued between the old squire and the young one, which had ended in the banishment of the young squire, who had left the Hall in disgrace and had taken lodgings at the Tawny Lion.

"In a day or two it was ascertained that the old squire had had a 'stroke,' and was not expected to live through the week.

"A servant from the Hall had brought the news to the circle at the ale-house, that a telegram had been sent to the solicitor of the old squire, Mr. John Ketcham, of Carlisle, to come immediately down to the Hall to remain with the squire until the end, and to take charge of affairs; also to bring with him the squire's last will, which disinherited the heir and left the estate to a hospital, and which was already signed and sealed.

"Lawyer Ketcham, the man added, was expected to arrive at Stockbridge, the nearest railway station, by the 9:50 express, and would come on to the Hall by the railway stage-coach, which ran twice a day between Stockbridge and Orton.

"The news brought by the servant from the Hall excited a great deal of indignation among the men present.

"Much foolish talk was indulged in. Many worse than foolish threats were made.

"In the midst of it all, Joe, who was as usual present, got up and left the place, and hurried home to Hayhurst Farm to take tea with Lil.

"He found the people at the farm all in a state of extreme excitement at some news brought by a cowboy, to the effect that the old squire had just breathed his last. Not that they were so much interested in the old squire as the young one.

"Mrs. Claxton, the farmer's wife, hoped that no will had been made, in which case the young squire would of course inherit as heir-at-law.

"Then Joe contributed his mite of intelligence gleaned from the circle in the tap-room of the Tawny Lion, to the effect that the obnoxious will had been made, signed and sealed, and that it was then in the hands of Lawyer Ketcham, who was on his way from London to Orton, to take charge of affairs at the Hall.

"And now Mrs. Claxton prayed the Lord might forgive her for hoping that some accident might happen to the train or to the stage coach, to prevent that wicked will ever coming to light.

"After tea, some one suggested that the report of the old squire's death might possibly be a false one, and suggested that some one else should go over to the Hall and ascertain the truth.

"Joe, the least tired of all the men present, because they had been hard at work all day and he had not been at work at all, good-naturedly volunteered for the service.

"Everybody thanked him, and he got up to go. Everybody laughed when he kissed Lil, as if he had been going on a long journey instead of a short walk.

"Ah me! how little we know what we do! Joe set

out to be gone half an hour; but he never saw the farm-house again.

"Joe went on to the Hall, gayly whistling and utterly unconscious of the impending tragedy of his life.

"At the Hall he found the servants closing the window-shutters, although it was not yet dark; from that circumstance he gained confirmation of the report of the squire's death, even before their words had given it.

" 'But Lawyer Ketcham is expected down to-night to look after affairs, and nothing more can be done until his arrival,' was the volunteered communication of the old butler.

"Joe thanked the man and turned to go back to the farm. Ah! if he had only gone back to the farm, what woe would have been spared him and all connected with him. Strange on what seeming trifles human destiny hangs. Venerable reflection that!

"If Joe had turned to the east instead of the west, on leaving the park gates, his whole life would have been different. The east path would have led him back to the farm and to safety. The west path led him to the gates of perdition.

"The reason why, at the last moment, he turned to the west was simple enough. He remembered that there was an evening mail due at the village, and thought it just possible that Joseph Wyvil, relenting towards Lil and Joe, might have written a letter, and that he should find it at the post-office and have the delight of taking it home to rejoice the heart of the young wife. So he turned to the west, instead of to the east, and so decided his own fate.

"Joe trudged all the way to the village, whistling gayly as he went.

"He found no letter in the post-office, and feeling much disappointed, he turned to go home to the farm-house, through the gathering darkness.

"The way was long, and the sky was black with night and clouds. Joe thought to take a short cut through some thick woods, but in attempting to do so lost his way and wandered about for some time before he came out on a part of the high road unfamiliar to him.

"He turned into this; but was utterly at a loss what direction to take.

"Presently, however, he heard footsteps and voices approaching, and he spoke aloud, asking to be directed the nearest way to Hayhurst Farm.

"By that time the approaching party had come up with him, and one of them, who had recognized his voice, called out:

" 'Is that you, Joe?'

" 'Yes, Thomas Estel, it is I, and I have lost my way in the dark, and want to be set on my right road for Hayhurst Farm,' replied the youth.

" 'All right. But come with us first. We won't keep you long. And you'll see some roaring fun.'

" 'But it is late, and I want to get home to Lil,' objected Joe.

" 'And so you shall in good time; but come with us first.'

" 'Where are you going?'

" 'Not out of your way home. Quite on the same road. This road. Such a lark! You'll never forgive yourself if you miss it.'

"Poor Joe! He was always ready for a lark. He joined himself to the half dozen boys, whom, as his eyes became accustomed to the darkness, he began to recognize as his village acquaintances; but more from their general appearance than from their faces, which were all half masked.

" 'Is it mumming?' inquired Joe.

" 'Something like that,' replied Estel.

"And they went on together down the road, which

deepened into a dark dell, or gully, between two high, wooded banks.

"Here they paused and waited.

" 'What are you stopping for?' inquired Joe.

" 'Oh! you'll soon see,' replied a boy named Burton.

" 'I wish you would let me go on. I know Lil will be anxious,' pleaded Joe.

" 'So you shall in a minute or two. Wait a bit.'

"Estel and Burton were stretching a rope across the road and tying its extremities to trees on the opposite sides.

"Joe watched them uneasily.

" 'What are you doing that for?' he anxiously inquired.

" 'Ax us no questions and we'll tell you no lies, youngster,' laughed Burton.

" 'I'm going home!' retorted Joe; and he turned to leave the party and to try to find his way to the farm alone.

"But at that moment the sound of wheels was heard rapidly approaching from the direction to which Joe had set his face, and at the same time the lanterns of the swiftly-rolling stage coach gleamed through the darkness.

"Another instant and the leaders had reached the unseen barrier, tripped and reared. At the same moment the bits were seized, the coach was surrounded, and oaths and curses, cries and screams, and dire confusion filled the scene. In the struggle with the rearing and plunging horses the coach was overturned, the lanterns extinguished, and utter darkness was added to the horror of the situation.

"Joe Wyvil stood at a little distance, transfixed with amazement at the suddenness of the catastrophe that he did not in the least understand. He never for a moment suspected that the stopping of

the stage coach was the 'lark' alluded to by his companions, for why should they stop the stage coach?
They were not highway robbers, even if highway
robbers were not utterly out of date in England in
this century. No; he supposed the whole affair to
have been an accident, unintentionally caused by the
boys stretching that rope across the road in pursuit
of some other 'lark;' to trip up some foot passenger,
perhaps, whom they meant to make the victim of
some practical joke.

"Only for an instant he stood panic-stricken, and
then he darted into the horrible mêlée to find out if
he could be of any assistance.

"At the same moment he perceived through the
murky darkness the figures of two men in silent,
deadly struggle, and then he heard, through the
groans and shrieks, the stern voice of some man saying:

" 'Hand over that wicked will, you villainous law
shark, or I will save the hangman a job by strangling
you with my own hands!' or compliments to that
effect.

"A fiercer, deadlier struggle ensued, and then the
flash and report of a pistol, and the heavy fall of one
of the men.

"Almost at the same instant the scene was filled
with a posse comitatus of constables and laborers,
drawn to the spot by the shrieks and cries that had
given the alarm.

"A murder had been committed, and Joe Wyvil
was found bending over the dead man, with the fallen
pistol on the ground at his feet, when he was rudely
collared and well shaken by the strong hand of the
constable who arrested him.

"But so utterly dazed and confounded was the boy
by all that had so suddenly happened to him, like
a hurricane or an earthquake in its swift destruc-

tion, that he was totally unable to give any intelligible account of himself.

"His companions had fled, and taken to the covert of the woods on either side. Joe, the guiltless, was the only one arrested.

"With the help of many hands the overturned stage coach was righted, and the passengers—all of whom, except the murdered man, were more frightened than hurt—got upon their feet and were helped to their places.

"The stage driver, somewhat bruised and shaken, was assisted to mount his box and take the reins once more in his hands, and so the coach resumed its journey.

"Nothing but the dead man on the roadside and the wretched boy in custody remained to tell the tale of the catastrophe.

"The dead body was placed on a hastily procured plank, and borne away to the police station to await the action of the coroner. And the boy, with handcuffs on his wrists, was marched off between two constables to the lock-up house.

"Poor Joe was no hero. This violent separation from Lil; this stern arrest and imprisonment; this sudden, overwhelming calamity was so wondrous, so incredible that he could not realize or believe in it, but rather imagined himself to be the victim of some horrible nightmare dream from which he tried to awaken.

"Yet still he told a pitiable tale to the constable of how he had been unconsciously drawn into that fatal adventure, and begged that some one might be sent to Hayhurst to his little wife, to tell her that he was only detained on business, and would return to her as soon as he possibly could.

"The officer, half in pity for the boy, half in impatience at his importunity, I suppose, promised to do all that he wished, and so locked him up for the night.

"Poor Joe was but a child, after all, and he cried all night long.

"In the morning he was taken before a magistrate, and charged with highway robbery and murder—the robbery of the stage coach and the murder of Lawyer Ketcham.

"Joe, to save the name of his adopted family from reproach, gave his own as John Weston, saying to himself that he had about as much right to the one as to the other.

"He told his little story, but no one believed it, and he was duly committed to jail, to take his trial at the forthcoming assizes.

"He had not seen or heard of his young wife since his arrest.

"Again he childishly implored constable and jailer not to let Lil know the truth of his misery, but to send her word that he was detained on business, and would come to her as soon as he could.

"And, as before, half in pity and half in impatience, they promised everything he required.

"Joe was too deeply humiliated to write to any one. It is all very well to talk about the support of conscious innocence, but it is reasonable to conclude that a man who is by his nature utterly incapable of crime suffers much more under its false imputation than does the darkest of criminals. Conscious innocence did not help poor little Joe much. He pined under the false charge, so ashamed of it that he could not prevail upon himself to write to any friend.

"But one day his prison door was opened and Joseph Wyvil entered the cell, his honest face full of sympathy, his kind eyes full of tears, his voice full of affection, as he stretched out his hands and took Joe's, saying:

" 'My poor, poor boy!'

" 'You don't believe I did it, Joseph?' said Joe.

" 'I know you did not. I know you could not!' answered Joseph, pressing the hands he held.

" 'And, oh! Lil!' cried Joe.

" 'Lil does not doubt you; but she is too ill to come to the prison. She is with me in the town here.'

" 'Not—not—dangerously ill?'

" 'Oh, no. Only prostrated; but confident in your innocence, Joe.'

" 'God bless her! God bless you! You have forgiven us, Joseph?'

" 'I forgave you from the first; I only intended to teach you a lesson by holding off for a bit. I wish I had not done it now. Perhaps if I had not, this would not have happened; but, Joe, it will all come right. I will take care of Lil until you are out again, and I will spend my last shilling in securing the best counsel I can get to defend you and to clear you, Joe, old fellow!'

" 'Oh, Joseph! I don't deserve it from you! Not from you!'

" 'You are my cousin and my brother!' said honest Joseph.

"It is nearly impossible to give the exact words of this conversation from memory; but such, at least, was its purport.

"He stayed as long as the rules of the prison would permit, and then, having cheered Joe with hopes of a happy issue out of his trouble, and with promises to stand by him to the end, and to bring Lil to see him as soon as she should be able to come, Joseph shook hands with the prisoner and left him.

"The next day the faithful brother returned to the jail even before the doors were opened, and waited until he could be admitted to see Joe.

"He brought cheering news that he had engaged

the services of one of the most distinguished lawyers in Carlisle, Mr. John Rocke, to defend the accused boy, and that the counsel would visit the prisoner in the course of the day.

"'But how is Lil?' eagerly demanded Joe, more concerned about the health of his little bride than about his own vindication and deliverance.

"'Lil is better since I saw you and reported well of you. Poor Lil feared that you would be as heavily prostrated as she has been by this sudden and overwhelming blow, but now since she knows that you bear it so bravely, she is more hopeful and consequently stronger. I shall bring her to see you tomorrow.'

"'Thank Heaven for that! But as to my bearing this infernal wrong——'

"'Don't swear, my poor boy,' Joseph mildly interposed here.

"'I'm not swearing. Infernal isn't an oath; but it is the truth. It is an infernal wrong, and I have not borne it bravely at all! I have not borne it in any way until you came to see me, dear Joseph!' passionately exclaimed the imprisoned boy.

"'Stop that and listen to all the messages that Lil has sent you,' pleaded Joseph.

"And then to attentive ears he repeated all the loving, confiding and encouraging words of the little bride to her imprisoned husband.

"The arrival of the counsel, Mr. Rocke, interrupted this tête-à-tête.

"Joseph Wyvil introduced the visitor to Joe.

"And then when the three men were seated—the lawyer on the solitary wooden chair and Joseph and Joe side by side on the narrow cot—the young prisoner told his story, of how he was returning home from the Orton post-office to Hayhurst Farm, when he accidentally fell in with a gang of boys who told him they were going on a lark and pressed him to join them; how, partly from curiosity to know what they were going to do and partly from willingness to oblige them, he joined the gang without the faintest suspicion that they intended to do any unlawful deed, and that the stopping of the stage coach and the murder of the lawyer came upon him with the sudden shock and horror of an earthquake.

" 'I said the murder of the lawyer, but I should rather have said the death of the lawyer, for I am sure it was an accident.'

" 'An accident! Why, he was certainly shot by one of the assailants!' said Mr. Rocke.

" 'No, he was shot by himself.'

" 'By himself!' exclaimed Messrs. Rocke and Wyvil in a breath.

" 'Yes; listen,' said Joe. 'Now that I can look back coolly on all that happened and put things together, I can understand much that at the time of the action was incomprehensible to me. And I am sure that no violence was intended beyond the seizure of a document in the green bag of the family solicitor. When the coach was overturned I thought it was an accident, and as soon as I recovered from the momentary shock I ran to the rescue. In the mêlée, through the obscurity, I saw two men struggling—one of the gang—Thomas Estel—the other a passenger of the coach—the lawyer. The first was trying to get possession of the bag, the second was holding it fast to his side with one hand, and with the other drawing a pistol from his breast pocket, which he leveled at his assailant. Estel struck the muzzle of the pistol up, and it went off, shooting the lawyer under the chin. There! I saw all that,' said Joe. 'And the next minute the posse was upon us and I was in custody. All the rest of the gang had fled.'

" 'And as usual,' added Joseph Wyvil—'as usual,

the only guiltless one of the party became the scapegoat for the guilty. Have any arrests been made
since?'

" 'Oh, yes! several noted roughs and poachers, on
suspicion, but every one proved an alibi and got off.'

" 'And Estel?'

" 'Estel and another chap, one Burton, both respectable young farmers, and tenants of Squire Hawkhurst, have disappeared from the neighborhood.'

" 'Do you know,' inquired the young prisoner,
'how it all goes on at the Hall? I cannot help thinking that all this came about through the old squire's
wicked will, and that it was only to get possession
of that will and destroy it that the stage coach was
stopped.'

" 'Very likely,' replied Mr. Rocke. 'But as for
affairs at the Hall, of course, after the death of the
lawyer, who was on his way down to take them in
charge, the bailiff, who was entirely in the interests of
the discharged nephew, notified Mr. James, who had
gone to town, and the young squire arrived in time to
take charge of his uncle's funeral. After which, as
heir-at-law, he entered into the undisputed possession
of the estate, inherited not only from his immediate
progenitor who had no just right to cut him off from
it, but from a long line of ancestors.'

" 'Well,' sighed Joe, 'I am glad he enjoys his own
again, though it costs so much, and though I never
would have joined them that helped him to it, if I
had known they were going to break the peace.'

"The lawyer questioned Joe farther as to his unconscious connection with the stage robbers of that
fatal night, and after noting down all his replies, retired to prepare his brief, leaving the boy cheered
with hope.

CHAPTER XXVI

THE MEETING OF THE YOUNG PAIR

Though losses and crosses
Be lessons right severe,
There's wit there, ye'll get there,
Ye'll find nae ither where.

Robert Burns.

"EARLY on the next morning Joseph Wyvil brought his young sister to the prison cell to see her husband.

"But notwithstanding the promise that the big brother had extorted from each of the unhappy little pair, that they would control their feelings and behave themselves, no sooner had Lil passed the grated door, entered the cell, and caught sight of her poor Joe, than she flew towards him, and the two fell into each other's arms and sobbed aloud.

"Joseph Wyvil withdrew from the cell and left them together, taking his seat on a bench in the corridor beside the turnkey.

"After the first paroxysm of sobbing, crying, caressing and pitying each other had exhausted itself and them, they sat down on the edge of the bed and began to talk and compare notes.

"And their conversation was something like this:

" 'When did you first hear of my trouble, Lil?' inquired Joe.

" 'Oh, not until next day. Do you think if I had known it that night I wouldn't have walked all the way to the lock-up house and made them let me in to stay with you?'

" 'Yes; but they wouldn't have done it, Lil.'

" 'But I would have made them let me. I would have screamed and cried so they would have been obliged to do it.'

" 'Poor little Lil!'

" 'But, you see, a man came and told me a passel of lies.'

" 'How was that, Lil?'

" 'Why, you see, we all at the farm sat up ever so late, waiting for you to come home, and never thinking any harm, and never feeling uneasy, because Mrs. Claxton said she reckoned as the old squire had died so sudden, and everybody had been taken so by surprise, and everything must be so upside down at the Hall, that maybe you had been called on to give some assistance, like going of a message, or something.'

" 'Yes. Well, Lil?'

" 'So we were not anxious about you. But just about an hour after midnight a man come to the house with a message from you, as you had been detained by business, but would come to me as soon as you could, and that I mustn't wait up, but must go to bed. And I thought you were at the Hall, as they said; and though I felt disappointed, and very lonesome, I went to bed.'

" 'Poor little Lil!'

" 'And it was all lies, Joe—all lies!'

" 'No, it wasn't, dear Lil; it was the truth. I was detained on business (detained in the lock-up house, on charge of felony), and I did mean to come to you as soon as ever I could. And it was I who sent that message to you. I did it so you could get some sleep that night, dear Lil!'

" 'Oh, Joe!'

" 'But how did you hear the truth at last, my poor Lil?'

" 'From Joseph.'

" 'From Joseph!'

" 'Yes. You see, Mr. Claxton heard the whole truth from the man who came the night before, though he never let on to me that he had heard it. And he sent a telegram to Joseph that same night. How lucky we had told him all about our brother, and where he lived! Well, I think Joseph must have taken the very first train after receiving the telegram, for he arrived the next afternoon.'

" 'Ah! after I had been committed for trial, and had set out for this place.'

"Yes; I suppose so. Well, he reached the farm about five o'clock; and he had so much self-control that I did not see that anything was wrong, but only thought that he had taken pity on us at last, and had forgiven us and come to say so. So, after he had kissed me a good many kisses, I told him I was sorry Joe wasn't home, but that Joe was over at the Hall, where the old squire lay dead. That was what I thought, you know.'

" 'Yes.'

" 'Well, then he told me that you had gone to Carlisle on business connected with the death of the old squire that would keep you there some time; he thought it best to take me on there, too. Oh, how cunning he was, Joe!'

" 'How wise and merciful, you mean, Lil.'

" 'Well, anyhow, I thanked him with all my heart. There wasn't another train that stopped at Orton that night, so we had to wait and take the early one the next morning; and that we did. And oh, Joe! I heard the peoplpe at the station, and on the train, too, talking about the highway robbery and murder, and saying such a thing had not occurred in that neighborhood within the memory of the oldest inhabitant; and talking about a stranger by the name of John Weston, who was the ringleader of it, and saying that he had been committed to prison the day before to stand his trial at the next assizes. And oh, Joe! while I listened with the greatest curiosity and interest to all that, I had not the least idea that John Weston was you!'

"Here Lil lost her self-control again, threw herself into Joe's arms, and burst into a storm of sobs and tears, in which her boy-husband joined her with all his might.

"When this tempest subsided, Lil, between gasps, resumed her discourse by asking a question:

" 'What made you call yourself John Weston?'

" 'To save the family credit, and because I had as much right to that name, or to any other, as to the one I wear.'

" 'Well, then, we got to this city yesterday noon, and went to a quiet inn. And I wanted to be taken at once to see you, never dreaming of where you were. But Joseph said you were engaged in business at the time, and that we could have some luncheon first and then go to you. I was half angry, but as I was hungry I agreed to take some coffee and sandwiches. And after that, when I insisted on going to you, Joseph told me you were in a little trouble. He didn't mean to tell me how bad it was, but just to prepare me to see you in prison; but somehow I seemed to guess all at once that you were the John Weston they had been talking about on the train, and though I never could believe anything bad of you for one single minute, and didn't then, Joe, yet somehow or other it floored me quite and left me for dead like, for when I came to myself it was dark, and there was a doctor and a nurse sitting by me. That was night before last. I believe they gave me something to make me stupid and sleepy, for I know I slept almost constantly day and night until this morning, when they let me get up to come to you—oh, Joe!'

" 'Lil! Lil! Don't cry any more! You will make yourself ill,' pleaded Joe.

"And Lil gasped, recovered and warded off a third attack.

" 'They all knew all about it before I knew a word. Mr. and Mrs. Claxton, and afterwards Joseph, as well as everybody else, I reckon, heard of your arrest and of your explanation of your presence with the party that stopped the coach that night, and they all believed you told the truth, Joe! Every one of them did, and of course I knew you did when Joseph told me about it.'

" 'Oh, it is so comforting to think my own friends and neighbors believe me,' sighed Joe.

"The two would have talked much longer, no doubt, but Joseph Wyvil spoke through the grating and told Joe that Mr. Rocke, his counsel, was waiting in the corridor to speak to him.

"Then Lil took leave of Joe, promising to come back as often and to stay as long as prison rules would allow.

"Joseph Wyvil showed Mr. Rocke into the cell and led Lil out, and took her home to the quiet lodgings he had provided for her.

"After this, Lil went every morning to see her boy-husband, and was permitted by the kindness of the governor to spend most of the day with him.

"Mr. Rocke, the counsel, and Joseph Wyvil, the brother, did all they could to keep up the spirits of the young pair, and succeeded better than any outsider could have believed.

CHAPTER XXVII

THE TRIAL

"AND so the time passed to the day on which the judges entered the town to hold the assizes.

"The docket was an unusually full one for this term, and many cases had to be tried before that of John Weston, charged with the murder of John Ketcham, was called.

"The remarkable feature in this case was the fact that it involved the first case of highway robbery that had occurred in that neighborhood for more than half a century, and seemed the revival of a phase of crime that had passed into history and should have been impossible in this age.

"The case drew a large concourse of people to the town, and on the first day of the trial filled the court-room almost to suffocation.

"But great was the surprise of the throng of spectators, when the atrocious criminal was brought in, to see a slight, dark-eyed and curly-haired boy, only eighteen years of age, and looking three years younger, placed in the dock.

"Many whispered comments passed through the crowd, as they gazed at the youthful prisoner. Here he stood lifted up in full view above everybody's heads, a target for all glances, looking, not frightened, but quiet, subdued, and deeply humiliated by his position; looking anything rather than the brigand and desperado they had expected to see.

"When the preliminaries of the proceedings were over, and the young prisoner was arraigned, he pleaded:

" 'Not guilty.'

"The opening charge of the prosecuting attorney was a tremendous assault upon the accused boy, as if in his slight form was incarnated the spirit of revolt, robbery, murder, treason, and all manner of evil, danger and perdition; and as if the safety of her majesty's people and dominions required the immediate death by hanging of the prisoner at the bar.

"Poor Joe was not at this time and in this place a

hero, it is sad to say! He was a very sensitive and
impressible boy, and hearing the prosecuting attorney go on at him at this rate, Joe was—so to speak—
psychologized by him and led to look upon himself,
the prisoner, as an incarnate fiend, though he had
never even suspected the fact before. Now, under
this scathing denunciation, the poor wretch bowed
his head and looked so guilty that men groaned and
women sighed to see such deep depravity in one so
young.

"At the end of the prosecutor's opening charge,
that officer called the first witness—Paul Cartright
—who, being duly sworn, testified that he was a
county constable, and about midnight on the night
of the 18th ultimo he had been alarmed by cries for
help coming from that section of the high road that
passes through Downdingle, and, with others, hurried
to the scene, where he found the stage-coach that
runs between Orton Village and Orton Station overturned and surrounded by half a dozen, or about
that number, of masked men. As he and his companions approached, he heard a pistol fired and saw
a man fall. The masked men turned and fled into
the thickets on each side of the road, and were soon
lost to the pursuers, who gave their attention to seeing to the wounded and righting the coach. He, Paul
Cartright, had caught one man in the act of flight—
had caught him, red-handed, grasping the pistol with
which he had just murdered the victim——

" 'Judge! Your honor! oh, your honor! I never
fired that pistol! I stooped to see if I could do anything for the fallen man, and seeing he was quite
dead, I picked up the pistol from the ground, without knowing what I was doing, and then the constable there took me!' burst forth poor Joe, before
any one could stop him.

"He was sternly called to order by the court, and

then instructed in a whisper by his counsel that he was on no account to speak again until he should be spoken to.

"Joe, crestfallen and despairing, subsided into silence.

" 'Do you see the man whom you took red-handed, as you say, standing pistol in hand over his slain victim?' inquired the prosecutor.

" 'Yes, sir; that is the man,' replied the witness, pointing to the young prisoner in the dock.

"Joe shook his head in desperation, but said never a word.

"The pistol was then produced, and identified by the witness as the one he had taken from the prisoner at the bar.

"A ball was produced, and identified by the next witness, Dr. Yorke, who performed the autopsy on the deceased lawyer, as the bullet extracted from the dead body. It was found to fit the empty chamber of the revolver, and to correspond perfectly with the other bullets with which it had been loaded.

"Pistol and bullets were handed to the jury, and passed from man to man—conclusive evidence of the guilt of the prisoner at the bar.

"Several other witnesses were examined, all of whom corroborated the testimony of the first one.

"Joe thought his case was gone, and he felt thankful that Lil was not there to hear evidence that might even have shaken her faith in him, since it had destroyed his faith in himself.

"But at length the case for the prosecution was closed, and the court took a recess.

"Then Mr. Rocke came around to the dock, and sat down and talked with his client, and encouraged him until his fainting self-esteem was in some degree restored.

"After recess the court reassembled, and the de-

fence was opened in a most eloquent speech by Mr.
Rocke.

"He told the whole story of 'John Weston's' purely
accidental connection with the party of young roughs
who had stopped the stage-coach, not either with
any intention of mail robbery, murder or any other
great violence, but merely to get possession of a certain document held by the deceased lawyer.

"He dwelt upon the young prisoner's total ignorance of their plans and incomplicity with their
offence.

"He described the purely accidental shooting of the
lawyer by the pistol held in the deceased's own hand,
leveled at one of the assailants, and knocked up by
the assailant in self-defence, so that it went off, send-
ing a bullet under the chin, and upward and backward
through the brain. He bade them see how easy,
natural and inevitable such an accident must be.

"He described the humane impulse of the boy spectator, now the unhappy young prisoner at the bar.
He told how he had seen the catastrophe; how he had
run to the rescue, had bent over the fallen man, but
finding him dead, had picked up the pistol, and without an idea of escaping, as the guilty ones had done,
stood there gazing at the dead in a sort of panic, no
doubt, until he was taken into custody by the constable.

"Was this, he asked, the conduct of a guilty man?
The guilty had fled—had finally escaped—had never
been recaptured. But had this young man ever even
attempted to fly?

"He would bring witnesses to prove the unblem-
ished good character of his client, and to prove that
on the fatal night of the robbery and the murder he,
the accused, so far from having any share in the con-
spiracy to stop the mail coach, had returned to his
home to spend the evening with his newly-married

wife, and had gone again only at the request of his landlady, and on a neighborly errand. It was after having executed this errand, and while he was on his way home, that he chanced most unhappily to fall in with the party of young ruffians who stopped the coach. He had no hand in their offence, and was taken while trying to render assistance to the victim.

"Then Counsellor Rocke called Joseph Wyvil, of Stockton.

"Joseph Wyvil, who had just come into court, being sworn, testified that he knew the prisoner at the bar, and had known him since he, the prisoner, was four years of age—that is, for fourteen years—and that most intimately at home and at school, and had never known him to be untruthful, dishonest or cruel in all that time, and could not possibly believe him to be capable of the crime for which he was there arraigned.

"Wyvil was cross-examined by the prosecutor as to whether he really never knew the prisoner to vary in the least from the truth, or to take liberties with the sweetmeats, or to tease cats, or to do any little thing that might trench upon the borders of false-hood, theft or cruelty.

"But all this only brought out the most positive declaration of the witness that he had not.

"Joseph Wyvil was then allowed to sit down, and Belinda Claxton was called to the stand.

"Being sworn, this witness testified that she knew the prisoner at the bar, who had been her lodger for two months up to the time of his arrest; that on the night of the highway robbery and murder he had come home to tea, and had arranged to spend the evening with his wife, and herself and her hus-band, to play a game of whist, but that news had come of the old squire's sudden death, and that she had persuaded him, the prisoner, to walk over to the

Hall and see if the report was true. That he went off, promising to be back in half an hour, or in an hour at most. When he failed to come she only thought that he had been detained at the Hall.

"Mrs. Claxton was also cross-examined as to when this whist party had been arranged. She answered that it had been settled before the prisoner had gone out to the post-office that afternoon, that he was to return to an early tea, and play whist all the evening.

"Mrs. Claxton was allowed to retire.

"John Claxton, husband of the last witness, was called, and corroborated her testimony in every item.

"Then the prosecutor got up to deliver the closing address to the jury. He made very light of the testimony for the defence, showing, or attempting to show, the jury that it really proved nothing, and had so little to do with the charge against the prisoner that it might well have been ruled out as irrelevant, impertinent and vexatious. He exhorted the jurors to do their stern duty as British jurors to punish red-handed crime; to—and so forth, and so forth.

"The judge arose to make the final charge. It was all against the prisoner. His honor considered the evidence for the prosecution as quite conclusive; the evidence advanced by the defence as weak and inconsequential. And charged the jury to bring in a verdict in accordance with the facts proven.

"Criminal trials of this sort are soon concluded in England. They do not waste so much time or spend so much money as we do over them.

"The jury retired to their room for half an hour, during which poor Joe waited in an agony of suspense as great as human nature can endure and live —in an agony that seemed to stretch that half hour into an eternity of suffering; and then the jury filed in and rendered their verdict:

" 'GUILTY.'

"Joe sprang up and fell back on his seat as if he had been shot.

" 'It will be a murder, you know, Mr. Rocke. Poor Lil!' he cried to his counsel, who came to his side.

"He was quickly called to order and directed to stand up.

"With as strong an effort at self-control as his boyish soul was capable of making, he obeyed and faced the court.

"He was then asked whether he had anything to say why sentence of death should not be pronounced upon him.

"He answered that he had a great deal to say. And then in eager, vehement, impassioned, yet most respectful language, he asseverated his innocence, and told again the often repeated true story of his connection with the young men who had stopped the stage-coach.

"The court heard him patiently, and then, when he had ceased to speak, the judge put on the black cap and proceeded to sentence the boy.

"He told him the enormity of the crime of which he had been guilty, the fairness of the trial he had stood, the ability with which he had been defended, the justice of the verdict, the justice also of his sentence, the hopelessness of any thought of mercy in this world, the necessity of seeking mercy from a higher tribunal, and finally he pronounced the ghastly sentence of the law, and ended with the prayer that the Lord might have mercy on his soul!

" 'Poor Lil!' was all the boy said, as the bailiffs led him away.

"And the court was adjourned.

CHAPTER XXVIII

IN THE TOILS OF FATE

"JOE was conveyed back to his prison cell and locked up and left there in a state of stupefaction.

"Joseph Wyvil, who had heard the verdict, was not able to get near the unfortunate boy, who had been hurried from the dock to the prison van by the officers in attendance. And though he followed the prisoner with all speed to the jail, he was not admitted to see him because it was after the hour of closing.

"He managed to see the jail chaplain and implore him, late as it was, to visit the desolate boy in his cell that night.

"The reverend gentleman willingly promised to do so, and Joseph Wyvil left the prison, with what a heavy heart! to go to his most unhappy sister and answer as best he might the agonizing questions she would be sure to put to him.

"Ah! the dreadful intelligence had preceded him to Lil's lodgings, and prostrated her frail frame to the very verge of death.

"He found the doctor in attendance, and the young wife, pale as a corpse, sleeping heavily under the influence of a powerful narcotic.

" 'How did she hear it?' was one of the first questions put by the unhappy brother.

" 'By the yelling of the people in the street. We could hardly keep her from going to the court-room; we couldn't keep her away from the windows, watching for you and her husband to come back arm in arm. She was so confident he would be acquitted! For she said he was innocent, and being innocent, could not be found guilty and must be acquitted,' replied their landlady.

" 'Ah! she knew nothing of the power of circumstantial evidence to convict an innocent man!' groaned Joseph.

" 'Why, sir, she even packed her trunk to return to Stockton, for she said that neither she nor her husband, nor her brother, would want to stay another night in the town where they had suffered so much, but would take the first train back to their cottage and be at peace.'

" 'Poor child! Poor child!'

" 'And then, while she was watching for you and him from the window, and turning round every few minutes to ask me to be sure to keep the water boiling so as to make tea the minute they should come in, or to please have the bacon grilled to a turn, or something of that sort, all of a sudden she heard the boys in the street shouting to one another that Weston, the mail-robber, was found guilty and sentenced to be hanged o' Monday week!'

" 'She heard that? Oh, poor Lil!'

" 'She heard that, sir, and afore any one could stop her she was out in the street, in the freezing winter night, without shawl or bonnet, to inquire into the truth. I just whipped a plaid shawl over my head and ran out to fetch her in. I found her prostrate and insensible on the ground, with a crowd of people gathered around her. We raised her and brought her in and laid her on the bed and brought her to. But as soon as she got back her senses to know what had happened, she fell into such convulsions that we had to send for Dr. Yorke, and he gave her summat to quiet her and put her to sleep. And that's all, sir,' concluded the landlady.

"The doctor gave directions for the treatment of his patient during the night, and left, promising to return early the next morning.

"The tired landlady went to rest, asking to be called at any time if she should be wanted.

"And Joseph Wyvil took his seat by the bedside of his unfortunate sister, to watch her sleep and dread her waking.

"A low taper burned on a little table behind a screen. And all the room was obscure and silent as a cave.

"Lil slept on quietly, and Joseph was almost tempted to hope that Lil might wake only in that happier world where 'there shall be no more death, neither crying nor sorrow.'

"Joseph Wyvil was a faithful Christian man, and found his greatest support during this long miserable nigl t watch in praying for Lil and for Joe.

"The late winter morning had dawned when Lil awoke.

"She awoke very quietly, and although she opened her eyes, looked about, saw her brother seated by her bed, and evidently by the change that passed over her face, remembered all that had happened since yesterday, yet there was no outburst of grief. The effect of the narcotic yet remained in the blunted sensibilities. But though her feelings were dulled, her intellect was clear enough; and although there was no outbreak of sorrow, yet the look of deep despair that settled on her face showed how profoundly she realized the situation.

" 'Lil! Lil, my darling sister,' muttered Joseph Wyvil, bending over her.

" 'Let me go to him, Joseph! Oh, please let me go to him. I will behave myself. Indeed I will behave myself, Joseph,' she pleaded.

" 'Yes, dear, you shall go just as soon as the doors are opened to admit visitors.'

"She put out her hand and pressed his.

" 'But, darling Lil, you need not give up hope. All

is not lost yet, Lil! I mean to get up a strong petition
in his behalf. He is so young. There are so many
circumstances in his favor. Lil, I am nearly certain
we can get his sentence commuted to transportation
for life. And then we also will go out to Australia,
to be near him. And if he conducts himself well,
as he will be sure to do, having so much at stake,
he will get a ticket of leave. And after a few weeks,
Lil, we'll not be any worse off than if we had emi-'
grated, you know. Are you listening, Lil?'

" 'Yes, Joseph. Oh, take me to him. I want to go
to him so much. I will behave myself so well.'

" 'Yes, dear. Just as soon as ever I can do so.
Keep up your heart.'

" 'If he dies I shall die too, and in a fortnight all
will be over, and we two shall meet on the other side,
never to part any more.'

" 'Don't speak so hopelessly, dear Lil. I feel sure
in my own mind that we shall win a commutation
of his sentence, and then the worst that can happen
to us will be that we shall have to go to Australia;
and that may turn out to be the very best that could
happen.'

"Their conversation was interrupted by a rap at
the door, followed by the entrance of the landlady
with a small bowl of beef tea for the poor girl.

" 'Oh, I thank you; but indeed I cannot take anything,' said Lil, when this refreshment was offered to
her.

" 'Come, now, I want you to drink this because it
will do you good. And you promised to behave, you
know,' said her brother.

" 'I will drink it then,' said Lil, with perfect
docility. And so well was the liquid seasoned that
on tasting it she drank it without reluctance and even
with benefit.

"The landlady had scarcely left the room, with the empty bowl in her hand, when the doctor entered it.

"Joseph Wyvil arose and bowed, and yielded his place by the bedside to the physician, who seated himself and proceeded to examine his patient.

" 'She is going on well, yet I would recommend a continuance of the same treatment for a while longer. She should be kept somewhat under the influence of sedatives to tide her over this trial,' was his whispered advice to Joseph Wyvil, as he arose to leave the room.

"He wrote a prescription and minute directions for its administration, and then took leave.

"Joseph Wyvil went down to his breakfast and sent up the landlady's servant to assist Lil in rising and dressing to go to the jail.

"Joseph called a carriage, but before he put her into it administered a dose of that merciful medicine sent by the doctor to quiet her nerves and blunt her feelings, if it could not obscure her intelligence.

"And so they drove to the jail and were admitted to the presence of poor Joe.

"The jail doctor and the chaplain had done their part, and the doomed boy was much calmer than he had been on the preceding day.

"The stricken young pair met without any violent outbreak of emotion. Each grew paler as they embraced, and neither could speak to the other at first. They sat down on the side of the cot, with their hands clasped together.

"Joseph Wyvil, after taking and pressing his brother's hand, drew the chair and seated himself before them, and began to talk of the petition for the commutation of Joe's sentence he intended that day to set on foot. Mr. Rocke, he said, would draw it up, and he thought that judge and jury would sign it as well as many clergymen and other citizens. He himself would take it up to the Home Secretary. He felt sure, he said, that the petition would be granted, and that transportation for life would be the very worst that Joe would have to suffer. Beyond every reasonable cause for believing this, Joseph declared that he felt an interior confidence that was prophetic, for which he could not account.

" 'And then, Joe, your fate will not be hard. It will depend upon yourself to make it easy. If you behave yourself, you will find it light enough, from all that I can hear. You will be taken as some gentleman's valet, or even secretary, and after a while get your ticket of leave, and in due time your pardon——'

" 'Pardon for what I never did!' said Joe.

" 'Be patient, dear boy! There be a deal of undeserved suffering in this world for which there must be compensation somewhere. And after all, Joe, there is many a free emigrant who has suffered and will suffer more than you need to do. And listen to this, Joe. After a year or two, just as soon as I have made money enough to carry us through, I will bring Lil out to you and we will all live out there together, and it will depend only on ourselves, under the Divine Providence, whether we prosper.'

" 'We have not got the commutation yet,' said Joe, despondently.

" 'But we will get it,' replied Joseph, confidently.

"At this moment Mr. Rocke entered the cell with the petition in his hand.

"Joseph ceded his chair and took a seat on the foot of the cot.

"After shaking hands with the prisoner, his wife and brother, Mr. Rocke read the petition, and producing a pocket pen and ink-stand, asked for their signatures.

"Joe signed his name first, Lil next, adding naïvely on the same line: 'Oh, please, please.'

"Mr. Rocke frowned, smiled, but let it stand.

"Joseph Wyvil then signed his name.

"And then the two men left the cell to go and take the petition around the town, leaving Lil with Joe.

"By this time all of the boy's history was known to the townspeople. Joseph Wyvil had given it to the lawyer, at first retaining him. The lawyer had given it to the reporter of the *Guardian* on the evening of the trial, and the whole story was published in this morning's issue, together with the report of the trial.

"There was a reaction in public sentiment. Much doubt was entertained of the prisoner's complicity with the crime for which he had been condemned. Much pity was felt for him and for his child-wife, in their extreme youth and utter despair. The petition for the commutation of his sentence was signed by judge, jury, magistrates, clergymen and citizens of all rank.

"Joseph Wyvil and Mr. Rocke took it up to London together and laid it before the Home Secretary.

"Three weary days passed before they could obtain a hearing. Then five tedious days before any action was taken on the petition.

"During all this time Joseph Wyvil wrote daily letters full of confidence and encouragement to his waiting, breathlessly anxious sister and brother.

"At length, on the ninth day, Joseph Wyvil and Mr. Rocke received the commutation and started with it for Carlisle.

"It was after the hours of closing the prison. But they could not easily consent to leave the prisoner, who was now the object of the royal clemency, one more sleepless night of agonizing suspense.

"So while Joseph Wyvil went home to gladden the heart of his sister with the good news, Mr. Rocke

LILITH

went to the house of the chaplain and with him to the governor of the jail, and so gained admittance to the cell.

"Joe, who had parted with Lil but an hour before, was sitting on the side of his cot staring into vacancy and on the verge of falling into idiocy, saw through his grated door the low light of the turnkey's lantern approaching, and roused himself.

"In another moment the door was unlocked, the two men entered, and Joe's eager, questioning eyes read the good news in their faces before the chaplain took his hand and said:

" 'Return thanks to the Lord, my boy! You are saved!'

" 'Oh, Lil! Lil!' cried Joe, and dropped his head in his hands and sobbed like a child.

"When at length he recovered himself he thanked the chaplain and the lawyer for all that they had done in his behalf.

"And then, as it was late, the two gentlemen shook hands with the prisoner and withdrew.

"The next morning the meeting between the young pair was a happier one than they had had since they had parted on that fatal night of the old squire's death and the lawyer's murder.

"Joseph Wyvil also kept their spirits up by hopefully putting the fairest view of the future before them. He reiterated that it depended on Joe himself whether his lot in Australia would be the hard lot of a convict or the ordinary lot of a hard-working emigrant. The chaplain of this prison, he said, would write a letter to the chaplain of the transport-ship and make interest with him for the young exile. And lastly, that, within a year, or two years at most, he would bring Lil out to Sydney.

" 'And by that time, Joe, you will have behaved yourself so well as to have got your ticket-of-leave and maybe your free pardon, too, and we will all, please the Lord, forget our troubles and live happily together.'

"And Lil and Joe believed all that their hopeful brother told them, and anticipated the brighter days that might be in store for them in the future years.

"The interval between this day and the sailing of the transport-ship was passed as calmly and hopefully as possible under the circumstances.

"Lil was allowed to be as much with Joe as the rules of the prison justified, and even a little more, perhaps, for governor, chaplain and physician all sympathized with them, despite the rigid discipline that would bind souls as much as bodies in such cases of officers and prisoners.

"The day came in which Joe and a fellow-prisoner named Jeremiah Hatfield, convicted of robbery and sentenced to seven years' transportation and penal servitude, were to be taken from the prison, hand-cuffed together and put upon the train, in charge of two armed keepers, to be taken to Liverpool, from whence the transport-ship Vulture was to sail.

"Lil, supported by the strong arm and strong heart of her brother Joseph, went early to the prison to take leave of Joe.

"Joe behaved pretty well under the circumstances, kept up his own spirits and kept up Lil's.

" 'Only look upon this as if I were going to sea, Lil! You know I am not guilty. I will not consider myself a convict. I will think of myself only as an emigrant. And I will behave so well, please the Lord, that everybody shall esteem me, whether they will or no. And shall believe that I have been wrongly accused. Cheer up, Lil.'

"The doctor had mercifully given Lil a sedative that morning to enable her to go through the ordeal, else Heaven only knows what sort of a scene of wild

hysterics would have been enacted in that cell. As
it was, Lil's heart only ached with a dull despair that
found no outlet in sobs or tears, or even complaint.

"The poor boy and girl were allowed to remain
together until the last possible minute, and then,
when they were warned that the moment of parting
had actually come, there was one long, clinging embrace, and then Joseph led his sister away—not crying, not fainting, yet half dead in her dumb anguish.

"The chaplain remained with Joe. And before the
wife and brother had reached the end of the corridor, another prisoner was brought from another cell,
handcuffed to Joe, and both were led off to the prison
van that was to take them to the railway station
en route for Liverpool and the transport-ship.

"Joseph Wyvil took his sister back to their lodg-
ing-house and made her go to bed, where, overcome
by all that she had done and borne that day, and
stupefied by the sedative she had taken, she fell into
a long sleep.

"Meanwhile the kind-hearted and helpful landlady
packed up all her lodgers' effects to save Lil trouble,
in anticipation of the journey that was to be taken
the next day.

"Lil awoke the next morning much calmer and
stronger than might have been expected.

"And the same day Joseph Wyvil, after thanking
and remunerating their landlady, took his sister back
to their cottage home at Stockton.

CHAPTER XXIX

DELIVERANCE

So, trial after trial past,
Shalt thou fall at the very last,
Breathless, half in trance,
With the thrill of a great deliverance,
Into our arms forevermore.

Browning.

"JOSEPH WYVIL took his sister home, but it was no longer the bright and happy home that it had been before Lil's stolen marriage and its almost tragic end.

"Lil fell into such dull and deep despair that her brother feared it would terminate in that most hopeless form of madness known as melancholia.

"He consulted their old family physician, who, after several visits to his patient, recommended an entire change of scene, occupations and interests for the despairing girl.

"Ah, poor Joseph Wyvil! And poor Lil! The doctor might as reasonably have recommended a yacht to the Mediterranean Sea and a palace on the coast of Sicily for this impoverished and embarrassed brother and sister.

"The expenses of the trial had absorbed all Joseph Wyvil's savings, and even compelled him to mortgage his house.

"For to the lawyer's fees and other legal costs there had been added the expenses of his own and his sister's board and lodging at Carlisle, and of his own and the lawyer's journey to London and back, and their hotel bills while in that city dancing attendance at Somerset House, and the loss of time and work.

"Joseph Wyvil was hopelessly embarrassed in money matters. The lately industrious, thriving and 'fore-handed' mechanic was financially ruined.

"Not by his own doings, but by the folly and calamity of his sister and brother.

"He had lost his work also, and could not recover it. This was a misfortune he had not in the least calculated upon. But another man had got his place, and there was no room for him.

"Joseph first sold his silver watch, and next the precious half dozen silver tea-spoons left him by his mother, to pay the interest on his notes and to bear current expenses. After that, piece by piece of the little parlor set went.

"But these could not last long. The crash came. The house was sold under the mortgage, and the little home was broken up. So much calamity may come of one little act of folly like Joe's and Lil's runaway marriage.

"Joseph took his sister and the remnant of his household furniture and moved into two rooms of a poor tenement house, and tried to get work even as a common laborer, but failed.

"He then sold more of his small stock of furniture, divided the money with Lil, and went 'on the tramp,' seeking work of any honest sort wherever he might get it.

"So he drifted to Liverpool. There he met with an old shipmate and friend of his late uncle, Zebedee Wyvil. This was George Poole, now captain of the fast-sailing Baltimore clipper Oriole, then in port.

"To Captain Poole poor Joseph Wyvil told his story.

"After hearing him to the end, the skipper said:

" 'There is always work for willing hands in America, and often fortune, too. Come out with me to America, Wyvil. I shall sail for Baltimore in ten days.'

" 'I have no money, and all my household goods would not bring ten pounds,' sadly replied Joseph.

" 'The more reason for your accepting my offer. Come, you can work your passage over if you insist upon being independent, and when——'

" 'But my poor little sister. I cannot leave her in her misery.'

" 'Of course you cannot. Who asked you to do so? Bring her with you. She shall have a free passage; or, if she has too much pride to accept a favor, she may help the stewardess mend the ship's linen, just as she pleases. Come, old fellow, take an old friend's honest offer and best advice. Run up to Carlisle. Sell out your sticks, and bring your sister down here. You have plenty of time to settle up all your affairs. And when we get to

"The land of the free and the home of the brave,"

I will look after you like a godfather until you get work. Come, what do you say?'

" 'I accept your kindness. But, oh! how shall I ever be able to express my thanks?'

" 'By holding your tongue, and getting ready to sail, my boy. You said your doctor recommended change of scene for the girl, didn't you?'

" 'Oh, yes! yes! But how was I to provide it for her, even though her life or reason might depend on her having it?'

" 'Exactly. But now you see it is provided for her. Hurry back to her, Wyvil. By the way, here. You must not dream of tramping back to Carlisle. Take this five-pound note. Pshaw! Nonsense! I am not offering to give it to you, man, but to lend it. There, hurry back to your sister, and fetch her down. I'll warrant her spirits will improve in a week.'

"Joseph Wyvil would have thanked this warm-hearted and generous friend and benefactor, but found no words, no voice to express himself.

"He took the first train back to Stockton, and returned to the poor lodgings where he had left Lil.

"He found her much worse than he had left her—paler, thinner, weaker and more melancholy.

"When he told her of the prospect opened for them by this free passage to America, her first words were those of disappointment.

" 'I thought we were to go out to Australia to join poor Joe.'

" 'And so we are to do, dear, just as soon as I can make money enough to take us out there. But I cannot make this money in England. And so we must thank Heaven for this free passage to America, where work is plenty and wages high. There it will require a much shorter time to make money enough to take us out to join Joe.'

" 'But will this voyage carry us any farther away from poor Joe than we are now?' was Lil's next anxious question.

" 'No; no farther. I do not think as far. Australia is at the antipodes, as we stand here, you know; so every thousand miles we sail must take us a thousand miles nearer in space, and the greater facilities offered in America will take us years nearer in time to our heart's desire.'

" 'Let us go, then! Oh! let us go! I begin to see light at last!' exclaimed Lil, rallying as she had never rallied since her parting with her husband.

"The need of activity, the prospect of a journey and a voyage, and conditions that were to bring her nearer in time as well as in space to Joe, infused new life into Lil.

"She rendered prompt and efficient aid to Joseph in preparing to leave home.

"The sale of their household goods brought exactly £7 5s. 3d., or about $37.56 of our money. Joseph had of the money loaned him by Captain Poole, £4 10s., so that when he had settled all his little debts he had still £10, or $50 of our money, left.

"On the day after their sale they took the train for Liverpool, and by the captain's advice, went immediately on board the ship, to save expense of board and lodging in the town.

"In a few days the Oriole sailed, and wind and weather proving very favorable, in two weeks the clipper crossed the Atlantic Ocean and anchored in Baltimore harbor.

"Within a week after landing Joseph Wyvil obtained work as a journeyman carpenter on a house that some contractor was in a hurry to finish by a certain date.

"Then he took his sister from off the ship, and conveyed her to a cheap, respectable boarding-house.

"Within a month after this the Oriole sailed again for Liverpool, and the brother and sister lost their kind friend.

"Joseph Wyvil and Lil had both written to their poor Joe before leaving England, telling him of their new hopes and plans.

"They wrote again on reaching Baltimore, telling him of their better fortunes, and of their one object in making and saving money as fast as possible to go out and join him.

"But ah! Joseph Wyvil's prosperity did not continue. When the house on which he had been at work was completed, he and his fellow-journeymen were thrown out of employment, and despite their utmost endeavors, remained idle for the rest of the winter.

"But about the middle of March a change came. A certain capitalist of Baltimore had found out a favorable part of the Jersey coast for the opening of a new summer resort that should combine cheapness with everything else that was desirable in life.

"He had leased the one large hotel on the place, and was about to build a number of small, rough cottages and bathing-houses there to accommodate visitors.

"All the carpenters who happened to be out of employment, and were willing to leave Baltimore for several months, were engaged at good wages on the work.

"Joseph Wyvil was among the rest, and he went to Seawood, taking his sister with him.

"The other workmen got accommodations in the fishermen's cottages scattered here and there along the shore, but Joseph Wyvil took his sister to a little inland village about two miles from the sea, lodged her in a farm-house for a few days, and then rented a cheap cottage with a little garden, furnished it with the bare necessities of life, and put her there.

"Gradually, as the spring and summer went on, he added little comforts to her store as his wages enabled him to do so.

"He went to work every morning, and returned every evening. He and his sister lived a most secluded life. They joined the Episcopal church at Seawood by letters from the rector of the parish church at Stockton, and as they were described as Joseph Wyvil, of Stockton, and Elizabeth, wife of Joseph Wyvil, a very natural mistake was made in their case—a mistake that they never thought of, and that no one else was aware of.

"They were taken for husband and wife instead of brother and sister; and as they went nowhere but to church, and received no visitors, this natural mistake was not corrected.

"They lived contentedly enough together, writing by every Australian mail to Joe, and looking forward to the time when they should have money enough to go out to him.

"They had not had a line from poor little Joe since he sailed in the transport-ship, on the fifteenth of the last December, nor had they expected to get one. They knew that months must elapse before the end of his voyage, and more months before a return letter could come to them. They even remembered how many months must pass before their first letter could reach him, though after the first long gap of silence the letters would come and go more frequently.

"To complicate matters more—to fill the situation with more of grief and more of joy—it was certain that little Lil was destined to become a mother. This fact was not written to Joe, for, said Lil:

" 'If I tell him it will only add to his anxiety and impatience to see us. If my child should live, it will only be the greater surprise and delight to him when he hears of it or sees it.'

"It was about the middle of August, ten months after Lil's marriage, and seven months after the heartbreaking separation from her husband, that the second catastrophe of her life came.

"You already know all about it—how, while Joseph Wyvil was at work on the shore, in the heat of an August afternoon, the little son of Major Hereward, while bathing, got out of his depth, and being unable to swim, was drowning and cried out for help.

"And Joseph Wyvil forgot all prudence in his manly impulse to rescue the perishing boy, and all overheated as he was, plunged into the water, swam to him and seized him; how he had just time to tow him in and fling him into the outstretched arms of a fisherman, when he was seized with cramp, sank and was swirled away by the under-current.

"You know all about that, and how the news of his sudden and violent death shocked the delicate young mother into a premature confinement, and how little Lil died within a few hours after giving birth to her daughter—died without being able to articulate one word of explanation to Major Hereward, who, brought thither by the minister, stood beside her bed ready to adopt the infant orphaned for his sake and for the sake of his son.

"Major Hereward was in no measure to blame for what occurred; yet he mourned as if he had been culpably responsible for the tragedy, and he did all that lay in his power—all that mortal man could do to atone for it. And not the least part of his work was his adoption and education of the orphan infant."

"That was his bounden duty. His most sacred duty. And in the object of this duty he found the greatest comfort and happiness of his life," said Tudor Hereward, breaking in for the first time upon Zuniga's narrative, and taking and carrying the hand of Lilith to his lips.

"I can well believe that! Lilith was a true daughter to her adopted father," said Zuniga.

"She has been true as truth in every relation of her difficult life," added Hereward.

"Will you tell us now, dear, what we most long to know—your own life after you left England under such a cruel and unjust condemnation? For even to me, your child, you have never told that story, consecutively," said Lilith, to divert the conversation from herself, for she was always embarrassed by such very direct praise.

"Yes, but still in the third person, if you please,

and still partly from the notes I have made from time to time," said Zuniga.

And he resumed his personal history as if speaking of another.

CHAPTER XXX

OUT OF THE SNARE AND ON THE WING

And all the time they hunted me,
From hill to plain, from shore to sea,
And justice hounding far and wide
Her bloodhounds through the country side,
Breathed hot and instant on my trace.

Browning.

"You know it was reported that John Weston was killed, shot dead, while trying to escape from Port Arthur. You will discover in the course of this narrative how that false report got out and how it secured his escape.

"John Weston was rather favored by the chaplain of the transport-ship on account, I think, of his youth and good looks, as well as his good behavior and the recommendation of the prison chaplain.

"When they were well out to sea he was taken from the convict gang into the chaplain's room to wait on his reverence, though the office was a mere sinecure.

"He had a good time of it all through the voyage, with nothing at all to cry for but the lost company of his Lil and his brother, and the cruel imputation of crime under which he lived, or seemed to live, for really you do not believe that anybody in that ship could look at the handsome little fellow and take him for a criminal. You don't, indeed!

"The Vulture was a very slow sailer, and we were five months at sea.

"It was the first of May when the ship reached Hobart Town.

"Here the convict gang were handcuffed, two and two, sent on shore under strong guard, and transferred from the custody of the ship's officers to that of the authorities in the town.

"They were lodged in jail that night, and the next morning assigned to their work.

"And now John Weston's troubles began. As a felon convicted of a capital crime, and condemned to death, who had had his sentence commuted to transportation and penal servitude for life, he was at once classed among the worst criminals and sent on to Port Arthur, the prison to which the most heavily sentenced of the British convicts were at that time doomed.

"True, the chaplain of the transport-ship had tried to interest the jail chaplain and the colonial authorities in favor of the boy; but all in vain. Chaplains have no authority and precious little influence in the convict settlements.

"So John Weston, who had done very little evil in his brief life, poor lad! was shipped off to that perdition of evil-doers—Port Arthur.

"It would be too cruel to harrow your heart with any description of his sufferings there, where everything that could revolt his nature surrounded him.

"No more of that. One day he was sent for to the office of the commandant, where he received the first letter that he had seen since leaving England. It was a joint letter from Joseph and Lil, telling him of their settlement at Seawood on the New Jersey coast in America. Also of the good wages Joseph was getting, and of their hopes soon to come out and join him.

LILITH 319

"Join him! How little they knew or suspected of his dreadful condition! They evidently thought that some chance of redemption had been given him, that he had been assigned to some easy duty as clerk, messenger, or bookkeeper in some of the officers' quarters; that he would soon get his ticket-of-leave, and only a little later his free pardon! And they would come out and join him and settle down to sheep-farming as hopeful colonists, as the too sanguine chaplain had led them to anticipate.

"When the real truth was—too horrible to dwell upon!

"By the allusions in this letter, John Weston learned that there must have been several other letters that preceded this one, and had never reached him.

"He did not reply to it; he had no heart to do so. He preferred to let Joseph and Lil dream their dream of the imaginary future a little longer, while he himself dreamed of escape or of—suicide.

"Early one morning after this he was at work under the timber cliffs, where many convicts were employed cutting down trees, and lopping off their branches, many others in rolling the huge boles down to the beach, and others still—among whom was John Weston—were toiling at the hardest work, up to their waists in water, harnessed like mules to these immense logs, and hauling them to the distant ship-yard.

"So early was the hour at which they had been called to work that it was as yet scarcely light on that cool autumn morning.

"John Weston, driven to desperation by the misery and hopelessness of his condition, suddenly determined to make a dash for freedom or for death. While preparing to harness himself to the great bole to be hauled, he suddenly threw ropes and chains over his head, leaped for the deeper water, and struck out for the open sea. He was a strong and skilful swimmer, whose muscular strength had been greatly developed by hard work in the open air; he was stimulated by desperate hope, and everything was in his favor. The tide was going out and the sea was calm.

"If he could only reach that rugged promontory nine miles distant up the coast, a point totally inaccessible by land, and almost so by water also, except by such a desperate wretch as himself.

"If he could reach that point, climb that cliff, lose himself in that impenetrable wilderness, why, then, he might starve or freeze to death in time, might be killed by the bushmen, or devoured by wild beasts; but he could never be recaptured, and he might eventually escape.

"A forlorn hope! But he seized it for all and more than all it was worth.

"Ah! but scarcely had he taken his leap for life before the alarm was given, and shot after shot was fired. One struck him, grazing the tip of his ear. He dived instantly, and that gave the rise to the report of his death—'shot while trying to make his escape!' No more shots were fired after that! When he rose again to the surface he was so far from the shore that his small cropped head was lost to view among the billows.

"He never reached the promontory, however. His strength gave out, or was giving out, when he swam for a floating log that had been washed away from the timber cliffs. Around this he clasped himself, and kept himself up, as well as he could, to put off death as long as possible.

"He was drifting farther and farther out to sea, and his senses were becoming benumbed and his thoughts confused; yet still he instinctively held on

to the log until everything else seemed to have left
him.

"When John Weston recovered his consciousness
he found himself in a comfortable berth in a ship
that he afterwards discovered to be the American
merchantman Buzzard, homeward bound from Calcutta to New York.

"Later on he learned the facts of his rescue. He
had been seen floating on the log by the man at the
look-out. A boat had been put off to his relief, and
he had been brought on board the ship, in apparent
death. All means known to science had been used
for his restoration, and they had proved successful.

"In a day or two John Weston was strong as ever,
and went before the mast a willing worker, in a-
short-handed ship, which had lost several of its men
by fever while in port at Calcutta.

"On reaching New York he discharged himself, and
glad, glorious with this realization of freedom, he
started at once for Seawood to give Joseph and Lil
a joyful surprise.

"Ah, how soon were his high hopes dashed to the
ground! He reached Seawood the same day.

"He inquired for Mr. Joseph Wyvil. He was told
the sad tragedy with which you are already acquainted—that Joseph Wyvil had been drowned in
rescuing the son of a Major Hereward, that Mrs.
Wyvil had died on the same day on which her child
was born, and that the orphan baby-girl had been
adopted and taken away to be brought up as his own
daughter by Major Hereward.

"Poor Joe—to give him back his familiar name
since his escape—poor Joe was nearly crushed to
death by this blow. He inquired about Major Hereward, but could not find out his address.

"The rector, who had been with Lil in her last moments, might have given him the information, but he had gone to Europe for his health.

"At last poor Joe gave up the search for the time being, and contented himself, on the child's account, by reflecting that she was in good hands and much better situated than she could be in his own possession, even if he, the fugitive convict, could dare to claim her.

"Satisfied as to his child's fortunes, but heartbroken for his wife's and his brother's loss, the poor fellow started on an aimless tramp over the country, getting a job of work here and there, just enough to keep him from starvation; sleeping in barns and outhouses, and faring as hard as he had fared in prison, except in loss of liberty.

"One day he fell in with a company of strolling players, and he joined them, getting nothing for his services except his 'victual and drink,' and very little and of very poor quality of that.

"But, after all, it was the small beginning of great things in that line. At first he was only trusted with small parts; but people were pleased to say he was handsome, elegant and attractive; he soon developed dramatic talent, and was charged with the leading parts in whatever might be afoot of tragedy, comedy or opera.

"After awhile he joined a circus company, where he learned to ride and to perform wondrous feats of equestrianism. He studied to improve himself in all these arts, of singing, riding, acting.

"He belonged, in succession, to many traveling companies, and he went all over the United States, the West Indies, Bermuda, and into several of the countries of South America. It took years, but at last he reached the climax of his fame as 'Mr. Alfred Ancillon, the World-Renowned,' and so forth and so forth! But with all this, he never made his fortune, and never, in all his life, had a hundred dollars over and above his expenses; no, not even when he was the proprietor of the Grand Plantagenet and Montmorenci Combination, etc., etc., which had the honor of playing before the enlightened audience of Frosthill, while all the crowned heads of Europe were pining for its presence.

"It was while at Frosthill that Mr. Alfred Ancillon chanced to hear of poor Joe Wyvil's little daughter, now grown to womanhood and married to her adopted father's only son, and that since the death of Major Hereward, and the departure of Mr. Hereward for Washington, she had been living alone at Cloud Cliffs.

"A very natural and most eager desire seized him to behold his daughter. He went to Cloud Cliffs and introduced himself, fearing the while that she would fail to recognize his claim and would deny him.

"But as fate would have it, she had, only that day, for the first time, overhauled certain old letters and papers, which had not seen the light since the day she was born; and in them she had read the story of poor Joe's life, and had even seen poor Joe's photograph.

"So when he revealed himself she recognized him at once. And when he explained that he was a fugitive from injustice, and that the extradition treaty was in force, she readily took the oath of secrecy her father prescribed for her—the oath that has been the cause of so much misunderstanding, suspicion and misery.

"Among the papers that he found in the old trunk, which had escaped his daughter's notice, was a diary kept by the old seaman, Zebedee Wyvil, in which was described, among other matters, the embarkation of Señor Don Louis Zuniga, with his wife, Donna Isabella Mendoza, and their infant son; and also the

Marquis of ——, the brother of the lady, on the Falcon, homeward bound from Havana to Liverpool.

"The diary, suddenly stopped and renewed ten days later, described the wreck of the Falcon, and the distribution of the crew and passengers into three boats; commanded respectively by the captain, the first mate and the second mate. The Marquis of —— found a place in the captain's boat, the Señor Zuniga, with his wife and child, in the third boat.

"The diary went on to describe the sufferings of the party in the last boat, and the subsequent death of the señor and señora, and the rescue of the only survivors, Zebedee Wyvil and the Spanish infant.

"This record, begun in a small pocket volume, was continued in similar books, and kept up to the end of the writer's life. And it contained a true record of the Spanish boy's adoption and education.

"Mr. Alfred Ancillon, thinking that he had the best right to this, took possession of it, without saying anything about it to his daughter. His silence on the subject was not premeditated, however, but the mere result of having so many more interesting things to talk of.

"When, however, Mr. Ancillon went to Washington to play at the Varieties he happened to hear that the Marquis of —— was minister from the Court of P—— to that capital. Subsequently he saw the minister in a public place, and certainly recognized a family likeness to himself.

"Then he laid his little plan. When his engagement at the Varieties ended, he did not go on to San Francisco as he was advertised to go, but sent a young man of his troupe, made up to personate him, while he stayed in the city and made himself up in his true, his only true, character, that of the Señor Zuniga, and so presented himself to the Marquis of —— as his nephew, the son of his deceased sister.

"The hidalgo was startled, amazed, incredulous.

"But the señor had his proofs, and these were corroborated by a strong family likeness.

"There was much cross-questioning, and close investigation. The marquis learned all the facts of the wreck of the Falcon, which, by the way, his own memory confirmed.

"He heard all about the death of his sister and brother-in-law, and the survival and rescue of Mate Zebedee Wyvil and the infant, Zuniga, by the Polly Ann.

"He heard all the details of the adoption, rearing and education of the young Zuniga by the mate, Zebedee Wyvil, and of the life of the youth at home, at college, and at sea, up to the time of his return from his voyage with Captain Pentecost.

"But he learned nothing of the runaway marriage, the trial for murder, the transportation to the penal colonies, the escape thence, the theatrical career and so on.

"In short, the marquis learned all of his young relative that it was expedient that he should know, and nothing more.

"And when he was satisfied that his nephew wanted nothing whatever from him, either of money, influence or preferment, or any other favor, and when he was pleased to see that the young man was fairly presentable in society, he graciously acknowledged him, entertained him, and presented him to his friends.

"You know the rest.

"But this must be acknowledged—that never, in his whole successful career as an actor, did the 'world-renowned artist, Mr. Alfred Ancillon,' undertake so difficult a part, or achieve so splendid a triumph, as when he caused himself to be introduced to his own daughter as the Señor Zuniga, and thoroughly deceived her in regard to his identity! For although, at first, she was startled out of her self-possession by what she considered a most amazing likeness, yet still in the end she was completely deluded.

"And now one word as to the fine art of success-ful disguise. It does not consist in coarse contri-vances, like staining the complexion of a different hue or wearing a wig of different colored hair, or any-thing of that sort, which does not alter the form of the features, or the character of the countenance. It consists in very refined touches, invisible to the naked eye, and yet capable of changing the whole individ-uality of the face, so that, though it may leave a likeness, it will seem only a likeness. These super-fine, magical touches are delicate strokes with a camel's hair pencil at the corners of the eyebrows, the corners of the eyelids, corners of the nostrils and of the mouth, changing the angles up or down as may be required, and so changing the very shape of the features so delicately that the art cannot be de-tected. Then, with a slight modification in the glance of the eye, the tone of the voice, and the gesture of the hand, the transformation is complete.

"In this artistic manner Zuniga deluded everybody as to his identity, so that if any one had ventured to raise the question whether or not he was the man known to the play-going public as Mr. Alfred Ancil-lon, his intimate friends must have scouted the idea, and while admitting the likeness, denied the identity, because, and so forth, and so forth.

"You know the rest of the adventurer's story quite as well as he does; so little more need to be added, except that he has bitterly repented all the sorrow his recklessness brought upon his daughter, and even upon her husband. It is not certain that his recov-ery of his proper name, Zuniga, will lead to any last-ing benefit to himself or any one connected with him.

As the only son and heir of Don Luis Zuniga, he would be entitled to large landed estates and much funded wealth, all held in abeyance. But courts of law would require more proof of his identity than it may be practical to produce, so it is very doubtful whether his estates can ever be recovered. That is all, friends."

As the Señor Zuniga concluded his story, he arose, kissed his daughter, and took a turn up and down the room.

"You have been more sinned against than sinning! What a life you have led!" exclaimed Tudor Hereward.

"And I am not yet forty years of age! An age at which many men, and women, too, actually first marry and begin life!" said Zuniga, pausing in the midst of his walk.

"You must begin a happier life from this time forth, dear," said Lilith, tenderly.

"I—I—I—think—— Don't you all think as we had better have luncheon now? Everybody looks so tired," said Mrs. Downie, wiping her eyes.

Zuniga broke into one of his hilarious laughs and seconded the motion, which was carried unanimously.

CHAPTER XXXI

CONCLUSION

The Herewards, Señor Zuniga and Mrs. Downie, according to arrangement, lived on in the house in the Champs Elysées during the month of the Prince and Princess Gherardini's bridal tour.

In that month they saw—they even became familiar with—all that was most worth seeing in Paris.

They also made excursions to all places of interest in easy reach of the city.

To well-read persons like the Herewards and
Zuniga, who from books were prepared for all things, .
there could be no surprise; but to Aunt Sophie every
day was a new life, every scene a new world, so that
she came into a chronic state of amazement.

At the end of the month the Prince and Princess
Gherardini returned to Paris.

As Mr. Hereward had still a few days of leisure
left, his host and hostess insisted on his spending
those days as their guest in Paris.

Mrs. Downie was easily persuaded to stay as long
as Lilith should stay.

The Prince and Princess gave a series of brilliant
entertainments at the commencement of the Paris
season.

Mr. and Mrs. Tudor Hereward always assisted them
in receiving. And the Paris world whispered together:

"So that was the distinguished statesman to whom
Madame Wyvil was betrothed—Monsieur Hereward,
of the American Legation at the Court of ——."

Mrs. Downie, in the same black satin dress, trimmed
with black Brussels lace and black bugles, with a
white point lace cap on her head—all of which had
been presented to her by the princess to be worn at
her wedding—was always present with the receiving
party, dodging a little behind whenever a great dig-
nitary, covered with stars, crosses and orders, or a
grande dame blazing with diamonds, approached the
circle; yet so thoroughly enjoying the splendid pageant that at length she grew really alarmed as to her
spiritual condition, and privately spoke her mind to
Lilith, as follows:

"I never was drunk in my life, honey, and I never
seed anybody else drunk, but I have read and I hearn
a heap about drunk; and I do think, for the last
week or so, since the princess have been giving these

high parties, and I mixed up into it all, I must feel just
like people do when they are crazy drunk. I ain't
myself, honey! I ain't indeed! I donno what Brother
Perkins or Brother More would think if they knew
the state I'm in. I don't indeed! Why, child when
I go up into my room and shut the door and begin
my prayers with reciting my hymn:

'Fading, still fading, the last ray is shining,
Father in Heaven, the day is declining—
Safety and innocence fly with the light,
Temptation and danger walk forth with the night,'

instead of the music of that comforting hymn, there
is sounding through my brain—

'Tooty-loo-loo! Tooty-loo-loo! Tooty-loo-loo!'

or some such sinful tune as them there misguided
young men and women waltz around to, with their
heads on each other's shoulders and their arms around
each other's waists in a way I can't approve of. And
so, honey, I think when you and Mr. Hereward leave
here, I shall go home and try to get back my sober
senses."

"But you have enjoyed it, Aunt Sophie," urged
Lilith.

"That's the worst of it, honey! I have enjoyed it
too much! It is a temptation and a snare! A delud-
ing snare.

'Tooty-loo-loo! Tooty-loo-loo! Tooty-loo-loo!'

There I am again with the waltz whirling round in
my old Methodist brain! Yes, honey, I am going
home!"

"But, Aunt Sophie, you must go first with Mr.
Hereward and myself to our home in ——. I know
you would like to see for yourself where I am to live,
so that you may be able to picture me in my home."

"Oh, yes! indeed I should, but——"

"But you will go! My father is to go home with us for a visit—and afterwards he also is to go back to America. And now don't you see that he who brought you out here should also take you home?"

"Oh, yes! Well, if the 'sinner' is going back so soon as you say, it would be worth my while to stay and go along with him. So I reckon I will."

At the end of the month of festivity, Tudor, Lilith and Aunt Sophie bade good-bye to their hospitable host and hostess, and left Paris for ——.

On their arrival at that city Mr. Hereward took them at once to the handsomely furnished house he had engaged, near the Royal Palace.

It was afternoon when they arrived.

And here a glad surprise awaited Lilith. As she entered the hall, led in by her husband, a great black beast flew to meet her and rolled joyously at her feet!

It was Lion, her faithful Newfoundland dog, who had followed her to the railway station, and from whom she had parted on that dreadful night of her banishment from her home, as she had supposed, forever.

Her joy at meeting her favorite was scarcely less than his own. She welcomed, caressed and talked to him.

"Loyal old Lion! We will never part again! Never again, dear old Lion! until death takes one or the other," said Lilith, as at last she disengaged herself from him and went upstairs to her room, conducted by Hereward.

Here another surprise awaited her.

As she entered the room her old nurse, housekeeper and lady's-maid, Nancy, came to meet her; but almost instantly became inarticulate in her words of welcome, and then burst into happy, hysterical tears.

When these had subsided, and Lilith and Aunt

Sophie, having laid off their wraps, were seated around the blazing wood fire of the bed-room, with Lion stretched on the rug before them, and Nancy standing leaning her head against the mantelpiece, Hereward explained:

"On the day after I met you in Paris, Lilith, five weeks ago, I wrote to Oxley, at Cloud Cliffs, to send Stephen, Alick, Nancy, and the Newfoundland dog, Lion, out to me by one of the French line of steamers that sail direct for Havre. I gave him minute instructions to see the party all the way from Cloud Cliffs to New York, and on to the ship by which they would sail. I directed him to carry out all these instructions without loss of time. And I inclosed a bill of exchange to cover all expenses. He acted so promptly and intelligently on my orders that the whole party reached here four days ago."

"But I can't get it out'n my head, Miss Lilif, as you and me has died and waked up in t'other world! I'm thankful it ain't the bad place; but it don't look quite like heaven nuther! And that's what puzzles ob me," said Nancy.

"Never mind, you will come around quite right in a few days," replied Lilith, consolingly.

Señor Zuniga stayed until after Christmas with the Herewards, and then, about the middle of January, sailed for New York.

Señor Zuniga succeeded beyond his sanguine hopes in recovering his patrimonial estates. He sold them for all they were worth and invested the money in West Virginia land near Frosthill.

Then he married his devoted admirer, Harriet Miles, who was never tired of telling her friends that she always knew that he was a young nobleman in disguise who was only playing at play acting for his own amusement.

Madame Zuniga's stepfather, old Jab Jordon, is a

very much subdued old man. First, he is "set upon" by Mrs. Jab, and secondly by Master Jab, their only son and heir.

Mr. Rufus Hilary wonders that his brother-in-law should ever have left the exciting and glorious life of a "world-renowned" dramatic artist, to settle down into a merely respectable farmer and father of a family Mr. Rufus Hilary is still an ardent admirer and liberal patron of the stage; he is still unmarried. and his pretty young sister, Miss Emily Miles, keeps his house.

The Herewards are still abroad—Mr. Hereward filling a very important diplomatic position at one of the highest courts in Europe, and Mrs. Hereward, at last his deeply loved wife, his companion in domestic life, his helper in official life, is one of the most brilliant and admired among les grandes dames who add lustre to the drawing-rooms of the empress.

THE END

www.ingramcontent.com/pod-product-compliance
Lightning Source LLC
Chambersburg PA
CBHW020942030726
47496CB00005B/1308